The
King James
Conspiracy

By Phillip DePoy

The Fever Devilin Mysteries

The Devil's Hearth
The Witch's Grave
A Minister's Ghost
A Widow's Curse
The Drifter's Wheel

The Flap Tucker Mysteries

Easy
Too Easy
Easy as One-Two-Three
Dancing Made Easy
Dead Easy

The King James Conspiracy

PHILLIP DEPOY

ST. MARTIN'S GRIFFIN
NEW YORK

This is a work of fiction. All of the characters, organizations, and
events portrayed in this novel are either products of the author's
imagination or are used fictitiously.

www.stmartins.com

Design by Phil Mazzone

The Library of Congress has cataloged the hardcover edition as follows:

DePoy, Phillip.
    The King James conspiracy / Phillip DePoy. — 1st ed.
        p. cm.
    ISBN 978-0-312-37713-7
    1. Bible—Translating—Great Britain—Fiction. 2. Bible. English—
Versions—Authorized—Fiction. 3. Biblical scholars—Crimes against—
Fiction. 4. Great Britain—History—James I, 1603–1625—Fiction.
I. Title.
    PS3554.E624K56 2009
    813'.54—dc22

                                                    2008043925

ISBN 978-0-312-62794-2 (trade paperback)

First St. Martin's Griffin Edition: May 2010

10 9 8 7 6 5 4 3 2 1

The King James Conspiracy is dedicated to Father Coleman. I took confirmation classes from him when I was eleven years old. At that time, news of the Dead Sea Scrolls was becoming popular. I remember how excited Father Coleman was when he told me what they would mean. "Once they're all translated, we can see what the Bible *really* says." Nearly fifty years later, as I continue to wait for the complete translation and revelation of the Dead Sea Scrolls (as well as the Nag Hammadi library, known as the Gnostic Gospels, discovered in 1945 and still not fully available to the public), it seems appropriate that this book should belong to Father Coleman.

Acknowledgments

Thanks to Keith Kahla for specific instruction and general help; Maria Carvainis for superior critique; Lee Nowell for first reading and constant support; and especially to the anonymous truck driver who pulled out in front of me on the expressway and nearly killed me. On his bumper was a sticker that said, "If it ain't King James, it ain't the Bible." When I saw it I stopped wanting to explain the rules of safe driving and started wanting to tell him everything that was wrong with that sentence. Instead, I came home and started this book.

1

Rome, 1605

"*Blood!*" The world's most significant ring dented the tabletop; the fist bore it crashing into the wood again and again with each word. "We must have *blood*."

The secret room, smaller than a bedchamber, offered a faint echo of the final word. In the shadows along the cold stone wall, a small black beetle clattered softly to the corner.

"But, Your Holiness," Cardinal Venitelli sputtered, his sleeve trembling as he held up his hand ever so slightly, crimson skullcap twitching twice. "This book is in *English*. Who would pay attention to that?"

"The book is circumstantial!" the Pope interrupted, bellowing. "If we are to win back that dirty little island, the time is now. We would never have attempted this with Elizabeth, but James has been handed the throne. He is a proud man, and now he has set his intellectual talents, such as they are, to work on this book. He is both overly assured and mentally distracted. The time is ripe."

"But—when you say *blood* . . ." Venitelli had no idea how to finish the sentence.

Pope Clement's red cape rose and fell with each labored breath. A white, translucent collar from the underdressing crested at the neck. Fire hissed in the hearth at the opposite end of the room.

"Blood will stop the book. Stopping the book will unravel James's plan for England. The plan unraveled builds a bridge from Rome to London. That bridge will bring England back to the Church. You must at least see God's humor, if not His plan, in this."

The small stone room in which the two men sat was quite hidden. It was unknown to all but the Pope's most intimate visitors. From the outside, the door was invisible, hidden by the stones in the long hallway. Inside, the room was bare of furniture save for a table and four chairs. Two large candles fixed to the tabletop illuminated the walls. The walls were draped floor to ceiling with thick tapestries, which did their best to absorb all sound. The images woven there were also red, stabbed with thorns: hunting scenes of startling violence. The characters seemed to move fitfully in the flickering light.

The floor was nearly covered with a deep, intricately patterned carpet that had been stolen during the Crusades, it was said, from Saladin himself. Cardinal Venitelli always fancied he could smell Saladin's encampment the moment he stepped on the rug. He had often struggled to explain the sensation to himself. The reason was just beyond his mind's grasp. The room itself seemed accustomed to harsh words.

"Yes," the cardinal managed, "but the exact meaning—"

"You need not concern yourself with exact meanings." Pope Clement relished thinking of himself as an impatient man: it prompted quick action on the part of subordinates. "We have already set certain plans in motion. They involve, in part, the man who is housing these translators at Christ Church in Cambridge—a minister named Marbury, a Protestant. Alas, he is an intelligent man in a mire of idiots. But to the point: a scholar of the Cambridge group is this night to be—what word is best? *Eliminated.* When that happens, we shall introduce into their midst our avenging angel."

That phrase was a code well-known to the cardinal, but to assure himself he began to ask, "By which you mean to say—"

"These tapestries are elegant, are they not?" Clement looked away.

The cardinal understood: His Holiness must not say the name of his chief assassin—his *avenging angel*. In this way he could honestly say, in future conversations, that he had not called for him—not by name—and had certainly never spoken with him. That task was assigned to the cardinal, who did not relish it. His face grew ashen and his voice quavered.

"I am to ask—ask the man in question to go to England, and kill—"

"Certainly not! Hush!" Clement rolled his head around his shoulders. "Tell him only that he is to be assigned to the translators of the King James Bible. Emphasize the *Bible*. Then say to him these *precise words*: 'The turning of the wheel by the tilling of the wheat.'"

Venitelli felt a fist tighten in his belly. How many times before had he conveyed such coded phrases to the man in question, subsequently leading to foul murder?

"The turning of the wheel by the tilling of the wheat," Venitelli repeated, nodding.

The Pope smiled, but did not look at the cardinal. "We are using the man in question for his special talents—abilities which only he possesses. He has a *telum secretus,* if We may be permitted a dramatic flair."

"But our brother's actual task—his assignment—"

"The reason We assign these administrative tasks to you, my brother Cardinal Venitelli," the Pope said soothingly, as if to a boy of seven, "is that you rarely grasp the import of any situation. You do, however, operate with *discretion*. You must understand that We will stop at nothing to reclaim England, bring her back to Mother Church. It is God's plan. We have in mind a series of events, in fact, though they may take several years to unfold, which will achieve Us this goal."

"Yes," Venitelli's voice betrayed his absolute confusion.

The Pope leaned forward, his face close to Venitelli's, and he barely spoke above a whisper, but the sound of his voice was thunder.

"This will be my legacy, do you understand? History will write me as the man who restored England to the True Church. And that *begins* with the destruction of this book—this folly to which James aspires."

The cardinal's nostrils were momentarily assailed by a scent of camels; his ears heard faint Islamic prayers. Though he did not speak Arabic, he believed that the prayers were calling for the blood of infidels. He glared down at Saladin's rug. Was it possible that a curse of the vanquished Islamic warriors lingered on the rug, infecting decisions made in this room? Perhaps that would account for the odd smells that attacked his senses, and the Pope's disconcerting passion.

"Are you attempting to think?" The Pope glared at Venitelli. "Are you giving second thought to Our words?"

The cardinal stood immediately. "A thousand pardons, Your Holiness." He reached for the papal ring. "God's plan is glorious, and your name will live forever."

The Pope offered his hand, sighing—Venitelli kissed the ring.

Cardinal Venitelli bowed, turned, and hastened toward the secret door. He peered once through a crack in the stones, cold and gray, his hand upon them, making certain no one was in the outer hall. When he saw no one, he pushed through, leaving his Pope behind.

Once in the hallway Venitelli realized that his hands would not stop trembling, and that his hairline dripped with sweat. He fought to quell his worst fear: that the Pope had lost his mind.

He slowed his pace only slightly, trying to decide which disturbed him more, the conversation he had just endured with his Pope, or the one he was about to have with the coldest man in Italy.

2

Cambridge, England

*W*ithout warning, Deacon Francis Marbury's slumber was shattered.

"Help! Murder! Someone!"

His eyes shot open. Moonlight, soft and clear, bathed his room. The April night was cold, the air still held a strong remembrance of winter, though winter itself had gone.

"Someone help!" the call came again, louder.

Marbury flew from his bedcovers, wrapped himself in a black, quilted cape, and thrust his head out the window of the tiny bedroom. One by one other windows all around him flickered from black to white; voices began to shout. Marbury stumbled back into the room, stopped to pull on his boots, then plunged into the hallway of the Deaconage, picking up his pace as he flew down the stairs.

Out into the night, several others joined him; faces blurred in the darkness. The peace of the common yard, surrounded by silent stone buildings, was destroyed by men running toward the sound of the cries.

As Marbury approached the Great Hall, from which direction the cries had come, he could see that one of the scholars, Edward Lively, stood barring the door. Lively was dressed in fine brocade, a soft silver that bent the moonlight his way. His hat was ermine, bold; new. He wore gloves of black leather whose cuffs were emblazoned with a scarlet letter *L*. His beard was as clean and soft as a rich man's bed. Others surrounded the doorway as Marbury came to a halt before him.

"What has happened?" Marbury, out of breath, touched Lively's arm.

"A body," Lively managed, swallowing. "A dead body. In there."

Lively stood aside, opening the door to the hall, his voice echoing against lifeless walls. The rest of the men flooded past him, lighting candles; whispering furious questions. The hall was a cave, cold and quiet. The far corners were obscured by an obsidian darker than the midnight. The air seemed filled with slivers of ice. They pricked the fingers and stuck the cheeks.

The men inched forward. Something terrible lay in a lump just ahead of them. After a moment one man cried out. Another began coughing, or vomiting.

Marbury breathed heavily. "God in heaven."

A bloodied corpse lay on the cold stone floor near one of the scholars' desks.

Marbury fought to control his breathing, repeating over and over in his mind that what he saw was not really there, it was a phantom. But his mind knew better.

Lively had apparently dropped a candle. It had come to rest against the leg of a desk and continued to burn on its side, casting a flickering light on the dead body slumped under the desk.

A corpse alone would not have so terrified the scholars. Thanks to the plague, each man in his time had seen many a vacant body. It was the face that provoked an impulse to scream; the sight of it churned the stomach.

That face had been cut perhaps a hundred times, long and deep lacerations gouged the flesh until no features were left, only raw muscle, peaks of bone, and dried blood the color of rotted plums.

There was no way of knowing the identity of the man from that face.

"Look!" Robert Spaulding cried, amazed. He was second-in-command of the translators, his position more secretarial than anything else. He seemed more fascinated than revolted by the scene that lay before him. His overcoat was plain, the color of a dead leaf, and cleaned so vigorously that it may have been in pain. He pointed to the intricate briarwood cross around the dead man's neck.

"That, I believe, is Harrison's cross," Marbury whispered.

"And that is most certainly Harrison's purple vest," Spaulding confirmed, cold as stone.

There was no doubt that the dead man was Harrison.

Marbury steadied himself against Harrison's desk, concentrating on his breathing. He watched in silence as the rest agreed with one another about the details of their conclusion.

"How is it," Marbury began slowly to Lively, "that you came across this horror at such a time of night?"

"My enthusiasm drew me here," Lively said quickly. "I was eager to work on my new pages—they hold an allure for me the magnitude of which you cannot imagine."

"Yes, but what I do not need to imagine," Marbury pronounced carefully, "is the anger Harrison would have displayed had he known you were looking at his work. He is given to fits of rage. We all know it. Perhaps he was here, you argued; he attacked you."

Lively's response was interrupted before it began.

"We must alert the night watch immediately!" Spaulding demanded.

"You are a man of letters, Dr. Spaulding, and would not know of such matters," Marbury answered, barely hiding his derisive tone, "but our constabulary here in Cambridge are, to a man, quite useless. You must permit me to handle this affair in another manner."

"Outrageous!" Spaulding squeaked. "We must not allow this night to pass—"

"I have already in mind a method for investigating this horror," Marbury said, his tones calming, almost hypnotic.

"But—" Lively began.

Marbury turned at once to the assembled and raised his hand. "Your pardon, gentlemen—I suggest we take stock for a moment before we speak further. Firstly, our Christian duty demands that we offer, each of us, a silent prayer on the part of our colleague Harrison."

Marbury watched as each living face registered its own brand of instant piety. Eyes closed, mouths moved; voices whispered.

Marbury used the moment of silence to take another look at the dead body, trying to examine it more closely. The blood on the corpse had not dried, but was not running. There was an almost complete lack of stain on the floor, the desk, or the chair around the body. The vest showed several torn places. Two were soaked in blood, but that blood was viscous—not oozing, not dry. Could Harrison have been killed somewhere else and the body lugged into the hall?

After a moment, Marbury forced himself to look again at the wreckage of the face. He prayed, then, that Harrison had been dead before it had been so mutilated. But as he finished his prayer, he noticed something else.

"Now then." Marbury's voice broke the silence in the controlled tone of a man of business. "I beg you all to keep silent about this incident. Let us not discuss it with anyone outside these walls until we know what has happened. Your work is too sacred, too vital, to be distracted by this. Perhaps my words seem cold, but I believe they are in the best interest of your scholarship, and our King. After all, is this hall a place of learning, or a house of murder?"

The most senior scholar of the group cleared his throat noisily. He was Dr. Lawrence Chaderton, a Hebrew scholar on friendly terms with many of England's notable rabbis. He radiated the deep calm of a man completely confident of his place in this world— and in the next. His coat was plain and black, buttoned, reaching nearly to the floor. His head was uncovered, his white hair all stray lightning and sparks.

"The man who did this to Harrison is not, by my definition, a human being." Chaderton squinted. "We must proceed with impossible delicacy."

"Does our elder colleague suggest," Spaulding piped up, a derisive grin mouthing the words, "that this may be the work of *demons?*"

"Devils may indeed enter into a man," Chaderton intoned, his eyes steel, in the voice of God. "They make a human hand perform inhuman acts. And we may be assured that the devil himself is opposed to our work here in this hall. He has doubtless sent his minions to distract us, or, dare I say, to destroy us."

Several of the men in the group began praying again. One crossed himself.

"Now, if I may be permitted," Marbury said slowly, inching his way toward the corpse, "I see that brother Harrison has something in his mouth."

All eyes turned toward the body, heads leaned in; the circle around Harrison grew smaller.

"Pardon me," Marbury continued, stooping close to the corpse, his hand hovering inches over the mouth.

"Do not touch it!" Lively whispered, sucking in a breath as if he had been struck in the stomach—with something of a dramatic flair, Marbury thought.

"Just so." Marbury's hand flicked without warning, speed and agility blurring the movement, and retrieved a crumpled, moist bit of paper from the dead man's mouth.

Everyone gasped. More men crossed themselves, whispering.

Delicately, with thumb and index finger, Marbury unwrinkled the bit of paper and held it closer to the candle. Words were written upon it, as several could see.

"What does it say?" Lively breathed almost soundlessly.

" 'Wandering through the world as God's hangmen,' " Marbury read.

He set the torn bit of paper on Harrison's desk. The men crowded around the desk. Candles were offered to illuminate the work. All read the note.

The words sound familiar, somehow, Marbury thought to himself.

"This ghastly note is clearly written in Harrison's own hand."

Lively tapped the bottom of his candle on the wrinkled, wet, torn bit of writing.

"I agree," Marbury asserted calmly.

Marbury's mind invented wild images of the murderer forcing Harrison's mouth open, forcing him to eat his own words.

"Is it a message?" Lively wanted to know.

"A warning?" Spaulding asked.

"This *is* the work of devils," Chaderton asserted.

"All the more reason," Marbury intervened, a bit louder than before, his voice a thin tissue of tolerance stretched over a chasm of impatience, "for us to shroud ourselves in a veil of secrecy. We should now return to our rooms. Please evacuate this hall. I would speak with Mr. Lively a moment in private, if the rest of you would excuse us."

Several of the men moved immediately toward the door. The rest followed slightly behind. Only Chaderton looked back.

As the last of the men closed the door, Marbury began, "Someone must investigate this monstrous event—and you know as well as I that the local watchmen are of no use."

"Are you suggesting that you—"

"No," Marbury assured Lively. "I am well aware of the political tempest that would ensue if I were the investigator. And this is to your advantage. If I were to follow the obvious line of questioning, you would be the first suspect."

"I?" Lively exploded.

"You found the body. You hated Harrison—"

"I called the alarm!" Lively snarled.

"A perfect gesture—"

"With the greatest respect imaginable," Lively said with no respect at all, "your perception is clouded by the brandy you drink. Everyone says so. One smells it on your breath."

Marbury's face offered an entire play, all five acts in quick succession: anger, constraint, consideration, calm, and indulgence. When he finally spoke, it was as if to a schoolboy.

"All the more reason, then, for an independent investigator, Mr. Lively." Marbury sighed. "And if I take a bit of brandy in the evening, it is so that I may sleep. The cares of this world evaporate in the fires of good drink, and I am delivered to my bed a calmer man. I am almost the child I was. For this I am grateful, as a good night's sleep dulls my response to the next day's insult. This allows me to return that insult with radiance rather than violence. In my younger days I would often stab the offender with my dagger."

Lively glanced at Marbury's left sleeve; it hung lower than his right, the perfect place to conceal a short blade. He suddenly realized that antagonizing Marbury was not a sound practice.

"So," Lively managed, swallowing hard, "have you a man in mind for this investigation?"

"Not exactly." Marbury's voice was crisp. "But as luck would have it, I know where I can find one."

3

The next night, on the most disreputable street in Cambridge, Marbury hesitated before he grasped the handle of a tavern door. He was dressed head to foot in sober, crisp black. The cape was thick and past his knees; the cap was low on his forehead. He could have walked away then. He even thought for an instant that he should. He had such a strange foreboding. He felt for his dagger, well hidden in the fold of his cape. Its solid handle reassured him. Still, at the exact moment he pushed open the door, he could not have explained why he'd done it.

Low ceiling rafters of the crowded public house made Marbury stoop as he entered. No one took notice of him. This was a place where eyes were deliberately averted, lest they be cut from the curious head.

The walls were smeared, streaked a putrid color that had no name. The noise was nearly comic, a jagged human racket. Men in torn black tunics, boys in soiled red doublets, old drunkards in brown rags, all crowded around the long tables. Smaller planks covered with relatively clean tablecloths might host a demi-royal in ocean blue, a minor earl with a red cap, a moderately wealthy shopkeeper draped in raw silk; a tinsmith in his slate-gray apron. They all sat at tables made of long, honey-colored wooden planks; their seats were single-timber benches.

The floor was hard-packed soil of England, covered with straw, old food, sleeping dogs. Where there was not a table, a bench, or a man, there was a column—six-by-six inches of rough wood that helped support the failing ceiling.

Here was an ideal meeting place for the rupture of dark souls, a haven for impious plots, the rough work of devils in flesh.

Marbury lifted his head a moment to a young woman in a gingerbread dress behind the bar. Her eyes darted to the right for only an instant: the direction of a little door in the far corner of the room. Without further interplay, she went back to her work. Marbury moved toward the door.

He clutched the handle, took a deep breath, and pushed the door forward with a sudden jolt of energy. He could see all three men inside the little room jump. Marbury stepped inside, closing the door behind him. The relative silence of the smaller room was unnerving. Worse, the three men, lit only by a single candle, all wore masks. Their monks' robes, black as a gun barrel, absorbed most of the candle's light.

"Good," Marbury said. "You received my note. I was not certain you would be here with so little notice. This has all happened so quickly. When last we communicated, some three years ago—"

"Shh!" the man in the middle commanded.

"I expected to see your faces this time," Marbury went on calmly, "as we have done business before."

"Sit." The man stood. "Please refer to me as Samuel. This is Isaiah, and that one you may call Daniel."

Marbury permitted himself a smile, one that barely indicated his derision. Petty men revel in espionage, he thought, false names they think might be clever, and ridiculous meetings such as this one. Perhaps these men from the Anglican Church, Marbury thought, are more laughable because they long to imitate the Catholics.

"And by which book of the Old Testament would you call me?" Marbury asked softly.

"Be seated." Isaiah indicated a chair. "We have agreed to assist you again only because our King's great work is in jeopardy."

The chair scraped like a shovel over the hard ground of a grave.

"And we must be brief." Samuel had a voice like a crow's. "We have found a man, perfect for your needs. We have told him of the murdered translator, Harrison. He has agreed to help you."

Marbury took his seat and said nothing. In a den of thieves, silence is an ally. But his right hand crept slowly up his left sleeve and touched the handle of his blade.

"The man, as it happens, is a former Catholic. By the grace of God, he converted to the Church of England some twenty years ago," Samuel's voice rattled.

Marbury drew in a breath, knowing a lie was hidden in Samuel's words. "Twenty years ago, in Queen Elizabeth's day, a man chose between conversion and death. A convert made from fear should always be suspect."

"In those years," Samuel continued, ignoring Marbury, "this man assisted Philip Sidney with his opus magnum, *Arcadia*. Sir Philip's estate recommends him. At that time, however, for reasons best kept secret from you, he worked under another name. That name has vanished from all records."

"How can we be certain, then," Marbury said, leaning back in his chair, "that this man—"

"He has vanished from *all records*." Without blinking behind his mask, Samuel's lips tensed.

"I see." Marbury nodded once.

"I hope you do," Samuel rasped. "Now to complete our story. We took our man to the Sidney family for a reference. An ancient servant named Jacob, whose memory for faces has outlasted his ability to recall names, knew our man. The family found, in certain payment records, that such a man had indeed been in the employ of Sir Philip, listed only as 'monk.' This monk is the man we want. We can produce certain records; he possesses certain qualities—"

"You mean to say that this man has credentials I might show to others," Marbury said evenly, "but which are, in essence, fabri-cated. They are in some way true but completely untraceable. And I assume you will not tell me this monk's real name, or anything else about him."

"We will not," Samuel confirmed. "Except to say that he was imprisoned for a time in Italy, but he is not a criminal. You are a clever man. This should tell you everything."

"The Inquisition." Marbury folded his hands and considered that the man he was about to hire had endured both Elizabeth's persuasion and the tortures of the Inquisition. He would be a man of iron.

"As you say," Samuel pressed on, "the necessary papers have been forged, documents signed, weak men bribed. Our man will infiltrate your translators and ferret out the murderer, as you wish."

"Possibly, but I must have an official reason for his presence. I too, you must understand, have documents that must be kept; petty officials to placate."

Samuel answered without hesitation, "He is a scholar. Say that he is to be your daughter's tutor."

"Anne's tutor?" Marbury coughed. "But she is an adult of twenty years; well past tutoring."

"Unmarried." Isaiah's single-word pronouncement was made from lead. "And fancies herself a religious philosopher."

Marbury's first impulse was to ask how this man might know anything about Anne, but he thought better of such a question.

"She is her father's child." Marbury's tone was not remotely apologetic. "And she will not accept a tutor."

"We are given to understand that she is interested in the modes of Greek learning as well as theology." Samuel let that sink in.

Marbury sighed. Of course these little men would know about Anne's religious leanings. She had voiced them often enough in public.

"She might be interested in such a thing," Marbury acknowl-edged.

"Perhaps you should insist." Samuel did not move.

"Does this man you have found know *anything* about the work of our translators?" Marbury's voice rose.

"Why is that important to you?" Isaiah asked, matching Marbury's volume.

"Anne's interest in the translation is keen." Marbury could not help raising his voice again. "If this man could know a bit about the work, it might help Anne to accept him more readily."

"He knows what any thoughtful person in his position might," Isaiah snapped. "King James has assembled a team of some fifty-four scholars. Eight of them reside with you in Cambridge."

"Only seven now," Marbury reminded Isaiah.

"The point is," Samuel went on, more irritated, "that they are translating the Bible from *original* sources. Our man's knowledge of Greek is what recommends him with regard to this translation as well as to your daughter. As many of the original texts are in Greek—"

"A little knowledge," Marbury interrupted, hoping to curtail further argument and quit the room as quickly as possible, "will fool neither our Cambridge men nor convince Anne—"

"He is a superior scholar!" Isaiah exploded. "He need *fool* no one."

Marbury could hear the menace in the man's words. He fought an impulse to escalate the argument, realizing that he must be careful with these men. Best to go along with their plans, but to be wary of trusting them completely. He formed, then dismissed, several questions before deciding on the most basic ones.

"How, then, shall I meet him?" Marbury leaned forward, ready to leave.

"He will arrive tomorrow morning and report himself to you at the Deaconage."

Samuel moved a sheaf of papers, tied with butcher twine, toward Marbury.

"By what name shall I call this man?"

"He is Brother Timon." Samuel's voice seemed momentarily hoarse.

Marbury noticed that the man referred to as Daniel—who had not spoken—shivered for a moment

"Who named him that?" Marbury wanted to know, failing to keep a fraction of amusement from his words.

The three men looked at one another, obviously without an answer to his question.

"I only ask because I find the name interesting. It is, you see, from a play I know. It is the name of a character who hates all men—hates them because they have been ungrateful for his good deeds."

The three men remained silent.

"Very well." Marbury stood up and pulled his cloak around him, feeling for the handle of his hidden dagger. "*Timon* it is. I look forward to meeting him."

Without another syllable, Marbury moved to the door, not quite turning his back to the three shadows. His ears were tuned to the slightest hint of movement from them as he slipped through the door.

WHEN HE WAS CERTAIN that Marbury was gone, Samuel slumped in his chair. Isaiah blew out a long breath.

The one called Daniel was the first to remove his mask. He mopped his face with it, and his hand shook as he did. "Thank God this business is done and soon I can return to Rome."

"Well, only . . . at least for the moment." Samuel glanced to Isaiah, mask still in place.

"Our brother Cardinal Venitelli does not have the stomach for back rooms and shadows," Isaiah sighed.

"Look how I am soaked in sweat, and yet what a cold place England is." Cardinal Venitelli tossed his dampened mask to the table. "You do not need to call me Daniel now?"

"I do not," Isaiah grunted. "We are alone."

"Of course." Venitelli shivered and crossed himself absently, holding his arms close to his chest. "I must tell you both that I am sorry for this Marbury. Sorry. He seems, from all I have discovered about him, an intelligent man. How have you been able to fool him for so long?"

"He is a Protestant," Samuel spat dismissively.

"He trusts us, and why shouldn't he? We have cultured his confidence for several years for our current purposes. He was our instrument, unwittingly, in destroying the Bye Plot against James."

"Was he?" Venitelli asked, shivering again. "I thought that our own Father Henry Garnet—"

"Our Pope wanted James to condemn all Catholics," Isaiah hissed. "Nothing solidifies us half so much, He feels, as opposition."

Venitelli struggled to understand. "His Holiness did not want James to repeal the anti-Catholic legislation?"

"Marbury is as much our instrument, though he does not know it, as is this so-called Brother Timon," Samuel sneered.

Venitelli closed his eyes at the mention of that name. "Timon," Venitelli repeated tensely, staring at the door through which Marbury had vanished. "What are we doing? We have handed this decent man Marbury over to a demon."

4

In an alley off another street in Cambridge, at that exact moment, a silver blade caught the moon's light. Then it pierced an old man's heart.

The dagger had skillfully been inserted just below the breastbone and thrust upward. The old man, whose name was Jacob, stared into the eyes of his murderer, an impossibly tall, obsidian shadow who seemed to reflect darkness. A black robe and hood made him nearly invisible in the night.

"Let me explain what is happening," the murderer whispered calmly. "I have slid my knife past your thin, thin skin and into your beating heart. Now, you could not feel the edge moving, but I have sliced your heart almost exactly in half. The wound in your chest is so clean that little blood will escape there, but your heart will keep pumping for a moment or two more, filling up your chest cavity with enough blood, at least in theory, to make your torso actually explode. Have no fear. You will be dead by the time it happens. But it will make identifying your body very difficult."

The monk's hood fell back, revealing a face that radiated cold brilliance. The eyes were the color of young green leaves, the curled hair was black and gray, tousled wildly about his head. His features seemed carved more than grown.

"I knew you—years ago—Giordano!" Jacob managed to say.

"Yes," the murderer answered soothingly. "That is why I have killed you: I must no longer *be* Giordano. I must vanish from all records, and you are a living record of my existence. From now on I shall be called Timon, you see."

Jacob struggled to speak more.

"Never fear," Timon interrupted. "You have given God and your masters in the Sidney family a good life of service. Your soul is crouched low now—I can feel it—waiting to leap into heaven. There it will find eternal delight. You were a good man."

The alleyway was short, the space of three horses. The stones underfoot were ice between two grumbling shops in this poorest part of Cambridge. One shop was a butcher's, fouling the air with rank decay. The other was a tinsmith's hovel. Cheap pots hung everywhere.

Jacob had forgotten where he was. He could feel nothing. He could only smell an overwhelming scent of nutmeg coming from his assailant.

"You may wonder why I have chosen this method of execution," the killer continued, his blade still in Jacob's chest. "I had a fondness for you, and my studies have indicated that you should feel nothing from this particular kind of wound. Ancient Greek doctors tell us that when a man experiences a sudden shock of this magnitude, his body refuses to believe it, and all senses are shut for a short span. You will soon sleep, never having felt anything more than the first brief insult of this dagger. I have offered you, Jacob, the only kindness I know how to give in a circumstance such as this."

Jacob's eyes rolled back in his head.

"Ah." Timon withdrew his blade.

Jacob's corpse slumped toward the stones of the alley floor just as Timon fancied he could see a burst of white steam fly upward.

"Good-bye, Jacob," he said to the steam. "I shall, alas, not see you again. We shall be spending eternity in separate quarters."

Just then a dog leapt out of the shadows, released from a side door at the butcher's.

"Get him, boy!" a voice growled. "He's killed Jacob!"

The dog went for Timon's throat.

Without a thought Timon swept his dagger forward, slashed deep, and sliced the dog's throat, nearly cutting its head off. The dying carcass continued to fly through the air before it fell to the ground beside Jacob.

Timon strode three long steps forward calmly and found the butcher crouching in the shadows, eyes bursting from their sockets.

Without a word Timon grabbed the man by his apron and thrust him backward through the side door, into his shop. The butcher crashed against a wooden table before crumpling onto the floor. In a blur Timon moved back into the ally to grab the dead dog by its tail, dragging it into the shop behind him.

"This will be a bit uncomfortable," Timon said calmly, tossing back his hood once more.

Immediately the butcher began to scramble backward. "Poor old Jacob. Villain! I saw what you did."

"I know," Timon answered reasonably. "That is why I must kill you as well."

Without another word Timon picked up the butcher's largest meat cleaver. The butcher froze. Timon raised the cleaver high. The butcher shrieked a sound so high-pitched that it was nearly inaudible. Turning the cleaver, Timon brought the flat part of it down savagely upon the man's head, only knocking him unconscious.

Carefully Timon placed the cleaver into the butcher's right hand. Then he picked up the dog, pulled open its throat, and drained a bit of its blood onto the butcher and the cleaver.

Timon cast his eye about the dark street for a moment. His ears strained for the slightest hint of any other witness. Satisfied that he was alone in his task, he wrenched open the dog's mouth, shoved it onto the butcher's ample neck, and clamped it down until the dog's lifeless teeth drew blood.

He searched the other knives in the shop until he found a long, thin fillet blade. He used it to carve several deep holes in the butcher's neck, holes that seemed to be the teeth marks of a dog. Two of them tapped the jugular vein, and blood immediately fountained, spreading dark red decoration over the floor.

Tomorrow people will say this was a shame, Timon thought to himself, standing back to admire his tableau. The butcher's dog attacked him and he was forced to cleave the dog's throat. Alas, the butcher bled to death before anyone could rescue him. Ironic in a butcher shop, was it not?

Timon watched for a full five minutes to make certain that the butcher had died. Only then did he examine his own robe for stains—but the advantage of wearing black was that blood rarely left any noticeable trace.

Without another thought for the dead men, Brother Timon turned toward the street and began to recite, from memory, the entirety of Aristotle's *Poetics*.

5

The next afternoon was warmer. Cambridge was verging on springtime, at least out of doors. The air inside the stone walls of the Great Hall was still bitter winter. Even the candle flames trembled, shivering.

The place was a cavern. High windows, softened by decades of dust, seemed designed to keep out the light. The walls showed evidence of moss in the shadows. Its scent hovered in the air. Floors as gray as rain clouds only sealed the chill.

Wooden beams the color of a crow's beak shouldered a high ceiling of fifty feet or more, urging it heavenward. Gravity, alas, did the devil's work, sagging the rafters and threatening to pull down the roof.

Brother Timon, easily six feet tall, his rough black robe almost a parody of an ascetic monk's, drank in—and memorized—everything. The placement of each man, each desk, the arrangement of candles, the small box by the door, a scent of brandy, all were cataloged in his brain. He found he was most fascinated by the sound of the huge room: a constant low humming. It was the product of whispered voices combined with the scratching of quills on paper.

Deacon Marbury led Timon past desk after desk. Many were empty; some were occupied by rapt scholars, seven in all. The men were scattered here and there among the fifty desks in the hall. The enormous study cubicles were arranged in rows of five, and no man sat directly next to nor across from any other man.

Timon followed silently behind Deacon Marbury to the appointed place, counting his footsteps and feeling the contours of the floor as he walked.

"Here we are," Marbury said at last. "I present my daughter, Anne. Miss Anne, this is your new tutor, Brother Timon."

The monk's eyes rose to meet Anne's.

He first noticed that her posture was perfect. The structure of her bones was a study in right angles, allowing a grace or easy comfort to relax her muscles. She sat at a small, rectangular table, not at a desk. Her ears were too small, eyes too big, lips too full, cheeks redder than fashion dictated. Taken together, these parts composed a whole that was strangely enchanting. She wore a black dress that choked at the neck, a clearly defiant gesture in a culture where courtly colors ran more to pale blues and bruised purples.

Without realizing it, Timon brushed back his hair, scrutinizing her every feature as if he were reading a difficult passage of Greek. He tapped his right thumb rhythmically with the fingers of his right hand over and over as he stared.

Anne had not yet recovered from the argument she'd had with her father earlier that morning concerning this new tutor. Her face remained stony.

The three stood silently for long moments before the young woman said, "Your staring, sir, is stark; quite disconcerting."

Instantly Timon looked down. "Forgive me. I was trying to memorize your features, and my first impression of you. It is an older man's foible: memory is essential to my work, of course, and memory fades. I find I must exercise mine constantly for fear of losing it altogether."

"You do not appear to be monstrously older than most men, only taller," Anne said plainly, "and certainly not in danger of losing your mind."

"I have, to my credit, over fifty years," he sighed, "and many of them were long ones."

"I have only twenty," she responded, "and yet, they are a lifetime to me."

"I told you she was clever," Marbury piped up. "I am blessed."

"My father loves me." Anne smiled, but barely.

"Brother Timon comes to us recommended by no less than the estate of Sir Philip Sidney." Marbury blinked.

"I had occasion to offer a groat's worth of assistance," Timon suggested, eyes downcast, "with a few of the more complicated structures of *Arcadia*. This was technical help, research, I hasten to say. I have no ear for poetry. And, of course, this was some years ago."

"Yes, as Sir Philip has been dead for twenty years," Anne answered steadily, only a lilt of suspicion in her voice. "Still, to be associated with the poet's greatest work . . ."

"Has it been so long?" Timon's voice softened. "The span of your entire life and yet only a moment ago to me. I count myself fortunate that his heirs have remembered, recommended me after so long a time."

"Here is a man of learning, years, *and* modesty, Anne," Marbury said briskly. "Highly recommended, indeed. Not to be taken lightly."

"Then he should realize," Anne began, speaking to her father, eyes on Timon, "that he is to be more my keeper rather than my tutor."

"Hush." Marbury shook his head.

"These great men." Anne's eyes drank in the entire hall. "All these great men are here in this place doing God's work—and the King's. I am not to distract them, so I have been told. My father hires a tutor to keep me occupied. I have bested seven other such men. Did he tell you that, Brother Timon?"

Marbury sighed. "She has done that," he confided to Timon. "Over the course of her younger life, seven men tried and failed to think faster than my Anne. They resigned—or were dismissed." Marbury's voice was clearly filled with pride. Not a hint of regret was in his words.

"Excellent." Timon leaned toward Anne. "Then I shall dispense with the basics altogether and select something to study which will amuse as well as enlighten."

"I like the theatre for amusement." Anne closed the book she had been reading. Her syllables were ice. "Shall we discuss your favorite play?"

"Good, I am away, then," Marbury said quickly, "leaving you two—"

"A moment, Father. If I know more about this monk's favorite play than he does, you will escort him back the way he came." Anne's eyes burned into Timon's.

"Daughter," Marbury admonished.

"In truth," Timon said evenly, "I do not attend a great deal of this modern theatre, and—if you will forgive me for saying so—only a weak mind has a *favorite* of anything. But I am quite fond, at the moment, of a certain comedy. Perhaps you know it for the beautiful lines 'O suffering mankind, lives of twilight, race feeble and fleeting like the leaves scattered! Pale generations, creatures of clay, the wingless, the fading.'"

Marbury looked to Anne.

Anne's face flushed, cheeks aflame, eyes black.

"A thousand pardons," Timon said, unable to prevent the touch of a smile at the corner of his mouth. "I thought you might know *The Birds*. It is the greatest comedy of the Greek playwright Aristophanes. I read it in its original language, quite naturally, but I am certain the passage I have just spoken in English is accurately translated."

Marbury let go a long breath. "And now," he said firmly, "I am gone."

Marbury turned at once and headed toward the door of the hall. Anne opened her mouth to voice further protest, but something in Timon's face made her stop short. It was a face devoid of any expression at all. It was the mask of a man who had something to hide.

6

Timon drew a chair to the side of Anne's table, opposite her, and sat.

"The play was first performed," he continued, not looking at Anne, "at the Great Dionysia in late March over four hundred years before the birth of Our Lord. If you like, I can recite the entire work. I have committed it to memory."

"You have cheated me!" Anne exploded. "This is not a real play!"

"It is, in fact, more real than your contemporary plays because it contains the basic building blocks for nearly every comedy written in the two thousand years since its production. You have, one assumes, studied Aristotle."

Anne's face cooled, as did her voice. "You must be proud," she sneered, "besting a *girl*."

Timon bit his upper lip for a moment, then leveled an icy eye at his adversary.

"Hardly a girl." Timon's gaze narrowed; his voice was barely above a whisper. "I have chosen to consider you a fellow scholar. And as I am a man of the cloth and have been celibate some thirty years, I scarcely consider your gender. You have a mind; it wants to learn. Acquire an arsenal of knowledge with which to arm yourself, Anne, if you are to be anything more than a distraction to the great men in this hall!"

Anne blushed to have been so easily read. Still, her mind caught fire at the prospect of learning from this man, though she could not determine exactly why at that moment.

"Yes." She nodded once.

"Then you must understand," he told her, pronouncing each word with great precision, "that our modern age is a time when learning is power. Every man in this room can translate Latin, write a poem, fight with a rapier, paint the dew on a rose, and sail a battleship if need be. Every man must know every *thing*. Ignorance is the curse of God, knowledge the wing we use to fly. You live at a unique moment in history, one that shall pass away all too quickly, I fear. You occupy an England that loves learning. A time like this? It comes but once in a thousand years. Your brain must hurry to eat all the facts it can hold, before the next age of darkness."

Anne was momentarily hushed, eyes a bit wider, by the urgency of Timon's speech.

Only when Timon read that awe on Anne's face did he realize that he had been making the speech as much to himself as to Anne.

She took that moment to study Timon's features. The eyes were not windows into the man, but mirrors, keeping everything out. The mouth appeared to be smiling even when it was a straight line parallel to the eyes. A mask, his expression revealed nothing of the inner content of the mind. And yet Anne knew, from experience, that such an expression always hid a secret.

She shifted in her chair. Finding out that secret would be her challenge.

"We shall begin with Aristotle's *Poetics*." Timon cleared his throat, as uncomfortable at her staring as she had been at his.

"Aristotle, then, wrote plays?" Anne's voice failed to hide her embarrassment at asking such a primary question.

"He did not, but his treatise is a clear set of directions for building a play. His rules are followed to this day."

"Then I must know of him, and his work." Anne brushed back a lock of errant hair. "Ours is a time when language dominates; men and women choose words over actions. Our tale unfolds in dialogue, and I must have direction from Aristotle."

"Yes, you must," Timon said softly, leaning forward onto the table between them. "To begin at the beginning, Aristotle tells us that the *plot* is primary to all dramatic effort. Our theatre exists to tell a story. However, that story must be told, of course, almost exclusively through the *dialogue* of the characters."

A small spider had achieved the tabletop and was making its way across, toward Anne. She did not appear to notice it, but Timon could see nothing else. Frozen, he stopped talking. He stopped breathing. His heart seemed to pound at his eardrums.

The spider was dark blue. A crimson pattern on its back was so intricate it seemed to be a tapestry. As Timon watched the progress of those eight legs, the tapestry undulated, making moving scenes. The images expanded, though the spider did not, and hung in the air, a sheer curtain, a bright fog whirling each scene until it threatened to break apart.

Without warning, Anne's milk-white hand brushed the spider off the tabletop. It was a single gesture, fingers perfect, as in a dance. The vision was gone.

Timon blinked. Suddenly remembering to breathe, he gasped, swallowed suddenly, and coughed.

"I have an aversion to spiders," Timon managed to explain. "Or rather, I had a fear that the spider might be of the poisonous kind and would do you some harm. Certain spiders can kill."

"It is the curse of this room." Anne scanned the huge room with a withering eye. "So many shadows and cold places for something poisonous to hide."

"Indeed," he answered, collecting himself. "But to return to Aristotle: his concept of any plot dictates that it must *begin* at a very specific moment, it must not have a haphazard—"

"I understand," Anne interrupted. "Let us say that *our* plot begins with the nexus of two characters. A young woman and a strange monk meet."

"Possibly." Timon allowed himself to smile. "The first moment of their meeting might be interesting, though the larger plot must include many characters."

"But, then, how does Aristotle introduce these further characters?" She leaned forward, locking Timon in her gaze.

"He does not," Timon insisted. "Aristotle tells us that they must introduce themselves."

Close by, a book slammed shut. A slap of thunder echoed through the hall. Everyone was startled by it. All activity ceased.

"How is a man to concentrate when monks and *women* are allowed to cavort freely about him?" The voice was pinched to the point of snapping off the tongue it used.

Timon turned to its source. He found a rail-thin, gaunt man— eyes gray, shoulders bent—seated at the desk closest to Anne's back. The man's eyes avoided contact, but his face was contorted by rage.

For a moment, there was not a sound in the room.

"Silence in this hall," Timon observed, turning back to Anne, "is louder than any sound, do you agree?"

"And yet I dare brave its oppression," she answered under her breath.

"Is that wise?"

Timon barely had time to ask the question before Anne stood.

"A thousand apologies, Mr. Lively." Her voice was not the least bit apologetic. "I know my enthusiasm must be a vexation. I shall withdraw."

She gathered the few items—pen, paper, several books—that were before her on the table.

"The fault is entirely mine," Timon insisted, also standing. "I am Brother Timon, newly established as tutor—"

"I must listen to more idiocy?" Lively stood with such fury that his chair toppled, clattering noisily on the stone floor. "How can I possibly work? God in heaven!"

Anne and Timon, indeed the entire assembled company, watched as Lively stormed over to the closest door, burst out into the daylight, and was gone.

Someone sighed, and pens began scratching on paper once more.

"That was Mr. Lively," Anne told Timon. "He is one of the translators. He often leaves abruptly by that door."

Without another word, Anne headed toward the same door. Timon followed.

"One hopes that he is the most tightly strung of the lot," Timon said softly.

"They are all tense. There has been a murder here. Lively is a suspect since he found the dead body, but all these men are worried. Can you not feel it?"

Timon paused a moment to take in all six of the remaining men, absorbed as they were with the documents before them.

"We must also consider," he told her softly, "the great weight they must shoulder, creating a new Bible for a king."

There was a hint at Timon's secret, Anne thought. He was clearly interested in the scholars' work. He was putting himself in the place of those great men. He had done that kind of work himself. Her father had not merely brought her a tutor. He was there for an additional purpose.

"King James will have his new *translation*," Anne whispered over her shoulder, "but surely the *Bible* remains the same."

Anne watched his face closely, looking for any unusual reaction.

Timon's eyes held her gaze, betraying nothing—but behind his eyes it was clear he read Anne's suspicion.

"Yes," he said, his lips thinned slightly. "Surely it must."

7

*E*arly that evening, Brother Timon stood in the hall outside Deacon Marbury's office, a high window above the back of his head. He had been watching a band of light from the setting sun shrink, watching it for nearly a quarter of an hour. It was almost gone. He had also used the time attempting to remove a bit of mustard spilled on his black robe, the product of a hasty supper. The spot remained, and he decided that he might clasp his hands in front of it, as if in prayer.

The appearance of piety may often hide a stain, he thought to himself, smiling.

Without warning, the door thundered open and Marbury appeared, leaning on the frame and shaking his head.

"Absolutely inexcusable, my keeping you waiting so long," he said briskly.

The deacon had changed from his afternoon clothes. He wore a comfortably loose blue doublet, no cap, and slippers instead of boots.

"Come in, come in," Marbury said warmly, stepping aside.

As Timon passed the man, he caught the scent of brandy. Was Marbury already in his cups?

The room was warm, embraced by low beams; paneled walls. The fire's light turned everything in the room to gold, even the air.

"My duties to Christ Church are never-ending," Marbury went on, "not to mention the trouble here with the translators. And on top of it all, of course, there is Anne. She is quite remarkable, thinks like a man, behaves like a criminal."

"Hardly that," Timon objected.

"Like a petty criminal," Marbury amended with a wave of his hand. "Do take a seat there."

The chair he indicated was a backless, cushioned bench. Marbury sat first, in the more comfortable armchair laden with pillows. Timon took the opportunity to survey the rest of the room. It was lined with bookshelves. The light was too dim for him to see titles, but the sheer number of books impressed. Apart from the table where Marbury sat, and the chairs in front of the fire, Timon saw no other furniture. It was a study, then, and a place to discuss delicate issues.

"To the point," Marbury said as Timon sat. "This is your key to the hall. Only scholars currently working on the translation have had such a key until tonight. Do guard it."

Timon stared at the key. It seemed to burn in the golden air. "But you have one, of course."

"Well—yes." Marbury shook the key impatiently. "Now, then. What did you make of Lively's outburst when you were talking with Anne? She reported it to me."

Timon took the key; held it in both hands. "Mr. Lively is the presiding scholar of this Cambridge group, one of the best linguists in the world, and a King's Professor of Hebrew. He was involved in the preliminary arrangements for the translation and has the confidence of the King. He has lost his wife, I believe, and must now take care of eleven children on his own. These are ample reasons, taken in all, for such a display as he gave us this afternoon."

"Mr. Lively," Marbury said after a moment, "is my chief suspect in the murder."

"Why?" Timon could not sit still. He stood and roamed the room as he listened to Marbury, running his hand over the dust of books. As he did, he memorized every detail of the room.

If Marbury found this wandering a distraction, he did not address it.

"For one thing, he was found in the room with the body," Marbury sighed.

"Though it was his alarm that called you and the rest to the scene." Timon let his hand rest on the marble mantel and gazed into the fire.

"But Mr. Lively is also, as you mention, a widower with mouths to feed, and the stipend for his work here is meager."

"You do not imagine that the motive for the murder was robbery?" Timon turned, eyes cold as the marble he caressed.

"I imagine, in fact," Marbury said, a bit more strongly than he should have, "that the motive was academic jealousy. Lively is the leader of the group, as you say. Harrison, a man barely in his thirties, tested all the rest of the Cambridge scholars."

"Tested?"

With a single glance Timon saw, by the dim light of the fire, that Marbury carried a knife hidden in his left sleeve. Marbury saw Timon's face and must have realized that his weapon had been discovered.

Timon turned his gaze to Marbury's glass. It appeared to be filled to the rim with brandy, but the brandy bottle on the shelf behind him was barely touched.

Marbury dilutes his brandy, Timon thought. The reason for this was uncertain, but Marbury would move more quickly than a drunken man. Would he be willing to use that dagger? That was the question.

The fire popped. A flaming ember leapt into the room. Timon bent and calmly picked it up with his fingers, tossing it back into the hearth. The action was meant to impress. Here was a man to whom pain was not even a nuisance.

"You were saying that Harrison tested—whom?" Timon's shoulders relaxed as he leveled his gaze at Marbury.

"Harrison's skill in Greek and Hebrew was so notable," Marbury explained, choosing to ignore Timon's display, "that he was responsible for picking the rest of the translators in his group. For this he did receive an extra stipend, money above what the rest were paid. It was, of course, an enormous burden. To make matters worse, Harrison did not have a doctorate."

"Ah." Timon brushed sooty fingers on his robe. "This provoked Mr. Lively."

"All of the scholars chafed," Marbury assured Timon, "but Lively was especially uncomfortable."

"Lively is a man more interested in academic credentials than in actual knowledge."

"Exactly. This may, in fact, have caused his reaction to you today. He heard you discussing Aristotle, about whom he knows little." Marbury sighed heavily—a bit theatrically. "He should apologize, but he will not."

Marbury's eyes, but not his head, followed Timon wherever he went in the room. Did he suspect a method in Timon's movement?

"I shall try my best not to disturb him, then." Timon came across an open book on the edge of one shelf. He was surprised to find that it was a copy of King James's treatise called *Demonology*.

"The humility you must exhibit as a monk," Marbury sighed, "surely it has a bitter taste for a man such as yourself, a person of your learning and achievement."

Timon's posture settled. "I have been the object of jealousy in my past. Envy is a poison which often kills. Surely you are not immune to such thoughts. I mean to say, how is it that a man of your scholarship is forced to *host,* but not to *head,* this team of translators from King James? Why is Edward Lively in charge of this group instead of you?"

"I am not a linguistic scholar." Marbury's eyes closed, avoiding Timon's glare. "I have been appointed—somewhat in secret—to guard over the men who do have such training. In fact, a guardian such as myself is ensconced with each of the groups of translators—"

"At Oxford and Westminster as well as here?" Timon pursed his lips. "Do you know these other men, know their names?"

"I do not. No one does. These translators here at Cambridge, they believe, as you have just suggested, that I am merely their host. It would be best if they continued in this belief."

"I understand. I am, perhaps, more capable of keeping such secrets than any man alive."

"Incidentally," Marbury said, opening his eyes, "the final reason Lively hated Harrison was a question of heritage. Harrison was a Scot. Some of his family members were apparently associates of our King's family in Scotland, though I do not know the nature of that association. It was another reason Harrison was chosen for his position here."

"I see," Timon whispered knowingly.

"Do not mistake my meaning," Marbury hastened. "Harrison was our most qualified scholar. His kinship only gained him notice, not favor."

Timon stood with his back to Marbury. "Possibly," Timon said to the man behind him. "Is there anything else you would have me know at the moment?"

"Yes." Marbury's voice filled the room. "There is the matter of the note found in Harrison's mouth. I have it here."

"I know what it said." Timon's hand flourished. " 'Wandering through the world as God's hangmen.' Written in Harrison's own hand."

"How could you—how could you know that?"

Good, Timon thought. He's off-balance. Now is the time to test him—an aggressive attack, I think.

Timon suddenly spun about facing Marbury, a small, dull knife in his hand.

Startled, Marbury gripped the arms of his chair.

"I know a great many things," Timon said softly. "It would be best not to ask how I know them."

With that, Timon's knife vanished.

Marbury had failed the test.

Timon nodded once. In that single, brief moment, he had established his dominance.

"The note is either a deliberate attempt to mislead," Timon

went on, as if nothing had happened, "or it is a genuine communi-
cation from the murderer. Time will reveal everything. But I do
not need to see the actual note. I find it distasteful to handle anything that has been in another man's mouth."

"Of—of course," Marbury murmured, quite unsettled, "then
there is nothing further to say for the moment. You have your key."

"I do." Timon held it up as proof.

"Good, good."

"Incidentally, where is Harrison's body? Are the laws of Cambridge the same as London's? Must the body be kept somewhere
aboveground for a number of days to make certain that the victim
is dead?"

"The law is the same," Marbury confirmed, "but the wounds
on Harrison's face, the loss of blood—there was no doubt that he
was dead. His body has already been laid to rest in our cemetery."

"Interesting." Timon moved to the door.

Marbury rose from his chair, following. "It means nothing. If
you think—"

"You may place your faith in me." The sound of Timon's voice
was crisp and cold as he stepped into the hall. "Lively is not the
murderer. I shall soon know more."

Timon strode into the darkness of the corridor and vanished.

8

*T*imon moved quickly through the candlelit hallways, down the stairs, and into the chill night air. Thin clouds shot through the stars above his head. The moon was not yet high. Timon hastened his steps toward the Great Hall, all the while clutching the key in his right hand so hard that it bit into his skin.

Immediately to work, he thought. No time to waste.

His boots clattered on the stone path, and in no time his key had found its way to the lock. The door gave the slightest discernible sigh as it swung open, as if the Great Hall had been holding its breath.

He stepped inside and closed the door; was immediately plunged into darkness. He felt for the flint he always carried—he was never without a means of producing light in the darkest places. He found it, struck it, and sparked the wick of the nearest candle. A halo of white gold surrounded him. Within its round perimeter there was illumination enough to make out twilight images: the tabletops, the neatly lined chairs, the books and notes and inkwells, all without color save the ghost light of the flame. Outside the candle's glow, the rest of the hall was pitch-black.

Timon moved deliberately in the direction of Harrison's desk. He glanced about for a second in the dim candle's light, taking in every translator's desk. So much work, and before All Saints' Day. He smiled as he thought of the Pope's code phrase, *the turning of the wheel by the tilling of the wheat.*

Clement loved such arcane phrases—thought them clever—but Timon's task was plain. He was to steal the King James Bible.

Timon could accomplish this feat without a soul in England ever knowing it had been taken at all. He was going to memorize it—every word, every comma, every footnote, every source, down to the very ink stains on each page. He was to be a human repository of *everything* written by the translators.

He was the only man on earth capable of such a task.

Timon had not been told what Mother Church hoped to do with such an ocean of words, but he could guess. The Pope somehow hoped to destroy the Anglican communion and restore England to the Catholic Church—England *and* its wealth.

It would never work, of course. All popes, all rulers, were mad—the very nature of ruling insisted upon it. Timon convinced himself that he did not care, he only relished being lost in his work.

Once he stood before Harrison's desk he drew a small wheel from a concealed pocket in his robe. He began to turn it, slowly at first, tapping the letters and symbols there, as he read the writing before him.

He focused his attention, a blade-sharp concentration, to the immediate task at hand and found he knew the first lines he saw. They were from Leviticus, chapter 26, verse 30: "And I will destroy your high places, and cast down your images, and cast your carcasses upon the carcasses of your idols, and my soul shall abhor you." A note in the margin insisted that the word *cut* should replace the word *cast.* What tedious work it would be if this was all that the translators were doing.

Timon knew his lips were moving as he read, a childish trait he had long struggled to snuff out. It seemed to help in memorizing long passages. His memory wheel was the primary instrument of his remarkable abilities. It was his own invention based on the Llullist system. It always seemed to be aided, however, by his whispering the words to himself. Timon suffered the sin of pride, but felt justly satisfied with his remarkable ability. No one on earth had greater powers of memory. It was his secret weapon, his *telum secretus*.

He was about to turn the page when a sharp crack in the shadows broke the silence of the empty room.

Timon smothered the candle with the palm of his other hand. Soundlessly he returned his memory wheel to its secret pocket. The building was old. The walls might creak. It was nothing.

Two heartbeats later, a sudden footstep shuffled in the darkness not twenty feet away.

Timon reached for his knife, straining his eyes for any movement. Moonlight did its best to help through the high windows, but was a poor assistant.

When light was not enough, Timon reminded himself, what other senses might be used?

Could he hear the intruder's breath? Could he smell the man? Could he feel the air swirl if the man moved?

The intruder had two advantages. He had been waiting in the darkness, so his eyes would be more accustomed to the lack of light in the room. He also knew exactly where Timon was because of the candle that had been lit. Timon willed his eyes to adjust to the darkness and slowly crouched down and away from Harrison's desk.

Without warning the intruder leapt though the air. He nearly landed on top of Timon, blade flashing in the moonlight. Timon rolled under Harrison's desk, kicking and grunting. The attacker landed on the floor with a thud, the point of his knife narrowly missing its mark. The killer spat and scrambled in Timon's direction, spiderlike.

Jabbing a boltlike thumb toward the man's face, Timon hoped to catch an eye. Instead he grazed the hairline, but it was enough to make the man jerk backward for an instant. Timon scrambled out the other side of Harrison's desk and stood. In a flash he found his flint and struck it, lighting the nearest candle. In its sudden glow, the intruder appeared. He was wrapped in a black robe, masked from forehead to chin.

Timon could only see the man's weapon, a long blade with two cutting edges and barbs on the hilt.

It was good that a thick oaken desk stood between them.

Timon drew in a deep breath and smiled, making certain that the man could see his face in the candlelight. It wore an expression of complete assurance, absolutely lacking in fear—or conscience. Timon had practiced it for years.

The man's blade hand began to shake.

Timon's foot flew forward then, kicking Harrison's chair from under the desk. The chair crashed into the man's legs. Timon sprang upward, leaping onto the desk. He seemed to fly. The intruder gazed up at him, momentarily stunned, and Timon kicked the blade from the hand.

The man stared at his empty fist for only an instant. Then he grunted and withdrew a pistol from some hidden fold in his robes. He cocked it and stepped back out of Timon's reach.

Timon, the smile never leaving his face, jumped over the man as if gravity did not apply to him. He landed on the next closest desk. The man spun, but found a heavy leather book headed toward his skull. He barely had time to duck.

When he recovered, Timon had vanished.

The intruder turned in wild circles, his lungs blasting out involuntary noises. He squinted desperately, but his pistol could find no target. Before he could realize what was happening, Timon appeared at his back. A razor's edge slid along the man's gullet, just enough to draw a thin line of blood.

The man froze and lowered his gun.

"Good," Timon told him soothingly. "Nothing sudden, that's the safe path when a man's got a razor at your throat."

The man's breathing was like a blacksmith's bellows.

"Now would you mind moving *slowly* toward Harrison's chair, just there?" Timon continued. "I believe you know the one. He was seated there when you murdered him and destroyed his face."

Still, the man did not move.

"I'm going to ask you some questions," Timon insisted, muscling the man forward. "It may take awhile. You want to sit down."

The man resisted, and Timon was about to slice deeper into the throat.

Behind them there was an explosion at the door of the Great Hall. A man holding a lantern plunged into the room.

"What is this noise?" the voice demanded, top volume. "Do not move. I have a musket!"

His attention momentarily drawn away, Timon lowered his knife. The intruder seized the opportunity, sank to his knees, and quickly slithered away. Too late, Timon lurched forward to grab him, but missed. Behind him, the man at the door called out.

"You there, I see you! Stand!"

The intruder slid farther into the shadows and rolled away. Before Timon could take a single step in pursuit he heard the unmistakable sound of a musket cocking.

"Do not move again," the man at the door called, "or I shall dispatch my weapon!"

Timon thought he recognized the voice; confirmed his guess as the man drew near and the candlelight revealed his face.

"Mr. Lively." Timon shook his head slowly, hiding his knife. "Excellent work. You have just allowed Mr. Harrison's murderer to escape."

9

*L*ively slowly lowered his rusted musket. His chapped lips fell open. He seemed to be trying to form words. Timon glared with all the revulsion he could muster, allowing his accusation to sink into Lively's brain.

"Murderer," Lively finally managed to sputter. "Escaped?"

"In fact, I had him well in hand," Timon sighed tensely. "Did you not see the man run from me?"

"I did see someone—"

"But the notion of firing your hopeless weapon at *him* seemed inappropriate?" Timon folded his arms. "You thought it a better plan to threaten an old monk, a young woman's tutor? It is an interesting choice."

"No," Lively began.

"If you will refrain from shooting me, I will follow after the killer at once."

Without further pronouncement, Timon turned to dart after the killer.

"I do not think it wise to run from me," Lively shouted. "Stand as you are until I can determine what has happened."

Timon sighed, looked back, and found that the yawning barrel was only several feet from his chest.

"I have told you what happened." Timon shook his head in disbelief. "What has happened is that you have let Harrison's killer escape. I can still catch him if you will——"

"I will pull this trigger if you move another inch!" Lively insisted.

Timon closed his eyes, mustering patience. "Have you ever shot a man, sir? At this distance, a gun like yours makes a hole in a man larger than a melon. Bits of bone and gristle fly in every direction. One finds these tidbits on the clothes and even in the hair for days afterward."

"I often shoot wild boar," Lively said unflinchingly.

In a blur Timon's hand flew out of the darkness. He grabbed the barrel of Lively's musket and pushed it once. The stock struck Lively savagely in the stomach. Lively staggered backward, losing his grip on the musket. Timon pulled hard, dislodging the weapon from its owner.

Lively regained his balance just in time to see Timon hold the musket up by its barrel as if it were a dead rat. Then the gun was tossed onto the empty desk next to Harrison's.

In three quick steps, Timon was beside Lively, a dagger in his hand. Lively found the point of the blade under his jawbone. He barely understood what had happened.

"You are, among the scholars who work in this hall," Timon whispered, "the chief suspect in Harrison's murder. Marbury has told me as much. He will want to know what has happened here—that the killer has escaped; that you helped him. I know you are not the murderer, but it would appear that you are in league with him. Now, come with me. We must disturb the deacon at once."

Lively closed his eyes and offered up a sigh to creak the rafters. "If I do not, do you think you will kill me? Because if I am not dead, I will only pick up my musket again."

"I have never shot a wild boar," Timon offered reasonably, "but I have slit the gullet of many a man like you—without regret, remorse, or recrimination."

To Timon's surprise, his words did not seem to alarm Lively.

"You have no idea what goes on within these walls." Lively's posture, demeanor, even the sound of his voice had changed. "Murder means nothing—even my own. We work in mysteries here that are known to fewer than twenty men in the world. The loss of any one scholar is absolutely inconsequential compared to the magnitude of the secret things we do as a group. Would you not like to know those secrets? Would it not be wise, before you kill me, to know the truth? If, as you say, the man who just fled this chamber was the murderer, you might wish to know his *true* motives in that matter."

The way Lively's voice had changed gave Timon pause. He was no longer the effete and offended scholar. He was a man who might know something important. That possibility kept Timon from dispatching the man and running after the murderer—for the moment.

"I have found," Timon said slowly, "that *truth,* in its purest form, does not exist in England."

"Then perhaps you should be seated at my desk," Lively said, having completely gathered his wits, "as I am about to offer you a purity of truth that will silence your impudence once and for all." Lively was the sword arm of God. That power was clear in his voice.

Timon hesitated, an event so rare that it momentarily confused his senses. He found himself baffled by Lively's demeanor. Other men might be quivering with fear. Lively was offering forbidden information.

"You will allow me to see your work?" Timon asked plainly.

"No," Lively said, his stare undiminished. "I will reveal to you a greater secret."

Timon's blade vanished and he clasped his hands in front of his chest. "Why?"

"Because when you know this truth," Lively said softly, "you will leave us to our work and never come back. That is what I want you to do, and I can accomplish it by sharing with you only a few of the terrifying facts at my disposal."

Timon understood the ploy. Show any ordinary monk some bit of secret information about the Church, and that monk would run, terrified, back to his abbey. Timon had, of course, seen so many hidden, illegal instructions from so many men of the Church that he was entirely immune to such a ploy.

"Allow me." Lively moved toward his desk in a stately, foolish fashion, as if he were headed for coronation.

Timon watched.

"Please." Lively indicated his own chair, a mask of solemnity pasted across his face.

Timon allowed himself the whisper of a smile. He deliberately took louder, slower steps than his usual gait. Gray stone walls amplified the insult.

If Lively understood Timon's intent, he did not show it. Instead, he lit three thick candles on his desk. Circles of dismal light surrounded the papers there.

Timon sighed as he lifted himself into the tall, straight-backed scholar's chair. An embroidered pillow was on the seat.

"What you are about to see," Lively rasped, "is known only to a handful of scholars in the world. I have no fear that you will reveal it, just as I have no need to hear you swear an oath. This single, ancient page reveals a hidden truth so completely unbelievable that you would be the object of wild ridicule if you mentioned it and arrested if you insisted upon it."

"Will you be making a very long speech, Mr. Lively?" Timon interrupted again. "I might still be able to follow the murderer's trail if—"

"Silence!" Lively blasted.

Without further ado, and with much heavy breathing, Lively produced a key and unlocked the drawer in his desk. He withdrew a sheaf of papers. They were clearly very old, greatly damaged; nearly transparent.

He placed a single tattered page before Timon, laying it on the desk with a delicacy Timon would not have thought possible from Lively.

"You can read Hebrew, one imagines?" Lively sniffed.

"I can." Timon allowed his smile to grow indulgently.

"Then read here." Lively's index finger fell to a single line in the middle of the page.

Timon moved a candle closer, squinted at the line. It was difficult to read. The page was torn and scarred.

"Read it aloud, would you mind?" Lively said plainly.

Timon thought he understood: Lively was testing his Hebrew.

"Very well." Timon sighed and focused on the letters. "Let me see. It says, 'And when eight days were accomplished for the circumcising of the child, his name was called Yshua, which was so named of the angel before he was conceived in the womb.'"

It only took Timon another second to recognize the text—or most of it. "This is the Gospel of St. Luke, chapter two, verse twenty-one. I have only read it in Greek"

"This is, we believe, the original text." Lively's voice quavered. "It was written in the same century as Our Lord died."

"But," Timon began, slowly realizing Lively's awe, "there is a very significant difference between this and all other versions of Luke I know."

"Exactly," Lively whispered desperately, afraid of the sound of his own voice.

"The name *Yshua*," Timon heard himself saying, temples pounding. "The Hebrew form of *Joshua*. Which means—it cannot be."

"The text is correct." Lively's voice was a wisp of smoke.

"This is a passage about the circumcision of Our Lord. His name—"

"Christ's name," Lively stammered, swallowing, "was not Jesus."

Timon sat frozen for a moment, not allowing the revelation to sink in. The hall seemed colder and more hollow than it had moments before.

"No." Timon finally slid the page away from him, sneering. "This is an obvious forgery."

Lively's answer was strained. "It has been authenticated to the satisfaction of every scholar here."

Timon quickly found the weight of those words sinking into his heart. All eight Cambridge scholars had agreed that the document was genuine. Eight men who could not agree on the best way to dip a quill had confirmed their belief in that page.

"Where did you get this?" Timon demanded, tapping the page with his index finger. "Why has no one else seen this?"

Lively looked about, pulled a chair from across the aisle toward him, and collapsed into the seat, weary beyond comprehension. He absently laid his hand upon the musket. It was still cocked.

"A Catholic archivist named Padget stole it from Rome many years ago. He had defected from his Church and was hiding in Scotland when James was king there." Lively avoided Timon's stare. "This man Padget sold it to James. That was the sort of man he was. Then he disappeared, perhaps to London. This was the first document that provoked our King to investigate certain . . . mysteries of our faith. This investigation eventually inspired him to commission the new translation. James is a man in search of answers. God help us all."

Timon studied Lively's face. The man seemed on the verge of collapse. This single Gospel, Timon reasoned, unsupported by any other evidence, would not be sufficient to disturb Lively so deeply. The conclusion was obvious.

"You have other such secret documents." Timon folded his arms across his chest.

Lively closed his eyes, nodding once. "Padget stole three, but eventually fifty-seven such secret texts were acquired by our King. I am in possession of them all."

In the silence that followed, Timon fancied he could actually hear Lively's heart thumping inside the bars of his chest. He wondered how much more agitated Lively would be if he knew that Timon was no stranger to the name *Padget*. That was a secret worth keeping.

"And over the course of these few months since the beginning of your work in this hall," Timon said, deliberately steadying his voice, "you have compared these ancient texts to a more current Bible—the Bishops' or the Geneva."

"Yes." Lively nodded, eyes wild. "Both."

"And you have discovered other such . . . anomalies?" Timon had to hold his breath to keep from exhaling too harshly.

"Yes, but how can it be?" Lively shuddered. "The Bible was written by God! It is infallible!"

"Yes."

"Then how," Lively croaked, barely audibly, "can there be over five thousand errors in translation?"

The cold in the hall seemed to press Timon's bones. "Five thousand?"

"More. We've stopped counting. Many date to the first Council of Nicaea."

Timon struggled to comprehend the information, hoping that his discomfort would not show in the dim light. Slowly, as he began to grasp the enormity of what Lively was trying to tell him, he fought a dull sensation of being dropped into a bottomless hole. In fifteen hundred years of the Christian Church, no human being had even considered questioning the *veritas* of its Bible. Yet here was proof that somewhere between the life of Christ and the reign of King James, that Bible had been changed—an unspeakable heresy.

If what Lively was saying contained even the whisper of truth, it would stagger the foundations of their religion. Small wonder that the Pope wanted to see what these men in England were doing. Conclusions were self-evident. If the Word of God could contain mistakes, what good were any other words? Where was there an atom of trust or faith in the world? What pope or king could hope to maintain any semblance of authority?

"Well." Timon drew in a long breath. "If you thought, Mr. Lively, that I might panic at this discovery, it was a well-founded attempt. No one I know would believe me if I repeated this information. Nearly any other man in Christendom would fly from this hall in terror. If my blood had not already been washed cold, if my heart had not been scrubbed empty, I too might have fled."

Lively recoiled, eyes wide. He was clearly stunned that his scheme had not produced the desired terror.

Timon was regaining his equilibrium. "The advantage of shedding one's soul, you see, is that no fear is of any consequence. The meaning of everything evaporates. All events are the same."

But here was information worth knowing, Timon thought, and terror worth exploring. The absolute necessity of knowing the truth of this matter was suddenly more vital, all at once, than water or air. Though Timon was uncertain of the exact reasons, he had heard in Lively's words the faint stirring of wings, the sound of his salvation. It was the first such sensation he had known in over twenty years.

"I must see them all," Timon buzzed.

"What?" Lively's head snapped back.

"I must see the other documents. All of them."

"N-no!" Lively's momentary incoherence betrayed a stark astonishment. "You cannot . . . I would never allow . . . God in heaven, have you not heard what I was saying?"

"I must have access to the ancient Greek and Hebrew texts which you possess," Timon whispered, his wits nearly restored. "I must see these errors for myself."

"No, I say!" Lively stood, his hand accidentally disturbing the musket on the desk.

The musket clattered to the floor, miraculously unfired.

In the silence that followed, both men could clearly hear a rustling in a far corner of the hall. It sounded very much as if someone had been frightened by the sound of the musket.

Lively froze.

Timon moved his finger to his lips. "The assassin."

"He is still here?" Lively's eyes darted everywhere.

"Shh," Timon insisted. "He may well be."

Timon crouched low to the floor, one knee on the cold stone. He took out his knife, inching forward, straining for any visual evidence of the killer.

Why is the man still here? Timon wondered. Is he so bent on killing that he *will* not escape?

In a far corner of the room, a scraping sound rang out. It sent Lively ducking under his own desk.

Timon peered through the forest of desk legs and saw a flash of movement caught by a sliver of candlelight. Gauging where the man might be, he rolled slightly in that direction on the icy floor.

Willing his movements to be silent, Timon eased himself in the direction of the corner where the killer hid. Once again Timon concentrated on all five senses, crawling slowly, slowly toward the killer. A sip of breath, a smell of rum, a feather of air, all betrayed the villain.

Suddenly a short gasp from Lively, the involuntary noise of dread, drew the killer's attention. Timon could make out gray motion in a blur of black air.

The man was headed toward Lively.

Timon drew himself into a crouching readiness; judged the distance between his place and Lively's.

He was about to pounce when Lively suddenly shot from his hiding place and seized the musket on the floor.

"Ha!" he exploded triumphantly, standing upright. "I have the musket! Show yourself!"

Without hesitation, a deafening blast and a flash of powder savaged the air. Smoke rose from the killer's pistol. Lively grunted and fell backward, crumpling onto the floor. Even by the dim illumination of the candles, Timon could see blood beginning to spot Lively's chest.

The killer was on the move, racing toward Lively's desk. Timon seized the legs of the tall chair closest to him. When he was certain that the killer was near, he burst upward, raising the chair with him.

His opponent was startled. Timon took advantage of the man's momentary pause, swinging the chair wide like a headman's ax. He chopped into the killer's side and the man flew backward, gasping.

Discarding the chair, Timon leapt toward his victim, grabbing the man's ankle. The killer kicked out with his other foot. Timon dodged it and twisted the ankle so that the man rolled. Drawing his knife, Timon cut through the man's boot. Feeling the knife's edge slice his flesh, unable to break Timon's grip, the killer threw himself forward. Timon barely saw him raise his pistol high. In the next instant it came crashing down directly onto Timon's skull. A searing pain momentarily blinded Timon, and he dropped his knife.

The killer scrambled away, crawling at first, then staggering to his feet. In the dim light, as his eyes barely focused, Timon could see the man pause at Lively's desk. Even then he appeared reluctant to flee. With one final glance at the documents on the desk, the killer finally roared away, through the main entrance, and into the night.

10

*T*imon clutched the top of the desk next to him, struggling to remain conscious. He took in deep breaths, held them as he prayed, then let them go. Just as his head began to clear, he heard voices. Fearing that the killer was returning with reinforcements, his eyes locked on the dark entrance to the hall. He felt his way along the floor with his feet until they found the musket. He dipped, clutched it, and crouched low behind the nearest desk, checking to make certain the musket was still ready to fire.

He could see tongues of orange and golden light through the open entrance. Men with torches drew near. He aimed the musket, glancing to make certain it was still cocked, and steadied his finger on the trigger.

Just as he was about to fire, Marbury's face appeared in the doorway. Torches aloft, others followed immediately.

"Who's there?" Marbury demanded.

Timon lowered the musket.

Torchlight did not fully illuminate the room from the doorway. Marbury strained to see in the shadows.

"Is anyone among you a doctor of medicine?" Timon asked calmly. "Mr. Lively may be dying."

"Timon?" Marbury's pace quickened.

The others remained behind him and slowed when they realized that Timon was holding a musket.

"What has he done?" one of the men whispered, terrified.

Timon laid the musket on the desk next to him. Retrieving his knife he moved toward the fallen Lively.

"Stay where you are!" an anonymous voice commanded.

"Please do not move, Brother Timon," Marbury echoed in steadier tones.

Marbury took a few steps forward. In the candlelight, Timon could see that Marbury held a blade of his own. It was longer than most, polished to mirrored perfection; thin—deadly.

Timon was momentarily perplexed by the thought that he would not like to kill Marbury. It was an inexplicable concept. He would not have minded killing anyone else in the room.

Something must be done quickly, however, Timon thought. There is a dead scholar at my feet and I have been discovered holding a musket.

From the muttering that filled the air, clearly the men behind Marbury had already judged Timon a murderer.

"We heard the gunshot," Marbury rasped. "It is not a common sound in our Cambridge nights, but one which is easy enough to identify—and to cause alarm."

As Timon opened his mouth to begin an explanation, he heard a groaning behind him.

"Brothers," Lively croaked, "will no one help me stand?"

Timon turned at once, without thinking, and offered his hand to Lively, marveling at the man's strength considering the pistol shot in his chest.

"Pray God," Lively continued, struggling to his feet, turning immediately to his desk in utter desperation, "nothing has happened to the pages—"

"Mr. Lively," Marbury ventured, moving quickly toward him, "are you shot?"

"God, God, God," Lively whispered violently, raking through the papers on his desk.

At first Timon supposed that he was trying to hide the secret text of St. Luke in his last moments of life. Then he began to realize what had actually happened.

Marbury arrived at Lively's desk, a kerchief in hand, intent on stanching the man's wound.

"Ah!" Lively shouted exuberantly. "His Name be praised!"

He held a single page up for all to see.

His colleagues gaped, blinking.

"Do you not need attention to your—?" Marbury began.

"It is undamaged!" Lively exalted. "I would never have forgiven myself if it had survived fifteen hundred years only to be destroyed in my care."

While others stared at Lively, Timon examined the desktop. The glow of the candles made it clear that the desk had been covered in ink, and several of the papers there had been ruined.

"I think you will find, Deacon Marbury," Timon announced, "that the stain on Mr. Lively's chest is not blood, but ink."

"Indeed." Lively exhaled noisily and sat. "The villain's shot failed to damage me, but instead performed its foul deed upon my workplace."

"The pistol seems to have put a hole in Mr. Lively's desk and upset his inkwell," Timon explained.

"Timon did not shoot you?" one of the men stammered slowly.

"Timon?" Lively glared. "He shot no one, though I nearly shot him."

A gaggle of astonished questions erupted in the room. Marbury put away his knife, and clearly hoping to avert chaos, he pounded his fist upon Lively's desk.

"Gentlemen, please," he insisted, "let us determine what has happened here in a coherent fashion!"

The room fell silent.

Lively's eyes met Timon's, silently imploring him not to reveal everything that had transpired. Timon took a moment, deciding what to disclose and what to conceal, a conundrum that often plagued him.

"We believe that Harrison's killer returned to his hall," Lively began, before Timon could speak. "Brother Timon was clever enough to have been waiting for him—how or why I do not know. I came to the hall after my dinner to do a bit of work in solitude, heard voices, retrieved my hunting musket, and nearly shot Brother Timon."

"In the ensuing moments," Timon interrupted, "the killer and I fought, he fired his pistol, causing the damage to Mr. Lively's desk; then used said pistol to crack my head, causing similar damage there. He escaped an instant before you came into the hall."

"The killer has returned?" someone whispered.

"He came to kill Lively," Marbury surmised, "the head of our project, hoping to further harm our work."

"I do not believe that the man's intent was murder tonight," Timon said slowly. "I believe he discovered something when he killed Harrison. It so astonished him that he returned to steal evidence of that discovery. I had bested him when Mr. Lively came in with his musket, and the man got away. But he did not then leave the hall, even with the two of us *and* a musket present. He wanted something in this room so badly that he was willing to risk all, despite being discovered and outnumbered. He attacked us hoping to get something."

The room was absolutely silent, which told Timon what he had hoped to learn. Every man in the room did, indeed, know the secrets that Lively had revealed to him. Each of them knew that those secrets were the killer's true motive.

"Deacon Marbury," Timon said suddenly, deliberately breaking the silence, startling everyone, "I believe it would be appropriate to pursue further inquiry a bit more privately. Perhaps you and I might—"

The others began to interrupt, voicing unorganized objections.

"Please," Marbury implored, "I think we would all be safer in our beds this night. Allow me to question Brother Timon further."

Lively sucked in a tense breath, but said nothing. The other men seemed to slowly absorb what had happened, mumbling to each other.

"May I remind you, gentlemen," Marbury insisted, "that there is still a killer loose in the night."

That was enough to propel the men, however reluctantly, toward the door.

Marbury indicated that Timon should precede him in the same direction. Timon acquiesced and started out of the hall. He did, however, manage to notice, out of the corner of his eye, that Lively was slipping the text from St. Luke into his coat. He made a noisy show of locking up some other piece of paper in his desk drawer, but he had stolen the secret document for himself.

11

*A*fter everyone else had gone, Timon and Marbury lingered just outside the door to the hall.

"I am certain that the killer has, at last, fled," Timon said softly, "but we ought to at least take a look around out here, would you not agree? It will give me the opportunity to ask you some questions which you shall answer fully and with complete truth."

"Do you imagine for the slightest moment," Marbury said softly, "that you intimidate me?"

I should, Timon thought.

"Although," Marbury continued, "I suppose I have hired you to investigate this—situation. If you've paid the devil, you may as well get a day's work from him. Please, ask whatever questions you like." Marbury moved away from the door. "Shall we?"

Again Timon had the uncomfortable sensation of liking Marbury. He fought it, concentrating on the greater issue at hand.

"I would like to see if we could find any sort of trail the killer might have left," Timon said quickly. "But Lively revealed to me some startling information that I feel would qualify as a motive for Harrison's murder."

"Yes?" Marbury's face gave nothing away.

The night, Timon thought, seemed determined to be as black as it possibly could. The moon was obscured by low rain clouds that tumbled in the sky like great waves in a storm. It was the perfect night for dark revelations and escaped murderers.

"Are you aware that Mr. Lively is in possession of a document that is the original manuscript of the Gospel of St. Luke?" Begin with the most shocking point, Timon thought; see what it stabs.

"I surmised," Marbury said, scratching the inside of his ear with his little finger, "that Lively had showed you a page from some ancient text. I saw it in his hand."

"That document proves that a great error was made in all subsequent renderings of the Gospel." Timon moved slowly away from the Great Hall, looking for footprints in the grass.

"This great error is the motive of which you spoke?" Marbury asked, not bothering to hide his derision. "Are you not aware that these men discover twenty such errors a day?"

"I see." Timon tilted his head, deciding to change the subject; let Marbury feel for a moment he had the upper hand. "Shall we look off the path, Deacon? I am trying to find any hint of the killer, perhaps in the wet grass—a footprint, a torn leaf, a bit of blood. I think the killer would have avoided the stone path—it clatters when anyone runs upon it. Our man would prefer silence, would he not?"

Marbury moved off the stone path distractedly. "But about these errors in translation—"

"Ah," Timon interrupted. Good, he thought, Marbury is thinking, he has not dismissed my suggestions quite yet.

"I—I mean to say that if you refer to the mistakes from older texts—"

"My concern hinges on a single word in the *secret* text," Timon snapped impatiently, "which is our current concern."

"No," Marbury insisted. "I must persuade you, Brother, that your discovery, whatever it is, is *not* current. It is hundreds of years old, most likely; exhausted by age. It is not remotely pertinent to our problem here in Cambridge in the year of Our Lord 1605."

Timon came to a halt in the dark night. "If you believe that, then you have not seen the text to which I refer."

"Perhaps I have not," Marbury admitted, glancing quickly in Timon's direction.

"The problem is not hundreds of years old, it is more than a thousand years old. The full revelation of the work these men are doing here in Cambridge would corrupt the very foundation of our religion. That is why Lively is frightened. That is why Harrison has been killed."

"Rubbish!" Marbury growled. "How could it possibly matter if Second Corinthians six: two should say '*a* day of salvation,' instead of '*the* day of salvation,' or where the comma rightly belongs in Mark sixteen: nine. The spirit of God's Word is unchanged."

"Yes." Timon bit his upper lip. Marbury's words confirmed that he did not know the magnitude of the secret kept in the Great Hall. How much to discuss and how much to conceal? Had the scholars deliberately kept Marbury in the dark? Were they afraid to share what they were learning with anyone but one another? It would not be an unfounded fear. The history of writing the Bible was, in fact, filled with stories of men who had discovered secrets far less dire and paid for the knowledge dearly, even with their lives.

In 1382, when John Wycliffe produced the first English Bible, the Catholic Church expelled him from his teaching position at Oxford and burned all his Bibles.

And when William Tyndale translated the New Testament into English in 1525, he was forced to flee to Germany. The Inquisition dogged his trail, out for his blood. Tyndale was caught, tried, strangled, then burned at the stake.

Timon attempted to untangle the knot of his thoughts and begin again. "Deacon Marbury," he said calmly, "shall I alter the course of your thinking?"

"What are you talking about?" Marbury asked hesitantly.

"Allow me to begin by asking you a question about the document that Lively showed me, the one you saw in his hand tonight. Was that document already here in Cambridge when the scholars arrived, or did Lively bring it with him?"

"That document, if I am correct, was delivered to us here by a courier from King James himself—an armed courier, to make matters more dramatic." Marbury cast his eyes downward. "I admit I did find that somewhat troublesome at the time."

"Yes, Lively seemed to indicate that there was much drama surrounding the manuscript." Timon had stopped looking for clues in the grass. "Would it surprise you to know that all eight scholars, before Harrison's death, examined the text and declared it authentic?"

"It would surprise me that those men would agree upon any matter, yes." Marbury's lips thinned.

"Lively showed me but a single sentence from *this* Gospel of St. Luke," Timon said plainly. "But it was a sentence that could wrack Christendom with chaos."

Marbury tried to see Timon's expression in the darkness. "You seem to have a flair for the theatre yourself."

"No, this is God's play," Timon said softly, "not mine. The sentence I read tonight named our Savior *Joshua*. The name *Jesus* does not appear on the page."

Marbury blinked, but did not otherwise move.

"The scope of our problem, you see," Timon went on, "goes beyond the placement of a comma."

"How could . . . how did . . . the document is a forgery." Marbury leaned forward, the cold wind chilling his cheek.

"All eight of your scholars agreed it was not."

"All eight," Marbury repeated, whispering.

"There is more," Timon hastened to say. "Your scholars here in Cambridge have in their possession many such documents containing many more secrets. Lively admitted to fifty-seven such texts."

"God in heaven." Marbury swallowed.

"I see that the enormity of the situation begins to sink in." Timon nodded. "Now, could all fifty-seven of these secret documents have come from the armed courier you mentioned? Did he bring such a large package, or make several deliveries?"

Marbury's brow twitched, and his eyes concentrated on a space somewhere between himself and Timon.

"No," Marbury said at last. "That courier came but once. He could certainly have delivered more than one document—dozens, in fact—but not fifty-seven."

"Well."

The high wind momentarily shoved aside the charcoal clouds that obscured the moon, and Timon was able to see Marbury's face.

Most men would not accept this news, Timon thought. Either the mind would be too small to encompass it, or the faith would be to weak to withstand it.

Marbury's face betrayed neither such thought. He seemed to stare at nothing. He was, Timon thought, weighing this new information against everything else he knew.

In that silence, Timon fought against that same impetus.

"I must know more," Marbury muttered at length, nearly to himself. "I must see all these documents. I must hear more of these *translation* errors, if, indeed, that is even the word that applies."

Timon smiled, an expression of kindred compassion. "Exactly my thought."

Before Timon could explore the warmth he felt toward Marbury, he was seized with a blood-drenched vision so violent that it silenced him. It was an old conditioning, something Timon had practiced over and over as a younger man: whenever he felt kindly inclined toward a man he might have to kill, he forced himself to imagine that man dead. That practice had become a reflex. Without even trying, Timon saw himself carving a hole in Marbury's chest, watching the heart beat there. Timon's training had combined with his great wariness of all men. It was a compulsion stronger than any fact or belief and was often triggered by any compassionate impulse he might have had. The vision passed quickly, its work done, and Timon eyed Marbury coldly once more.

Timon could see that Marbury had been studying his face.

"Brother Timon," Marbury began, obviously misinterpreting Timon's expression, "I see that you are as unhinged by these revelations as am I."

"No," Timon said, exhaling. "I am in the process of realizing that King James already knows what you and I have only now discovered."

"Yes, of course." Marbury glanced about in the darkness. "He sent Lively the documents."

"I have a thousand questions." Timon began to pace in the cold, wet grass. "Clearly these secrets were the cause of Harrison's murder. But are these secrets, in fact, what motivated King James to commission his new translation?"

"Yes," Marbury said instantly.

Timon held a finger to his lips. "Are we overlooking anything? We must be thorough in our thoughts. Men kill each other for so many reasons, and the most obvious answer is not always correct."

"By which you mean . . . ?"

"One man may quarrel with another in the street," Timon explained, "because the first bumped the second. They fight. One dies. All others would say, 'He died because he bumped another man in the street.' They would fail to take into account that the killer had been jostled a hundred other times and taken no offense. What made that particular moment different? What gave that day a funeral? Perhaps the killer quarreled with his wife earlier in the day, or his finances were in disarray, or his mistress had been taken by another man. Any one of a dozen nuisances may change a man's disposition from courtesy to murder."

"I had never quite thought of things in that light," Marbury marveled. "But you appear to be trying to talk yourself into believing there may be some other motive for Harrison's murder."

"Because my true suspicion, that the crime concerns these secret texts, leads us toward too many other troubling questions."

"Especially King James's reason for commissioning his new Bible," Marbury asserted.

"Exactly. What man would want to investigate a king? If only I could discover more about the King's motives."

"I may be able to help with that," Marbury said softly. "As it happens, I had a hand—a very private hand—in aiding James against the Bye Plot. The details are boring. I chanced to overhear these English Catholics discussing their plan to kidnap King James and force him to repeal anti-Catholic legislation. I reported it to the King, and he was saved. As a result, I have a bit of the King's favor."

"But that plot was revealed by English Jesuits," Timon objected. "Father Henry Garnet, specifically, fearing retribution against Catholics if the plan failed—"

"That was the public face of it," Marbury interrupted, looking away.

Timon's thoughts raced. "It *would* have been more politic to let it be known that Catholics themselves condemned the plot."

"If you say so." Marbury's face was a mask.

"And yet James used the plot as an excuse to order all Catholic clergy to leave England."

"Did he need an excuse?"

Timon stared at Marbury. "You amaze me, Deacon. Who would have suspected that you were a man of such mystery?"

"Indeed I fancy that I may be, in my world, what you are in yours."

"Which is why you mention your work for the King," Timon surmised. "You have some relationship with His Majesty that might allow you to ask him certain questions."

"In fact," Marbury whispered, "I have a coach in our stables which the King has given to me for the express purpose of keeping His Majesty informed of any dire news. A murder among his translators would seem to be of such a nature, especially since James knew the deceased. I could take advantage of such a visit to—"

"You must leave at once," Timon insisted. "I know what I must do."

Before Timon could finish his thought, sweeping footsteps in the darkness startled both men.

They had been watched; the killer had lingered. Someone was running in the shadows that surrounded them, running directly toward them.

12

ather!"

Both men turned in the direction of the harsh whisper. Marbury held his hand up imploring Timon not to speak.

"Anne?" Marbury called softly.

"I heard a gunshot," she insisted.

"All is well," Marbury ventured. "I heard it too. It was nothing. Please return to your bed."

Silence.

"Anne?"

After another second, Anne appeared out of the shadows. She carried a single taper and was dressed in a thick, azure, quilted robe. The perfection of her cheek reminded Timon of a painting by Giotto, Mary after the Annunciation.

"Has someone been shot?" Her voice was solid as the stones in the wall.

"Anne, go back to bed!" Marbury snapped. "Why on earth would you—?"

"Brother Timon," Anne continued, breezing past her father, "have you shot someone?"

"Brother Timon was nearly shot by Mr. Lively," Marbury corrected. "Why would you assume that it was Brother Timon who—?"

"Did you imagine that I would believe, even for an *instant,* that this man was actually to be my tutor?" Anne's face was crimson in the moonlight. "The scholars in the hall will be fooled because they don't care about me and they won't pay attention to my tutor. But I can tell the difference between this man and any other teacher I have ever had, because I am not an idiot!"

"I thought you liked Brother Timon." Marbury shivered a bit and wondered if there were enough logs beside the hearth in his study.

"I like him very much," she snapped. "I can learn from him; he is exceedingly wise. But he is hardly here in Cambridge as my tutor. And I wonder why he smells of nutmeg so strongly."

"I cook," Timon responded.

"Your response comes a bit too immediately," Anne insisted accusingly.

"Anne!" Marbury's voice hardened.

"Where did you find him, Father?" Anne demanded.

"I would prefer to remain primarily anonymous," Timon said quickly. "Mistress, with great apology, you must at least pretend to believe that I am here in Cambridge as your tutor."

"But you are in charge of this *investigation,* are you not?" she demanded.

"A coincidence," Marbury assured her before Timon could respond.

"No!" Anne exploded. "Brother Timon's mental dexterity, which I witnessed yesterday in the hall, will prove a discomfort to the translators. If one of them is guilty of this horrible crime, that one may reveal himself unbidden in some ill-advised trick to hide the truth. Nothing so confounds a clever man as his attempting to be too clever. Timon is just the person to provoke that sort of behavior in these scholars. You must believe that the assassin is one of the translators."

"Yes," Timon lied.

"Splendid." Suddenly Anne could not hide the thrill she felt at the possibility of having stared into the eyes of a murderer.

"Not necessarily," Marbury insisted hastily. "I would have Brother Timon eliminate them first, of course."

"Not to put too fine a point on it, Brother Timon," Anne began, holding up her candle, staring into its flame, warming her fingers over it, "you do recall my interest in the theatre?"

Both men were obviously bemused by her change of subject.

"Of course," Timon responded hesitantly.

"I was just now thinking of a beautiful line from one of our plays—something more recent than your ancient Greek one, a bit of dialogue in which you and my father may find some solace at the moment. It says, 'That which we call a rose, by any other name would smell as sweet.' "

Anne leveled a bold stare, over the flickering candle's flame, directly into Timon's soul.

"Your meaning?" Timon demanded softly.

"Does it really matter what *name* we call our Savior?"

The full import of her words struck Timon with the same force as the killer's pistol had hit his head. Anne had been listening in the shadows. She had heard everything.

"You are a brilliant student," Timon confessed. "You have taken to heart my first lesson: that the plot of our play is revealed primarily through dialogue—dialogue which, it would seem, you have overheard, making your character a tacit part of it."

She nodded once, a thin smile upon her lips. "But if the play is all talking and no forward action, then the plot lies dead upon the stage. And to provide us with that action, I believe, my father is away tonight—to London."

Timon found himself transfixed by the color of her hair, in disarray about her shoulders, even as he realized he would have to kill her as soon as he killed her father.

13

In his rooms, Marbury gathered up several necessities and crammed them into a leather pouch.

James sent the secret documents to the translators, Marbury thought, his mind racing, and those documents may well be the cause of Harrison's murder. The King's instruction when he sent his royal coach was to use it in the event of an emergency. If our troubles do not constitute an emergency, I cannot imagine what would. And surely His Majesty would know the true import of the documents he sent us. Could it be that the King could solve the murder?

Thus preoccupied, Marbury hastened down the stairs and into the night, through the cobbled courtyard, to wake a certain coachman.

The boy's hovel was adjacent to the stables. He was well paid from the King's coffers, in secret, to rouse himself and have his horses ready at a moment's notice.

Marbury moved silently past the horses and tapped on the boy's door with the fingernail of his index finger. He had never availed himself of this particular service before. The King had commissioned one such coach for each of the three groups of Bible translators, to be used for anything deemed too urgent or too delicate for a courier's pouch. It had always seemed a foolish extravagance—until that night.

The boy appeared. His smudged face could have belonged to a cherub or a demon, there was no way of telling in the dark. Marbury had expected someone older, with a bit more experience, a king's man, not a stable boy.

"London," Marbury mumbled. "Hampton Court."

The boy only nodded.

Twenty minutes later the coach pulled out of the stable. Marbury was its only passenger, his few travel items tucked under the single seat. The horses picked up speed, kicking back gravel and mud as they flew through the pale moonlight. Marbury fell into a tumbled sleep.

HOURS LATER HE AWOKE with a start. It took a moment for him to remember that he was inside a clattering coach bound for London. He glanced out the window. Low clouds, gray as a widow's tears, hid any hint of the sunrise.

Those are snow clouds, Marbury thought to himself. And here I am on a frantic trip to visit the King instead of in my nice warm bed. Why does God hate me?

Snow in April would be unusual, but the Thames had nearly frozen at Christmas. Winters were getting colder and lasting longer. Perhaps it was a sign of the last days.

Shivering, Marbury pulled a heavy burgundy cloak around himself. He wondered how far the coach had traveled; how long he'd been asleep.

He stared out the window again, trying to wake up. The colorless gray of the sky pervaded every scrubby bush and tree, the very ground underneath the battered carriage wheels.

The interior of the coach was no better. The plain wooden box was constructed for speed of conveyance rather than comfort of passenger.

Few more than forty miles lie between Cambridge and London, Marbury calculated to himself, and this coach has been known to travel five or even six miles in an hour. At this speed we would have to have changed all four horses somewhere—while I slept, I suppose. We can't be far from London now. Better start thinking about how to behave in front of a king.

James had only been on the throne for six months when Marbury had first visited the Great Hall of Hampton Court Palace. The King had presented Christmas and New Year festivities— endless feasting and dancing. The actor William Shakespeare had written a fine piece, *A Play of Robin Goodfellow*, for New Year's Day. Beyond that, Marbury's memory of the event was overshadowed by his meeting with the King. He had done his best to keep Sir John Harington's advice, though it was nearly forty years old, foremost in his mind.

Harington had always said, as to dress for a meeting with a king, "be well trimmed, get a new jerkin, well bordered, and not too short—diversely colored." As to deportment, "you must not dwell too long on any one subject, and touch but lightly on religion."

It is good to remind myself of such advice, Marbury thought. Those words aided me the last time I saw the King, January a year ago. It was the conference that resulted in James's decision to commission this new Bible.

The carriage raced around a tight bend in the road, threatening to overturn. Marbury fell sideways across his seat. He heard the driver shout and felt the carriage drawing to an abrupt halt.

Marbury drew his blade instantly. There would be only one reason for these horses to stop on the road. He slumped onto the coach floor. Hand on the door handle, he strained his ears.

The driver was silent. Or dead.

The howl of the morning wind made it impossible to hear footfalls or whispering.

Marbury held his breath. His head shot upward for an instant. He saw no one on the road beside him. He opened the door as silently as he could; eased out onto the ground.

Through the legs of panting horses he could make out a single figure in the middle of the road.

Marbury was startled by the driver's growl.

"Get out of the way, you pile of snot."

"Stand and deliver," the highwayman stammered.

That voice had barely reached twelve years, Marbury realized.

"What do you think you can do with that little staff you're holding?" the driver taunted. "Throw it at me?"

"I could blind your two front horses," the boy said, his voice steadying, "and be off into them woods. Then, while you stood here in the road trying to figure what to do, I'd be back with a hundred other boys and we'd be on you like hornets on a dead mole."

"What the hell do you want?" the driver sighed. "I don't have any money, and there's no one in the coach."

"I could take the coach," the stranger suggested.

"Christ, I'll *give* you the coach if you leave them horses alone," the driver snarled. "I can walk to London from here. Come on up; take the reins."

Silence.

Marbury could see that the boy did not move from in front of the horses.

"The thing is," the driver explained, "this coach is registered to King James himself. Only two others like it in England. It's built to fly on royal business. If I let it be known that a pile of snot's got the King's harnesses, you'll be hanged by the neck until dead before sunset."

Marbury could just make out the robber's profile. The boy was dressed in a single piece of cloth, wrapped around him and tied in several places. His head was bare, his skin was smeared, his hands were raw from the cold. He held a quarterstaff in front of himself as if it were a shield. Curiously, his boots were perfect, well made, and the heels were high as was the fashion.

In a flash Marbury leapt forward, vaulted onto the driver's step, and flew up to the carriage seat beside the driver.

The sudden explosion of activity startled the driver almost as much as it did the boy.

The driver fell backward, gasping.

The boy dropped his staff and hollered, "Blood!"

Marbury's dagger was cocked in his right hand, clearly ready to throw directly at the boy.

"Get out of my way, now!" Marbury commanded. "Or this knife goes right through your forehead."

The driver sat up suddenly, eyes imploring Marbury not to throw the knife. Marbury winked at him and the driver exhaled.

The boy stood frozen where he was, staring, eyes wide, at Marbury's blade. "Give you my new boots if you don't kill me, mister."

Marbury gazed down at the terrified face. "Yes, where did you get those boots?"

"They was a gift of the plague," the boy whispered desperately. "On my life I didn't steal them. The man was dead, swole up like a plum and runny. I got the boots. Somebody else got the hat."

"I see." Marbury put his knife away. "And are there really a hundred other boys like you in those woods?"

The boy sniffed. "Not quite twenty, truth be told." He scratched his backside.

"And you were elected to rob this coach?"

"I don't know what *elected* is, but I'm the oldest." The boy coughed once. "It's up to me."

"Then here is my offer." Marbury reached into his cloak and produced a golden coin. "I shall give you this angel if you do *exactly* as I say."

"That's what an angel looks like?" The boy's eyes nearly rolled to the back of his head at the sight of the coin. "That's—"

"Ten shillings!" the driver groused. "Don't give him that much."

"That's more than I could steal in a month," the boy managed to sputter. "Or six!"

"It's too much for the likes of him," the driver whispered.

"I'll give you this gold," Marbury repeated to the boy in the road, "if you promise to do as I say."

"Give me that coin," the boy vowed, "and I will murder the Pope."

"I had something less complicated in mind."

"Anything!" the boy swore.

"All right." Marbury tossed the coin.

The boy caught it with both hands, bit into it; shook his head in wonder. "It's real."

"It is." Marbury suddenly leapt to the ground, landing directly in front of the boy.

The child's skin was raw, the lips were chapped, the cheeks were smeared with dirt, but the eyes were clear—possibly a worthwhile human being was behind the mask of that face.

"If you disappoint me," Marbury insisted, "I will find you. I will hunt you down. I will either take back my shillings or have your life. Do you believe me?"

The boy nodded once.

"Are we agreed, then?"

"What do you want me to do?" the boy rasped.

Marbury leaned close to a filthy ear and whispered his instructions, then looked the boy squarely in the eye. "Say back to me what I have just told you."

The boy took a breath and mumbled low, repeating almost word for word what Marbury had said.

"Clever boy," Marbury said brightly. "Off you go, then."

The boy had vanished into the low shrubs beside the road before Marbury's last syllable had gone from the air.

The driver sat scowling. "What could you possibly want him to do that's worth ten shillings?"

"I pray we never find out," Marbury said softly.

"He won't do it, whatever it is," the driver complained. "He's gone and so is your coin. You'll never see either again."

"Well," Marbury answered, looking down, "what could be the worst of that? I lose a bit of money, but one less boy starves to death this month."

The driver's face changed, slowly at first, but with a dawning realization. "You *gave* him that coin," he said haltingly.

"We should hurry along," Marbury said, taking hold of the carriage door. "I really do need to get to Hampton Court almost immediately."

"I never met anyone like you, Deacon Marbury, and there's the truth." The driver's face was briefly illuminated, as if an invisible candle had been held close to it. "I'll have you to London inside of an hour."

14

*E*very street in London seemed to thunder as if the entire world ran on wheels of carts and coaches. Hammers beat, tubs rolled; pots clinked. Porters, as if at leapfrog, skipped out of one shop and into another; tradesmen, as if dancing lust-legged galliards, never stood still.

Hampton Court Palace lay fifteen miles southwest of London on a curve in the Thames. The main entrance was built to intimidate the uninitiated. Huge wooden doors arched between two walls; those walls, in turn, were flanked by thin brick spires that shot heavenward. Two larger octagonal turrets rose nearly four stories above the ground. Marbury counted four enormous brick chimneys, all doubles, rising higher than the turrets. No Tudor structure in England could match it. Going through that gate, a small man felt smaller, and a great man was humbled.

Such is the aim of all palaces and cathedrals, Marbury thought as he approached the great edifice.

The morning watch, though uncertain of the exact importance

of the coach, knew the King's markings on the doors and flew to hold the horses as soon as they came to a halt in the stable yard.

Marbury climbed from the interior, pulled off one of his gloves, and handed it to the captain of the Guard.

"Please present this to His Majesty as quickly as possible," Marbury said in as commanding a voice as he could muster. "I have urgent business with the King."

The captain only hesitated for an instant.

"He will know the glove," Marbury assured the captain sternly. "He gave it to me."

Immediately Marbury was ushered across the yard, through the gardens over huge white paving stones, and into the Banqueting House. Built for Henry VIII, the high, arched beams of the main hall seemed to Marbury to make it more like a cathedral than a dining room. The hall was dark, and Marbury was rushed through it and into a corridor black as a cave.

Down the narrow stone hall, he was eventually admitted to a small kitchen. The perfectly square room had stone for floor and ceiling. Nondescript, utilitarian, uncluttered, it somehow managed to seem inviting.

The captain pointed to a certain chair at the single dining table in the room. "You are to sit in the same spot as Dr. Andrews."

The captain could only have meant Lancelot Andrews, Bishop of Winchester and president of the London company of translators; also elder brother of Roger Andrews, one of the Cambridge translators. Much had been made of the enmity between the two brothers, a contest made more bitter by the disparity in their positions.

So Lancelot Andrews had already been to see the King. Marbury burned to know more about that.

The captain whispered something to one of his men. That man hurried to a cupboard at the far end of the room and brought Marbury a plate of sweet cakes and a large tankard of pear cider.

"Do not leave this room," the captain said. It was as much a threat as an instruction.

Marbury nodded.

"I cannot assign men to stay with you," the captain continued, "but if I return to fetch you and you are not here, your next room will be considerably less comfortable than this."

Marbury smiled. "I have urgent business with the King," he repeated. The instructions he'd been given the year before were fairly narrow. He was only allowed to say certain phrases.

The captain blinked once and vanished, followed, somewhat less smartly, by his men.

Marbury sat back in his chair and looked around the room. There was only one stove; it was warm; the kitchen was lit by no other flame. The stone walls, the sturdy wooden table, the relatively small size of the room, meant that this was the Privy Kitchen, the one that Elizabeth had commissioned. The rumor had been that the Queen would meet certain men in this kitchen in order to disorient her victims. A woman in a kitchen was not a queen in a palace—and the subsequent confusion in her visitor's mind could prove a useful tool of interrogation for Her Majesty. Marbury suspected, as he settled into his chair and looked down at the golden cakes on the plate before him, that the room had been built for a simpler reason: it was comforting. It warmed Marbury's bones, eased his thoughts; gave peace to his soul. He was suddenly seized with a desire to devour the cakes. He thrust one of them, whole, into his mouth. Instantly the burning delight of fresh ginger and the numbing ease of cloves filled his mouth. The pear cider fizzed on his lips.

He was done with the food in an instant and immediately wanted more. Alas, the combination of the warm coals in the stove and the warm food in his belly conspired to make Marbury drowsy. God help him if he were asleep when someone came to fetch him.

Marbury stood deliberately and paced the room. He brushed his front three times, praying he'd rid himself of any hint of crumbs. He'd worn his best clothes, and he shook his head absently to think what his costume, including sleeves, breeches, and cloak, had cost. Fifteen shillings had gone to the tailor for his work, and nearly fifteen pounds spent for materials: velvet, silk and fustian lining, double taffeta, gold braid and gold lace, hose, and three

dozen buttons for the doublet. It was a shameful indulgence—
more money than three household servants would see in a year—
more than that boy on the road was likely to see in his short
lifetime. Still, the King favored fashion, and clothes were as essential to this meeting as a dagger would be in the London streets.

Long moments stretched into half an hour. Try as he might, the
waiting did nothing to abate his sense of chaos. His heart nearly
leapt through his shirt when, at last, he heard a rattle at the kitchen
door.

A pale young man rushed in. He was dressed in ice white and
cold blue, and his face had been made up: a bit of powder, a bit of
rouge, and just the touch of shading at the eye.

"A thousand pardons, Deacon Marbury." The young man
winced. "Insufferable and inexcusable to keep you waiting so
very long. It was entirely my fault. There has been some lengthy
discussion . . . if you would not mind, the King would prefer to
meet you here. He comes by and by."

The servant shook his head as if he had just told a joke but forgotten the final line, then shrugged once.

Marbury tensed. He had never heard of the King coming to a
visitor. Why would he do it? A visitor went to a King—always.
Something was amiss. Marbury found that his head was pounding
and his lips were dry. Clearly, others had been just as surprised by
this turn of events and attempted to dissuade the King from such a
breach of precedent.

Before any other thought could plague Marbury, two armed
guards burst in through the door, each in armor, scowling.

"King James!" one of them bellowed.

The sound of the guard's voice battered all four walls of the
small kitchen, and Marbury forgot how to breathe.

15

Guards parted smartly and revealed His Majesty. He had Marbury's glove in one hand, waved it once, then gave it to the nervous servant behind him. The servant squeezed past the King and thrust the glove in Marbury's direction just as Marbury was attempting to bow as low as he possibly could without falling over.

The King watched with a distant eye. The long white lace of his royal collar seemed to accentuate the reddish tint of his beard. His doublet was ash white, piped in rust-colored patterns, a design echoed in his cape. He wore no hat. A long, downward curving nose gave the King's face regal bearing, and he affected a weary look. That expression was the product of long years of instruction.

Marbury looked up from his uncomfortable bow to see his own glove dangling before his face. He was momentarily uncertain whether to stand upright and take the glove or to remain in his correct posture until the King spoke.

"For God's sake, Dibly, take that damned glove out of the deacon's face," the King sighed.

The glove disappeared. Marbury straightened. The King took two steps forward.

"We are happy to see you," James said slowly.

"Your Majesty," Marbury answered tentatively.

"Well, then." The King swung his arm wildly. "Leave us!"

The guards stood a moment, perplexed.

"We would speak with Deacon Marbury alone," the King assured everyone. "Leave us."

The guards turned at once and moved quickly. Dibly remained.

"I only," Dibly began, his lower lip trembling, "a thousand pardons, Your Majesty—the glove, I wonder—should I—"

"Please take your glove from Dibly," the King said to Marbury, "or we will spend the rest of the morning sorting out the protocol of the business."

Marbury snatched the glove from Dibly, who retreated toward the door, nearly at a run.

The King listened to him go. "It doesn't pay to have personal servants who are overly intelligent, because they begin to think, and thinking can only lead them into trouble. But there are drawbacks to such a philosophy, do you agree?"

"Indubitably, Your Grace," Marbury sighed.

When Dibly's noise vanished, the King himself closed the door to the kitchen, took a seat at the head of the small table, and turned a different face toward Marbury. He spoke in startlingly familiar and confidential tones.

"I am certain you will forgive this bizarre setting for our meeting, Deacon." The King looked about for a moment and sighed. "But I confess that I find this place comforting. When I was a boy in Scotland, and my sleep was troubled by nightmares, I would often come to our kitchen, sit by the fire, have a bit of cake, and consider the world of dreams."

Marbury smiled indulgently, uncertain how to proceed.

"But to the business at hand." James tapped the tabletop. "Please sit down."

Another breach of courtly etiquette. How could he sit in the presence of the King? Even in a kitchen, certain rules must be observed.

"You have urgent news of my Bible," James said sternly, "or you would not have appeared so suddenly, without forewarning, in my coach. I beg you, dispense with this mincing courtly courtesy and speak plainly. That is one reason we are meeting here, alone. I can barely stand the modes of the court today, and when a man such as yourself brings what I suppose to be news of a holy nature, I would rather stew in boiling grease than to hear obsequious speeches."

The King's eyes burned into Marbury's. Marbury, against every courtly instinct in his training, sat down and did his best to keep a steady voice.

"Here, then," Marbury began in hushed tones, "briefly and without adornment, is the reason for my visit. One of our translators has been murdered. I have hired a man to investigate the crime. That man has uncovered troubling evidence of great confusion in certain texts from which our scholars are translating. He has concluded that these texts may be at the root of the murder. There are larger issues at stake, he believes, than the killing of any single man."

James's face did not change.

The silence in the Privy Kitchen was alive. It seemed afraid to admit any sound after such a rush of disturbing information.

"Who is this investigator?" the King said at last.

"I know him only as Brother Timon. Surely an invented name, but I acquired him through certain members of the Anglican communion whom I have trusted before—a group of men recommended by one of Your Majesty's counselors on a previous—"

"Yes, yes!" James stopped Marbury short. "I would know more of him and his investigation. But you must first expand your news. Do you know the nature of this *evidence of great confusion,* as he calls it?"

"Yes."

"Go on, then. Give me the worst." The King did not breathe.

"It would appear," Marbury continued, steel in his voice, "that our translators are in possession of an ancient text of the Gospel of St. Luke in which our Savior is named Yshua—Joshua—not Jesus."

Marbury found, when his words were out of his mouth and in the air, that he could scarcely believe he'd said them. He had the dizzying sensation of a dream rather than a waking moment. The kitchen's warm comfort had turned to hot sweat.

"I see." James did not appear to move the slightest atom of his body.

"So I thought it best," Marbury continued hesitantly, "to bring the entire matter—"

"Your assumption," James interrupted, "is that I was already aware of this startling information, since I delivered the text in which it was found. You came to ask questions as much as to deliver news."

Marbury opened his mouth to protest, though the King had spoken utter truth.

James held up a jeweled hand. "And I have answers for you. But first things first. Tell me which of the translators has been killed."

"Harrison," Marbury said instantly.

"Oh."

Marbury was astonished to see a very human face on the King of England.

"Harrison, you may know, was my countryman—though I did not know the man." James looked down at the tabletop. "Our families, I have been told, were acquainted."

"So I was given to understand," Marbury said, surprising even himself with the sympathy his words betrayed.

"Do you see now the wisdom of meeting here in this private place, instead of at court?" James asked quietly, looking around the room for a moment.

"Absolutely, Your Majesty," Marbury answered confidently.

"I knew or sensed—even feared you might be bringing news of this ilk. I had reason to believe you were here on a delicate mission. You see, I have recently spoken with Dr. Lancelot Andrews. Andrews, the presiding scholar of our London translators. Alas, he came to me two days ago with similar concerns—odd occurrences."

"God in heaven," Marbury whispered before he could prevent himself.

"Praise Him, no one has been murdered there," James assured Marbury quickly, "but there have been incidents of theft, and then several bizarre notes. These are matters which we will not discuss at this time. I only mention them to assure you that you are not alone in your troubles. There is more at work here than you can possibly imagine. The details of these ancient documents—several of which were delivered to each group of translators—have vexed me from the first moment I read them. How I came to possess them is a tale itself. You see, Deacon Marbury, I have a mind that will not quiet itself. It has come to my attention that certain facts pertaining to the Savior have been hidden from us, even altered to suit some dark motive. This is the work of the Catholics. These popes are insane, of course, but there is more to it than that. Something has *strangled* our religion from the very beginning, since the days when our Savior walked this earth!"

The King shot up from his chair, his eyes were white flame. Marbury scrambled to stand himself, tossing his chair backward with a clatter on the hard gray stone floor.

"This is the true reason you have commissioned the new translation," Marbury concluded, amazed.

"Oh," James answered, waving his hand, "I have a desire for a new translation to replace the Bishops' Bible also for petty political reasons. I know that the Geneva version is more popular, but I do not care for the marginal notes in it which proclaim disobedience to a king necessary, if the king be like Herod. And as you know, the public face of it is that we are creating a Bible for all England—all the world—a translation to end all translations. And it must be favorable to Our political ends. But there is much more to the picture."

The King took three strides toward the oven coals, seized an iron poker that leaned against the wall, and stabbed the red glow until it yielded flame.

"I see that," Marbury said hesitantly, "though my brain seems unable at the moment—"

"In the first place," James declared, bashing the poker against the sides of the oven, "our new translation will open a window to let in the light. It will break the shell so that we may eat the kernel;

pull aside the curtain, that we may look into the most holy place; remove the cover of the well, that we may come by the water, even as Jacob rolled away the stone from the mouth of the well by which the flocks of Laban were watered. Indeed without our translation, the unlearned are but children at Jacob's well, without a bucket—lost. But that is only the first step."

The King whirled, pointing the steaming poker directly at Marbury. Marbury stared at it. James was trembling with rage.

"Did you know, Deacon Marbury," the King whispered savagely, "that when I brought my Lady Queen Anne home from Denmark, a tempest of ghastly proportions nearly destroyed us? We were given last rites on ship, certain of our deaths. Several able seamen cast themselves overboard in anticipation of our ship's going down. We only made land by the grace of God, barely alive. And do you know the *cause* of that great storm?"

Marbury began to speak, but was interrupted by the merest breath from his King:

"Witches."

Embers shot upward in the oven fire; several popping explosions sent red devils in all directions. Marbury began to form a sentence in his mind, thought better of it, and exhaled silently. The King paced back and forth in front of the fire, tapping the poker on the floor as if it were a walking cane. His voice was hotter than the sparks that sprayed.

"In the town of Trenent in Scotland," James went on, his voice hoarse, "there lives one David Sarton. He was a bailiff and had a maidservant named Geillis Duncan. She was often secretly absent from her master—every other night. During such time she helped the sick people of that town. In a short space of time she did perform many matters most miraculous. This, quite naturally, caused her master to be curious. He suspected that she did those things not by natural and lawful ways, but rather by some extraordinary means."

Marbury shifted his weight. The strain of standing in the increasingly hot kitchen, especially after the torturous coach ride, caused a sudden sharp cramp in his right leg. He struggled to hear his King's voice, which continued at a whisper, occasionally obscured entirely when the King turned away in his restless dance.

"Her master inquired of this maid by what means she was able to perform matters of such great importance. She gave him no answer. Her master and I—for he had called upon me for help—did then torment her with the torture of clamps in her mouth. When that failed, we bound her head tightly with a rope and strong men pulling it. Yet she would not confess a thing. This lead us to conclude, of course, that she had been marked by the devil. Witches commonly are. We tore her clothing from her and indeed found Satan's mark! It was a wine-red blemish upon her throat. When this was found, she confessed that all she had done was by wicked incitements of the devil. Do you see? That she had done them by witchcraft! Have you not heard this story?"

"Ah," Marbury stammered, "no, Your Majesty, but—"

James bashed the poker against the back of the stove again, and bits of flame flew onto the King's coat, his legs, his shoes. They were cold in seconds, but left visible dark points. James seemed unaware of them.

"She confessed!" the King declared. "She said she kept a black toad hanging by its heels for three days. She collected the foul venom that dropped from the toad's mouth into an oyster shell. She then obtained a napkin which I had used and dipped it in this venom. This she did in order to cause the storm which nearly killed Us!"

"She *confessed* to this?" Marbury managed to stammer.

The King spun suddenly and bore his gaze into Marbury's eyes. "Now you see the importance of my work! Many—too many have been licked by the tongue of the devil since this world began and borne such a mark as was found on the throat of that poor maid."

Marbury stumbled backward, startled by the King's vehemence. He rattled the chair behind him and swallowed.

"The devil's minions are everywhere!" The King's eyes were wild. "And they are most certainly found inside the present Catholic Bible. Which means they are also in your scholarly libraries in Cambridge; in the London and Oxford offices of our translators.

They have killed Harrison, do you see? No one is safe. *Now* do you understand the true nature of our work? We labor to destroy the ancient demons which were provoked by the birth of our Lord! These devils live in the very ink and paper of wicked, corrupted translation. They feed on the ignorance they produce. This new translation will be my legacy to the world! We must open the window and let in the light; burn these demons with illuminating truth, or humankind is lost!"

Marbury realized that his hands were trembling. His hairline dripped with sweat. He fought to quell his worst fear: that King James had lost his mind.

16

I see by your expression that you are amazed." The King nodded once. "It would seem that you have not read my work on this important subject."

"I beg Your Majesty's pardon," Marbury stammered, racing to collect his thoughts, "if you mean—"

"My seminal work on the subject," James continued, ignoring Marbury completely.

"Demonology," Marbury rushed to insert. "I have indeed read it."

"Ah." The King smiled "Then you may know the three passions that incite a human to witchcraft."

A test.

"Curiosity, revenge, and greed." Marbury answered his King with calm assurance. "These, I believe, are the passions to which His Majesty refers."

"Indeed! And the worst of these is the first. If a man is curious, he will try to find answers. And answers, for small minds, are holes in the brain through which Satan will enter. Thinking is the worst thing a man of limited intellect can possibly do. Translate our Bible into an easy language, and you rub out a portion of that curiosity. A mystery makes men curious, you see. The Catholic Church is filled with mystery, the secret Latin words, the whispered vespers unheard by the common congregation. Our translation removes that mystery. That is its first cause. Therefore we must know all there is to know about the hidden secrets of the Bible and expose them to the light of day. Or eliminate them completely. Some of the texts I sent to your scholars must be eliminated completely—expunged from human knowledge. They are too vexing for the ordinary mind. Your plowman, wheelwright, glove maker—their skulls would swell and pop like melons in the sun should they learn what lies in some of these texts."

"I do beg the King's pardon," Marbury began, at sea, "but you are saying there are some documents that should be entirely eliminated from our Bible?"

"Yes," James snapped. "Some of these works will not translate properly no matter what a scholar does. They contain information too complex for most minds."

"These are," Marbury ventured cautiously, "actual *books* of the Bible?"

"Four unknown gospels were sent to your group." The King sighed impatiently. "Surely your scholars have discussed them. You have alluded to the Gospel of Luke. There are also gospels attributed to Philip, Thomas, and Mary the Magdalene. The other groups received other texts. They may be sharing with each other now—one cannot say what men of the academy will do."

Marbury swallowed hard. "There is a gospel written by Mary—"

"It must be dismissed!" Clearly the King would say no more on the subject. "Have you not heard my accusation? The Bible has been tainted by the work of demons. This Magdalene was almost certainly a witch herself. One of a species of Original Witches that beset Our Lord Christ from the beginning. Her words must not be translated, but destroyed!"

The heat in the room seemed to increase. Marbury stared at the blistering coals in the oven, trying to find the best response.

"Alas," Marbury managed, sweat pouring down his chest, "I have not the King's wit for such matters."

"Witches, you see," James continued, almost gleefully, "are servants only—slaves to the devil. It is easy to see why women become witches."

Marbury responded by slumping against the wall.

"Deacon? Are you ill?" James peered objectively into Marbury's eyes. "Your face is pale. Your brow is quite wet."

"I—I"—Marbury struggled—"have journeyed all night with little sleep in order to bring my news to Your Majesty. I beg pardon: I am but exhausted."

"And the sudden rush of my knowledge has unsettled you. I should have been more sparing. My thoughts are too overwhelming for most men."

"Indeed." Marbury clutched the wall beside him to keep steady.

The King was mad, and Mary wrote a gospel. A thousand walls would not be enough to steady a man who knew those two facts. Still, the wall did its best and Marbury did not succumb to the allure of the floor.

However, as he attempted to stand without support, Marbury realized that the room was insubstantial. A rising fever scratched at his neck and ears. He was suddenly seized by a piercing pain, as if something alive in his stomach began to stab him with razor claws from the inside. He recognized the sensation.

"Your Majesty," he rasped. "This is poison. I fear someone has given me poisoned cakes and perry—here in this kitchen."

The King squinted. "Are you certain?"

"I have been poisoned before. I must have—" Marbury's thought was interrupted by another violent pain, and he crashed to his knees.

"Dibly!" the King bellowed

Dibly instantly appeared in the doorway, crouched low, dagger in hand.

Even in his dizzy state, Marbury realized that Dibly had feigned walking down the hall or had silently returned. He had been waiting for his King, just outside the kitchen door.

"Put that away," James said quickly, glancing at the blade, "and take out one of Our blue vials."

Dibly sheathed his blade and reached into a hidden pocket. He produced a vial the size of the King's thumb.

"Give it to the deacon," James commanded. "He has eaten food intended for me."

Dibly moved silently across the stones in the floor and uncorked the vial. "Drink this at once," he said gently to Marbury. "And pray we are not too late."

"The effect of this elixir is unpleasant," the King added, "but I have had occasion to use it several times with, as you can see, a good end. You may step into the hall, with Dibly's assistance. You will not be able to walk further."

Dibly helped Marbury up and the two men struggled through the door and into the hall before a churning sensation overcame Marbury.

"The vial contains an instant purgative," Dibly began.

The remedy was instant and effective. The rest of Dibly's explanation was as lost as it was unnecessary.

17

*F*or ten interminable minutes, Marbury could do nothing but expel poison and cough. For that same amount of time, Dibly wiped Marbury's face, uttered soothing sounds, and assured Marbury that shortly everything would be fine.

At last Marbury stood, light-headed, and nodded his thanks to Dibly. Only then did he notice that the captain of the Guard and the men who had taken Marbury to the Privy Kitchen were standing at the door, stone-faced, barely breathing. How they had gotten there, when they had come, Marbury could not have said.

Marbury leaned his head close to Dibly's and whispered, "I saw how quickly you came into the kitchen when the King called you; how easy the dagger lay in your hand. And the fact that you were equally adroit with this antidote for poison assures me, Mr. Dibly, that there is more to you than meets the eye."

The mask of the sycophant vanished from Dibly's face for an instant. "There is an advantage to being underestimated, Deacon Marbury."

"Do you believe that the poison was intended for the King?"

"His Majesty often comes to that kitchen to think, to drink, and to be alone. No one knew you would be there this morning."

"They knew," Marbury said, his eyes darting in the direction of the captain and his Guard. "They knew I was to be brought here."

"Are you quite recovered from your illness, Deacon?" the captain of the Guard asked, his voice a bit louder than it needed to be.

"The foibles of travel," Marbury said, clearing his throat.

"Captain," Dibly said, assuming his mincing character once more, "I would know what prompted you to offer Deacon Marbury food. I feel there may be something spoilt in the cakes that has caused our guest to be so stricken."

"Royal order," the captain said, his disdain for Dibly dripping from every syllable. "I was instructed by my superiors on direct command from the King. I am to escort *any* visitors who arrived in a royal signet coach to this kitchen. Then I am to offer them what refreshment might be available in the cupboard."

"And when did you receive these orders?"

"No more than a week ago."

"From which of your superiors?" Dibly took a few steps in the captain's direction.

"Baxter."

"I see." Dibly turned to Marbury. "Shall we return to His Majesty?"

Marbury nodded.

"And, Captain," Dibly continued, "see to it that this corner of the hallway is cleaned before the King emerges from the Privy Kitchen, would you? There's a good man."

The captain let go a harsh breath; said nothing.

Dibly made his way past the guards and into the kitchen; Marbury followed. Dibly closed the door. Marbury noticed, from the corner of his eye, that the cupboard had been cleared: doors open, shelves empty.

"You heard, Majesty?" Dibly whispered.

"I did."

"And your orders to Baxter?"

"Were to bring the men here to this kitchen," James answered. "Nothing more."

"Your Majesty," Marbury began, swallowing, his face a bright vermilion, "words fail to express my great humiliation at this unforgivable—leaving the royal presence—"

"Do not apologize," the King said grandly. "Imagine how much more uncomfortable it would have been for both of us if you had died in my presence!"

Dibly managed a troubled laugh.

"And my gratitude—," Marbury attempted once more.

"Pish!" James insisted.

"You have been poisoned before, Deacon?" Dibly asked, his voice returned to a normal volume. "You seem to have recognized the symptoms in good time."

"I have been poisoned." Marbury nodded, beginning his story. "I was involved in some matter—"

"Yet you lived." Dibly cocked his head, willing Marbury to cease his tale.

"Barely. My young daughter nursed me. I was delirious for several—"

"I have been poisoned five times," the King said proudly. "This concoction which Dibly carries has done the trick each time."

"It is a wondrous potion," Marbury admitted. "I feel remarkably steady considering what I have endured."

"Scottish kings have never been without a remedy for poison," James declared at a stage whisper. "This is an ancient medicine."

"To the matter at hand," Dibly insisted, "if the poison was intended for His Majesty, we must move quickly to ferret out the culprit. If the poison was intended for Deacon Marbury, he should, if his business here is concluded, return to Cambridge, where he will be more secure. And perhaps the deacon might employ the journey to consider who would want to kill him, and why."

Why is Dibly so anxious to curtail my meeting with the King? Marbury wondered. I have only just arrived.

But the King seemed ready to agree; nodded once. "Exactly. Marbury, return to your home at once. Consider all that I have told you, and keep your translators well in line with what I have said. Do you understand the urgency of the matter?"

"Absolutely, Your Majesty."

"I would know more of this Timon, incidentally—the investigator you mentioned. Please give Dibly the particulars as he escorts you to your coach."

Instantly and without a glance, the King strode to the door, pulled it open, and began bellowing questions at the captain of the Guard.

"Follow me," Dibly said softly.

The last words Marbury heard, as he exited the dark hallway back into the astonishing dining hall, were the King's.

"Bring me Baxter!" His Majesty roared.

Marbury began to consider, as he walked through the great dining room, that the poison might, indeed, have been intended for him, not the King.

Only three people know where I am, he thought. Anne, of course—she knows everything. Obviously the coach driver knows where I am, though he would have had scant opportunity to communicate anything to the palace: he was on the journey from Cambridge with me. That leaves only one man.

"Now," Dibly whispered, interrupting Marbury's train of thought. "Who is this *investigator* whom His Majesty mentioned?"

Brother Timon tried to have me poisoned, Marbury realized slowly, only half-hearing Dibly. What in God's name have I brought into my house?

18

*M*arbury was surprised to find his coach waiting for him when he arrived at the royal stables. The courtyard was bustling with people coming and going. The stones were clean and the noise was pleasant. Except for its size, it was not unlike the stables at Cambridge—and there was his coach, ready to leave.

That efficiency alerted Marbury's suspicions. If a message could travel the breadth of the palace with such speed, and in such secrecy, it would have been possible for this coach driver to say something to a servant that would result in poisoned cakes. Perhaps Timon was *not* the only suspect in that regard.

Marbury offered Dibly a few superficial particulars of Timon's hiring. This included a scant mention of the secret Anglican brotherhood that Marbury had consulted on several other occasions. He was quick to remind Dibly, however, that the group had been recommended by the King himself. Without a word of farewell, Dibly turned with a flourish and vanished into the shadows of the courtyard.

Marbury drew near to the coach and caught his driver's eye. "That's done, then," he said briskly.

"Quick business for such a long trip."

"Brevity is the soul of wit," Marbury assured the driver. "Let me see—I wonder if you would mind my riding beside you for the first leg of our journey? I have been cloistered in a rather stuffy kitchen."

"Suit yourself," the boy said, moving to one side of his seat. "It's cold up here."

"I could use a bit of fresh air." Marbury climbed up beside the driver. "Shall we?"

The driver nodded once and the horses lurched forward.

"We were in such a hurry last night," Marbury began over the noise of the carriage, "that I obviated amenities. I would now like to know your name."

"Thom."

The coach creaked its way to the grand entrance. The gate was opened and they were on the road before Marbury spoke again.

"How did you get this job?"

"I saved a man's cat from a bull."

The coach picked up speed. The day was attempting spring— still cold, but the sun was out and the air was clear. The wind did, indeed, feel good on Marbury's face.

"Might you elaborate?" Marbury asked.

"The owner of the stables, he loves his cat. The cat got into the bull's pen just at the time that bull was about to stud. This is a time when a bull is what they call *antagonistic*. Especially to little annoyances like a mewing cat. The bull was intent on stepping on same to smash it flat. I slipped in, grabbed up the cat, and got out. Good thing too. The bull had become antagonistic toward *me*. The owner saw all, and I was rewarded with this job."

"A job that likes you?"

"Aye, that." Thom nodded. "It's not many stablemen my age that gets paid to sleep in a nice warm bed with only the occasional hindrance of a midnight ride. And even that is likable, truth be told: commanding a coach like this is a damned sight better than mucking out a stall."

"Do you know who I am?"

"I do now. Everyone in the stables is guessing about your work. I listen. You're Deacon Marbury."

"Did you know me before last night?"

"Heard the name."

The road bent, following the bank of the Thames, with its swans, salmon, and sewage. Icy waves peaked in the wind to the left side of the racing coach. Here and there a waterbird fished the river. The coach rolled over the Bridge, where severed heads on poles sat side by side with houses and shops.

Once the weavers and brewers of Cripplegate were behind them, the outskirts of London and the open field of Finsbury quickly faded into greener pastures. The city was gone.

To the right was a small rise, lined with trees. Beyond the trees were more open fields—some already planted with turnips and beets, some being tilled in the stark afternoon sunlight. When the coach was up to its full speed, the racket was deafening. The road narrowed, barely wide enough for the coach. The seat upon which Marbury and the boy were perched was hard as a gravestone, and the wind whipped their noses and cheeks and ears.

"How?" Marbury asked above the din.

"Pardon?"

"How had you heard my name? In what manner?" Marbury had to shout to be heard.

Thom turned to look at Marbury. "Truth?"

"Yes." Marbury's eyes bore into the boy's.

"You're Anne's father. She's perfection, if you don't mind my saying so."

Marbury took in a breath. "How do you know Anne?"

"Go on." Thom laughed. "Everybody knows Anne. She's the smartest girl in England. Bested three men, including my stable master, at mathematical computations. That was something to see, her summing before him. Then there's the matter of her riding. She rides better than any girl I ever saw. Better than most men."

"You've seen her ride?"

"I work in the stables."

"But—"

"Beg pardon," Thom said, lowering his voice so that Marbury could barely hear. "I couldn't help but notice that there was a rider behind us. Could be nothing, just another traveler. But considering that you was poisoned in the King's own palace, I thought it might be something worth mentioning."

Before he could think, Marbury craned his neck around. Some fifty feet behind the coach was a single rider, hat drawn low, cloak wrapped tightly around him.

"You shouldn't have looked," Thom sighed. "Now he knows we've seen him."

"How did you know that I was poisoned?" Marbury demanded.

"You can't be serious," Thom answered tensely. "Everyone in the palace was talking about it. Poison intended for the King, served to you. Your life saved by a magic potion, they say—an elixir known only to the King. It makes him invincible against all such treachery, they were saying."

"Everyone knew?"

"So, things being what they are," Thom drawled, "perhaps we ought to consider that the man behind us—"

"Can you pick up speed?"

"We can't outrun a man on horseback with this coach," Thom objected. "I mean, it's fast, but—"

"Well, there's no room to turn around. And we don't need to outrun him, we only have to make it to a certain stretch of road before he overtakes us. Can you speed to the stretch of road where we stopped on our way to the palace earlier this morning?"

Thom took a moment. Marbury watched as several realizations swam behind the boy's eyes. At last a conclusion emerged from those waters.

"You suspected something like this might happen," Thom concluded. "*That's* what deal you set up with our rummy little high-wayman."

"Indeed."

"Well." Thom grinned. "Pardon my saying so, but it's very difficult to see where Miss Anne gets her brains—certainly not from you. That boy won't be there. We're for it."

"If the boy is there," Marbury said calmly, "we have help. If he is not, we have the best stretch of road upon which to defend ourselves. That is why the boy chose that part of the highway, you see: flat, easy to maneuver, easy to dash into the woods if need be."

"We'll see," Thom grumbled.

"And there are two of us to his one. Do you carry a weapon?"

"Me? Christ, no. I can barely—"

"Take this." Marbury held out a dagger. "Hold it in front of you and squint one eye."

"I can't—"

"Our attacker will have no way of knowing your level of skill. If you swagger and move about distractingly to one side of him, I may be able to get him from the other. Unless he has a pistol. Then he will likely to shoot us both."

"Lord God in heaven! What the hell have you got me into—flying to London, poisoned in the palace, and now pursued by Christ knows what demon!"

Thom slapped the reins hard against the horses' backsides, and the coach lurched forward. The man on horseback picked up his pace to match. He was not attempting to overtake, only to follow closely.

"Curious," Marbury mumbled. "He is not trying to catch us."

"Maybe he's waiting for a good stretch of highway to make his stand," Thom said, eyebrows arched.

"Are you absolutely certain that you were given this job as a reward?" Marbury growled. "You seem the sort of person whose cheek merits punishment more than gratitude."

"True, that, sir," Thom said, barely keeping a grin from his face. "And so I beg your pardon once again. But as to this job, well— one man's hell is another man's cook fire."

"You mean you love this job."

"Not at the moment, no," Thom yelled. "But on the ordinary day—"

"Faster?"

Thom called out something to the horses—a sound meaningless to the human ear but clearly encouraging to the horses. They picked up their pace quite remarkably.

The coach flew along the water's edge until the road veered inland, through a small forest. The man on horseback stuck like a shadow in their wake.

Marbury's heart quickened when he saw, in the distance, the patch of ground where the young boy had waylaid them. He could find no sign of a lookout, no hint of the other boys in the wood. It seemed he would have to face the shadow alone.

—

19

Thom slowed the coach as they drew onto the flat part of the road. "Here we go," he sighed loudly, his face a mask of resignation.

"No one in those woods." Marbury's eyes searched the trees and shadows.

"Right." Thom looked around. "I told you he wouldn't be here. Your angel's gone."

The coach came to a halt.

"You have my knife," Marbury whispered.

Thom held it aloft, hands still on the reins.

"Keep it low, at the waist, flat out, as if you meant to sweep it upward into his gullet."

"God." Thom pulled back on the reins to steady the horses.

Marbury looked back. The man behind them had come to a halt, apparently perplexed that the coach had stopped.

Thom cast his eye about the wooded landscape once more, mumbling to himself.

Marbury climbed down from the seat and thrust open the coach door; rummaged under the seat and drew out his rapier.

"Let go of the reins and get down on the other side of the coach," he instructed Thom. "You stay on that side of the road, I stay on this. Say nothing."

"Can I make a noise like a bear? It's a very frightening sound."

"Say *nothing*."

"Exactly." Thom secured the reins to his seat and slid down onto the road.

The man on horseback did not move, but Marbury began to stride quickly in his direction. Thom had to scurry to keep pace, trying not to look foolish, straining to harden his face.

"Are you going to make me walk all that way?" Marbury called out to the man. "Very inconsiderate. Poke your horse a bit, would you? I am in a hurry; I should like to kill you and be on my way."

Thom growled, very much like a bear.

The man on horseback leaned forward. His horse began to walk slowly. Only then did Marbury hold out his rapier.

The man on horseback smiled.

Thom continued to growl.

Marbury strode more quickly and the stranger's horse picked up speed.

A sudden gust of wind blew the stranger's cloak aside for the briefest of moments, but long enough for Marbury to see that he was wearing the plain red robe of a priest, and Marbury had a sudden pang of doubt.

This man is a priest, he thought, only a fellow traveler—the poison has affected my reason. What am I doing?

"Friend," Marbury began, lowering his rapier.

The priest nodded. A pistol appeared in his hand. It fired.

Thom grunted, more surprised than anything else. He stared down at his chest. A rose had erupted there, spraying red petals into the cold air. Thom sank to his knees, dropped the dagger in his hand. His head tilted in Marbury's direction before he fell, hard, facedown onto the road.

Marbury sucked in a breath, staggered to one side.

The priest produced a second pistol and cocked it, his lip curling upward. Before he could take aim, the air around him was filled with stones. His face and chest were pummeled relentlessly by them. In seconds he was bleeding in a dozen places.

Marbury dove to the ground and rolled out of the line of pistol fire. From his vantage point in the ditch at the side of the road, Marbury watched as the priest was battered by what seemed to be hundreds of rocks, thick tree branches, several crude arrows.

Then the air was filled with high-pitched curses, and the priest slumped, sagging sideways, and slid off his horse.

At once a dozen or more frail ghosts were upon him, kicking, stomping, or beating him with rough-hewn clubs.

Marbury lifted his head and shouted, "Enough!"

The boys froze.

A familiar face looked up from the horde. "Like that? Is that what you wanted?"

The innocent highwayman and his cohorts, some as young as six or seven, all stood.

"Sorry we wasn't in time to save your driver," the boy continued.

Marbury's eyes shot to Thom, whose body lay over a growing circle of rust. Otherwise, nothing about him was moving.

Marbury dropped his rapier and scrambled to Thom's side, lifting him up. The body was limp, the eyes were rolled back in his head.

"*Sangre.*" The priest rolled onto his side, holding several of his wounds and staring at the wild boys. His accent was Spanish.

The young highwayman kicked the priest hard in the head.

Marbury stood. Three quick steps placed him between the priest on the road and the sun in the sky. "Get up."

"No." The priest coughed. He held the back of his hand to his mouth as he did, an odd bit of courtly manners in a desperate wood.

"Get up!" Marbury repeated, icy menace in his voice. "I mean to know more about you."

"I am very tired—one of these arrows has cut into my liver and bowels. I face the prospect of an agonizing death within the week." He smiled as his hand dropped away from his mouth. White powder was evident on the lips; a broken ring on the hand was similarly stained. "I choose this moment to end my work."

The priest had taken poison.

"God," he stammered to the boys, "sit him up."

The boys moved at once, and the priest was sitting up, choking and gurgling. Marbury stuck his gloved finger into the priest's mouth to make him vomit. The priest bit down so ferociously that his teeth broke through the leather and gnashed into Marbury's skin, drawing blood. Only when one of the boys picked up a rock and broke it on the back of the priest's skull was the finger released.

The priest was dead moments later, his body quaking on the side of the road. The boys stared down at him with absolute indifference.

When the twitching stopped, the young highwaymen smiled.

"Job done," the boy said. "Fast poison."

Marbury was at a loss for words.

"You thought I wouldn't show," the boy went on, "but I earned my angel."

"Yes," Marbury managed, "you did."

The other boys stood silent—waiting for their leader to make the first move.

When Marbury realized what they were thinking, all he could do was reach into the hidden pocket of his doublet and produce more coins—three crowns. He held them out. No one moved.

"Help me get both of these bodies into that coach," Marbury croaked, "and these coins are yours."

"Come on, then," the leader said to the others, taking the coins from Marbury.

Silently, like the ghosts they imitated, they lay hold of the priest and dragged his carcass toward the carriage.

Marbury let go of a long, staggered breath and went to Thom's body. He gathered it up and carried it to the other side of the coach.

The boys lay the priest on the floor. Thom was put to rest on the seat.

Thom's blood stained Marbury's new, expensive doublet.

When Marbury finally closed the door and looked around, only the leader, the bold, young highwayman, stood in the road, holding the priest's horse.

"Tie this horse to the back of your coach?" he asked Marbury.

"Yes. Thank you."

The boy found a convenient hitch, fastened the horse's reins tightly, and stood back.

"I never thought . . . I never meant for you to——," Marbury began.

"Fact is," the boy said quickly, looking down at the road, "it's not the first man we've killed on this road."

"Oh."

"But with the money you give us," he continued, "who's to say? Life turns like a road. Not all of it looks like this stretch, does it now?"

"Indeed it does not." Marbury sighed brokenly. "Listen, you must come with me now."

"What?"

"We could arrive at my home by morning. I cannot leave you here."

"I think you'll find you can," the boy say incredulously. "I can't go bounding off with you. These others, some of them's not five years old. They depends on me. I'm the leader, see? I can't leave."

Marbury stared at the stain in the road where Thom's blood was drying. "My name is Francis Marbury, can you remember that? I'm the dean of Christ Church in Cambridge. If you could manage to get your lot there——"

"Cambridge?" The boy shook his head.

"Will you at least consider——"

"It's a kind offer," the boy said, squinting his eyes, "and I don't know what to make of it. But I'll bring it up with the others."

"You must tell me your name."

The boy stared into Marbury's eyes, clearly at war in his mind. At last he said softly, "Doesn't matter."

Without another syllable, he turned and was off the road, loping into the little bit of wood and shadow beyond the bloody ditches.

20

*I*n Cambridge the next morning, Brother Timon's right hand played across the surface of the small wooden wheel the way a master's hand might play a lute. Though it was morning outside, midnight's shadows still clawed at the candlelight inside. The room was on the ground floor, an unused servant's place, far away from the family quarters, windowless and cold.

Timon's fingers moved with lightning speed, hitting precise symbols, adjusting the wheel, turning the outward circumference or the inner surface. The wheel was smaller than a dinner plate, yet it contained an infinite universe of words. His left index finger raced along words before him, a manuscript bearing notes in Harrison's handwriting. Timon had stolen it from the dead man's desk. He had been up all night reading and memorizing each word and every mark of punctuation perfectly, flawlessly—owing to his memory wheel.

Timon's chamber was not unlike most rooms in which he had spent his lifetime. It contained only a bed, a basin, and a book desk.

The desk in the corner was high; the student was meant to stand: a seated man might fall asleep. The bed was along the wall opposite the door: flat boards, a single blanket, no pillow. The basin was two pieces: one held water, the other was a chamber pot. One was filled every evening, the other was emptied every morning.

Three tapers had burned down while Timon worked his alchemy. He read as quickly as he could so that he could return the papers to Harrison's desk before anyone saw that they were gone.

Memorizing a document of this magnitude would be difficult if he became too interested in the contents. It could cost him pages of memorization—time spent thinking instead of absorbing words. So, with great irritation, he snapped at the urgent, early-morning pounding upon the door of his cell.

"Please go away!" he shouted. "I'm working!" Or trying to work, he thought.

"Brother Timon, this is Dr. Spaulding," the urgent voice responded. "You must come quickly!"

"I am praying," Timon insisted.

"There has been another murder! And I believe we have found the culprit!"

Instantly Timon slid his memory wheel into a hidden pocket in his robe. He kicked up a loose stone in the floor beneath the desk—a stone that he had himself freed—and he hid the stolen papers under it, replacing the stone perfectly.

He strode to the door and pulled it open. Dr. Spaulding stood straight as an iron pole. His coat was an unadorned umber, smooth lines reaching nearly to the floor, and so clean that it seemed more a painting of a garment than actual clothing. His cap was likewise simple: a dark golden skullcap, also without design or insignia. His face looked as if it had been sucked forward by some invisible force. The nose was pointed, lips pursed, eyes a bit beyond their sockets. His hands seemed incapable of rest. He folded them, unfolded them, scratched the back of one with the other, tapped fingertips together. All the while his breath kept pace: shallow, huffing, demonstrably impatient.

"Another body!" he exploded. "In the hall. But we have caught the killer! I found him with his bloodstained hands upon the corpse. The body was still warm. And you will not believe your eyes, Brother. He is one of us!"

Timon stepped quickly out of his room and closed the door behind him. A vague scent of nutmeg wafted outward from the cell. Before Timon could ask a single question, Spaulding was off, running down the hall toward the door.

"Of course I first sought out Deacon Marbury," Spaulding chirped over his shoulder, "but he is not in his rooms. He is nowhere to be found. I am beginning to fear the worst, in light of the events—"

"Who has been killed, Dr. Spaulding?" Timon demanded, catching up with the man.

"Did I not say? Mr. Lively! Our leader! *He* has fallen."

Spaulding slammed the palms of his hands into the door, and the two men burst into the morning sunlight.

"Naturally, as his second, I have immediately assumed command of our group," Spaulding reported breathlessly. "The work of the scholars must continue apace. This is essential. We must not lose momentum. That is precisely what the devil desires. This man, this murderer—his treachery must not be allowed to hinder our progress."

"And you have caught the murderer?" Timon asked, unable to keep his doubt from his voice.

"I myself caught the man in the act!" Spaulding repeated as his pace quickened.

The morning sun was a golden coin—not enough to purchase much warmth, but sufficient to brighten the air.

"And you say that the killer is—"

"One of us! Yes. A scholar—a demon in our midst." Spaulding was nearly running.

"Name the man," Timon demanded impatiently.

"Wait. You shall see. The eye can scarce believe the scene."

"And he is in the Great Hall with the body." Timon strode gracefully, easily keeping pace with the more frenzied Spaulding. "You placed a guard."

"No." Spaulding slowed, but only slightly.

"You somehow secured him to a desk or a chair?"

"I commanded him to stay where he was. He agreed." Spaulding's irritation blossomed.

"Certainly you understand," Timon began, not quite realizing that his smile revealed his derision, "that he will be gone by now. A man who has committed murder would scarcely—you spent some time looking for Marbury?"

"Nearly an hour."

"Then you took more time in finding me."

"Perhaps the half of another hour," Spaulding snarled. "But you seem not to grasp the fact that I caught the man as he was working his foul deed. He is known to us all. There is no escape. An old man does not travel well or quickly."

"An old man?" Timon bit his upper lip.

"Look for yourself!" Spaulding exploded.

They were only a few feet from the doors to the Great Hall, and they flew the distance. Spaulding grasped both handles and flung wide the portals.

A lone figure sat, a bit slumped, at Mr. Lively's desk. A nearly spent taper's halo embraced him.

As Timon drew nearer he saw that the old man was in prayer, eyes closed, lips moving.

On the floor at his feet lay a body.

21

*I*s that Dr. Chaderton?" Timon whispered.

"The very same!" Spaulding responded vociferously.

Chaderton, startled, sat upright, eyes popped open.

"As you perpend," Spaulding sneered, "the man saw the wisdom of my command and has remained as I instructed."

Chaderton craned his neck, squinting. "Is that Brother Timon?"

"It is, sir," Timon answered softly.

"Good." Chaderton lifted himself off the stool and brushed flat his black robe. Without a hat, his hair obeyed no law. "I have been meaning to speak with you. Deacon Marbury has the utmost regard—"

"Deacon Marbury may well be another of your victims, sir!" Spaulding shouted, scurrying to Chaderton's side. "This is known to us."

"Marbury is in London on urgent matters with the King," Timon told Chaderton calmly, ignoring Spaulding. "When he returns, I believe we shall have a greater understanding on these crimes, and their dark purpose. That is Mr. Lively on the floor?" Timon glanced to the corpse.

"I found him more or less as he is now." Chaderton folded his hands, upon which, Timon noticed, there was no blood. "My first thought was that he had fallen asleep. It happens to all of us. I myself have spent more than a few hours napping on these cold stones when some animated nepenthe has overtaken me. I went to wake him and discovered the blood, just there."

Chaderton pointed to a sticky spot on the floor, as if someone had poured brown honey onto Lively's side.

"Nothing more?" Timon asked.

"I realized that he was dead and I determined to fetch Deacon Marbury—and you," Chaderton answered, the hint of a smile at the corners of his mouth. "Then Dr. Spaulding bounded into the room and *ass*ailed me with his *ass*ertion: his *ass*umption that I was the *ass*assin."

Timon was taken off guard by Chaderton's low humor. The old man had called Spaulding an *ass* five times—twice in one word. Without warning, Timon burst out laughing.

"Who would expect this schoolboy humor, sir, from such a distinguished scholar?" Timon asked Chaderton.

Chaderton only offered a shrug.

Spaulding seemed not to understand what had happened, which made Timon even more amused.

"I caught him bending over the body!" Spaulding sizzled.

Timon's head snapped in Spaulding's direction. "Do you see, Dr. Spaulding, that Lively has been stabbed? Where is Dr. Chaderton's weapon? And do you see that the blood on the floor is not running? That means it is old, not fresh. Lively has been dead all night, I surmise. Finally, the man whom Mr. Lively allowed to escape from this very room the other night, the actual murderer, was young, agile, smaller than Dr. Chaderton, and, incidentally, left-handed."

Spaulding sputtered but produced no actual English words.

"You pointed to the victim with your right hand," Timon confided to Chaderton.

"And I do not, alas, count agility among my current talents," Chaderton admitted, sinking back down to the stool at Lively's desk. "You should have seen me, however, when I was sixty! Lithe!"

"Now then," Timon said, primarily to himself.

He stepped around Chaderton and knelt beside the body. The face was still obscured by shadows.

"Have you seen the face?" Timon asked.

"I confess," Chaderton said wanly, "that I was afraid to look. Harrison's face, so disfigured, has appeared more than once in my dreams."

"Marbury told me." Timon drew in a breath and rolled the body onto its back.

The face was mutilated, but scarcely to the extent that it could not be identified.

Three stab wounds killed Lively, Timon thought: two at the heart and one at the liver. There was less blood than there should have been.

"Dr. Chaderton, Dr. Spaulding," Timon sighed, "may I ask you to examine this face? I believe it is not nearly so destroyed as was Harrison's, am I correct?"

Spaulding, grumbling, shuffled his way to the body. Chaderton stood once more and held his breath.

Both men stared.

"This is monstrous," Chaderton whispered, "but nothing compared to Harrison's mutilation."

"Harrison could only be identified by his clothes and his cross," Spaulding confirmed in full voice. "Lively's face is readily discernible."

"This may mean that the killer was interrupted in his work," Timon said. "Someone else may have seen this body before Dr. Chaderton did. Someone may even have witnessed this murder."

"But—," Spaulding began.

"And Marbury told me," Timon said slowly, "something about a message . . . the mouth."

Timon's hand reached out.

"No!" Spaulding objected.

"There was a note in Harrison's mouth," Chaderton whispered.

Timon's lips thinned. His right hand moved deliberately toward the dead man's lips. Hovering for a moment, his fingers worked open the mouth, the teeth, and plucked out a bit of paper. It was still wet with saliva.

"Yes." Timon held up the note, wincing. "A very unpleasant—"

"What does it say?" Spaulding insisted.

Timon unrolled the note and held it closer to the taper on Lively's desk. The words were difficult to read, the wet ink had blurred.

"I believe it says," Timon ventured, " 'The enemy of man's salvation uses all the means he can.' "

"It is a warning from the killer!" Spaulding snapped. "He will do anything to stop our work!"

Timon knew he had heard the words before—a dim memory, a vague image, the corner of a forgotten room.

"If our work is indeed the salvation of man," Chaderton said softly.

"Could these lines," Timon mumbled, "be from some ancillary text or excluded volume—"

"Apocrypha," Spaulding snarled. "Why would Lively waste his time with *that*?"

"No." Timon stood. "I would recognize a line from any of the apocryphal books I know. Mr. Lively was the presiding scholar for this Cambridge group. Would he have had access to documents that other scholars would not?"

"Not likely," Spaulding sniffed.

"Most definitely," Chaderton said at the same time.

"And Harrison was the—I beg your pardon," Timon said to Chaderton, "he was the primary judge of all the other scholars' qualifications. So he too might have been privy to certain information—"

"Never," Spaulding insisted. "Harrison was a *Scot*!"

"Your point is not clear to me," Chaderton admitted to Timon, ignoring Spaulding.

"The killer may be eliminating scholars in a certain order," Timon explained. "First he kills the first man to see all the documents used in these Cambridge translations: Harrison. Second he strikes down the director of the project, the second man with such knowledge."

"There will be a third victim?" Chaderton whispered.

"Precisely," Timon affirmed.

"Nonsense." Spaulding's word seemed sneezed more than spoken. "We must remove this body from the hall at once, before anyone else sees it. And I must insist upon the same silence concerning this murder as we agreed was best when Harrison was killed. No one must mention this event."

"Mr. Lively was the director of this project," Chaderton said patiently. "Certain proprieties must be observed, certain personages informed."

"I suppose you could be right," Spaulding wheezed. "Authorities must be assured that I am in command of the group; I am in charge. I wonder if it would be best to take a brief hiatus in our work at this juncture."

I must know who is killing these men, and the precise reason for these murders, Timon thought. And I must prevent more bloodshed if I am to complete my own task—or there will soon be little left for me to commit to memory. If I am to fulfill my orders, these killings must cease. What an unusual circumstance for me. God must surely be laughing.

"Brother Timon, rouse yourself, man," Spaulding squeaked. "This is no time for reflection. Lug these guts from this hall at once."

Timon allowed himself to gaze into Spaulding's eyes just long enough to see Spaulding shiver and look away.

"The door at the end of the room," Timon said, "does not appear to be an exit."

"A cellar," Chaderton answered.

"Lively will keep down there until Marbury can see him."

Timon moved to take hold of Lively's ankles, staring up at Spauld-ing. "Are you persuaded, now, Dr. Spaulding, that Chaderton is not the murderer?"

"Certainly not!" Spaulding glared down at Timon. "I expect you to use all your wiles to interrogate Dr. Chaderton and obtain a confession. I leave him in your care."

"I see." Timon pulled on the dead man's ankles. Neither scholar made the slightest move to help.

22

When Timon returned from the cellar, only Chaderton remained in the Great Hall. He was still seated at Lively's desk.

"Dr. Spaulding," Chaderton intoned, "has scurried off to inform anyone who will listen that he is now in charge of things. If I were an alchemist, I would turn myself into a bee that could float behind him and watch the rich pageant. Alas, my talents are more practical."

"Why would Dr. Spaulding be so quick to suspect you of this murder? I wonder." Timon paced a bit in front of Dr. Chaderton.

"He does not like me. Everyone knows it. And I confess I may have slighted him upon occasion. Surely you see how easy that would be to accomplish. And how tempting. Apart from that, I could not say—"

"Will you walk with me, Dr. Chaderton? You and I must make a show: I must appear to interrogate you, and you must appear to defend yourself against a charge of murder."

Chaderton stood. "You do not concur, then, with Spaulding's conclusion. Should I be grateful, or insulted?"

"As I have said, the true murderer is more lithe, younger, and of slighter girth than yourself."

"Insulted, then." Chaderton smiled.

"And there is the fact that Spaulding is an idiot," Timon continued, avoiding Chaderton's eyes. "We must consider that."

"His understanding of Hebrew is quite complete," Chaderton protested.

Timon ceased his pacing and stood in front of Chaderton. "Complete but not *artful*. Whereas your reputation for the same subject hangs in the very air around Cambridge."

"That is the odor of old age," Chaderton corrected. "Please do not mistake it for an accomplishment."

"I am unused to modesty. It makes me uncomfortable."

"Then let us go out into the Cambridge air and clear our heads." Chaderton made for the door. He was quite vigorous for a man approaching his sixty-eighth year.

"If you are of a mind," Timon said, striding beside the older man, "I would first like to walk around the outside perimeter of this building. We may find something that tells us more about our killer. Deacon Marbury and I attempted something like it the night before last."

"You found nothing?"

Timon studied Chaderton's face. "I believe that the killer lingered last night, after killing Lively, after nearly being apprehended twice. The demon is bold, reckless, and seems immune to capture."

"And you believe that I can help?"

"I believe that two sets of eyes are better than one for this sort of work." Timon hid a slight smile. "You may see something that Marbury and I did not."

"Excellent! I am to aid you in your investigation. I shall enjoy that."

They picked up their pace and were out the door.

"What are we looking for?" Chaderton said, his eyes darting everywhere about the foundation of the building.

"Anything that does not seem in its place, any footprint, all discarded items—"

"Everything, in short," Chaderton concluded.

"Yes."

The two men kicked and pawed over every inch of earth around the Great Hall. They considered and discarded rocks, snails, rusty nails, gopher holes, buried chestnuts, a squirrel's skull. The walls of the Great Hall rose high into the air, topped by amber tiles. It sat at the end of a common yard that was surrounded by several such buildings: the deaconage, several dormitories, a chapel. The walkways between the halls were dotted with trees and shrubberies, but no garden relieved the severity of the yard.

"You are a Protestant," Timon said distractedly after half an hour's fruitless activity had passed in silence.

"You surmise this by my black robes or by my rusty reputation?" Chaderton asked, bending to examine and then to pocket a bit of paper in the dirt.

"When I was quite another man, a younger man, I heard your sermon at Paul's Cross, in London. I believe the year was 1578."

"Just so." Chaderton straightened and rubbed his back. "I was quite proud of that sermon."

"Your father was not."

"Marbury said you knew everything." Chaderton's expression softened. A bit of zeal for the investigation left his eyes. "And now you drag out that old ghost."

"He was a Catholic, your father."

"Devoutly. Sternly. He was greatly disappointed when I rebelled—some fifteen years before you heard me speak. I applied to my father for some pecuniary aid shortly after my religious awakening. Our estate was quite vast. He sent me a torn purse with a groat inside and told me to use it for begging. And then he disinherited me."

"You did not go begging."

"If I stare at this wall long enough," Chaderton said barely above a whisper, "I can conjure him, you know. In my mind's eye he is raging, impenetrable as these stones. He never heard me sermonize. I did not attend his funeral. I am an old man, and yet I am reduced to a child's incomprehension whenever I am visited by my father's ghost."

"And for the sake of a disagreement over something so insubstantial as words."

Chaderton raised his face to the sun and folded his hands in front of him, near his heart. "I see. You *are,* in fact, interrogating me."

"I have absolutely no suspicion," Timon protested, "that you are a murderer."

"I do not refer to that." Chaderton stood frozen. "Your investigation goes in many directions."

"I do not know your meaning."

"Do you not?" Chaderton laughed. "You are attempting to lead me into a discussion of 'something so insubstantial as words.'"

"I only—"

"Hush," Chaderton commanded. "I must think for a moment."

Several large crows sat in the bare hazel that stood on the other side of the path from the Great Hall's wall. They appeared to be listening. Timon indulged Chaderton and remained silent, attempting to stare down the black birds.

"You believe that there is something about our translation, our work here, that provokes these murders." Chaderton's eyes were narrow, his breathing shallow. "You wonder if a Protestant might have reason to object so vehemently that he would be driven to madness. Such a man would perform Satan's task."

"Mine is a much larger question," Timon snapped back. His eyes bore into Chaderton's. "I wonder if a conspiracy of lies has shrouded our Bible since its origin. Only last night did Lively show me evidence of this grand deceit."

That should pop his eyes, Timon thought.

Chaderton, however, smiled and took in a long, slow breath. "Well, Brother Timon," he answered at length, "it would appear that we have much to discuss."

The cold wind picked up. Timon barely noticed. Chaderton knew something. It was written on his face.

"We must not speak here," Chaderton whispered. "Anyone could be listening. What we have to discuss is of the utmost secrecy. I would never consider sharing certain information with you unless you had already begun to suspect. What we are about to explore is of paramount relevance to the recent savage events in this hall, these murders."

"Where—"

"If you are not too cold," Chaderton suggested, "we ought to stay out of doors, someplace where we can see for ourselves that no one is about."

"I am indifferent to the weather. And you are warmly dressed."

"Still," Chaderton sighed, "I wouldn't mind if we found a place out of this wind."

"Can you suggest such a spot?" Timon asked patiently.

Without another word Chaderton strode toward the walls of an inner courtyard garden. Timon followed.

"When it is convenient," Timon said, catching up with Chaderton, "you might show me the piece of paper you picked up a moment ago and deposited in your pocket."

"Ah, you observed."

"I did."

Chaderton fished for a moment and produced the shred in question. "You must believe that I intended to share this with you."

Timon took it. "This is the same type of paper used by all of the scholars in the hall. It is on every desk."

Timon studied the scrap with the intensity of a hawk watching a mouse. He held it up to the light and nodded. "This piece is freshly torn," he said steadily, "and was stuck to the bottom of a boot."

Chaderton slowed his pace. "How could you possibly—"

"See here." Timon held out the shred. "The tear is still ragged, not smoothed. That's fresh. And this corner has the distinct imprint of the heel of a boot."

Chaderton squinted, zigzagged his neck, and at last agreed. "I believe you are correct."

"This could be a portion of the same piece upon which the odd quotation was written before it was placed into Mr. Lively's mouth."

"I suppose that is possible," Chaderton said, picking up his pace again, "but what does it matter?"

"We might find, in the hall, the page from which this was torn. It could be matched, if we do not wait overlong. That, in turn, might lead to other discoveries."

Chaderton shook his head, smiling. "Marbury was right to place such faith in you. You *will* find this killer."

23

They reached the end of the stone pathway and arrived at an arched opening in the wall. The wall was perhaps fourteen feet high, the archway half that height. Through it Timon could see a small, perfectly patterned garden with several stone benches at the center. Those benches surrounded a circular pool, five feet or so in diameter, that was partially frozen. Several wrens were scraping delicately across the ice to sip water from the pool.

Variegated privet had been planted in concentric circles around that small body of water. Beyond lay four flower beds whose base was curved, parallel to the outermost rim of privet. In those beds, thickly planted crocus bloomed bloodred.

The two men walked quickly toward the benches.

"In less than a month," Chaderton said, his words rapturous, "hyacinth and tulip will overtake that crocus. By spring who knows what delights our gardener might plant there. Last year: nasturtiums!"

"I fear that the love the English bear for this style of gardening is a primary cause of fear in the rest of the world."

"You really think so?" Chaderton seemed genuinely surprised.

"Bending nature this far from its true course," Timon answered, "makes everyone suspicious. It seems a metaphor, begging the question, what else might England do to subvert the world to its patterned will?"

Chaderton stopped dead still. "Spoken like an Italian."

Timon too came to a halt. "I beg your pardon?"

"I have studied languages for fifty years. Your accent is nearly flawless, but you are not English. I wonder if Deacon Marbury knows this fact."

"I could not say what Deacon Marbury knows," Timon said calmly, "but despite your years of learned study, I must report that my father was in diplomatic service when I was young. I spent formative years in Genoa. This scarcely makes me Italian, though it may have had an effect on my speech—and my appreciation of wilder horticulture."

"A fine answer," Chaderton shot back. "I wonder if I believe it."

"I wonder if it matters at the moment. We have larger issues to explore."

"I wish I were certain—"

"Then I shall begin." Timon headed for the closest bench.

"Yes," Chaderton said instantly, "perhaps you might tell me about the evidence that provoked you—"

"Lively showed me, shortly before he was murdered, the most ancient text of St. Luke—that the very name of our Savior has been incorrectly translated for well over a thousand years."

"I see." Chaderton drew in a breath. "For me, it began with a camel."

Chaderton reached the bench and seemed happy to sit down.

Timon stood, waiting for the scholar to continue.

"Perhaps you are familiar with our Lord's admonition that 'it is easier for a camel to go through the eye of a needle, than for a rich man to enter into the kingdom of God'?"

"Matthew nineteen, verse twenty-four."

"And did you never wonder at the strangeness of the image?" Chaderton could not contain his grin.

"It seemed to me that our Lord was attempting to illustrate the impossibility—"

"No," Chaderton snapped. "Nowhere else in the Testaments does He use such far-fetched imagery. His words are simple. His analogies are plain. That is the beauty of His words. That passage alone provokes the senses. I was quite young when I surmised that something was amiss."

"But—"

"And so I turned to the original Greek—copies of St. Matthew's testament. I discovered, my dear Brother Timon, that the first testament speaks of *kamilos*—not *kamelos*."

Timon caught himself taking in a sharp, sudden breath. "*Kamilos* is 'rope'—*kamelos* is 'camel.'"

"An absurdly easy error to make. I could almost see the bent monk, the darkened chamber, the single candle by his table. There he was, working past midnight, eyes bleary, mistaking an *i* for an *e*—and an image more appertaining to strange dreams than the words of Christ is introduced into our Bible."

"It is easier for a *rope* to pass through the eye of a needle," Timon said to himself. "This is the metaphor of a desert messiah."

"It was innocent, surely, an error of this sort. But it made me wonder. And when I wondered, I became hungry. And when I became hungry—"

"Has it not been argued that the phrase *eye of a needle*," Timon offered, "referred to a city wall in Jerusalem, a narrow gate?"

"In Mark the word for *needle* is a *rafic*; in Luke it is a *belone*. Both are words for sewing needles, not architecture. But what does that matter when the word our Savior used was *rope*, not *camel*?"

"Yes." Timon found he could not stand still. He resumed pacing aimlessly.

"That discovery—a single letter out of place in the ocean of words—began an adventure for me," Chaderton continued. "How could I have realized I was opening a door that would close behind me? I have been in a labyrinth of doubt now for some thirty years."

"Because you have discovered other errors—less innocent." Timon slowed his pacing for a moment. "Lively told me that the group had uncovered some five thousand errors in translation. He said that they dated to the first Council of Nicaea."

"What many of my brother scholars seem to ignore"—Chaderton cast his eyes downward, suddenly weary—"is that the first Council of Nicaea was, in fact, something of a battlefield. In the year of that council, 325, the Christian Church was little more than an aberrant sect of Judaism. Some erroneous choices were made. Some of the documents we now possess were the casualties of that conflict. Many were destroyed. Others were hidden by men—and *women*—who believed that they were valuable. Nicaea determined the direction of the Church. I believe it led us away from Christ."

"Spoken like a Protestant." Timon smiled. "The primary function of the Nicene Council was to determine the exact nature of Christ, not to destroy books of the Bible."

"You must realize the magnitude of this," Chaderton insisted. "In deciding the nature of Christ—whether He was primarily a spiritual entity, or essentially a physical being—the council created a filter. That filter was used to expurgate *ideas*. When they decided that Christ was a man, with a body that died and rose intact from the grave, nearly half of Christendom was excluded."

"The half that believed Christ was primarily a spiritual being." Timon nodded. "The half that found the reanimation of dead flesh abhorrent, even pagan. The Resurrection was, to them, a mystical event."

"*That* half is the source of the secret texts."

"You have studied them all."

"And I believe that they are more accurate," Chaderton answered vehemently, "and more particular to the true words of our Lord than any Bible currently in existence. There are secret teachings that have been deliberately kept from us by the popes!"

Before Chaderton could continue, both men were startled by a sudden figure bounding into the garden.

24

*B*rother Timon!" the shadow called.

"Anne?" Timon could scarcely believe his ears.

Anne was running, her black cloak fanning out behind her. When the wind blew back her hood, it revealed a pale face, a mask of desperation.

"You must come at once," she demanded, stopping at the outermost circle of hedges. Her eyes implored. "My father is in the stables. He is in a desperate state. Something terrible—you must come *now*!"

Without waiting for a response, she turned and fled, clearly expecting Timon to follow.

Timon turned to Chaderton.

"Go," the older man said. "Did you not say that Marbury had gone to London only night before last? If he is back so soon and Anne is distressed, there must be grave news. I shall follow as quickly as these bones allow."

Timon nodded and set off. Once out of the garden, he saw

Anne flying across the stone path toward the stables. He raced after her.

They both ran madly between tall buildings, past bare trees, and at last into a cobbled courtyard surrounded by stalls. The yard itself was only a hundred feet across, a circle open on two opposite sides for entrance and exit. Around each half circle sat four stalls, a total of eight barely nine feet tall, but one was larger than the others. It was a coach house with an odd insignia over the entrance. The stable wood was a whitewashed gray, and the unmistakable scent of new hay and old manure filled the air. That smell assailed Timon's senses and dug into some long-suppressed memory.

Most of the stalls were empty, or quiet, but the coach house was crowded and noisy. Anne, barely out of breath, stopped suddenly a few steps shy of the open door. Timon caught sight of Marbury inside, unharnessing the horses.

"Deacon Marbury?" he called out.

Marbury froze. His head shot out from the shadows of the stall and he said quickly, "Brother Timon. Good. Help me with this, would you?"

"Father—," Anne began.

"Please!" he shot back. "I have asked you twice already. Stay out!"

"You want me to help you with the horses?" Timon asked, confused.

"God," Marbury swore, and moved instantly out into the court-yard.

Anne took a quick step backward.

"Anne," he said, the sound of her name straining the air around it, "would you mind very much going to find the stable master. We need him. Brother Timon, I need your assistance in here—"

"But are you all right?" Anne insisted. "And where is Thom?"

At the mention of Thom's name, all energy seemed to abandon Marbury. His shoulders sagged and his eyes closed.

"Was he not your driver?" she asked, her voice less vigorous than before.

"He was," Marbury choked.

"What has happened?" she whispered.

Marbury found himself without words and nodded in the direction of the coach.

Timon stepped into the stall. His hand felt its way along the side of the coach until he found a handle. He turned it and drew open the door.

Even in the shadows he could tell that the occupants of the coach were dead. He could also see, out of the corner of his eye, that Marbury was watching him with a curious intensity.

"Might I speak freely?" Timon asked with a slight glance in Anne's direction.

"Is Thom in that coach?" Anne asked, her voice icy.

Marbury nodded, his eyes still locked on Timon.

"And the other man?" Timon asked calmly.

"There is another?" Anne interrupted.

"Can you not see who he is, Brother?" Marbury did not move.

Timon moved a step toward the back of the stall and pulled the door of the coach open wide. A bit of sunlight found its way into the gloom where the bodies lay. It was only a candle's worth of light, barely enough to discern the features of the other man's face.

Timon bent down. Before he could prevent it, a shock of recognition played across his face, and he took in a sudden breath.

Marbury folded his hands across his chest and clenched the fingers. "I have no idea what made me consider that you might know the man. I gambled—or, more than gambled, really. At times I have an intuition for this sort of thing."

Timon stood, pinching his lips together. "And this, it would appear, is one of those times. I do, in fact, know the man. He is Pietro Delasander—an assassin."

Disarm suspicion with the truth, Timon thought. Though perhaps it would be best not to mention that I taught the dead man his craft.

"Assassin?" Anne exploded. "What has happened? I demand— Thom?" She rushed forward.

Marbury caught her arm. "He is dead."

"As is Pietro Delasander," Timon sighed. "Which is a shame. He could have told us many things."

"He is dead by his own hand," Marbury blurted—and instantly regretted it.

"Why would he do that?" Timon stared down at the body. "You must tell me everything. And I have news to report as well. There has been a lamentable occurrence in your absence."

"Anne," Marbury said calmly, eyes locked on Timon's, "you understand now why we must fetch the stable master. Please find him and bring him here."

Anne knew the tone of her father's voice—knew it was an absolute command. Without a word she turned and headed for the stable master's room.

As soon as she was gone from sight, Marbury grabbed his dagger. He moved slowly, as if he were joining Timon in the stall to further examine the dead bodies.

Without warning his hand flew out toward Timon's throat, the blade flashed in the dim light, and the cold cutting edge drew a thin line of red across Timon's gullet.

"Who are you?" Marbury demanded, his voice a guttural, animal sound. "What are you doing in my house? Why did you try to poison me at Hampton Court?"

"I am called Brother Timon," Timon responded, dead calm, full-voiced. "You hired me. I did not try to poison you. And if you do not take your knife away from my throat, I will be forced to make Anne an orphan, which I would not relish."

Marbury felt a sudden pain in his solar plexus and looked down. Timon held a dagger that seemed nearly as long as his forearm. It was pointed almost straight up. Its tip had cut through Marbury's expensive doublet. It was piercing the skin beneath it.

"At this angle," Timon continued, "the blade will slide beneath the rib cage and very nicely into the heart. Once there, if I twist it just right, I can actually cut the heart in half. Apparently the heart keeps pumping; fills up the chest cavity with so much blood so quickly—"

"Enough," Marbury barked, stepping back and withdrawing his blade. When he looked down, Timon's blade had vanished.

"I must assume that your journey to London was not a pleasant one," Timon sighed. "You return with a sickly pallor and two dead bodies in the royal coach. You are exhausted, that much is clear, and apparently you have been poisoned. For these reasons I forgive your temporary lapse in manners. Though I must assure you that no other man has held a blade so close to me and lived. I am uncertain why I did not dispatch you. I have an inexplicable fondness for Anne, and a somewhat grudging respect for you. Or perhaps it is the smell of these stables. It reminds me of my boyhood home, a place I had all but forgotten until a moment ago. Who can say? These are puzzling days for me in general. I am not myself. And, incidentally, there has been another murder here."

25

*M*arbury felt that all life had been kicked from his body. He grabbed the stable's support beam to keep from collapsing.

"Might I suggest that we discuss a few matters before we try to kill each other again?" Timon concluded. "But here is Anne—she was quick."

Marbury twisted his body enough to see Anne running a bit more slowly than she had before, pulling the stable master by his sleeve, toward the stall.

"Another murder?" Marbury whispered. "Here?"

Timon stepped past Marbury and into the light of the courtyard. "You are the stable master?"

The man Anne led was Timon's age, though much less vigorous, completely bald, and bent as if he'd carried the horses on his back. His clothes were the color of straw and mud; his hands were raw leather. His face, masked in ruddy red, revealed nothing about his character, but the eyes evidenced a hidden intelligence, a guarded power that, Timon guessed, few around him saw or understood.

"I am the stable master," the man repeated, out of breath, when he drew near to the patient horses behind Timon. "Name of Lankin."

"Well, Mr. Lankin," Timon began, "we have something of a difficulty. It will require your utmost discretion. Deacon Marbury has returned from London with an unfortunate cargo."

"Thom is dead," Anne cried, "and there is another body in his coach!"

Lankin froze. "Thom?"

"I might have broken the news with a bit more care," Timon said tersely with a glance in Anne's direction, "but Anne has told the bare facts."

"What did he do?" Lankin demanded.

"I am uncertain," Timon began, "as to the exact events—"

"We were attacked on the road home," Marbury croaked, making his way out of the stable. "The other man in the coach shot Thom. He would have shot me too, but for Providence."

"Let us leave details for a less delicate moment," Timon interrupted. Best not reveal everything to daughters and stable masters, he thought.

"Yes," Marbury said softly. "Would you see to Thom's body, Mr. Lankin? Brother Timon and I shall extract the other."

"Thom's body," Lankin repeated, unable to quite grasp the reality of the words.

"I will help," Anne said softly, her hand on the stable master's shoulder.

Before protest could erupt from either Marbury or Lankin, Anne brushed past her father and peered into the coach.

"Miss—," Lankin attempted.

"We shall need a sheet in which to carry the body," she announced, "and I would appreciate an apron to cover my dress. There is a good deal of blood."

She popped her head up and searched the stable walls.

Lankin took a moment to register what had been said, blinked, and turned away, headed back for his room. "Sheet."

Marbury glared at his daughter as if she were a stranger.

Timon stepped back into the stall. "I believe I observed a leather farrier's apron in the corner. Would that do?"

"Where is it?" Anne asked.

Timon stepped to the back wall of the stall, bent, and retrieved a single item from a tangle of hay, rags, and aprons.

"This?" He held one aloft.

"Thank you," Anne answered primly, taking the dark brown apron from Timon with one hand delicately. "It will, at least, protect my skirt."

"Anne," Marbury began weakly.

"You and I should remove Pietro's body now, Deacon," Timon interrupted. "That will make it easier for Anne and the stable master to care for Thom."

Marbury rubbed his eyes with the palms of his hands, blew out his lips, and nodded. Anne stepped back, slipping into the stiff, oversize apron. Timon moved to the coach and unceremoniously locked his wrists into the dead man's armpits. Marbury hurried to join him, going to the other side of the coach, opening the door gingerly, and staring down at Pietro's ankles.

After too long a pause, Timon said softly, "You pull, I'll move through the coach and come out that door. We'll lay him in the sun out there so we can get a better look at him."

The stable master had returned by the time Timon and Marbury were both standing on the outside of the coach, holding the body, waddling toward the light on the cobblestones.

Anne and Lankin went to work at their own gory task more gently. Thom was wrapped in a sheet, the sheet was tied, and the body swung from the seat as if it were resting in a hammock.

Marbury and Timon stood in the courtyard, panting.

"What now, exactly?" Marbury stammered.

"How do you mean?" Timon swallowed.

"What do we do with the bodies?"

"We prepare Thom's body for an honored burial, in the service of the King," Timon answered, making certain he spoke loudly enough for Anne and Lankin to hear. "This one we examine." His toe tapped the body at their feet.

"Examine?"

"Mr. Lankin," Timon said, moving to the front of the stall, "would it be possible for you to see that Deacon Marbury and I were not disturbed here for the span of an hour?"

Anne and Lankin emerged from the relative darkness of the stall with their shrouded burden. They laid it gently on the stones, the sun adding blinding white fire to the sheet.

"I'll need to see to a few things for Thom anyways," Lankin sighed. "And I hope you mean it, that about the King's service. Thom got little enough in this life—it would be nice for him to have honor in death."

"I personally assure it," Marbury answered solemnly.

"Good." Lankin brushed his hands on his thighs. "Now, Miss Anne, I believe you and I ought to fetch a few of Thom's things out of his hovel."

Anne nodded, taking off the leather apron. "But I shall know the full story of this day before nightfall."

Marbury sighed heavily.

Without further conversation, Anne and Lankin were off. Once they had disappeared around the corner of the stables, Lankin could be heard shouting stern orders, presumably at the stableboys, to stay clear of the courtyard all morning. They would surely be happy at the news. It meant far less work than usual.

"Where to begin?" Timon asked brightly.

"Who among our translators is dead?" Marbury whispered.

"Yes. That." Timon bit his upper lip. "Mr. Lively has been murdered. His body was found in a state similar to Harrison's."

"The face mutilated?" Marbury gasped.

"Yes, though not so severely, it would seem, as was Harrison's. Lively was readily identifiable. You should also know that Dr. Spaulding has assumed command with all the assurance of a man who is entirely ignorant of his task and has accused Dr. Chaderton of the murder."

"God in heaven." Marbury leaned back against the outer stable wall.

"As with Harrison," Timon continued breezily, "there was a note in Lively's mouth: 'The enemy of man's salvation uses all the means he can.'"

"What to make of these notes?" Marbury muttered.

"They are an attempt to tell us something, but it may be that the meaning is known only to the killer. These facial mutilations appear to be the work of a deranged mind."

"Is Lively's body still—"

"I removed it to the cellar of the Great Hall," Timon assured Marbury. "Now I wonder if you would tell me, in a nutshell, what happened at Hampton Court that made you want to kill me, and where you acquired the dead body of this notable assassin."

Marbury did his best to marshal his forces. "Our King is mad, witches are abroad, Mary wrote a Gospel, I was poisoned, then pursued on my way home by this creature, Delasander, who shot Thom and would have killed me but for boys who are starving in the woods outside of London."

Timon stared at Marbury for the span of several long seconds.

"It might be best," Timon began carefully, "to dispense with the nutshell and speak a bit more elaborately."

"Your immediate task is to examine this sack of bones."

"Yes." Timon looked down at his student. "It is."

"You cannot imagine how I am in need of a change of clothing, a splash of water upon the face, and a gallon of brandy." Marbury sniffed, rubbed his hands together, and took a step into the sunlight. "I ought to stay with you while you examine this assassin, but I propose that I repair, instead, to my rooms and gather my thoughts. Come to my study in, shall we say, an hour?"

"You will need a full night's sleep and a good meal if you have been poisoned, though I concur with the concept of a large amount of brandy. However, time is of the essence. I would prefer to meet you in the cellar of the Great Hall within half an hour. I am eager to hear what the King told you, and you will be amazed, in turn, at what I have learned here in your brief absence. If your tale and mine concur even in the slightest, then I believe that we will have uncovered a plot to rattle the world. It is an ancient deception whose revelation could shake down the firmament; could change, I say without hyperbole, everything we know and do. Everything."

26

*F*orty minutes later Marbury discovered that the cellar beneath the Great Hall was made of ice. He was certain that he could feel his blood slowing down. The marrow in his bones seemed to be snapping as he walked toward the dead body. Timon had brought down several candles, but their light only emphasized the cold. Marbury could almost see it hanging in the stale, dank air of the place.

"One benefit is," Timon said, reading Marbury's mind, "that at this temperature the body does not offend the nose."

The cellar was a stone box, barely twice the size of Timon's room. The ceiling was low, the floor was filthy. One wall was a rack, floor to ceiling, primarily containing claret and sack. Two of the other walls were similarly arrayed with bins for root vegetables. Carrots, potatoes, radishes, onions, and beets all lay in state with their fellows.

Lively lay on a table against the fourth wall. The body was illuminated at the head and foot by tall tapers. Timon held a third in his hand.

Timon had laid the body with great care, folding the arms across the chest. That made no difference to Marbury. He was still shocked to see the man's face. Even in the dim, flickering candle-light, Lively's face was a nightmare. Curled gashes opened like hellish red mouths. Eight or nine of them erupted from his cheeks, his forehead, across the bridge of his nose.

Without warning, Marbury's brain echoed with recent words of the King of England: *too many have been licked by the tongue of the devil.*

"Would you care to hear, Brother Timon," Marbury croaked, "our King's theory concerning these murders?"

Timon set his candle down on the table, at Lively's side.

"James believes that the devil's minions, as witches, are every-where. He believes they killed Harrison. He will think the same of Lively's death. He feels these demons live in the very ink and paper of our work here."

"King James has long pursued witches," Timon said softly. "When he was King of Scotland he burned hundreds. One of his first efforts as King of England—"

"Yes, he devised the sternest act against witchcraft in England's history." Marbury shivered. "But if you had heard him speaking, seen the look in his eye—"

"Your own face betrays your fears about the King."

At that Marbury stopped, realized what he was saying. He shiv-ered, looking down at Lively's face. "I would spend as little time in this cellar as possible."

"Yes." Timon sniffed. "Then please examine Mr. Lively's face and tell me how these lacerations compare to those found on Har-rison's."

"Harrison could not be identified by his face. It was entirely obliterated by wounds, perhaps ten times the number on Lively's face."

"This is what both Spaulding and Chaderton have told me. Good."

"You surmise," Marbury responded, "that the killer may have

been interrupted in his work. Which could mean that there was a witness."

"Exactly. But what to make of the note found in Lively's mouth," Timon said, failing to hide an admiration for Marbury's powers of deduction.

"As you said"—Marbury nodded—"a message from the killer?"

"Possibly."

"Tell me what you discovered in examining the body of Pietro Delasander."

"He died of poison," Timon answered. "That much is certain. It came from a ring on his left hand. Many such men wear hidden potions."

Marbury stared. "You found something else. I can tell by the sound of your voice."

"I did." Timon's face remained expressionless. "He had on his person a certain missive, secret instructions."

Marbury squinted, hoping to hold back the cold through sheer force of will. "Secret instructions."

"Later," Timon responded perfunctorily. "They do not have immediate bearing on our circumstances."

Marbury's face betrayed his belief that Timon was lying.

"Incidentally," Timon continued, as if he had not noticed Marbury's expression, "I did not find any pistols on his body, but he had about him a pouch with shot and powder."

"His pistols were taken from him by highwaymen." Marbury smiled. "The very same men who saved my life."

"You did, indeed, have an eventful journey." Timon did his best but failed to understand Marbury's delight at the mention of the highwaymen.

"May we leave this frigid place?" Marbury asked. "I have seen Lively. I concur with your sequester—this room will preserve him well until we decide what steps to take. What purpose does it serve to bring me here? Why did you not agree to come to my study when—"

"Chaderton has convinced me that invisible eyes and ears are everywhere. I do not believe that they are of a demonic nature, but I do believe that they are listening, watching—gathering information. I would make it clear to them that you and I are not easily dissuaded. We are men of iron whose tasks are not the least averted by hideous wounds, pistol shots, poison, pestilence, or witches. They must see that nothing will stop us."

"Agreed," Marbury responded, teeth clenched, "but could we be iron heroes in a slightly warmer room?"

"Please indulge me." Timon leaned casually against the table upon which Lively lay. "Tell me about the poison *you* took."

"I did not take it," Marbury snapped, rubbing his hands together. His suspicions alerted once more, he did his best to ignore the cold. "I was given it in sweet cakes and pear cider."

"Yet you survived."

Marbury glared at Timon before he would answer. Timon returned the gaze without emotion of any sort.

"Surely the poison was intended for the King," Marbury began slowly. "It was in his Privy Kitchen. An aide had about his person a remedy so potent—"

"A purgative," Timon interrupted, nearly to himself.

"Yes. Very powerful. I may have vomited up my spleen. I was forced to perform this humiliating task in the hallway outside the kitchen."

"With the King waiting inside?"

"I have never been so embarrassed in all my life."

"Where and when were you given the food?"

"As soon as I arrived." Marbury's irritation was gravel in his throat. "In the Privy Kitchen, as I have said."

"And you waited there for His Majesty for the span of . . . ?"

"Less than half an hour."

"Long enough to feel the sting of the poison," Timon said quietly, "but not quite so long that it could complete its work."

"Sorry?" Marbury's displeasure abated a bit in the face of a newer curiosity. "What manner of—"

"Did you not find it odd that this aide had an antidote with him?"

"It was explained to me," Marbury said slowly, "that His Majesty was in constant danger of being poisoned. In fact he had been poisoned and saved by the very remedy which restored me."

"But the King was not coming to dine with you, am I correct?"

"It was explained to me," Marbury answered weakly, "that this aide kept the potion on his person at all times."

"A stroke of salvation for you."

"Yes."

Without thinking, Marbury too leaned on Lively's table.

"But surely," Marbury continued, "you don't imply—"

"I only observe that you were poisoned in the King's presence, then saved by the King. It is a ruthless but not unprecedented manner of establishing a sense of overwhelming gratitude coupled with a deep humiliation. It is a perfect combination to produce, in many, a certain loyalty."

Marbury folded his arms, his shivering nearly constant. He realized that Timon had captured some important bit of information. Before he could completely grasp its meaning, Timon continued.

"You told the King secrets; told him there had been a murder. You said or implied that documents here in Cambridge—which he sent—may have been the cause of the crime. In turn he shared with you his war on witchcraft, the confession that he had been poisoned before—"

"And the accusation," Marbury whispered, "that there are hidden or suppressed Gospels of our Bible, books which have not come to light in more than a thousand years."

"After which," Timon said, pounding the flat of his hand on the table, "you are pursued by one of Europe's great assassins—the instant you leave Hampton Court! If the King wished to silence you, to keep his secrets hidden, there could have been no better executioner than Pietro Delasander."

"You must tell me how you know him," Marbury hissed.

"You must tell me how he died," Timon shot back.

"I've already told you!" Marbury exploded.

"Highwaymen?" Timon responded with equal volume. "Very selective highwaymen who killed him and helped you?"

"There is more to the story."

"Then tell it to me."

"My blood is freezing!" Marbury's shiver quickened, every muscle in his body twitched with the cold.

"We shall go upstairs, back to your study," Timon explained patiently, "as soon as you have answered my questions."

Marbury took in a breath to offer his hasty summation of the encounter with the boys in the woods—which seemed more like a dream than an event—before he realized what Timon was doing.

"I had given thought to the notion that you were a victim of the Inquisition," he said, managing a smile at Timon. "You now confirm that fact, at least to my mind. I realize that you are, in very subtle ways, using Inquisition techniques to obtain information from me. There is no actual reason to bring me to this ice room, standing beside the dead body, except to say that I might be relieved of that circumstance if I would only answer your questions."

Timon smiled, folding his hands. "I wondered how long I could employ that tool before you realized what I was doing."

"I no longer trust you, nor the men who gave you to me," Marbury said plainly. "You have discerned that, perhaps, and thought it best to ferret out information in this manner."

"And I am a single-minded man. You hired me to find a killer. I will do it. The more facts I have, the sooner that task will be completed. I will stop at nothing."

"As you have suggested."

"But I will confess," Timon said more softly, and with some difficulty, "I may have been excessive in my manner because I find that I admire and respect you. This is unwise for me. It can become an impediment to my work."

Is this the truth, Marbury wondered to himself, or another ploy? It seems clear that he is not the one who poisoned me at Hampton Court, but how can one be certain with this man?

"I suggest a truce of sorts," Timon continued. "I will tell you—perhaps tomorrow—the details of everything that has happened here in your absence. I have discovered things which, as I have told you, will roil the waters of the world."

"I, in turn," Marbury sighed, "will reveal, after a good night's sleep, everything about my journey to court, a tale to strain even the most vivid imagination."

"Then for God's sake let us leave this dungeon," Timon responded quickly, heading for the stairs. "I can no longer feel my feet."

"I fear I might shatter a bone if I do not stop this quaking," Marbury said, rushing to follow Timon.

Both men ran up the stairs into the Great Hall.

Marbury was reflecting on the strangeness of his day.

Timon, on the other hand, was reliving one of a hundred or more nights when he had been dragged from a torture chamber back to an Inquisition cell, a room the size of a coffin.

27

*W*ithout a word of farewell, Marbury was gone. Timon was left to stumble through the enormous darkened hall past vacant desks where only ghosts could study. Timon hastened toward his room, all the while clutching the hilt of his dagger in his right hand as if it were his crucifix.

Black shadows raked past his face as he quickened his steps; a desperation gripped his mind. Pietro Delasander—that close. And the return of Inquisition nightmares. His hands began to quiver and his lips formed soundless words.

The pale moon rowed its silver boat across a darkening sky, its ease mocking Timon's panic. It offered Timon white ropes, beams of light through tree limbs, an escape from the earth, if he could climb them. But the bare limbs were blood vessels, the veins of the earth bleeding night into the sky. Timon understood that the moon offered false hopes. There was only one true salvation, to be found in the oil of nutmeg.

That was obtained through steam distillation and could be consumed in a variety of ways. Nutmeg was an important item of trade in England. In certain Jewish communities, especially the Yemenites, it was used as a folk medicine and as an ingredient in love potions. It was also useful against vomiting, colds, fever; diseases of the liver, spleen, and skin—all wonderful ancillary benefits to any love potion. Nutmeg had other practical uses, notably as a flavorful culinary ingredient, but also as an aid to abortion. Women employing the latter usage were derisively called *nutmeg ladies,* whereas those employing the former were generally referred to as *cooks.*

Timon smoked it in a clay pipe. He had learned of its more peculiar properties from Jews with whom he had been imprisoned. They had told him about the soothing qualities of large portions of the spice, distilled and smoked. Nausea reigned for a while, and the mouth was as dry as sand; the skin flushed, eyes were red and wild. The hours that followed, however, were filled with unearthly delights. Great visions would take him away from his misery and into another world. Timon had depended on the spice to make his time in prison bearable, to increase his perceptions and insights; later to allow him to render his own personal brand of horror on his hapless victims.

He reached the Deaconage, crashed through the outer door and down the hall to his cell. Though the room was cold, Timon was sweating. He had been holding back the cravings, but the events of the day had finally broken his defenses. Every atom in his body was shrieking for the spice.

He stumbled toward his bed and found the wooden box. A vial of oil and a clay pipe rested there. He sat on the bed, threw the box aside, poured the thick brown oil into the pipe. He found the flint he carried in his robe and struck it feverishly. Mad seconds blithered by before the oil ignited and the smoke began to sting his eyes, then his lungs.

In the darkness of his room, the scent of cooking nutmeg was more comforting than any other sensation in the world. He sucked in the needles of smoke as if he were drawing his last breath—over and over.

At last the panic began to subside. He set the pipe on his lap and leaned back against the wall. His stomach churned and he longed for ale to wash the sand from his throat.

Then, without warning, a vision overtook his mind. Timon found himself in another room, a brighter and more terrifying cell in Rome, near the Campo dei Fiori square.

28

In his vision, Timon was once more in captivity, by the hand of an employer—his betrayer—in January of 1600. Zuane Mocenigo, a wealthy, lazy young man, desired to be taught the art of memory. That was a talent for which Timon—though he was not yet called by that name—was widely known. Timon had been hoping for the vacant mathematics chair at Padua, but that exalted post went instead to Galileo Galilei. Timon served instead, with no small measure of disappointment, as tutor to Mocenigo.

Mocenigo was, in turn, greatly disappointed to learn that Timon's system of mnemonics required diligent work and earnest concentration. Mocenigo had expected easily acquired magic. He believed that Timon's prodigious ability to remember the infinite was an effect of sorcery. No matter how many times Timon explained it was mere science—a plodding, exhausting game of making one small fact link to another, a chain that could hold the enormous weight of facts—Mocenigo did not believe him. At first despondent, Mocenigo grew more angry with each passing lesson. Where was the magic?

When he'd had enough of the tedious schoolboy study, he thought absolutely nothing of denouncing Timon to the Inquisition.

Timon's trial had been overseen by the famous inquisitor Robert Bellarmine. He was a stern interpreter of his task, and his assistant was Cardinal Enrico Venitelli. Timon was quickly condemned as a demon and given over to secular authorities. He was to be burned at the stake in Rome, Campo dei Fiori square. He waited in his cell there, hearing the common noise of the people strolling by, vendors calling out how fresh the salt mussels were, how white the turnips. And, at last, listening to the construction of his own dry funeral pyre, heavy, rough-hewn logs planking and scratching together.

Every waking moment had been spent either in prayer or in killing the thousands of spiders that were his cell mates. Some of them bit and raised red welts that burned and itched. Timon had endured hundreds of such wounds. They had not bothered him at first, but as their number increased, and the constant pain and itching grew, he thought he might go mad before his execution. The tickle of a spider's legs across his skin—real or imagined—prevented all but the most fitful moments of sleep. His sanity came and went, a kind visitor from another country.

As he knelt in that cell, praying on his last day, an uncommonly warm February morning, he wondered at the approaching footsteps.

This early? he thought. The sun has barely risen. There will only be a small crowd in the square at this hour.

This was puzzling because the primary objective of burning a man at the stake, aside, of course, from serving as popular entertainment, was to warn would-be sinners. An early execution defeated both aims.

He opened his eyes.

The cell was scarcely larger than he was: room enough to lie down only if he curled like a child, room enough to stand only if he stooped like an old man. The walls were green with moss. The odor of the uncleaned corner that served as his chamber pot was nearly overwhelming. He had been blessed with a small, high window. It faced the east so that he could meditate on the changing of the hours. Sometimes he sat for days watching a square of morning light chase shadows slowly up the wall; watching a silver ghost of moonlight do the same in the long spider-hours of the night.

He heard the door groan as it opened. He did not rise from his knees or even turn around to face it. A doomed man is free of such manners.

"My son," the gentle voice whispered in crisp, formal Latin.

My confessor, he assumed. "Father." Timon closed his eyes again.

"Please rise," the voice urged.

Timon sighed, held out a hand to the wall, managed his way to his feet, head brushing the ceiling.

When he turned around, he was presented with an image that branded the forefront of his brain.

His Holiness Pope Clement VIII stood framed just outside the doorway of the death cell looking like a dagger held straight up: gleaming in white robes, his miter coming to a knife point above his head.

Timon was too stunned to move.

"Giordano," the Pope said, the kindest pronunciation of his real name that Timon had ever heard.

"Your Eminence," Timon managed, still foolishly standing.

Holy Father turned slightly and dismissed whoever stood behind him with vague gesture. The departing attendant left a stool upon which His Holiness sat in the hall outside the cell.

"This is a terrible day for Mother Church," Clement began without looking at Timon. "We despise your sins but we disagree that you, yourself, are a demon."

"I understand, Your Grace," Timon mumbled, though he did not.

"The most serious charge against you—"

"I have discovered an interior structure to the world of ideas."

Timon held his gaze steady until the Pope looked at him, looked him in the eye. "I can, therefore, remember anything. It is true."

"In your eagerness to speak," the Pope responded, a slight smile twitching at the corner of his mouth, "you have degenerated into Italian."

Timon smiled, realizing that he had, indeed, reverted to his mother tongue. "Cold Latin will not contain my fervor, and I have become an Italian instead of a Dominican."

"A man becomes himself on the morning of his death," Clement agreed softly. "Bellarmine and Venitelli were right to condemn you, with your science of memory." The Pope shifted uncomfortably on his stool. "And yet it is precisely this science of memory that prompts Us to visit your cell. As of this moment We lay aside your execution. Your death is not a thing We would have upon Our soul. We have therefore made other arrangements. You are to go into hiding and do as We bid you."

Timon felt as if the stones from the wall had collapsed on him. He could not find his tongue nor unsnarl the knot of his brain. "You are laying aside my execution?"

"We know this stupid Mocenigo," the Pope said with a wave of his hand, "the man who denounced you and condemned you to your fate here. We understand he was angry that you did not instruct him in some magical arts, but rather attempted to teach him your tricks of science. We know you are not an alchemist. You are a scientist. The very thing that condemned you now saves you. Ironic, is it not?"

"Your Holiness." Timon heard the relief in his own voice.

"These tricks that help you remember," Clement continued impatiently, "this scientific device or some apparatus of the mind, We must have you continue to perfect it. You must grow in your abilities so that you will have the power to accomplish great work which We will require of you one day soon."

"Power?"

"The power of language," Clement said simply, "and the power of memory. You will be taken to a place of safety where you will learn several difficult languages as quickly as you are able, and you must come to know them better than any man on earth. You will also be given a knot of codes and instructions which no mortal man could possibly untangle. And you will be given further instruction in certain . . . other skills, which we know you once possessed—before you became a monk. We choose you, a man who will die and come back to life, for great work, my son."

An alien smile touched the lips of His Grace.

Before Timon could form his next thousand questions, a shuffling came down the black hall outside his cell. He cringed, still expecting to be dragged to the stake.

"But here are your protectors," the Pope said, rising.

"I do not understand," Timon rasped. "I am to leave with these men? I am not to be executed today?"

"You must bring your remarkable brain back to life, Giordano," the Pope snapped impatiently. "Preparations have been made."

"But," Timon said hastily as the Pope turned to leave, "my father, my earthly father—he will be here to collect my body."

Holy Father sighed. "We have selected another man," Clement said, eyes watching the men who approached him. "You must leave immediately."

With that, the Pope was gone. Vanished as if he had not been in that horrible place at all.

Three men appeared out of the darkness. Timon could not see their faces. They pulled off his tattered brown robe and replaced it with another like their own: black as night, clean.

"But my poor father," Timon mumbled helplessly to one of the strangers, "my real father, will know I am not the man at the stake."

"Everything has been arranged," one said in Italian.

A second, kinder voice whispered, "The man selected to take your place has had his tongue nailed to his jaw so that he cannot speak. And he will have a sack of gunpowder around his neck, which will obscure his face."

"What?" Timon stammered.

"It is often done as an act of kindness on the part of clerical authorities, so that a man may die more quickly and not suffer burning. It—explodes."

29

*T*he vision of these events continued to roll over Brother Timon as he lay in his bed in Cambridge, more than five years after they had happened. He leaned back against the wall behind him, turning his head so that the bare stones could cool his burning cheek. His breathing was labored. His eyes flushed constantly, and all the white in them was gone, replaced by red fire. He replaced the pipe and vial in its coffin. He hid the box once more and lay down across his bed.

Before long, another, more dreaded memory overtook him. He recalled the reason that the name *Padget,* which Lively had spoken just before he died, so burned the brain.

He closed his eyes, feeling the memory begin to roll over him. He clutched the bedsheets, helpless to prevent the vivid images from appearing in his mind's eye. At first he only saw transparent strings of rain, dangling in the night. Then, more clearly, he felt himself walking the Southwark street where a certain old man was living. The street had materialized out of the insubstantial air, and

Timon was there, walking down that dark corridor. As far as he could tell, the street had no name.

Timon came to a pocked, brown door, half-eaten by worms. Before he knocked, a woman came to the door. She was wearing an apron the color of the rain outside. Her face was lined and sooty, and her eyes were slits. A crumpled bonnet hung on the top of her head. Her hands were red and raw, and she winced when she saw Timon, as if his presence caused her pain.

"What?" she demanded.

"I have come to see Robert Padget, please," Timon said politely.

He had learned that courtesy often startled the London populace. He could turn that shock to his advantage.

"No use," the woman said, utterly impervious to manners. "If he gets any money at all, it goes to me, see? He owes me three months' rent now."

She swung the door toward Timon, shooing him away.

"I do not want his money. I have some questions, only."

"He doesn't *have* any money," she insisted.

"Then you may find it a good thing I am not here for it."

She stood in the doorway, sulking for a moment. Greasy hair dribbled from her stained cap. One eye looked slightly more westerly than the other.

"I suppose you can come in," she grudged, stepping back. "Top of the stairs, first door you see."

"Thank you." Timon nodded and squeezed past her as quickly as he could. Her breath was like the remains of a bird ten days dead in the hot sun.

"You can't stay long, mind," she called. "He needs his rest so's he can work. To get my money!"

Timon shot up the black stairs.

"I will not keep him long," he assured her, hand on Padget's door.

If he had known what that room was going to be like, he might not have gone farther.

The door croaked open.

Padget's room was dark; no candle lit it. The lack of light made those four walls a crypt.

The odor of the room mangled the senses, shoved Timon backward like a fist in the chest. The air reeked of sickbed sheets, old ale, cheap tobacco, unemptied chamber pots, and a palpable, heart-stopping fear. Without thinking of how it might offend, Timon put a hand across his face, covering his mouth and nose.

"Who is it?" The voice could have come from a dying animal; it was barely human.

"Robert Padget?" Timon asked, unable to see where the voice had come from, peering around the room without going in farther.

"Close the door," Padget croaked. "There is a draft."

Timon found he could not move, fearing what more darkness and less air would bring to that room.

"Who are you?" Padget asked, exhausted by the words.

Timon heard the rustle of bedsheets and tried to focus his eyes on the bed. As they adjusted a little to the darkness, he could see a hulk shifting on the wooden frame several feet to his left.

"May I light a taper?"

"I have none," Padget sighed.

"And you won't!" came a sudden voice from the hallway.

Timon spun around.

The landlady had followed up the stairs, silent as a ghost. Her voice was a nail in the skull.

"No candles until you pay me!" she finished her short tirade.

"I will pay for a taper," Timon said quickly, digging into his pouch. "Here is a farthing, bring several, and a tankard of ale for Mr. Padget."

She took the money, stood a moment trying to understand what was happening, gave up, and disappeared.

"Are you buying me candles and ale?" Padget managed, his voice gathering a little strength.

"I am."

"You have no idea," he said, almost like a little child, "how long the nights are in this room without a bit of flame."

Timon shuddered, knowing all too well what it would be like.

"What is your business with me, then?" Padget sniffed. "Surely Mrs. Isam has told you I have no money."

"Is there a place for me to sit? A chair?"

"No," Padget said curtly. "I have only this bed."

Mrs. Isam appeared at the top of the stairs, three tapers in one hand and a lead tankard in the other. Money, it seemed, made her quite fleet of foot. She shoved past Timon as if he were not there and thrust the ale in Padget's direction.

He took it and drained half the tankard before she turned in Timon's direction.

"Here," she said, handing Timon the candles. "There's a flint on the windowsill. I'll come back up if you're not gone in half an hour."

"Yes," Timon assured her.

She eked past and was gone down the stairs.

"Delightful woman," Padget intoned, then finished his ale. "God, I have a thirst. Burning up with fever."

"Mr. Padget," Timon said calmly, "I am an emissary from His Holiness Pope Clement the Eighth."

"Mrs. Isam!" he bellowed, his voice stronger than one would have thought possible. "You have let in a *Catholic*!"

"Shut up!" she hollered from the bowels of her house.

Timon moved toward the windowsill, barely visible in the fading light. He felt around, found the flint, struck one of the candles, and pocketed the flint.

The room whitened. Timon instantly wished it had not.

The walls were spotted and stained where they were not crumbling; the ceiling was a nest of spiderwebs. Crumpled paper filled the room, piled two feet high or more in the corners.

Three stomach-churning chamber pots overflowed at the side of Padget's bed, the only stick of furniture in the room.

The covers around the man were smeared, blood-spotted, torn, and fouled. A pile of filthy clothes covered his feet. The bed's wooden posts were splintered, cracked; the whole frame threatened to give way at any moment.

Leering at Timon from this haven was the oozing face of a

bloated corpse. His skin was yellow, pocked; blistering. His eyes were rimmed crimson, no white to be seen. Fewer than ten strands of gray hair twisted around his otherwise bald, liver-spotted skull. Parched lips curled back over gray teeth; his tongue was nearly black.

Every breath was a labor of Hercules; the little light from one candle stung his eyes. Yet he had the strength to sit up and examine Timon's features, his eyes taking Timon in with lewd abandon.

"You have come into possession of a document that does not belong to you," Timon said, advancing a step or two. "What is worse, you have written a pamphlet about it."

"I have written a thousand pamphlets," Padget wheezed.

"Not like this one. You acquired a document which was illegal to possess, and then quoted it. The document begins, 'I am the whore and the holy one—'"

"No!" Padget exploded. "It begins, 'I am the first and the last; I am the honored one and the scorned one'; then, 'I am the whore and the holy one—'"

"From whom did you acquire this document?" Timon insisted, ignoring Padget's pedagogy.

"This is actually quite a blessing." Padget coughed. "Come over here." He began to struggle with the sheets, trying to peel them back.

Timon did not move.

"Come on," Padget encouraged with a dead hand, "I want to piss on you, and I can't do it if you stand that far away. You are, in my opinion, a gutterful of spittle."

Timon smiled.

"No?" Padget rasped. "Well, then bugger a bunghole and get out. You can see how badly I need the money. Look there, at that chamber pot." His eyes shot downward.

Timon had already seen enough of Padget's chamber pots.

"What is in those pots is more useful to humanity than anything your Pope has to say on any subject," Padget said sweetly, as if he were talking to his grandchild.

A fit of coughing suddenly racked Padget's body. Rust-colored phlegm flew from his mouth. The lead tankard fell from his fist, rolled off the bed, and clattered on the floor between two chamber pots.

"Take a good look at me, whoever you are. Light no more candles, I want to save them. But take a gander at what I am. This is what you have in store for you. I am your future, poxed and unable to piss; parched and poor. My wife left me, my whore ran off with my money, and my children recoil at the sight of me. Such is the inheritance of all men."

The effort of so much bile had spent him. Padget closed his eyes and began to snore almost instantly. Drool like an egg yolk escaped the corner of his mouth.

Timon stood a moment, trying to think what to do next. His assignment was clear, but this man would never say where or how he acquired the secret text. Best to move on to the rest of the task.

Timon picked up the taper and searched the room until he found a rotted leather pouch. In the pouch, as expected, he found a sheaf of papers, among them the document for which Timon had been dispatched.

All that remained was to burn the document and kill its current owner.

He stood in the hellish room for long, silent moments, reading the document enough times to memorize it. It was short enough that it did not require his wheel. It was also beautiful enough that it required no effort. It seemed to be a revelation from Mary Magdalene, but Timon pushed that idea to the farthest recesses of his mind.

When he was done, Padget's snoring had reached a thunderous level. Timon took three long steps to the bedside, produced a dagger, and sliced Padget's throat from ear to ear. Padget made no sound whatsoever and was dead instantly. Thick brown blood erupted from the wound like pulp from a rotted pomegranate. It was the first of a hundred such wounds that Timon would inflict.

Timon tossed the offending document onto Padget's chest and lit it with the candle. Then he touched the flame to Padget's hair, his bedshirt, the stinking sheets. Fire was slow to catch, but it grew, and flesh began to boil.

Timon put the taper in Padget's liver-spotted hand and was down the stairs in the next instant.

Out in the street, he strode toward the river before taking his first deep breath in a quarter of an hour. Needles of cold air stung his throat, and they were glorious.

He had the odd sensation that he had just played his own death scene in a play no one was watching. Had Padget correctly foretold the future? Would the man called Brother Timon end up dying in such horror?

Over and over a circle of questions ran about his head like buzzing flies. Why kill a man who would have been dead within the week? Why burn the document? What in that document so threatened the Pope that he would send Timon to London to murder a man and burn a holy revelation?

But the questions soon dissolved into the satisfaction derived from a job well done.

My first murder, Timon thought as he emerged from the back street onto a main thoroughfare. It wasn't as difficult as I had imagined. It seems easy enough to kill when you know you are doing God's work.

30

*A*ll the visions were gone by morning. Night-mares retreated to their hidden places. A single lark announced the rising of the sun.

Timon was awakened by a commanding series of thumps upon the door of his cell.

"Please go away," Timon managed weakly. "I am asleep."

"Brother Timon, this is Dr. Spaulding," the angry voice responded. "You must come to the door immediately."

"I am at morning prayers," Timon mumbled, turning over.

"I believe that I have now deduced the *true* identity of the murderer," Spaulding insisted coldly.

Timon licked his lips and opened his eyes, blinking them like bat's wings.

"Have we already played this scene?" Timon asked, trying to sit up. "Did you come to my door yesterday morning with the same . . ." But he trailed off, suddenly afraid that he might actually have imagined the similarities between the two mornings, or confused reality with his dreams.

"Will you come to the door?" Spaulding snarled.

"The door is not locked," Timon sighed. "If your brain burns to confer with me, come in."

Immediately the door swung open. Light from Spaulding's taper charged into the room. Illumination from the high windows of the hallway admitted a greater gold. It was, indeed, morning.

Timon sat up. He dipped his hands into the water basin beside his chamber pot and splashed the water onto his face, which only made his thirst more desperate.

Spaulding strode into the room like an army of men. Even in his desiccated state, Timon could see that hundreds of thoughts were battering about in Spaulding's head. The weasel eyes squinted and he seemed to be pointing his nose at Timon's face. His perfect, unwrinkled robe and skullcap only added to Timon's suspicion that he was, in fact, death incarnate.

"Stand!" Spaulding demanded.

Timon remained seated, calculating how much effort it would take to kill Spaulding at that moment, dismember his body, and hide the pieces inconspicuously around Cambridge.

"Too much trouble before breakfast," Timon mumbled, rubbing his eyes.

"Eh?" Spaulding snapped.

"You have been saved by a boiled egg and a bit of ale," Timon yawned.

He stood, at last, towering over the Spaulding, whose stooped height was no match for Timon's six-foot frame.

"What are you saying?" Spaulding demanded.

"Let us confer upon the matter of your latest theory," Timon explained, headed for the door, "over breakfast."

"I think not. We are expected in Deacon Marbury's office immediately."

"If I do not have an egg and an ale first," Timon allowed, nearly out the door, "I shall be distracted, and there is no telling what I might say or do."

Spaulding hesitated, watching Timon leave. "Quickly, then," he said, a bit less vigorously, following after. "The deacon is waiting."

"Why not invite him to join us for breakfast?" Timon called over his shoulder as he moved lazily down the hallway into the honeyed sunlight.

THE KITCHEN IN THE DEACONAGE was scarcely more than twelve feet square. It had been built well away from the main living quarters of the house. This was so that cooking smells and noises would not disturb the rest of the household. All black and gray stone, it had one window through which the morning sun bisected the darkness of the room; cut it exactly in half. There was space for a fireplace, a stove, a large table for food preparation, a cabinet that served as a larder, and a small table with four chairs. There, at mealtimes, servants might gather to eat off wooden platters.

The preparation table was laden with food, medicines; sweet-smelling potpourris. The fireplace was large and wide, almost the entirety of the outside wall. Candle burns on the timbers of the window evidenced a thousand early-morning preparations.

The stove, to one side of the fireplace, had been used earlier that morning to cook sausages and oatcakes. It was still warm, and the smells lingered.

Timon breathed in the rich air of the room, glad to be alone to collect his thoughts. Spaulding had gone to fetch Marbury.

After a moment's investigation, Timon gathered hot embers from the hearth and placed them in a firebasket on top of the stove. As luck would have it, a dozen or more eggs lay in a bowl on the preparation table. He found a saucepan underneath the arch below the stove.

The kitchen was well stocked with a large collection of earthenware cooking and storage pots. Huge decorative platters, obviously used to present food at the deacon's table, took up space on the preparation table. An array of mugs and three-handled tygs lay on the floor, more basic in design than those used in the dining room. In one of the mugs Timon found ale. He poured some of it into a saucepan, in the absence of good water, and set the pan on a trivet over the firebasket. Ever so carefully he slid his egg into the dark brown liquid.

He also found several oatcakes drying in a rack above the fireplace. He grabbed one as if it might save his life.

Spaulding stormed in. "I have sent for Deacon Marbury," he told Timon in pinched syllables.

Timon answered by waving his oatcake in Spaulding's direction. "This is the perfect companion for my egg." Timon swallowed the cake whole.

"You are cooking your egg in ale," Spaulding said crisply.

"Yes. And I am drinking the rest." Timon hoisted the mug with the remainder of the ale and drank heartily for a full minute.

"There," Timon gasped. "Now—we wait."

For Spaulding the wait was interminable, and he paced the short breadth of the kitchen nearly one hundred times before Marbury appeared in the doorway.

Timon suffered for what seemed like hours waiting for a five-minute egg, though a bit more brown ale had worked to ease the agony.

Marbury alone was cheerful when he burst into the room. "I slept like an infant." He beamed. His eyes were clear; his face was washed. He was wearing his comfortable clothing: gray tunic and pants, old leather boots, and a blue, quilted coat.

"You needed it," Timon acknowledged as obligingly as he could manage. "I hope you were not troubled by dreaming."

"I dreamt that long stacks of paper were flying out of my mouth whenever I tried to speak," Marbury answered, a bit amazed at his own imagery. "Whatever could it mean?"

"That dream owes itself to your humiliating experience outside another kitchen yesterday morning, no doubt," Timon suggested.

"Of course, that must be it." Marbury clapped his hands. "Speaking of which, I am famished. Good idea, this meeting in my kitchen. What is that cooking on the stove?"

"I am boiling an egg," Timon answered.

"Excellent," Marbury roared. "I shall have six. And an ale."

Marbury moved toward the larder perhaps three or four steps before Spaulding exploded, "We are not here to discuss your dreams or to cook your breakfast! We are here to confine a murderer!"

"*Confine,* did you say?" Marbury stopped in his tracks.

"This monk," Spaulding responded, pointing a bony finger at Timon. "He is the assassin. We must, together, confine him to this kitchen until we can alert the local constabulary."

"Timon is the murderer?" Marbury asked, barely containing himself.

"I have concluded that a man of his ilk could not possibly know all the things he knows with only a church education. He is not of the proper class to be able to accomplish such thoughts, nor to deduce anything about our present troubles. Let him deny it. I see clearly now that the only reason he knew Dr. Chaderton was not the murderer was that *he* was, in fact, the murderer himself! I have assumed command of our group since Lively's death, and I demand that you call the constables!"

"Stunning logic." Timon yawned, getting up. "I think my egg is ready. Shall I drop in half a dozen for you, Deacon?"

"Please," Marbury answered.

"No, but do you not see—," Spaulding sputtered.

"My dear Doctor," Marbury said calmly, "perhaps I should remind you that the first murder—that of dear Harrison, may he rest in peace—was committed before Timon arrived. And, Brother Timon?"

"Yes, Deacon Marbury?" Timon scooped his egg from the boiling water.

"Who are you? What are you doing in my house?"

"I am called Brother Timon, as I was happy to tell you yesterday when you asked me the same question," Timon responded brightly.

"History runs in circles," Marbury said, equaling Timon's cheer. "Go on."

"I seem to be repeating myself quite a bit this morning—but to completely answer your question, I was hired to find the man who murdered Harrison. And now I must work harder, as the killer seems bent on destroying all the King's translators here in Cambridge."

"Yes." Marbury turned to look Spaulding in the eye. "And he seems particularly bent toward killing anyone in charge, does he not?"

"That he does." Timon caught his boiled egg with a wooden spoon and laid it gently on the table beside the stove. Then, daintily, he selected six more eggs from a basket on the same table; dropped them slowly in the rolling boil of the pot.

The silence gave Spaulding a moment to consider his next question.

"How did you come to hire this Timon, Deacon Marbury?" Spaulding folded his hands in front of his chest. "Where did you find him? Did you know him?"

"I do not know this man," Marbury said slowly. "I found him through the auspices of other men I met while doing the King's work. More than that I cannot say, by royal decree."

"But you must surely admit the possibility," Spaulding continued, a bit less steadily, "that a man of his sort might have murdered Harrison and then put himself in a position to be assigned the task of finding the killer. It would be the perfect post from which to carry on his mayhem."

Timon picked up his egg, burning his fingers, and began to blow on the shell. "You must decide, Dr. Spaulding, if I am not clever enough or too clever. What you suggest would require a significant degree of planning and intelligence."

"Yes." Marbury's face had changed.

Timon began to peel his egg, placing the bits of shell neatly on the table, watching Marbury, wondering what he was thinking.

He is remembering my blade as it cut into his skin, Timon guessed. He is thinking how easily I discussed cutting a heart in half while it was still beating in a living body. He believes that I could, in fact, be murdering the translators. Perhaps he is even wondering how I knew Pietro Delasander.

Timon watched as those thoughts played across Marbury's face. It was not difficult to read. Timon's mask was better armor. He had long ago trained himself to reveal nothing. But he was surprised to find that he wanted to tell Marbury his true mission. He had not been sent to kill anyone. He was merely to memorize the King James translation by the time of the early wheat harvest. He could also, in fact, solve the murders and was willing to do so. How much of *that* could he tell Marbury?

"Dr. Spaulding," Timon said after a moment, "you may certainly fetch whatever local men you feel might confine me. It certainly would not be you and Deacon Marbury. But when I am gone, the murders will continue, you will be the next victim, and I will be deprived of the satisfaction of pointing out your error—at least to everyone else. You, of course, will be dead."

Spaulding shivered at the sound of ice in Timon's voice.

"By all means, Dr. Spaulding, seek out the town guard," Marbury added, eyes on Timon. "I will wait with Brother Timon. Despite his opinion, I may be able to hold him here until you get back."

"I—," Spaulding began.

"Go!" Marbury snapped.

Spaulding jumped. He turned to see Timon staring at him and biting heartily into the egg. Spaulding took two steps backward, felt for the door, and flew from the kitchen. Timon listened for a moment to the sound of Spaulding's running.

"Will he bring back the guard," Timon asked, mouth full, "or not?"

"Difficult to say." Marbury grinned. "How are my eggs coming along?"

Timon finished his egg and was seized by a sudden, inexplicable desire to tell the truth.

"I was a prisoner of the Inquisition five years ago," Timon blurted, startling himself as much as Marbury. "I was released on the condition that I perform certain tasks. One of those tasks was to train men in the art of murder; one of those men was called Pietro Delasander, the man who tried to kill you on the road home from London."

Marbury stared.

Timon could see that the deacon had been utterly disarmed by his obvious candor.

Marbury began to speak several times and stopped, clearly considering and then discarding questions.

"I have caught you off guard," Timon said softly. "Under other circumstances, I would have done this as a ploy, to gain some advantage. In this particular instance, I cannot say why I am being honest with you. It is unlike me. I had a difficult night and was troubled by dreams, of a sort. Still."

He waited upon Marbury's response.

Marbury seemed at last to settle on one, possibly at random, doing his best not to sound as astonished as he was.

"How did you acquire such ability at this *art,* as you call it, that you could instruct other men?"

"I have not always been a monk," Timon said quietly.

"No." Marbury found the sound of Timon's voice heartbreaking. "I suppose not."

"I have told you too much, but I have done so in a spirit of honesty." Timon glared at Marbury with such intensity that his face ached. "I want you to believe me: I am not the man who is murdering these translators."

"Who is the killer?"

"That," Timon assured the deacon, "I shall discover."

"But it is not your only duty here in Cambridge." Marbury sat back in his chair.

Timon finished his ale and said nothing.

"I wonder if you would tell me something else."

"I wonder," Timon answered.

"There are three dead bodies very near this little kitchen," Marbury said softly, all his previous mirth washed away. "Lively is waiting, Thom is taken care of, but what, I wonder, have we done with the body of Pietro Delasander?"

31

*T*hree minutes later, with a pocketful of hard-boiled eggs, Marbury was moving as quickly as he could to keep up with Timon. They raced toward the stables.

"After you left me with the assassin Delasander's body," Timon said over his shoulder, irritated at Marbury's slower pace, "I examined it most thoroughly. Then I moved it back to the stall."

"You found nothing, of course," Marbury said, breathing hard, "or you would have told me in the cellar, over Lively's body."

Timon heard the tone of Marbury's voice: sounds that defined Marbury's suspicion. Marbury was certain that Timon had in fact found something he was not revealing.

The two men arrived at the courtyard of the stables. The smell of hay, the distraction of wrens hopping about the cobblestones, the warmth of the sun—all combined to offer Timon another vision, a ghost of his own boyhood.

"Have I told you that I was a stableboy when I was nine or ten?" Timon's voice had grown with a warmth to match that of the sunlit air. "Or that I fell into—into another line of work when I became a driver for a certain man? I was a boy not unlike the one whom took you to London."

Marbury had pulled an egg from his pocket, but it was frozen in his hand. Timon's voice was so filled with the longing for days gone by that Marbury was momentarily unable to move.

"Ah." Timon rubbed his face with the palms of his hands. "What would make me think of that boy? Delasander's body is this way."

Timon moved more slowly into the stall where the royal coach was kept. The coach had been cleaned and the harnesses were gone. A pile of horse blankets was at the back of the stall. Timon knelt and flung them aside, revealing the dead body in its plain red robe. Two black beetles, interrupted in their own examination of the dead man's face, skittered away into the straw on the floor and waited.

Marbury looked away. "Why did he take his own life? Did he think I would kill him?"

"This man?" Timon shook his head. "You could not have killed him."

"Then why . . . ?"

"He killed himself so that he would not have to endure, in a wounded state, an encounter with me."

"You?" Marbury swallowed.

"He knew I was working with you. He knew who you were."

"How could he possibly—wait. Was that the nature of the secret missive you say you discovered on his person?"

"You observe that this man is dressed in red," Timon sighed, as if he had not heard Marbury's question.

"What?" Marbury asked, confused by Timon's apparent change of subject. "They are his priestly robes, are they not?"

"Not exactly." Timon assumed a tutor's tones. "The average red kite has a breast that looks covered in blood. Its pale gray wings are knife blades that slice through the air. They are carrion birds. This man, this dead man, loved those birds. He thought of them as his colleagues, his collaborators. That is why he wore red."

"Who was he?" Marbury asked softly, standing over the body, egg still in hand. "Will you tell me more about the man?"

A wren just outside in the sunlight found a worm, swallowed it, sang out, and darted away into the air.

"What if I told you," Timon began slowly, "that this man was Queen Elizabeth's chief physician."

Marbury dropped his egg. "Lopez?"

"Dr. Rodrigo Lopez saved the life of the Queen on numerous occasions and then was convicted of trying to poison her. Lopez was hanged, drawn, and quartered in the streets—to the delight of a cheering throng who continually chanted, 'Jew, Jew, Jew.' "

"Dr. Lopez *was* a Jew," Marbury insisted. "Though no one believed him guilty of the crime for which he died."

"But I am asking you to consider a hypothetical question." Timon sighed. "What if he did not die that day? What if he died yesterday on the road from London?"

"No. This is not Lopez." Marbury collected his wits. "Thousands saw Lopez die."

Timon looked up at Marbury. "You must believe me when I say that it is possible to substitute one man for another in such executions. The head of the man whom everyone thought was Dr. Lopez was covered with a black sack. He was dressed in the favorite color of Dr. Lopez: bloodred."

"But who would save his life in such a manner?" Marbury found he had to lean against the royal carriage for balance. "And why?"

"Many powerful men," Timon answered steadily, "find it useful to recruit from among the dead."

"I do not believe that this man was Dr. Lopez!" Marbury snapped. "And even if I did, I do not believe that he would be an agent of the English Crown. Lopez was a Jew and a man accused—however wrongly—of an attempt on a royal personage. An English sovereign would not recruit such a man. Such a man, likewise, would neither trust nor serve an English sovereign. And who else but a king could be powerful enough to take a man out of a death cell—"

Marbury stood bolt upright. He was afraid to look at Timon. Timon too looked away.

"What is it, Deacon Marbury?" Timon drew the horse blankets over the face of the dead assassin.

"The Pope." Marbury's lips barely moved. "Are you trying to tell me that this creature was an agent of Pope Clement?"

What am I doing? Timon thought to himself, sitting down on the hay. Am I *trying* to lead him to know what I truly am? Why would I do such a thing?

32

Shortly after midnight that night, Timon found himself walking past a certain butcher shop in Cambridge. A hastily written sign told everyone that it was closed until further notice. A funeral wreath was on the door. In sympathy, it seemed, the nighttime sky above the shop was black. No moon, no star, not a single light in heaven shone down upon that street.

The day had passed in a blur for Timon. Marbury, he supposed, had spent the morning wondering how to tell Lively's eleven children that they were orphans. Timon had spent the same hours wondering why he felt more affinity for Deacon Marbury than his student Pietro. In the end, Timon buried Pietro Delasander in a shallow grave and did his best to forget him.

By nine o'clock that night Timon had gone to his bed hoping for sleep, but found instead a note on his blanket.

"We await, praying."

It might have appeared, to anyone else, a message from one of the translators, or even Marbury. The meaning was obscure, but the note seemed innocuous. Timon knew better. He recognized the handwriting. When the hands of a clock are pressed together at midnight, they appear to be praying. Timon knew that three men would be waiting for him after that hour at a prearranged meeting place: a public house on the most disreputable street in Cambridge.

Little minds think words like these are clever, Timon had thought as he'd stared at the note.

He knew he should have rested or prayed for the few hours before he was to meet with these men, but instead he had taken out his pipe and breathed in a bit, just a bit, of the devil's foul breath.

The visions were gone by the time he walked past the stinking butcher shop. Timon was left with a burning tongue and a frightening mood, an air of reckless abandon. Every possible circumstance was equal in Timon's fiery brain. A pint of ale down his throat or that same throat sliced open, it just didn't matter. Whatever awaited him at the public house, his meeting with the demon trinity, was of little consequence to him in such a mood.

When he arrived at the tavern, he shoved open the door and cast a careless eye about the room. No one looked his way.

He hid his angular grace, walking a bit stooped to appear shorter until he sat at the wooden bar. He leaned on it and caught the eye of a young woman in a gingerbread dress. She was, he knew from previous visits, the daughter of the owner. Jenny was her name, and she was barely sixteen, the object of many a furtive glance in the room.

"Ale, please," Timon said in a hoarse voice that barely rose above the din. He thought, I am certainly not going to face those men back there with a dry mouth.

"Please?" The young woman's eyes met his. "A gentle soul in a wooden city. Ale it shall be. I've seen you before, Father. Not many dresses in black around here."

Without another word, she turned, scooped up several tankards from the bar, and slid away. He watched her go, aiming toward the kitchen. Her body moved like a skater's over frozen water. He thought it possible that her feet never touched the floor. Her skin was alabaster with a blush of pink. Her hair was plaited gold silk.

She vanished into the kitchen and returned almost instantly with a tankard. Timon handed her twice the amount that was due.

"You gave me too much," Jenny stammered.

"Little enough for such service." Timon had no idea why he had given her the money.

"I mean to say," she went on uncomfortably, as if she'd done something wrong, "it's the biggest bonus I ever got in this place. In my whole life."

"That's hard to believe," Timon told her, smiling, "a girl with your charms."

Her shoulders relaxed. That was the sort of comment she understood.

"Go on." Her eyes flared bright. "You a priest, flirting to a young girl like that."

"Not flirting," Timon said plainly. I am deliberately delaying my meeting with the men in the back room, he thought.

Jenny's eyes welled with a certain softness that had not been there before. "I'm not meant for a life in this place," she said, a slow yearning taking hold of her voice. She leaned forward, her face only inches from Timon's. She rested her elbows on the bar and her head in her hands, staring out across the foul smoke, the grimy faces, the filthy floor. "I was to be married, you see. But that's off now."

"I am very sorry to hear that. The man was a fool who left you."

"Oh," she sighed. "He didn't leave, not like you mean it. He's dead. Killed by his own dog whilst he was working late—only a few nights ago."

Timon's hand stayed on his cup of ale. He stared down into the brown foam at the bottom and let go a long breath.

"He was a butcher," Jenny went on. "Made a good living. I would have been mistress of his shop."

"Yes," Timon managed to say softly.

"Funny thing about that dog," she mumbled. "He was so friendly. But there's life: everything turns on you in the end. Something bright as the morning star can burn your face by noon and leave you cold by the end of the day."

"I am heartily sorry, Jen," Timon said softly.

Jenny seemed to rouse herself from her mood. "Tosh. Don't waste your sympathy on me. I didn't love him—nothing like that. It was just a way out of this room. You know."

"Still," Timon mumbled.

"More ale?"

"No, alas." Timon cast his eyes toward the squat door at the back corner of the room.

"Well," she said, smiling, "don't be a stranger."

Before Timon could respond, she vanished into the throng. Try as he might, he could not even see a bit of her gingerbread dress.

33

*T*imon drained his cup of ale at one swallow. He stood and aimed for the dreaded door. In ten steps he grabbed the cold iron handle. He held his breath, felt for his knife, and threw open the door.

All three men jumped. The two wearing masks, the ones with the penchant for code names and secret messages, recovered quickly. Cardinal Venitelli, however, continued to shake while Timon eased the door closed behind him.

"So," Timon said before anyone else could speak, "what are we calling ourselves tonight?"

"Please be seated, Brother Timon," Samuel said crisply. "You will remember Brother Isaiah, to my left, and at the far end Brother Daniel is—"

"Good evening, Cardinal," Timon said, staring into Venitelli's eyes.

Venitelli looked down at the table in front of him.

"I prefer to stand," Timon said softly. "I may have to pace."

Isaiah looked as if he might protest, but before he could voice his objection, Samuel forged ahead.

"Very well," Samuel growled irritably, "but this is of the utmost importance. Please try to concentrate."

Timon's right hand shot forward until his fingers were less than an inch away from Samuel's eyes.

"You have no idea what powers of concentration I can muster," Timon whispered. "These fingers, for example, can move with the speed and precision needed to pluck out a human eye. I can do it so suddenly as to show it to my victim before he faints away."

Venitelli feared he might faint at the mere suggestion. Samuel, to his credit, Timon thought, barely flinched.

"I am well aware of your gruesome magic tricks, Brother Timon. Those abilities are, in fact, the primary reason for this meeting."

Timon's hand disappeared into the sleeve of his robe. "Yes, why have you called me here?"

"You are to give us anything you have memorized," Samuel answered quickly. "Write it down, what you have committed to your brain, and we will take it to His Holiness."

"Write it down? When?"

"Now. Tonight. Before you go."

Timon glanced at Samuel, who was studying his own fingernails. "Why?"

"We would know of your progress," Isaiah snapped.

Timon smiled. "Surely you mean that *Holy Father* would know of my progress."

"There is another issue!" Samuel interrupted, nearly rising from his seat. "Without knowing it, you are threatening other plans we have set in motion."

"Go on," Timon said steadily.

Samuel cocked his head in Timon's direction, like a dog. Cardinal Venitelli, it seemed, had stopped breathing. Timon's reaction had not been what they had expected.

Timon realized that he had been stooping since he had entered the public house. He straightened his posture slowly. Bones shifted; joints cracked. The men at the table watched as if it were a play—a play about a man who could grow five inches taller before their very eyes. Timon took in all three sets of eyes slowly. A satisfying snapping sound at his neck punctuated the final motion as his gaze returned to Samuel.

"Go on," Timon repeated, a slight smile at his lips.

"You—you endanger the other half of our plan," Samuel managed, the bite gone from his words. "We had no way of knowing—"

"Why His Holiness did not leave the entire matter to you is a mystery to us," Isaiah snarled.

"No, but you see," Venitelli broke in, laying a flat hand upon the table in front of him, "Brother Timon's full powers of memory are required for his task. Holy Father did not wish to have him distracted—"

"And yet he now threatens the entire—," Isaiah began.

"Stop," Timon said calmly, still smiling. "You must tell me what the problem is."

Samuel swallowed. "You are interfering with the elimination of the translators."

Timon folded his hands behind his back patiently. The bulk of his dagger tugged at his forearm. "Yes."

"You must stop it." Isaiah absently picked at the cuticle of his thumbnail.

Timon exhaled, suddenly understanding. "The man killing the translators is also an agent of Pope Clement."

"He is emphatically *not*," Venitelli insisted immediately. "Never would His Holiness command such a thing."

"Exactly," Samuel joined in. "But we do not wish to interfere with this man or his divinely inspired work."

" 'Divinely inspired work,' " Timon repeated.

"Surely God's plan is to eliminate these so-called men of knowledge," Isaiah sang out, "before they can further desecrate His divine word. This man—whoever he is—acts on God's behalf."

"By killing the scholars," Timon said, as if he were seeking confirmation.

"Exactly," Samuel said.

"But surely you see the irony of the matter," Timon continued, his smile growing. "I was brought to Cambridge for the express purpose of discovering and stopping those murders."

"Incorrect!" Samuel responded, drumming his fingers on the table, barely controlling his ire. "You were brought here to memorize what the translators were producing. You were brought here to be a human library, a repository of all the vile book that these Englishmen would compose."

"But you told Deacon Marbury that I could save them from the killer." Timon began rocking, every so slightly, back and forth on the balls of his feet.

"What does that matter?" Isaiah demanded.

"What does that matter?" Timon spoke the words to himself as if they had been uttered by an idiot. "If I do not at least appear to be making some progress in that cause, Marbury will quickly dismiss me. If your man succeeds in killing all the translators soon, there will be nothing for me to memorize. And there are two other groups of translators. There are other men to keep the King's work alive. I feel certain that Marbury would have heard the news if anything had befallen any of them. No such news has been reported to me. And these are only the first concerns that come to mind. If I take a moment, I am certain I could discover several hundred other holes in the fabric of your *plan*. Venitelli, you, at least, must realize the insanity of this thinking."

"Brother *Daniel* is only here in an advisory capacity," Samuel snarled. "His opinions have no bearing upon our efforts."

"What would you have me do?" Timon asked, his voice aflame. "How, exactly, would you have me proceed?"

"That is precisely why we brought you here tonight," Isaiah sniffed. "To give you additional instructions."

"Stop trying to capture or kill the man who is murdering the Cambridge scholars," Samuel began, as if he were reciting from a legal document. "Continue to memorize everything these men have written, and when you have done that, aid the killer in his work."

"What?" Timon's shoulders sank. It was a barely perceptible motion. Only Venitelli noticed.

"Finish them off," Isaiah went on. "However many are left when your memory work is done, eliminate them as quickly as you can."

"Tonight, however," Samuel broke in, reaching underneath the table, "you must write down what you have memorized thus far."

Samuel produced a bundle of blank pages, an inkwell, and a quill.

"You may sit there." Isaiah pointed to the chair in front of the table, the one in which they had expected Timon to sit from the beginning.

Timon glared at the pale paper. "It may take some time to write down everything." He did not move.

"We shall watch." Samuel sat back, offering a gargoyle's grin. "And, praise God, *here* you will not be distracted by crawling spiders or the knotted lash. As you were on similar occasions in our mutual past."

Timon instantly locked out the memory of the spiders before its power could have any effect. The lash wounds, which he still carried, were unimportant. Samuel's attempt at intimidation had completely failed.

Timon felt the handle of his knife against his bare skin. His eyes moved across the faces of the men seated next to one another at the table. One move, sudden enough, could cut all three throats.

"To clarify my task this night," Timon said lightly, "you wish me to write down everything I have read that the scholars have translated thus far?"

"Yes," Samuel sighed, utterly devoid of patience.

Then I may eliminate from my writing tonight anything that the scholars have not yet translated, Timon thought to himself. I shall therefore keep knowledge of the secret Gospels to myself. I need not report what Lively showed me from the ancient text.

Timon then weighed his two choices carefully: kill these men and leave London or sit down and write out his assignment.

If I kill these men now, he thought, the girl, Jenny, will have to clean up the mess. She has had a difficult week.

Timon put his hand on the empty chair beside him.

"Make yourselves at ease, gentlemen," he said, moving the chair toward the table. "This will take the rest of the night."

34

*M*orning came as a tap at the door. No one entered, but a man's voice from the other side whispered, "It's well past sunrise. Will you gentlemen be wanting the room for the day as well?"

Timon did not appear to hear. Samuel groaned and scratched his cheek. Venitelli and Isaiah were asleep.

At first there had been a fascination at the sight of Timon's turning the strange wheel with his fingers. They watched if he were playing a musical instrument. He wrote for hours, mumbling to himself, without the slightest pause.

But as the night had worn on, Venitelli had given up. He had long since retired to a corner of the room, curled up like a small child, and fallen asleep. Isaiah had followed him into the sea of dreams, laying his head on the table; snoring like a wild boar.

Samuel was roused by the man at the door and called out, "Yes, we will be wanting the room a bit longer."

"Then . . . ," the hesitant voice on the other side of the door began.

Samuel yawned; managed to stand. He shuffled toward the door and opened it a crack. He held out a hand filled with coins.

The man at the door took them all. "Breakfast?"

"Yes," Samuel mumbled.

"For three?"

"Four."

The man stood at the door for a moment in silence. "Four?" he repeated at last.

Samuel took a moment to rub his eyes before he realized that the man was waiting for more money. He reached into his pouch and produced enough coinage to feed ten.

The man took it all and vanished.

"Seven hours, Brother Timon," Samuel said, clearing the gravel in his throat, "or eight. How do you do it?"

"Perhaps the Inquisition was correct to think that I was in league with the devil," Timon answered without looking up.

Before Samuel could respond, Venitelli sat up. "Breakfast?"

Isaiah awoke with a start, threw himself backward in his chair, and produced a small, thin blade, the kind generally used for gutting fish.

"Brother!" Samuel snapped.

Isaiah looked around the room, unable, for an instant, to remember where he was. When he did, he glared at his hand and seemed to wonder where the knife had come from.

"Thus begins a morning for my Unholy Trinity." Timon's lips betrayed the ghost of a smile. "Hunger, fear, and greed."

"What?" Venitelli struggled to his feet.

"I say, 'Good morrow, gentlemen,'" Timon sighed, sitting back and pushing the thick stack of papers away from him on the table. "There you have it: the ancient ceremonial gesture of completion. I push these pages away from myself because I have done with them."

His memory wheel had disappeared.

"You—you are finished?" Isaiah stammered.

"You may put away your knife, Brother," Timon said, his smile becoming more substantial. "I believe we will be having oatcakes and eggs for breakfast. Neither requires cutting."

Isaiah spent another foolish moment staring at his knife before he put it away. Venitelli came to the table, staring at the large stack of pages.

"So much work already done in Cambridge," Venitelli whispered.

Timon licked his lips. "I shall be very happy to have breakfast. And a bit of ale. It is thirsty work, my labor."

"That you can concentrate for so long," Venitelli began, still not himself, not quite awake, "it staggers the imagination."

"That you can sit at a table and write *anything* for so long," Isaiah grumbled.

"I tell you, Brothers," Timon said happily, "I was not in this room for most of the night. I was in another country, a land whose map is made of words, whose boundaries are punctuation marks. I had no body in that other place, no weight. I had no sensation at all save the keen, constant shower of sentences, like a spring rain washing me over. I drank the sweet liquor of the mind and was refreshed, intoxicated but invigorated. I was, in short, a resident of my true home."

"I do not understand your meaning." Venitelli again searched the room for answers. "You left the room while I was asleep?"

A solid rap upon the door prevented further conversation.

"Ah!" Timon stood. "A speedy landlord. What a rare creation."

"I paid enough money for it," Samuel groused, pulling open the door.

The landlord, along with a rounder, older version Jenny, burst into the room. Each bore two trays and busily set about transforming the writing table into a dining table. Venitelli barely had time to grab the manuscript of Timon's work before it was used as a mat for tankards of ale.

Timon stared at the woman. There was Jenny's fate before his eyes.

"We'll be back in a nonce," the landlord said briskly, "with manchet bread and some very nice apricots."

"Apricots and manchet?" Timon said to Samuel. "You did pay well."

"Always happy to have fine men of the clergy," the landlord said with a slight, unconscious bow.

Timon stood, seized by a sudden compulsion. "A moment, landlord. I understand that your young daughter Jenny has recently lost her husband-to-be."

"Well, news does travel," the landlord sighed philosophically. "I expect everyone's heard the story by now. Fancy his own dog going for him like that. Some say it's the devil's work. They found another body close by—looked like it was hit by a cannon shot. Nothing left but bones and guts. And not a cannon in sight. Not to mention the matter of the missing wheelbarrow and the baker's assistant—"

"Yes," Timon interrupted, staring at Samuel. "As a token of Christian compassion, under the circumstances, Brother Samuel, here, would like to contribute to her welfare. What is the price of your finest room?"

"Depends on how long it's occupied," the landlord said slowly, not quite grasping what was happening.

"Shall we say two months?" Timon asked lightly. "That is often a customary period of grieving these days."

"Two months?" the landlord exploded. "That's ten shillings!"

"It is the least we can do for the poor girl," Timon said briskly, holding out his hand to Samuel.

Samuel stood frozen, wide-eyed in disbelief.

"Their daughter Jenny," Timon explained to Samuel, "was about to marry a butcher whose shop is not far from here, when he met with an unfortunate accident. He was killed by his own dog. Only a few nights ago. People are saying it may even have been the work of some dark demon—or an avenging angel."

Venitelli sucked in a breath. The Pope's avenging angel, he thought, clutching the crucifix around his neck. Samuel's eyes betrayed a dawning understanding of Timon's choice of words.

"Pray God that same angel does not take after us," Timon concluded, his eyes boring into Samuel's.

"Ten shillings, was it?" Samuel said immediately, plunging his hand into his pouch.

"God in heaven," the landlord whispered.

"There," Timon sighed. "That's better."

The wife crossed herself.

The landlord grabbed the money and backed out of the room as if he had been drawn away by a typhoon.

35

*S*ilence pervaded the room.

Timon broke it by sitting back down. He dragged a tankard of ale across the table toward him. He drained it at once.

"Now," he said, dabbing the corners of his mouth with his index finger, "let us discuss the rest of our business."

Venitelli clutched the manuscript to his chest as if it might shield him from further realizations. The phrase *avenging angel* burned his mind. Isaiah reached for a hard-boiled egg.

Samuel remained standing. "The butcher," Samuel began at last, "is another man you have killed?"

"Do not proceed with your inquiry in that matter," Timon advised. "I will not discuss the incident except to say that it occurred in conjunction with the disappearance of an old servant, Jacob by name, who once worked for the Sidney family. Looking back, I wish that events had unfolded differently, and second thoughts conjure old ghosts in this case. We can, however, discuss my other duties if you like."

Samuel seemed to waver in his opinion, but he sat down finally and grabbed an oatcake.

"As to your other duties," Isaiah growled slowly, "I think they were made quite clear last night. You must stop trying to capture the killer of the translators."

"No," Timon disagreed, "your instruction went further. You said that you wished me to aid him."

"Yes," Isaiah interjected quickly, bits of yellow egg yolk dotting his chin. "Once you have copied the translators' work, you must eliminate however many that remain."

Timon grabbed another ale. "And then? You will send me to the Oxford group, or to Lancelot Andrews's amalgam in London?"

"Possibly." Samuel did not look at Timon.

"You will keep me working," Timon continued, half to himself, "constantly exposing me to greater risk of capture myself, until I have done my work. Or until I have, myself, been eliminated."

"Hardly that," Venitelli began quickly. "His Holiness has the greatest regard—"

"I am already dead," Timon said simply. "My life belongs to Pope Clement. He can do with it what he will."

"Brother Timon," Samuel said earnestly, "you must realize that you work in the greater service—"

"I shall tell you what I have realized," Timon interrupted. "I have come to think of this body—this flesh, these bones—as a prison. And I know something of prisons, thanks to the likes of you three."

"Prison?" Venitelli stammered.

"I am saying that I feel trapped in corporeal matter," Timon explained calmly. "The sensation is terrifying if I allow it to be. I find that in my worst moments I can barely breathe, drowning in skin and blood and marrow. When that feeling overtakes me, I am in such a mood as to long for death. So your threats to that effect would not move me in the least. Alas, I lately also find myself wondering what will happen to my spirit once it is released from this earthly cell. Something needles my memory, raises the face of every man I have sent before me to the grave. When that happens, my only salvation is the daily exercise of memorizing *other* things. I must use so much of my brain that it crowds out the burning thoughts, eclipses them. True, that eclipse leaves me in darkness, but it is a darkness that is kind to me. Lately I find that I would rather bear the horrors of this life than endure the retribution that awaits when I have shuffled off this mortal coil. I fear my punishment will be Promethean. And so, Brothers, I am at a crossroads, you see. On the one hand, I can no longer bear another moment trapped in this living body, and yet something in my spirit fears the body's death. How to proceed? You see my dilemma."

The room, the very stone walls, seemed staggered by the weight of Timon's speech.

Timon punctuated the end of it by peeling an egg.

Samuel began to speak three times, each time taking in a breath and then thinking better of what he was about to say.

"So," Timon finally concluded after finishing his egg, "you would have me allow the killer in Cambridge to continue murdering scholars there. And when my memory work is done, you want me to help kill the rest. It is an ill-conceived plan. The timing and logic of which boggles the mind with its sheer incompetence, but that does not matter. I discover, upon reflection and a bit of egg, that I do not care."

He stood so abruptly that the other three quaked. Isaiah struggled to produce his dagger once more.

"The truth is, remembering a Bible phrase, killing a butcher, standing idly by as men are murdered," Timon sniffed, "it is all one to me. All one. Rest easy. Your orders are communicated."

Isaiah had his knife in his hand. Timon stared down at it.

"My little speech meant nothing to you?" Timon asked Isaiah. "You must understand that I am not, at this moment, afraid of death. Throw your knife. Aim for the neck, though. Something that small would only be a nuisance unless it cut a vital vein."

"Put that away!" Samuel ordered Isaiah.

Isaiah blinked.

"You shall have word from me soon," Timon assured the men.

At once he turned his back on them—a gesture of clear, fearless contempt—and moved to the door with the grace of smoke.

If it had not been for Jenny and her butcher, Timon thought as he grabbed the door handle, I might have agreed to do their bidding. Now I am forming other plans—plans of my own. Why would this stranger, Jenny, have such an effect, instead of any other of a dozen human beings?

Timon was in the street heading back to his room, eastern sun in his eyes, before he understood that Jenny and her landlord father were the low-character equivalent of two high characters in the play in his mind: Anne and Deacon Marbury.

That sky is a backdrop, he thought. The things I have just said are lines written by God; the men I left behind in that room: minor players.

Understanding the characters, their relationships—in fact, the play as a whole—was the reason, somehow, that he would not kill the translators; that he would eventually confess everything to Marbury. It was the reason he would stop the murderer, defy his Pope, and see King James's work to fruition.

He thought of Anne's observation on the night her father had gone to see the King: "If the play is all talking and no forward action, then the plot lies dead upon the stage. And to provide us with that action, I believe, my father is away tonight—to London."

When dialogue ceases and action begins, a character has made up his mind. All doubt vanishes. He may move forward toward his inevitable end with grace as well as haste.

Timon shielded his eyes from the blinding passion of the sunrise and thought suddenly of a hymn, his favorite when he was a stableboy.

Bright morning stars are rising, the song said. *Day is awaking in my soul.*

36

In a darker corner of Cambridge, Deacon Marbury was raked away from his dreams by a furious pounding on his door.

"Father! Quickly!"

Marbury sat up. His blue bedcovers were strewn about him, discarded after great abuse. The single window in his bedroom admitted ivory, slanting light through the rough glass. Beneath the window stood a washbasin, and on it someone had left a small pot filled with primroses to assure the deacon that, despite the cold in his room, spring had come somewhere. The oak bed creaked like an old boat when he managed to throw his legs over the side.

"A moment!" he hollered.

His feet hit the floor, and the realization crept upon him that he had slept all night in his boots and clothes. Though he had slept deeply, he was waking to an overwhelming exhaustion, conversations with Lively's children still roaring through his brain.

He staggered out of the bedroom toward the hallway door, twice kicking things in the relative darkness of his parlor.

He grabbed the handle, threw open the door, and scowled down at his daughter.

"You dressed in a hurry," she said.

"What is it?"

Anne was spotlessly attired: black dress from chin to floor, hair pulled back, face scrubbed.

"Timon was not in his room all night." She started away from the door, down the hall.

Marbury stood in the entranceway. "Stop."

She turned. "You must come and see what I have found."

"Found where?"

"In Timon's *room*. Did I not make it clear that he was gone the entire night?"

"You went into Brother Timon's room?"

She sighed impatiently. "I saw you both come back last evening. I knew something was afoot. I heard you go to bed. Then, an hour before midnight, Timon left!"

Her face was flushed with a growing excitement. Marbury knew the look. It only meant more difficulty.

"You did not sleep?" he asked Anne.

"How can you sleep," she answered breathlessly, "with everything that is happening in this place?"

"Was I ever as young as you are now?" he wondered, mostly to himself.

"No," she answered curtly. "Now, are you coming with me to see what I have found or not?"

"Not." Marbury began to pull the door to his rooms closed.

"Father! You must see quickly, before he returns. It is morning."

Marbury looked through the high windows of the hallway. "Only just."

"You will want to see what I have found. And you may want to call for the constable or at least the beadles."

"What have you found?" Marbury asked, the door almost closed.

"Come and see!" Anne sang. "Brother Timon has stolen papers from the Great Hall!"

Marbury's brain rid itself of the last dust of sleep, and he drew in a great breath. He squeezed his eyes shut tight for a moment to clear his vision, then he stepped into the hall, closing his door behind him.

Anne was already ten feet ahead, not looking back. She was halfway down the stairs before Marbury overtook her.

"I must severely protest your invasion—"

"I watched him leave by moonlight. I waited. I knew that he was gone and I might safely—"

"Your safety is hardly the issue! *Propriety*—why did you do this thing? Why would you presume—"

"He might be the killer!" Anne whispered harshly, pausing on the stairs. "So my safety might *well* be the issue."

Marbury rubbed his forehead. "You've been listening to Spaulding."

"One can scarcely prevent hearing him. He rails constantly."

"Timon is not the murderer."

"Please, Father," Anne said softly. "Come and see what I have found. Perhaps you will be able to explain it to me."

Marbury wavered between bed and daughter for only a moment before he descended the next step toward the ground floor.

Anne ran ahead of him and Marbury watched her, wondering when she would begin to behave as a woman instead of as a child.

It is my fault, he thought to himself. I could not be a mother to her. I was barely a father. And her earliest impulses were to imitate me. What could be worse for a young woman in England than to argue the virtues of Puritanism at the age of nine?

He did his best to keep up, but Anne had already weaved through the back halls of the downstairs. She was into the servants' section, then Marbury saw her burst into Timon's room.

He quickened his pace. By the time he stood in Timon's doorway, he saw his daughter kneeling beneath the writing desk. Taper in hand, she was tearing up the floor.

"Anne! Stop it. What are you doing?" Marbury rushed into the room.

Anne tilted a single stone and held the candle closer.

There, on the floor under the stone, was a portion of a manuscript.

"That is in Harrison's hand," Marbury said slowly.

"I discovered it quite by accident," Anne gushed. "I was standing at the desk looking for anything I might find interesting, and I was trying to pretend that I was as tall as Brother Timon. I stood on tiptoe and faltered. The stone came loose, and I saw this under it."

Marbury knelt beside his daughter. "It is Harrison's work."

Anne bounded up, taking the candle with her. The manuscript pages that had been hidden under the stone were plunged into darkness. Anne was at Timon's bed and slid her free hand under the cover.

"Look!" she breathed.

The illumination from the candle showed a small wooden box.

"What is it?" Marbury mumbled, coming to his daughter. "And what in God's name did you think you were doing when you were going through the man's bed?"

"I saw a lump in the cover," she answered defensively.

"Well?"

"Well *what*?"

"What is in the box?"

"You shall never guess."

"Christ help me," he said softly, taking up the box.

He opened it; saw the pipe and several vials. He was momentarily overtaken by the smell of burnt spice.

"I checked the vials," she said excitedly. "They contain oil of nutmeg, that is my guess. Does he cook with it? Is that a clay pipe?"

"It is." Marbury stared down at the box. "What can it mean?"

In the black hallway out of the candle's influence, a hoarse voice answered, "Shall I explain it to you?"

Anne dropped the candle and fell back upon the bed, gasping. Marbury fumbled with the box, trying to hide it and wondering how quickly he could draw his dagger.

Timon stood framed in the doorway, stooping his head, the ghost of a shadow.

37

"*You* should pick up your candle, Anne," Timon said calmly. "I only have one blanket, and if that one scorches . . ."

"Brother," Marbury stammered, dropping the box onto the bed where Anne sat.

Anne's breathing got in the way of her words, but she managed to make her accusation clear: "You have stolen documents from the Great Hall!"

Timon glanced once at the loose stone beneath his desk. "Also, Anne, would you mind rising? As a man devoted to celibacy, I am uneasy when there is a girl in my bed."

Anne shot up from the place where Timon slept, glad that the dim light hid her crimson blush. She stooped, grabbed the candle, and held it close to the box on the bed.

"And what is this?" she demanded.

"Anne!" Marbury snapped.

"I do not mind," Timon said. "She lashes out because she has been caught doing something she ought not to have done. It is a common human reaction—especially in the young. I assume she came into my room while I was gone, made her several discoveries, and fetched you."

"Yes, exactly," Marbury muttered.

"I have not slept this past night." Timon blinked. "My moonlight work was taxing. I need to sleep, but perhaps it would be best for me to deal with matters at hand first."

He moved suddenly. Anne held the candle in front of her as if it were a sword, her breathing more labored. Marbury planted his feet and felt for his knife. Timon's hand shot between them and he grabbed the small wooden box. Anne stepped back, gasping. Marbury's blade appeared.

"This box," Timon announced, ignoring both blade and candle, "contains a world. In that world anything may happen, because it is a place unconfined by walls such as these stones around us. Its only borders are the limits of my brain. It is a land where I may fly, may distill and evaporate from my body entirely. There I am a king of infinite space. In short, this box is my best freedom."

Anne lowered her candle. Marbury clutched his knife, but released his breath.

"But a more mundane explanation," Timon continued, staring at the box, "is that the vials contain a certain oil of nutmeg, which may be ignited. The smoke may be drawn through a pipe into the lungs. The lungs take the smoke, absorb its chemical properties, and relate those properties to the brain. The brain interprets those elements in various ways, the way a man might interpret another language. In the details of that translation, I find the truth."

Anne looked to her father. "I do not understand."

"A man may drink wine," Timon explained, "and become drunk. In that stupor he may perceive the world in a different light. He may see things that other men do not. You have witnessed this phenomenon?"

Anne's brow furrowed. "Yes."

"That is similar to my experience, except that mine . . ." Timon struggled to explain. "Ah! My experience, Anne, creates a theatre in the mind. My brain becomes a stage upon which many parts are played. In that theatre I am a playwright—as in *this* world God invents our parts."

Anne stared at the box with new eyes.

"As to the documents you discovered in my hiding place, Anne," Timon concluded, "they are Harrison's. In my effort to investigate his murder, I found it useful to read a bit of his work. I believe that your father and I agree that the murders have more to do with the *work* of the translators than the translators themselves. It therefore seemed appropriate to examine that work more closely."

Everything I have said is true, Timon thought to himself, but it is not the complete truth.

"Brother Timon," Marbury said quickly, hiding his knife. "Our trespass has been inexcusable. Please do not think that Anne and I are the sort who—"

"Deacon," Timon asserted, "we have matters of much greater import to discuss. This is your room; I only stay here at your whim. One cannot trespass property of one's own."

"How very gracious," Marbury began.

"I do not fully understand about the oil of nutmeg," Anne stammered.

"Daughter!" Marbury warned.

Timon's head snapped in Anne's direction. "Your father worries that my tutelage will explore areas of your education best left unrevealed."

"But—," she complained.

"There is a world of earthly endeavor from which every father would shield his child." Timon held out the box. "It is unlikely that I shall ever understand that impulse. If your curiosity is of an overwhelming magnitude, please be my guest. You pour only a few thick drops of the oil into the pipe."

Marbury put his hand on the box. "Brother Timon thinks that his confrontation in this fashion will cause you to demur. He does not know you." He looked to Timon. "She would do it."

Timon sighed. "I am tired in my blood and bones. Perhaps my judgment is compromised."

"You wish to sleep," Marbury said instantly, stepping away from Timon's poor bed.

"Yes," Timon said, staring down at his bed, "but I fear what dreams may come. And I feel an equal need to share information. There is a coming darkness. We must work quickly."

"Something wicked this way comes," Anne said softly. "I have felt it too."

Both men stared at her.

"Something more wicked than two men murdered within view of my bedroom?" Marbury asked.

"There will be more killing," Timon said. "But the murders are nothing compared to the treachery of—compared to the larger forces at work."

Timon tossed the box onto his bed and rubbed his eyes with the cold palms of his hands.

"Christ," Timon exhaled. "I must rouse myself."

He stepped quickly to his basin, scooped his hands into the water there, and threw it against his face. "Chaderton," he mumbled, again splashing himself. "Anne, would you mind fetching him? He told me certain things that must be examined further. We must do so immediately."

"And then you must leave us, Anne," Marbury told his daughter firmly.

"No, Father," she responded reasonably. "The best way to keep me from breaking into strange rooms is to keep me well-informed. A mystery makes me curious. Remove the mystery and you remove the curiosity. The best way to eliminate my difficult behavior is to educate me. I must, therefore, come with you to this discussion or else prove a nuisance in so many other ways: crashing into more rooms, listening at keyholes, peeping over hedges."

Marbury sighed, knowing that what she said was true. He struggled for a moment, trying to understand why her words seemed familiar—and so strange.

But Timon interrupted, saying with only a hint of humor, "As your tutor, I deem it essential to your education that you be present as we converse. Now off you go to find Chaderton."

Anne shot toward the door before her father could think of how to protest.

38

*M*arbury spent a useless few minutes trying to make amends with Timon for disturbing his room. Each time Timon protested that silence was a better ally to them both than any conversation could be. Timon seemed to need silence to absorb energy from the air. That same time seemed to tax Marbury to the point of pain, tensing his brow, straining his joints, adding brass weights to his lungs.

Chaderton arrived behind Anne at last, breathing heavily. He was dressed in a dark purple coat. A hat to match, faintly embroidered in gold, covered his head. Marbury nodded to Chaderton, who continued to gasp for breath trying to speak.

"No preliminaries!" Timon said loudly. "I believe that there has been a conspiracy since the death of our Savior to lie to all Christians. Some of these prevarications may have been the result of innocent mistakes. In the main, however, they represent a deliberate effort to pervert the life and death—the very meaning—of the man called Jesus. From this time forward, we must spend all our efforts to stop the forward progress of these lies. They are over a thousand years in the making. We must find the truth."

Chaderton, without thinking, crossed himself.

Timon smiled sympathetically. Years of being a Protestant had not rid the old man of his father's Catholic ghost.

"The lies of which I speak," Timon continued, "are in the process of being sanctified in James's Bible. No monarch on earth has ordained such an effort. Others have tried, to be sure, but they have proceeded grudgingly, or with half a heart or a third the scholarship of the present work. We must see to it that King James's Bible tells the truth as it has never before been told. To do that, we must prevent the translators from being killed. Their deaths aid these ancient lies."

"We are being murdered to prevent the revelation of Christ's true meaning." An instant of stunned silence had separated Timon's comments from Chaderton's realization. "This means trouble for the other translating groups. Clearly something could happen to them."

"It already has," Marbury said softly. All eyes turned to him. "James informed me that Lancelot Andrews visited Hampton Court before I did."

"Yes, you saw the King, I nearly forgot," Chaderton moaned. "I should have asked you about it immediately."

"The King mentioned the other translators?" Timon began.

"Only to say that the Westminster group had received strange notes," Marbury hastened to tell everyone. "No one there has been killed. Texts have been stolen."

"Wait!" Anne demanded, stunned. "What lies?"

All eyes turned her way.

"Tell me what you mean about the lies!" she exploded.

"As you already know, because you overheard, our Savior's true name was Joshua," Timon said flatly.

"But," Anne sputtered, "there must be more to it than that."

"Mary Magdalene may have written a gospel that has long been suppressed," Marbury offered tentatively. "Why it was kept from us, I do not know."

Anne held her breath.

"Christ's resurrection could have been, in truth, of a more spir-itual than physical nature," Chaderton sighed. "He might have dis-carded his body and presented his True Self, his spirit, to the disciples after his crucifixion—not his earthly form."

Anne clasped her hands so tightly that they turned colors: rose red at the tips, bone white at the joints. She opened her mouth, but no words came out.

"A woman wrote a gospel," she whispered at last.

"And not just any woman," Chaderton added.

"And the resurrection of the body—," Anne gasped.

"Brother Timon and Dr. Chaderton have expressed *opinions*," Marbury said uncomfortably. "There are no facts to support his rash and, incidentally, extraordinarily illegal speech."

"On the contrary," Timon responded at once. "Facts abound."

"Yes, but these facts may be interpreted in a hundred different ways," Marbury argued feverishly.

"The mistake was in soliciting language scholars," Chaderton interrupted, "men whose academic spirit of competition might get the better of them. That is where James went wrong."

The comment seemed out of place; Chaderton appeared lost in a world of his own.

"I only mean to say," the old man told everyone when he saw the way they were staring at him, "that James made a mistake hir-ing men of keen intellectual curiosity. We are all, alas, scholars who will follow the idea more than the assignment."

"Yes. Even if all these men were told to copy the Bishops' Bible word for word," Timon agreed, "they could not curtail their pur-suit of the truth, their thirst for knowledge—"

"And their desire to be one step ahead of everyone else," Chaderton interjected. "We are, I admit, a competitive group."

"Pause a moment." Anne bit her upper lip. "The men hired to translate the Bible could not stop at clarifying what had already been translated. They sought to return to the original texts, trans-late from ancient documents. And some of these contain the infor-mation you have just revealed."

Timon did his best not to stare at Anne. Her zeal matched his. Her eyes burned with a similar fire. Her questions were in his mind too.

Is this what Marbury feels? he wondered to himself. Is this the pride that every father knows?

"In so far as was possible, we did revert to original texts, yes," Chaderton said to Anne, the strength returning to his voice. "We have all found or been given texts that we believe were written within a hundred years of our Lord's lifetime."

"There are other Gospels," Anne struggled to say. "There are books of the Bible—written about Christ—that I have not read. How is this possible?"

"Decisions were made in the year of our Lord 325," Chaderton began.

"The Council of Nicaea." Anne nodded.

"The documents to which you refer were casualties of that conflict," Timon said quickly. "Many were destroyed. Others were hidden."

"Years of research in the matter," Chaderton asserted, "have provoked me to disagree with the Nicene decisions."

"But you said you were *given* certain texts." Anne's eyes had not left Timon's. Clearly she still suspected him of hiding something.

"By James himself," Chaderton said. "He too has had a lifelong interest in spiritual matters. His tastes differ from mine, but his thirst is the same as mine, I believe."

"I have read *Demonology*," Anne sniffed. "You differ in more than matters of taste. Your level of scholarship—"

"What is the point of this speculation?" Marbury exploded.

"If the physical body of Christ was not resurrected," Anne replied with equal force, "then our religion would be fundamentally different. I am willing to call Christ by whatever earthly name I may, but if his body did not rise from the grave—"

"Certain texts I have read," Chaderton interrupted in a bid to ease the tension between father and daughter, "find the concept of a body coming back to life revolting—the province of necromancy! They suggested that the fathers who prevailed at the council were possessed by devils. Their grotesque insistence on the re-animation of a corpse was made more monstrous by the concept of ritual cannibalism: eating flesh and drinking blood. Who but a demon would suggest such behavior?"

"You are talking about Holy Communion," Anne railed.

"Yes." Chaderton tried to smile.

The very air stood still around his word. Atoms refused to engage it. Anne found she could not exhale, and Marbury was beginning to sweat in the cold room.

"I can see the truth of this," Anne said slowly. "Christ had a body on earth, but it was unimportant, as are all bodies. When He died, He had no further need of it. His *spirit* arose from the grave."

"The fire of the spirit is essential," Timon agreed. "The flesh is only a prison."

"The miracle of Resurrection is essential to Christian belief," Marbury insisted, dabbing his hairline with his fingertips. "And the body is a *temple,* not a prison.*"

"My body is a nuisance," Anne muttered. "Every third woman in the world would agree."

"I must see these hidden texts!" Timon said abruptly. "I must see them for myself. I must see them now or my mind will capsize. I must know the truth of these matters today! This morning!"

The urgency of his voice stopped all further conversation.

Timon charged toward his doorway, leaving Anne and Marbury to stare.

He did not turn their way as he crossed the threshold. "I find myself at a crossroads, you see," he told them, vanishing down the hallway. "I feel a new season is about to begin."

39

The others followed Timon into the common yard, the bright air, headed for the Great Hall. The morning wind raked its bone-cold fingers across the sky, cleaning it of clouds.

Marbury struggled with one sentence after another trying to find the exact words that would make time stand still. He needed time to think.

Anne caught up with Timon and matched his strides, staring at the side of his face.

Chaderton brought up the rear, talking to himself. "We could begin with the secret documents I received," he offered reasonably, "and then ask each one of the others to present. In this manner, Deacon, you will soon see what we are facing. But will they share their work with Brother Timon? There is a question."

Anne listened to Chaderton with one ear and whispered her first question to Timon at the same time.

"What has happened to you?" she asked plainly.

"Pardon?" Timon murmured, his eyes locked on the entrance to the Great Hall.

"You bear a new aspect this morning."

"I do?" But he smiled.

"There. That smile is different from the one you gave me when we first met."

"How is it different?"

"I cannot say, but it would seem to be the smile of a man let out of prison."

Timon stopped dead still. Marbury almost ran into him. Anne continued for several steps before she realized what had happened. Marbury glared at his daughter, wondering what she had said.

"Yes," Chaderton said, joining the group. "We had best agree on a plan before we proceed further. Some of the men will already be in the hall working this morning."

"Deacon," Timon said, staring into Anne's eyes, "your daughter may well be England's best secret weapon. She has the bold mind of a man and the subtler perceptions of a woman."

"We had a queen like that," Anne reminded Timon, "until recently."

"Yes," Chaderton said, lost in thoughts of his own, "our plan must not be too bold."

All eyes turned to him.

"I suggest," he continued, "that I show you what documents I have, and you all gather around me eagerly. Make such praise as you might if you were surprised. Such attention is honey to our bees. We all are drawn to it. If one of us has discovered something that would cause the three of you to convene, then I can assure you that the others will horde around."

"Let them think that they must compete with you for our attention." Anne folded her arms and smiled. "Perfect."

"It will provoke them to show their work." Timon nodded. "Even to me. They will believe it was their own idea."

"So," Chaderton clapped his hands, well pleased with himself. "Follow me."

He headed at once for the door with a greater speed than he had managed before. The others surrounded him.

"You did not answer my question," Anne whispered to Timon.

Timon nodded. "Let my actions be your answer."

Chaderton grasped the cold iron handle of the tall oak door, but hesitated.

"We must be careful, of course," he whispered, "not to reveal too much. The killer may be near. And, as I believe we have considered, there may be demons at work."

Without further conversation, he thrust forward, jolting the door open with a loud scraping noise.

The hall was, indeed, occupied. Three of the remaining scholars were hard at work, each at his separate desk. The thunder of the door disturbed them only slightly, but the sight of Chaderton followed by the odd trio piqued interest.

Chaderton began his gambit in an all-too-theatrical voice. "Right this way, Deacon," he said vigorously, and with enough volume to echo through the hall. "You will soon see for yourself that what I have told you is the truth!"

The strange quartet moved almost as one directly to Chaderton's desk. He made great show of unlocking his top drawer and pulling out several documents.

The other scholars in the room glared. Timon was glad to see, out of the corner of his eye, that Spaulding was not among them. His intrusion would muddy the waters of Chaderton's efforts.

"Here, for example," Chaderton announced, "is the gospel most curiously excluded, in my opinion. It is perfectly in line with Matthew, Mark, Luke, and John. I have no idea why it should not be included in our King's Bible."

He held the document aloft for all to see.

"By Thomas?" Marbury asked, staring at the top page in genuine wonder. "Is my Greek correct? The apostle Thomas?"

"Exactly!" Chaderton shouted. "Why was this eliminated from our Bible?"

"What could it say that was so offensive?" Anne whispered.

"Read here!" Chaderton pointed to a phrase a few lines down from the top.

Timon read them aloud. "'We asked him, "Do you want us to fast? How should we pray? Should we give to charity?" And He said, "Do not lie, and do not do what you hate. If you know what is in front of you, then what is hidden will be disclosed."'"

"Why would such words be kept from us?" Anne gasped.

Chaderton sighed. "In two sentences, our Lord eliminates the need for rules, laws, and priests to interpret them for you."

"Which eliminates the money," Timon said softly. "A decidedly un-Catholic sentiment."

"The simple perfection," Chaderton began.

"Stop!" a voice from behind them exploded.

They all turned to see Roger Andrews bearing down on them from his desk a few rows away.

"Stop this at once!" he demanded, a scowl burning his face.

Andrews was dressed in his academic regalia, a pretension that Timon found as laughable as it was telling. He was the only one of the translators who exhibited his credentials on his sleeve. His deep blue robes carefully avoided the appearance of being black. Gold piping and an ornate family crest emphasized the color of the material. His cap, foolishly cascading over one side of his forehead, bobbled wildly, threatening to fly away. He was thin, and the bony finger he pointed at Chaderton was a twig of birch in the dim light. His blond hair and fair complexion exaggerated the flush in his cheeks. The total effect made him seem younger than he was.

"Dr. Spaulding has given express instructions," Andrews continued as he marched toward Chaderton's desk, "that we are to avoid this monk. He is not a scholar, he is a stranger among us, and he is the likely murderer of our fallen comrades!"

"Dr. Andrews," Marbury began, his voice pitched perfectly to soothe and calm, "our Brother Timon is here to help."

"And I am astonished that there is a woman in this hall gawking over our secret texts!" Andrews seemed close to violence. "A *woman!*"

"Dr. Andrews!" Chaderton's volume matched his comrade's. "Cease yelling in this holy place!"

"Do you not find it curious," Anne said to Timon, a devil dancing in her eye, "that Dr. Andrews objects more to the presence of a woman than that of a murderer?"

"A murderer," Andrews stammered, his throat closing on the words, "who should be in our prison, not our hall. This is a place of scholarship, not a haven for misbegotten children and vile assassins!"

"A place of scholarship," Timon mused. "Anne, did you know that Dr. Roger Andrews was not *chosen* for his duties here in Cambridge?"

"I—," she began.

"The departed Harrison was, I have been told, the man who selected the rest of the scholars for this group. He did not choose Andrews."

"The matter is more complicated than you can imagine," Marbury interjected, realizing what Timon was after. "Harrison was— shall one use the word *encouraged?*—to include Andrews here."

"What word, in truth, would fit the situation better than *encouraged?*" Anne smiled calmly.

"Well," Marbury answered back, a grand wave of his hand flaying the air around him, "say *forced,* then. No one would argue."

"Who could force such a decision?" Anne did her best to manufacture an innocent pronunciation of her words.

"When Harrison rejected Roger Andrews, there came a decree inclining Harrison to change his mind," Marbury asserted. "A brief but precise letter, royal seal affixed."

"The King insisted?" Anne stared into Andrews's eyes.

"More likely it was Roger's brother, Lancelot Andrews, who affected this turn of events," Marbury responded. "Lancelot is the bishop of Winchester, and the man who presides over the *first* company of translators."

Andrews's face had grown from crimson to mauve. His shoulders began to shake involuntarily.

"But it was the King," Marbury went on lightly, "who commanded that Roger Andrews be a part of the work here at Cambridge."

"Unfortunate," Timon said, his smile growing. "The rest of the scholars resent it. They have no regard for Andrews as an intellectual force and do not seem to care for him outside of the working environs."

"Dr. Andrews, alas, made matters worse by accusing Harrison of slighting him," Marbury added. "Which claim lacks all meaning since Harrison slighted everyone equally."

Timon exhaled noisily. "There you have it."

Andrews was so enraged that he could not speak. His entire body quivered, and his face pulsed with an ocean of blood. Low, growling sounds disturbed the air around his head.

Chaderton seemed confused. "What do you mean, Brother Timon, by saying, 'There you have it'?"

"I mean," Timon said, taking a quick step toward Andrews, "that Dr. Andrews has the best reasons for murder. *He* is our killer."

Roger Andrews struggled desperately to speak. His breathing was labored. His eyes were popping.

Timon could see that his goading plan was about to work. Andrews would bolt from the hall, unable to respond to derision, and Chaderton could continue with his plan.

Alas, Andrews had other ideas. He took an unsteady step forward, reaching for Timon's throat, then collapsed. He lay like a sack of turnips on the floor at Timon's feet.

40

I only meant to make him leave," Timon apologized, kneeling on the floor beside Andrews.

"You do not believe that he is the murderer?" Chaderton whispered.

"I only thought of it while we were talking. A bit of improvisation. But considering his reaction, have I made a discovery?"

"He *is* the killer," Anne whispered. "He was humiliated that Harrison did not choose him, that this group was forced to take him. He lashed out with a jealous heart."

"May I point out," said Marbury, the only one of the quartet not bending over Andrews, "that Andrews would have no reason to kill Lively?"

"But you see," Anne responded, "Lively, for all his faults, was a competent man, a man bent on finding the truth. He would have eventually found Andrews out. Spaulding on the other hand—"

"Call the constables," Andrews mumbled weakly, his eyes still closed.

"Ah, good," Timon said briskly, helping Andrews to sit up, "I have not slain you."

"I am a sensitive man," Andrews whined. "Occasionally my brain erupts and my body collapses. I am better now. Call the constables."

"For what purpose?" Chaderton asked.

"To arrest this Brother Timon," Andrews shot back, gaining strength.

The other two scholars in the room had joined the group, gazing down at Andrews with what appeared to be amusement.

Timon knew them. One, Dillingham, was known as the great Grecian. The other, Richardson, considered himself the most superior scholar in Europe, or so Timon had heard.

Richardson spoke, barely hiding his delight. "Andrews, are you on the floor?"

Richardson was dressed in a most royal manner. His dark coat was exquisitely quilted, stitched with a fine filigree. His clothes beneath were satin, pale cream, and spotless. His shoes were dyed to match the coat. The cap was white but so heavily embroidered in gold that it appeared to be a halo, an appearance, no doubt, that had been calculated. He also sported the best-trimmed beard in England.

"Dr. Richardson," Timon said, standing, "you are, I know, the foremost Latin expert among your fellows, perhaps in all the world. I am greatly honored to meet you."

Andrews exhaled noisily, and Dillingham looked downward.

"I *joust* with the great Latin experts." Richardson's head leaned forward eagerly. "I unhorse them all. Even the Italians. Mine is the sword of knowledge, the shield of absolute confidence. I am, in short, a knight of old: true to a grail, a quest. I would have sat with Arthur, you know. No man on earth is my equal in this language of emperors and poets."

"Quite so." Timon folded his hands in front of himself.

"I do not boast in this matter, I only announce the facts."

"Dr. Chaderton is sharing our secret texts with a murderer and that woman!" Andrews protested.

"Well, if we *all* know about these things," Richardson drawled languidly, "then they can hardly be called *secrets,* can they?"

"And it has always been our intention to *share* our work here, Dr. Andrews." Chaderton raised his eyebrows.

Richardson clapped his hands. "Only last week I delighted in sharing with the group my discovery of an ancient text in Greek written by none other than—"

"Dr. Richardson!" Andrews exploded.

"Yes?" Richardson asked, irritated.

Andrews struggled to his feet without aid. "I demand that you cease this discussion with these *persons!*"

"You have made certain discoveries, Dr. Richardson?" Timon asked, deliberately vague. "Discoveries that would alter the content of the King's Bible?"

"Thousands!" Richardson asserted. "And nearly all result from deliberate suppression or addle-brained interpretation by Catholic monks. I could have discovered more, but *Mr.* Harrison refused to allow me any latitude. He provoked us to wander in the darkness, do you see? He would not permit me to go over all the texts, the entire Bible. But you must see that a man with my breadth of scholarship must take, as it were, the entirety of the . . . how does one say it?"

"You must see the whole to better understand its parts."

"Exactly!"

"And Harrison was a little man," Timon needled, "unable to see a grander scheme."

"Incapable of it."

"One wonders how such a man came to a position of selecting the others for their assignments," Timon goaded conspiratorially.

"Search the body politic," Richardson whispered, suddenly hushed, "for answers there."

"I have been told," Timon responded in similar tones, "that Harrison somehow had the support of our King in this regard."

"You refer to the fact that Harrison was a Scot, as was our King." Richardson pursed his lips. "But his appointment was never the King's, surely. It was the work of some minor court clerk, someone who wrote a recommendation with one hand when he discovered that his other was filled with coins."

"Doubtless." Timon glanced quickly at Marbury.

Richardson noticed the glance. "You understand, of course, that what I say is mere speculation."

"I demand—," Andrews began at the top of his lungs.

"I wonder, Dr. Andrews," Richardson bellowed, "that you have not yet discovered the reason Marbury set Brother Timon upon this investigation."

"He told us that it was to discover a murderer," Andrews answered simply, "but—"

"No!" Richardson adjusted his coat. "You have been duped."

"Duped?"

"Brother Timon," Richardson said in soothing tones, turning his gaze Timon's way, "you have been misled and misused. Mr. Lively, before he died, tweaked your interest in academic matters of which you doubtless have little comprehension. I can see that he did. He was distracting you of a purpose. He was in league with Marbury, you must realize it."

"In league with Marbury?" Timon stared, utterly unable to see where Richardson was going.

"You have not fooled me, Deacon," Richardson said to Marbury, waving his hand grandly, "though I dare not reveal all of my knowledge until the time is right. You chose this *Timon* to investigate for one reason and one reason alone: so that the real killer could have some pawn to blame for the murders!"

Timon fought back laughter, turned it into a brief moment of coughing.

"I see you are stunned, Brother Timon." Richardson nodded sagely. "But that is the way of it! I have determined that you have been set upon your task in the belief that you will stumble, fall, and be revealed *as if* you were the killer. The particulars of Marbury's scheme I do not yet know, but shall discover them by and by. He is a clever man, but as you see, he is not my match. No Puritan could be. I have found him out."

"Are you out of your mind?" Marbury stammered, barely controlling his derision.

"Dr. Richardson, your mind is peerless," Timon interrupted, managing to hide part of his face behind his hand.

"You have not yet realized the full import of my deductions," Richardson said, tapping Timon's forearm with a single finger, absolutely delighted with himself. "You do not realize that I know the *true* identity of the murderer!"

"God in heaven!" Andrews gasped

"Or, in truth, I should say *murderers*," Richardson sniffed. "I have deduced it almost from the start."

"Pray tell me instantly, sir, what is your meaning?" Andrews demanded.

Richardson closed his eyes. "Let me see if I can lead you all to my conclusions with a few well-chosen questions, as I often attempt to do with my students." He took a moment to gather his thoughts. "Who hired Timon as Anne's tutor?"

"Marbury, of course." Andrews folded his arms tightly.

"And who assigned him to the task of finding the killer?"

"Marbury."

"Just so. Now. Who now first railed most adamantly against Timon?"

"Lively," Andrews answered, softening a bit.

"Exactly!" Richardson exploded. "You have your answer!"

"I do?" Andrews responded weakly.

"Marbury and Lively are the guilty parties, man! They conspired to murder Harrison."

"Why?" Andrews stammered.

"For his gross insults to us all. Harrison was removed from this project in the only manner possible. He was a King's assign, after all, and could never be simply dismissed."

"But, then—Lively—," Andrews gasped.

"Ah! Marbury disposed of Lively in order to assure his *own* safety. Now he has Timon to play the fool—a poor monk, an outsider, a pawn, as I say."

"God in heaven," Andrews whispered, taking a step away from Marbury.

Richardson turned his benevolence toward Timon. "Never doubt it, Brother Timon. Marbury will formally accuse you of the murders ere long."

"So Marbury hired me," Timon began hesitantly, "and then set me to find the dead body, only to have Lively accuse me, vociferously, of the murder in order to plant the seeds of my supposed guilt."

"There you have it." Richardson folded his arms in front of him, a mask of great satisfaction refining his features.

Timon looked to Marbury, whose lips were thin and whose shoulders were shaking with barely controlled silent laughter.

"What am I to do?" Timon asked meekly. "I am lost."

"Fear not," Richardson answered valiantly. "When the time is right, Sir Galahad will come to your aid and set all aright."

"You?"

"Precisely. I am your salvation," Richardson assured Timon. "In the meantime, continue your investigations. Who knows, you may stumble upon evidence that could be of some small use. I shall strike when the perfect moment presents itself, when Marbury least expects it."

"Well." Marbury cleared his throat. "I may expect something *now*."

Anne, no longer able to contain herself, burst into laughter.

"See how the daughter reacts with hysteria," Richardson confided in the silent Dillingham. "Tragic, is it not?"

Dillingham responded by closing his eyes and sighing. "I believe," he said, his tolerance obviously strained to the limit, "that I shall return to my work."

Without another word, Dillingham shuffled to his desk, the hem of his long brown coat whispering across the stone floor. He sat, ran a hand through his unwashed auburn hair, and picked up his pen.

Timon knew Dillingham's reputation. Everyone in England had heard of the debate conducted in Greek between Francis

Dillingham and William Alabaster. The disputation was so famous that it had already become a benchmark of the age: Greek scholars were considered old if they came to prominence before the argument; new if they came after.

Certainly Dillingham had a greater understanding of Greek and its subtleties than any other man alive. That he appeared uninterested in murder, politics, or competition made him more interesting to Timon.

"Well, then," Chaderton grumbled, his plan of getting the others to share secrets in an obvious shambles.

"I do not trust myself in the presence of this company," Richardson announced grandly, glaring at Marbury. "I may forget the proprieties and lash out before I am entirely able to prove my thesis. So I take my leave."

Richardson turned as a monarch would turn, hand clutching his bosom, and rolled toward the door.

Timon addressed Andrews. "Calling for the constable at this moment may be ill-advised," he said confidentially, "since you and I *and* Deacon Marbury are suspects."

"God in heaven!" Andrews bellowed. He gathered up his academic robes as if he were carrying a half bushel of apples in his arms and ran from the room to catch up with Richardson.

41

*I*s it worth pointing out that I was in London when Lively was killed?" Marbury asked once Andrews was out the door.

"Probably not," Timon answered.

"As entertaining as that was . . . ," Anne began.

"Entertaining? This is the devil's work!" Chaderton lamented, his head swaying like a tree limb in the wind. "Satan is making fools of these men. Brother Timon, I see the wisdom of your assertion that some great force is at work to hide greater truths from the world. What shall we do?"

Timon leaned against the desk closest to his hip, a wave of exhaustion rolling over him at the prospect of the task before him. "We must work with all our might to assure that this Bible—the entire project—is completed without interference from anyone or anything. The King James Bible must be perfectly translated, free of errors. It must also contain all of these hidden books. We must not allow another year to pass on this planet in the darkness that has been created by the lies and deceits of the past."

"We should visit Lancelot Andrews," Marbury said nearly to himself. "He has the King's favor above all other scholars. He presides over the first group, and his men have been threatened. He is the ally we need."

"I do begin to think that Roger Andrews," Anne said softly, "despite his obvious inabilities, may be the man who is killing translators here."

"Could a man with so weak a stomach have carved Harrison's face?" Chaderton wondered.

"A man seized by a moment of rage and fear," Timon answered quietly, "is capable of a thousand things which he would never ordinarily consider."

"What must we do?" Anne demanded. "What else can be done to assure that this Bible tells, at last, the Truth of truths?"

"Speed the work," Chaderton suggested.

"Protect the men," Marbury added.

"And stop the killer," Timon concluded.

Timon kept other silent decisions to himself, locked in the darkest chambers of his heart.

Suddenly, in one of the hidden shadows at the far end of the hall, Timon saw a sickly blur.

The others saw Timon's face change. His muscles tensed and all mirth left his eyes. Something had alerted him.

"Someone is watching us," he whispered.

Chaderton's head shot back.

"Where?" Anne whispered. "Is it Andrews?"

Timon raised a finger to his lips.

"Let us not make a show," he cautioned urgently, his voice barely audible. "Dr. Chaderton, would you please lock the Gospel of Thomas back in your drawer? The intruder may want to destroy it."

Marbury's eyes shot in the direction of the cellar door. He saw something too.

Timon nodded once, acknowledging the likely position of the intruder.

A stark stillness filled the hall. Every shadow, every flicker of the candles, the very air, seemed frozen for a moment; all eyes strained for signs of movement. Anne's breathing was shallow, trying not to make a sound. Marbury's fingers twitched in the direction of his hidden dagger. Chaderton's wide-eyed gaze was a grotesque counterpoint to Timon's intense stare as he explored the darkest corners of the far wall.

Without warning the cellar door flashed open and clear footfalls could be heard on the stairs. Someone was plummeting into the lightless room below.

"We have frightened him away!" Chaderton called out.

Timon broke into a run. The blade in his hand seemed to come from nowhere. He careened around tables and chairs, flying toward the open cellar door.

Marbury set out behind him, reaching for his own knife, gasping deep breaths.

Timon hit the top step peering downward into darkness. He paused for a split second, willing his eyes to adjust to the lack of light below. A strange scraping sound at the far end of the cellar assured Timon that the wraith was not waiting for him at the bottom of the stairs. He plunged ahead, nearly blind, spilling down the steps.

His foot hit the solid stone floor as a slap of icy air stunned his face. More scraping and a low grunt told him where the intruder was. He lunged, but hit only stone wall.

Wood on stone betrayed the intruder's whereabouts again. Timon flailed, spitting out a sharp breath.

The intruder grunted, dodging Timon's blade, and the scraping sound intensified.

Timon fell forward in the direction of the noise, hoping to land his bulk against the man, careless of any weapon the intruder might have. His head cracked on the cold wall, his knee caught an edge of other stones. Around him there was only air.

Was the intruder a ghost? It was a maddening nightmare, fighting something unseen.

Timon's eyes were beginning to adjust to the complete absence of light, and he thought he could make out the bulk of the man beside the potato bin. He kicked high, hoping to catch the man's stomach. The man's breath exploded, but Timon's blow had not connected, and the shadowy image of the man was gone.

Where was he? The sound of his breathing seemed to come from everywhere. The movement in the cellar was some invisible force, not a man.

Abandoning all caution, Timon leapt again, throwing himself in the direction of the scraping sound. The potato bin stopped his forward motion; he cracked his right elbow hard against it.

Timon jumped back, waiting for an attack, trying not to breath, trying not to give away his position. He stood in utter silence, hoping that stillness might accomplish what frenzy had not.

His tired muscles twitched. He willed himself to close his eyes, to depend on other senses. There was no sound, no smell, and the taste of the air in the cellar was stale against Timon's tongue.

The killer is holding his breath too, Timon thought, waiting for me to make a move.

A sudden noise at the top of the stairs announced Marbury's arrival.

"Timon?"

Timon did not respond for fear of giving away his position.

"Bleeding hell," Marbury muttered.

He stepped on the second stair. It creaked.

In the cellar there was no sound. Timon's lungs pounded, his blood throbbed in his ears, he had no breath left.

"Timon!" Marbury called again.

Nothing.

"Well, then!" Marbury bellowed, and leapt forward. He landed close to Timon, lunging wildly in all directions with his blade.

Timon realized that Marbury might easily stab him mistakenly in the dark.

"Deacon," he exhaled, six inches from Marbury's ear.

"Uh!" Marbury exploded, startled.

Both men froze.

Timon knew they had given themselves away, but his eyes were slowly adjusting to the darkness.

"Can you see anything?" Marbury whispered.

"Shh!" Timon commanded. He took several steps sideways toward the table where Lively's body lay. With his free hand, he struck his flint and quickly lit a candle.

The flame flickered, revealing all.

Marbury was crouched low. His left hand was a fist; his right hand clutched a dagger.

Timon stood upright, knife held in his fingertips as a painter might hold a brush, ready to throw.

Lively lay still on his cold table.

No one else was in the room.

42

*I*n the gray light of the candle, it was all too obvious that the intruder was not in the cellar.

"How could he have gotten past us both?" Marbury whispered.

Marbury's breath was a white ghost of words. The cellar was deadly still. Lively's face was tinged with blue. The candle flame seemed frozen in the air.

Timon's eyes searched everywhere in the grim room. An answer to Marbury's question quickly presented itself.

"There." Timon pointed.

Marbury focused his gaze on the floor. A freshly made quarter-circle pattern disturbed the dust of the floor beneath the vegetable bin.

"That is the result of the scraping I heard," Timon continued. "This bin moves."

Both men moved to the stacked wooden shelves and tugged until it began to give way. Once opened, its hidden hinges were easy to find. Through the opening they could see a low hallway behind the bin.

Timon headed straight into it, heedless of the impenetrable darkness.

Marbury went to grab the candle at Lively's head as Timon's footsteps receded into the hollow stone cave. Clutching the candle in front of him, he followed the increasingly faint sounds down the tunnel.

The cellar had been cold; the tunnel was frozen hell. Marbury felt his joints freezing; his lungs burning. Still, he moved as quickly as he could, the candle sputtering in his left hand, his blade shivering in his right, until he came upon Timon standing at what appeared to be a dead end.

Timon was running his hand across the surface of a solid stone wall.

"Somewhere there is a release or a handle," Timon muttered.

"How did you run down this hallway without light?" Marbury asked, staring at Timon.

Marbury's breath filled the small space with white vapor, but Timon barely seemed to breathe at all.

"I spent a great deal of time in darkness when I was imprisoned," Timon answered tersely. "Instead of going blind, I acquired a kind of preternatural sight. The brightest sun burns my eyes, but they can see in the darkest recesses of night. Damn this wall!"

His sudden outburst startled Marbury.

"Our man has surely vanished now," Timon hissed. "But where?"

"Could this lead to some kitchen?" Marbury guessed. "A convenience for the cook—so that he might fetch things from the cellar without having to brave the elements?"

"When did a builder ever care about a cook's ease?" Timon shook his head. "And I am an imbecile for not wondering until now why there would be a root cellar in the Great Hall."

"Wait." Marbury massaged his forehead with his fingertips, as if encouraging some thought to free itself from the tangle of his memories. "The Great Hall is one of the oldest buildings of the university. It was—am I remembering this correctly?—a chapel or even a monastery at one time. Is that possible?"

"Some of these buildings are four hundred years old," Timon answered, staring back down the hidden hallway toward the cellar, "and many monasteries of that day had escape tunnels. Which, it would seem, is exactly what this is: our man has eluded me. Again."

"Are you certain it was the killer?"

"I suppose it could have been anyone." Timon leaned against the wall for a moment. "But who else would have run?"

"Well, we're no worse off than we were: we already knew there was a killer lurking nearby."

"Yes." Timon's head snapped back suddenly and he started back down the hall toward the cellar. "Anne and Chaderton are alone in the hall. We have lost our man here. I would like to make certain he has not returned to—"

"God!" Marbury exploded, breaking into a run, past Timon, back down the tunnel and into the cellar.

Timon caught up with Marbury and they raced together up the stairs, into the Great Hall.

Anne and Chaderton sat side by side, reading something on Chaderton's desk.

Anne stood, startled by their entrance, but her eyes were wide for another reason.

"Mary Magdalene wrote a gospel. I am reading it!" She could barely breathe.

"I have come to a certain conclusion with which I hope everyone will agree," Chaderton interrupted, addressing Marbury and Timon. "I believe that we should hide as many of the secret books as we can gather—and I believe that Anne should be their custodian."

"No!" Marbury exploded.

"Hear me," Chaderton continued, holding up a solid hand. "Andrews expressed an attitude toward her that I believe the other scholars all share to some extent. None of them can believe that a young woman could have any understanding of these matters. They will never consider that she might be hiding the texts."

"What you suggest," Marbury growled, arriving at Chaderton's desk, "places my daughter in the utmost jeopardy. I will not allow it."

"I am already in harm's way," Anne responded, iron in every syllable. "And I am sufficiently invisible to these scholars to ward off scrutiny. I believe that Dr. Chaderton's plan is perfect."

Anne's primary concern was obviously complete access to the volumes she so desperately wanted to devour.

"Deacon," Timon said quickly, "I agree that we must hide these secret books. Leaving them with Anne is a sound idea. It is a woman's advantage in an age of men that she is often invisible."

"No!" Marbury insisted. "If they are to be hidden, let me take them!"

"You do not have the time!" Timon shook his head. "Your suggestion that Lancelot Andrews must be consulted is also a sound one. He will surely have more influence with the King than anyone else. He may even have come to some of the same conclusions as we have."

"It *is* likely that Lancelot has come to some understanding of these matters himself," Chaderton suggested. "He is possessed of an exceptionally keen mind. I have conferred with him many times over the years. We remain eager colleagues."

"How can I leave for Westminster with my daughter's life in danger and the men here in Cambridge—," Marbury began

"I will remain here," Timon said, only then putting his dagger away. "Lancelot Andrews will speak to you alone more readily than he would if I were there. I will remain here, vigilant. I swear to you that no harm will come to Anne."

Clearly no one in the room doubted Timon's determination.

"Go to Westminster this moment?" Marbury asked, tapping his fingers on Chaderton's desk.

"The men will work in groups," Timon snapped, "and Anne will remain in her room. I assume there is a lock on her door."

"There is," Anne said, "though rarely used."

"Make good use of it now," Timon said firmly. "I envy the reading you have in store. What servants are your most trusted?"

"Say no more. I know best how to secure myself in my quarters."

"And I will be everywhere," Timon announced loudly, as if someone might be listening.

"But are we *certain* that the documents ought to stay with Anne?" Marbury insisted desperately, his voice lowered.

"I am not a child!" Anne rasped. "I can take care of myself."

"Dispense with coaches, Deacon," Timon said briskly, ignoring both Marbury's concern and Anne's ire. "You have no need of royal display at this point. Lancelot Andrews will see you, will he not?"

"Yes, but," Marbury said, then moved closer to Timon to whisper, "if there are more like Pietro Delasander after me—"

"I should have told you before," Timon answered softly. "When I searched Delasander's body, I discovered a document—a coded missive—that told me his true purpose."

"So you said." Marbury's brow furrowed.

"You were not his target. He was only following you back to Cambridge so that he could kill me. I have no idea why, but I know who sent him: the same men who told you to hire me; the same men who told me to work for you. The missive was in their code."

"God in heaven," Marbury swore. "We are swimming in madness."

Anne took in a breath, clearly on the verge of asking a hundred questions.

"Dr. Chaderton," Timon snapped in full voice once more, "you know Dr. Lancelot Andrews well, did you say?"

"Quite well," Chaderton answered, a bit confused.

"Well enough to know where he might be of a late afternoon?"

"Let me see," Chaderton said to himself, thinking as quickly as he could. "When I am in London, and we meet, we often walk in the College Garden before sunset. I believe he told me that it was his custom every evening before prayers and dinner. Why do you ask?"

"Time is of the essence. Deacon Marbury may not wish to waste it searching Westminster for the man. The College Garden is as good a place as any to start."

"I know that garden," Marbury affirmed.

"If you ride at top speed and exhaust the first horse," Timon said, his words racing, "you can exchange mounts at the halfway point. You could arrive at Westminster by late afternoon, would you say?"

Marbury hesitated for only an instant, but it was too long for Timon.

"You *must* speak with Lancelot Andrews." Timon insisted. "We must have him as an ally in the cause of saving our religion!"

"He may also offer some information," Chaderton added, "in the matter of his brother, Roger, the man who may well be the killer."

"Make haste, Deacon," Timon encouraged. "The sooner you finish your work at Westminster, the sooner you can return and help me catch a killer."

43

*T*wenty minutes later Marbury threw his leg over a worn brown saddle, wondering how he had gotten there, when only moments before, it seemed, he had been asleep in his bed—in his clothes.

Another trip to London, he thought exhaustedly, and this time to another group of translators, as if my bunch were not trouble enough. How have I offended God?

Marbury sighed, urged his horse forward, out of the courtyard and into an open green field. The air was filled with red birds. The sky through the trees was a stained-glass window, blue and hard. Cowslips were blooming, nodding in the morning breeze.

Gathering his strength from the sight, Marbury leaned down and whispered something to his horse. The horse shot forward. The wind against his face was cool but soft, its scent now and again sweetened by early-spring pleasures: narcissus and daphne, the loam of leaf mold, a riot of birdsong, the early green on every tree.

He was glad to be on horseback because it allowed him to take a route no coach could travel, through thick woods and over rolling hills. The trip would be quicker than before thanks to the less traveled roads, and Westminster was closer than Hampton Court.

But the best reason to take this particular way, Marbury thought to himself, is that it avoids the woods where those boys live. Best not to be distracted, more important work was at hand. There will be another time, another day, to think about them.

He occupied himself, instead, with the ten feet of road in front of him, then ten more, the trees and fields flying by. The sound of his horse's breathing was everything.

By four o'clock that afternoon the road turned west before Shoreditch. Marbury stayed north of Red Bull and Gray's Inn so as to skirt the worst of the city's afternoon chaos and avoid a Thames crossing. He finally turned south to head through Charing Cross and onto King Street.

Before too long he made out the towers of Westminster, not far away in the haze. Marbury had come to the outskirts of London and slowed his horse to a walk. Only then did he allow his fears for Anne, and the translators, to distract him. They mixed with his apprehension of the coming conversation with Lancelot Andrews. Those twin concerns bled into one another. He found he was more fretful than he had been in a decade.

On the larger open grassy spaces, here and there, sheep grazed and almost gave the illusion of bucolic peace, but in the distance Marbury could hear, piercing the blue fabric of the air, city voices screeching: "Mussels lily-white? Herrings, sprats, or cockles? And Wallfleet oysters!" They were throats rattling, in want of grease. "Old shoes for new brooms!" They were distant sparks of the hot coal of London, searing the sky and smearing the wind. "Boy, works cheap! Has no tongue!"

Marbury began to imagine the faces from which those distant sounds emerged, marveling at how far the voices carried in the spring air. After a moment he began to wonder if he was imagining them, not really hearing them at all.

HALF AN HOUR LATER, Marbury was seated on the stone bench beside the infirmary beds at the College Garden of Westminster. The open expanse between the grand buildings was abundant with grass, already tall, soon to be made hay feed. Its green was matched by the sky's cloudless blue. Soft winds had polished the air, rid it of all clouds. Everything in that great open yard was clear. At the far end stood aged buildings of the college whose walls seemed to glow with a sort of golden vapor, a kind of complicity with the more ancient past discussed and argued within them.

Lancelot Andrews appeared in short order for his daily constitutional. If he was surprised to see Marbury, he did not show it. He moved deliberately, his great blue coat and robe trailing behind him. His white beard grew to a perfectly groomed point.

Marbury stood. "Dr. Andrews," he began quickly, "we met at the Hampton Court Conference, though you would surely not remember me. I am Deacon Marbury from Cambridge."

"I will not say that I have been expecting you," Andrews called, his voice a low, solid bell. "But I am not surprised to see you, Deacon Marbury. I would not have recognized you. You have changed since I saw you at Hampton. But your reputation is greatly to be admired."

"Your Grace," Marbury said with only the faintest hint of irony.

"I assume," Dr. Andrews said, coming to take Marbury's hand, "that you are here to tell me what strange things have been happening with Mr. Lively's group of translators in Cambridge."

"Mr. Lively is dead," Marbury said instantly. "As is Mr. Harrison. There is a monster loose in Cambridge. But that fact means *nothing,* you must believe me, compared to the primary reason for my visit."

"I know." Dr. Andrews did his best to make his face a stern mask where nothing could be read.

"You know of the murders?" Marbury asked. "Then the King told you about my visit."

"He did, though I confess I did not know of Lively's lamentable death."

"The entire translation is in danger." Marbury's words burst from him like a pistol shot. "The work of generations is at stake. I have been convinced that this is, indeed, of greater import than any man's life. The very nature of our religion may be in grave danger."

Dr. Andrews sat down on the bench.

"Someone is killing the translators to stop their work," Marbury said, still standing. "It is only a matter of time before the same thing happens to the group here at Westminster and to the Oxford men as well. I came to tell you this news—and more."

"In the hope that I will speak with His Majesty." Dr. Andrews scowled. "But he already knows about—"

"We hope that you will convince him to produce a complete Bible—a *true* Bible."

Dr. Andrews looked up from his place on the bench. "I do not take your meaning when you say 'a true Bible.'"

"The men in Cambridge have discovered so many things," Marbury whispered, eyes darting. "Surely your lot here have done so as well."

"Discovered?" Dr. Andrews folded his hands in his lap.

"Thousands of errors in translation dating back to the time of Christ," Marbury said impatiently. "There are dozens, perhaps hundreds, of gospels and genuine ancient texts which have been expurgated from the various Bibles over time. Yes, we must prevent the translators from being murdered, but we must also see to it that the true Bible—"

"I see." Dr. Andrews stood abruptly. "We must work quickly."

Marbury exhaled. "Then you see the import of this, Dr. Andrews. I am relieved. Dr. Chaderton speaks so highly of you, I should have known your decisions would be swift."

"Of course." Andrews seemed deep in thought. "First, to the murders. How may I help?"

"I must be bold to ask you several questions," Marbury stammered, "concerning your brother Roger."

"What?" Dr. Andrews's hands dropped to his side; his face slacked.

"This is a part of the investigation," Marbury rushed to invent. "We fear that he may be the next victim."

"I see. Well, Roger is my younger brother. Have you siblings?" Marbury shook his head.

"They are a blessing and a curse," Dr. Andrews said, smiling. "When he was younger, Roger used to copy everything I did—to the point of distraction. He would dress the same, walk the same—and when I was talking to my school fellows, he would often repeat what I said, verbatim, under his breath until the other boys shrieked and drove him away. If I had been more aware of the nature and the intensity of his adulation, I might have been kinder, but brothers argue—even wrestle—and there is nothing to be done."

"You have made amends as an adult, surely," Marbury said, looking away. "You saw to it that your brother was taken on as a translator."

"He resents my success." Andrews sighed. "He laments my high position; my nearness to the King."

"Indeed it has been said that you are to James what Burley was to Elizabeth." Marbury looked down at the tall grass that enveloped his boots.

"But enough of my troubles. You have questions about Roger."

"You may have just answered them," Marbury mumbled.

"Curious." Andrews looked Marbury up and down. "Then perhaps you will tell me about your plans to insure—how did you phrase it?—this *complete* Bible."

"It must include all points, all of the rediscovered books," Marbury answered instantly, "the ancient texts, if they are true and verified by all the translators. All errors, no matter how small, must be corrected."

"To what end?" Andrews folded his arms. "You do not agree, in general, with the Bishops' Bible?"

"This goes well beyond disagreement with—"

"What is the point?" Andrews interrupted, demanding a direct response.

"Well," Marbury answered uncomfortably, "we have discussed the nature of Christ's body. The insistence that he was primarily *flesh,* and that his flesh rose from the grave, is a concept that enabled so many of the other decisions made by the early Church."

"But this is the foundational belief of Christianity," Dr. Andrews roared, startling Marbury. "If we do not believe that Christ rose from the dead as flesh and blood, then we cannot partake of the miracle of the Eucharist! The clear words of the Bible are that 'the Word was made flesh.' The flesh and the Word may not be sundered. We celebrate both; honor both by taking His flesh so that He may replenish us with His grace and truth."

"I do know—I have heard your sermons on the value of the Eucharist," Marbury stammered, trying to gather his thoughts in the face of Dr. Andrews's power.

"Christ's flesh is the cornerstone of our religion!" Dr. Andrews turned his overwhelming gaze upon Marbury.

"Your friend Dr. Chaderton," Marbury answered, "made bold to suggest that an insistence on the reanimation of dead flesh, and the cannibalistic ritual of eating that flesh, was the province of demons rather than of our Lord."

"No!" Dr. Andrews growled. "Dr. Chaderton never said such a monstrous thing."

"He did, in fact."

"God in heaven." Dr. Andrews ground his fingertips into his temples. "Too much to take in. My mind is at sea. I do comprehend the grave import of your concerns. I must find myself. Please, be seated. I must collect what men we have here and—and we all shall meet. You must dine with us—yes—and we shall work out what can be done. Wait here. I shall send for you shortly."

Without another word, Dr. Andrews turned, his blue robes rising in a flurry, and sped away toward the nearest building.

What to make of that? Marbury observed to himself, watching Dr. Andrews disappear through a black door.

Even when he saw the armed guard, only moments later, he did not realize what was happening—until it was too late.

44

Cambridge, That Night

*T*imon stood frozen outside Anne's door. He had been standing there for ten minutes unable to knock. Finally he called out, "Anne! I have forgotten a name."

A silent pause hung in the air for a moment, then her voice answered, "Brother Timon?"

"Will you come to the door?" The panic in his voice was obvious.

There was a clatter of bolts, the click of another lock, and the door inched inward only slightly. Anne peered out. "Forgot whose name?"

"The stable master!"

"Lankin?"

"God!" Timon rolled his head and took an unconscious step sideways. "Lankin!"

"You seem upset." Anne opened her door a few inches more, puzzled.

"I could not remember his name." Timon's face was drained of blood. "You have no idea what this means."

"That you could not recall—?"

"My memory is my life!" Timon snapped.

Anne read genuine terror in Timon's eyes, though she could not understand it.

Timon began mumbling to himself, pacing back and forth in front of her door.

After a moment Anne felt she must ask, "Is that Greek you are whispering?"

"I am reciting a certain passage from Erasmus."

"Why?"

Timon looked into Anne's eyes. "Something is happening to me." His words shook like new leaves in the wind. "I am not myself."

Anne's lips thinned. "You have not slept."

"I have not."

"The mind often betrays itself when it wants rest," she chided. "And when did you last eat?"

"Did I have a breakfast this morning?" Timon answered, still dazed.

He stared at the floor. He swallowed, licked his lips, eyes darting furtively all about him.

"Then perhaps a bite of food," Anne suggested.

"I am not myself because I feel my life may have changed its course. Abruptly. Rather abruptly."

Anne's face was a stern as any nun's. "I have no idea how your habit of smoking nutmeg in that pipe might disturb your brain, but I do know that when my father has had a bit too much brandy-wine in the evening, he is in a mist the next morning."

"Yes," Timon began, but stopped himself. He was loathe to admit that he had taken a pipe instead of dinner. It had not helped his fever. How to explain what was burning in his mind? What to reveal and what to keep secret?

"Did you come to my room so late at night just to ask me the name of the stable master?" Anne's hand on the door tensed without her realizing it.

Timon clutched the hilt of his knife and breathed slowly, silently, stilling his heart, readying his hand.

Anne did not move. "I watched the way you dealt with two dead bodies. Perhaps you are unsettled by death."

"I have seen death many times. I was impressed with your ability to take charge of moving the boy's body. You seemed—"

"I have tended men who died," Anne said simply.

"And I have killed men," Timon said before he thought. He did not recognize his own voice.

"You have fought in battle," Anne assumed.

"No. I have killed men as a part of holy work—or work which, at one time, I thought of as holy."

Anne's breathing became more shallow. Her eyes longed to blink, but she thought, somehow, she should not. "A man who thinks that murder is holy is lost to darkness."

"Yes" was all Timon could manage.

"Are you the man who is killing these scholars here in Cambridge?" Anne leaned her weight forward, scarcely believing that she had asked such a question.

"I am not," Timon assured her unsteadily. "I am the man who will stop those murders."

"Why?" It was a simple question.

"I *am* puzzled by that," Timon admitted, slowly regaining his composure. "So many great comets collide in my brain, such disparate elements as to drive a man mad: a kindly old servant's heart, a faithful dog, a disappointed barmaid, the loathsome nature of a certain trio of men, the many strange things revealed by the work of your scholars—the entire depth of—the history and scope—we must not allow the truth to be hidden any longer—because—" Timon found, to his great surprise, that he could not continue. His hands were shaking and his eyes stung.

Anne stared.

"I feel the very atoms of my flesh transposing," Timon whispered, staring at his fingers. "I last felt this way on the day of my death."

Anne swallowed. "There's a sentence that needs an explanation," she said tentatively.

"Well, then plainly: I was sentenced to die by the Inquisition." Timon still watched the creases and folds in the palms of his hands. "On the morning of my execution, Pope Clement came to me. He knew everything about my life, and he was aware of my powers of memory. He instructed me to perform his work, which I have done for five years. Now—for reasons that are battling in my brain and which I barely comprehend—I am turning away from his instruction in favor of . . . you told me that I seemed to be a man newly released from prison. You may have been correct. It is possible that I am somehow released from my vows to the Catholic Church—to do other work."

Anne could see that Timon was struggling to find the perfect words. "In his time a man plays many parts on the stage of this world."

"How odd." Timon smiled. "Only this morning I was considering how like a play my life seems."

"You need sleep and food," Anne insisted, distinguishing each word from every other. "Your eyes are wild, your hands are shaking, and you are developing very strange ideas."

"Very strange," Timon agreed, nodding.

Anne only took a second to decide her course of action. "Then let me take you to the kitchen," she said firmly, "and fix you some supper."

45

Westminster, That Night

Marbury watched in disbelief as the iron bars of his prison door slammed shut and the armed guard marched away.

The cell was large enough for ten prisoners. It was well lit by torches in the hallway. There was gray stone in six directions, but there were also several elevated pallets with blankets, and a high, thin window through which one might at least imagine the setting sun.

I was a fool, Marbury thought to himself. An absolute imbecile. How could I ever have believed that King James's favorite adviser would—what was I thinking? And now here I am in a prison cell while my daughter is left defenseless against a madman.

He went to the cell door and took hold of the bar closest to the lock. He shook the door, felt the lock with the tip of his finger, his cheek pressed against the cold iron of several other bars, and stuck out his lips. He closed his eyes, realizing how easy it would be to pick the lock. A few clumsy clicks with his knife, and he could be free.

A sudden voice in the darkness of the hall startled him.

"Shall we take an early dinner together?"

Dr. Andrews appeared out of the darkness, his right hand on the cell door. "I do beg your pardon for detaining you in this unhospitable manner," he continued, slipping a key into the lock.

The door swung open.

Marbury stared suspiciously.

I have no idea why he locked me up, Marbury thought, and I have no idea why he would let me go. This is some sort of trick.

He absently checked his hidden blade.

Dr. Andrews seemed not to notice, turned, and led the way down a long hall to a great, empty dining room. It was a third the size of the Great Hall in Cambridge and dotted with candles swirling small circles of light around the dining table. Only two places were set; plates and bowls and tankards were all empty.

The long plank table was made finer by an embroidered golden runner down its middle. The floor of the place was inlaid with a single symbol too huge to take in, obscured by the darkness. The black rafters thirty feet overhead were thick and crossed, holding up their ceiling lost in shadow.

Dr. Andrews walked a few feet ahead of Marbury, silent as the grave.

Marbury did his best to form several perfect questions in his mind before he gave them voice. Where were the rest of the translators? Why had he been put in jail? Why had he been released? Was he in danger?

The last question was answered when Marbury was able to make out, barely, the outlines of hidden guardsmen at each door.

Dr. Andrews sat at his place, at the head of the table, and indicated that Marbury should take the place on the right-hand side of his host, which he did. Andrews seemed to be waiting for Marbury to speak. Marbury was determined to remain silent. The first man to break such a silence would be the man to lose the advantage of it.

Both men sat in absolute stillness, then, for long minutes. No food came. No one seemed to breathe. The men guarding the doors could have been made of granite for all their movement.

Suddenly Dr. Andrews pounded the table with his fist, sending plates aloft and toppling tankards.

"Who are you?" he bellowed. "Tell me this instant! You are *not* Deacon Marbury!"

Marbury was only at a loss for an instant. When he recovered, he settled back into his chair and smiled. He determined to let Andrews go on.

"To call yourself Marbury," Dr. Andrews snarled. "I *knew* you did not remotely resemble the man. I only saw him once, but his bearing and grace were enviable—unlike your slouch and sneer."

"Who am I, then?" Marbury asked, feeling for the knife hidden in his sleeve.

"Guards!" Andrews called out.

Instantly twenty men surrounded the table, blades unsheathed.

"You," Andrews announced triumphantly, "are the well-known assassin Pietro Delasander!"

Marbury could not stifle his momentary grin.

Andrews continued, quite satisfied with himself. "And now you will tell me the true meaning of your visit to Westminster, though I think I know it."

Marbury sat silently, slowly realizing that he would not be reported to the King. The man whom Andrews would report as a visitor to Westminster—the assassin Delasander—was, in reality, already dead. All that was left for Marbury now was escape. And for that, all that was necessary was to return to the flimsy cell, wait until everyone had gone to bed, pick the lock, and ride home.

Marbury's stomach growled—a good sign, he thought. Fear had been replaced by hunger.

"Speak!" Andrews demanded, his head snapping in Marbury's direction.

"Pietro Delasander is, as you know, the greatest assassin in Europe. If I were he, I would be forced to kill you. That was not his goal here, but it may be a necessity."

"Kill me?" Andrews laughed. "My guard may have something to say about that."

Several of the men in the guard laughed too. Marbury noted them for future reference—laughter betrayed overconfidence in such situations. One man stepped closer to Marbury, his rapier poised to strike. He was obviously the captain of the guard.

"And pray," Andrews went on, "what was your original goal here?"

"As you know, there are odd rumors abroad," Marbury explained calmly, "concerning the work of all the translators for our King's Bible. I am working for the King. We are to discover if there is treason afoot here in Westminster by positing such treason to you as a fact of the Cambridge group. If you had agreed with our rebellious suggestions and offered to help, we would have— reported it."

"Do not mince words," Andrews objected. "You were to execute anyone who evidenced betrayal in this regard. Why else would the King set an assassin upon the task? And the King's great awareness of how the supernatural is at work to subvert his plans would only lend more reason for such executions."

"I could not say," Marbury drawled, looking away.

"Come, come, sir." Andrews shook his head. "You have already done as much in Cambridge. Are there not two men dead in that place?"

"One hears strange stories," Marbury agreed.

"Clever," Dr. Andrews muttered to himself. "King James is clever."

"Is he?" Marbury shrugged.

"I understand," Andrews said at once. "You are not at liberty to say."

"And now I wonder," Marbury said delicately, "if there will ever be anything on these supper plates. I am ravenous."

Andrews stared at the plates, trying to make up his mind.

"No," he said at last, "I think not. To be on the safe side, you understand, I must insist that you return to a temporary imprisonment until I seek council with the King. I must affirm the veracity of your claims. Captain, please take this man to the lower level now."

"You are returning me to cell?" Marbury asked before he could think. "Without dinner?"

"Not exactly, Master Delasander," Andrews answered, standing. "The room wherein you were detained briefly is not as secure as the lower levels, but have no care. You shall be well looked after while you are there—only several days, I should imagine." Andrews turned to the captain. "And see to it that he is given the dinner—the complete meal—that we were about to receive at this table."

"Of course," the captain answered instantly.

This will never do, Marbury thought, his blood rising. I must not be placed in a secure cell for several days. He grasped the handle of his knife.

"Well then." Andrews stood, patting his chest once. "I go to compose a brief query to a king."

Without warning Marbury sprang from his chair in a blur. He landed behind Andrews, dagger pointed upward under Andrews's chin. With his other arm he had pinned both of Andrews's arms from behind.

In the next second, the point of the captain's rapier was half an inch from Marbury's right eye.

The tableau held for a single breath before Marbury pricked a bit of blood from the throat of his captive. The captain did not move.

"Both of us will be dead," Marbury whispered into Andrews's ear, "if your captain does not lower his rapier now."

Andrews nodded. "He will. But you will never leave this room."

The captain took a step backward, lowering his blade slightly, but a chaos of other cutting edges and points surrounded Marbury.

Suddenly Marbury shoved Andrews forward, grabbed a leaden plate from the table, and tossed it directly at the captain's head. Other guards lunged, but Marbury leapt onto the table and fended them off, kicking. In their confusion, Marbury pounced upon the hapless captain, who thudded to the floor, hand over eye. Marbury jumped on top of him, grabbing his rapier, and was on his feet instantly, rapier in his right hand and his dagger in the left. He began turning slow circles and breathing hard. Most of the guard surrounded him.

"You know that Delasander is someone who could kill your men," Marbury announced loudly. "All of them. You know his reputation. You will die, Dr. Andrews, unless you call off your guards *now*."

Each word seemed so filled with truth that Andrews held up his hands immediately. "Stop!" he commanded. "Put down your arms, all of you. Stop!"

The confused guard turned to Andrews, saw the way of things, but hesitated to lower weapons.

"Captain!" Andrews shrieked. "This is the world's greatest assassin. He is not human!"

From the floor the captain groaned, "Down."

Marbury backed carefully toward that door.

"Pause a moment," Dr. Andrews said, a desperation edging his words. "If you are bound for Cambridge—if you have a mind to—please—I love my brother Roger, but I know he is jealous of my achievements. Such jealousy has caused him to do foolish things in the past. I beg of you, do not kill him. Arrest him if you must; hold him. I will see to his confinement; I will consult with the King to assure it. Please."

"I will do what I can." Marbury nodded.

"Thank you," Andrews said, though it obviously hurt his throat to utter the words.

Marbury found the cold, black door handle at his back, grabbed it, and gave it a tug. Sometimes a clever captain would lock a room behind him to trap his prey. As luck would have it, the guard at Westminster, though numerous, were not so thoughtful. The door pulled free.

Within a heartbeat Marbury was outside under the stars. He used the rapier to secure the door, wedging it into the wood so tightly that it would hold for at least a few minutes. The sun had abandoned Westminster.

As he ran for the stables, Marbury realized why Lancelot Andrews had begged for his brother. It was obvious. Roger Andrews was murdering the translators.

46

Cambridge, That Night

*T*he kitchen in the Deaconage filled with delectable smells as Anne poured red wine over the cooking onions. She had taken down several wooden platters and sat Timon down in front of them. One had held nearly an entire loaf of manchet, but it was gone.

"You are adding rosemary and sage?" he asked dreamily.

"I am." She nodded pertly. "Not many men I know can identify those herbs with one sniff."

Good, she thought, the rosemary has covered the scent of the other herbs I added.

She clutched her hand around the vial she had brought from her room.

"I have not always been as you see me now." Timon sighed. "I once operated a dispensary for a local hospital and, of course, directed the planting and cultivation of all the various herbs needed for the infirmary—fennel and hyssop were my favorites."

"Those herbs grow in our garden as well."

"And you have a kitchen garden, one supposes," Timon said, smiling. "Leeks, broad beans, a radish or two."

"Yes."

"Some people cannot imagine what bliss there is to be found in pulling a radish you have planted yourself," Timon said, his lips barely moving, "after you have lived a life of blood and bile."

Only then did Anne consider the full import of the words *I have not always been as you see me now.*

"Timon is a name that you have taken," Anne said, not turning to look at him. "It is not your given name."

"The Greek word *timos* means 'value,'" he explained distractedly. "Whereas the noun *timoria* means both 'assistance' and 'vengeance.' It is a name that finds value in both assistance and vengeance."

"No," Anne said quickly. "There is a story of another Timon, a man who knows no middle path. He is given to extremes, first loving all humankind and then hating everyone that lives. Perhaps you know it. He ends by taking his own life." Anne stirred white beans into the cooking pot.

"You are trying to understand the connection between that story and the man who is seated here in this kitchen. What you do not understand is that the men who gave me this name have only a fraction of your intelligence—and twice your sense of theatre."

"What I do not understand is why any man, monk or misanthrope, would confess to a young woman that he has killed many men."

"I am not myself," Timon groaned.

Anne glanced his way for an instant. He was not looking at her. She took that moment to add the rest of the black powder from her vial to the cooking pot. Stirring the pot slowly, she held her breath as it dissolved.

"Well," she said briskly, taking a step back, "you may begin with these beans. They will go well with your bread."

"My bread is gone," Timon lamented, staring down at his empty plate.

"I see." Anne did her best to keep her voice calm. "Help your-self to the white beans. I shall fetch more bread."

Timon stood without a word, picked up a plate, and lumbered over to the stove. Anne watched him carefully. She turned and moved deliberately to the pantry.

Timon sat and began at once to devour the beans with a large wooden spoon.

"These are wonderful," he managed to say with his mouth full. "It must be the rosemary."

Anne found another full loaf of bread. She walked slowly to-ward the table, saw that most of Timon's plate was already gone.

He looked up at her. She took in a quick breath and held out the bread. "Here."

He nodded and went back to his plate, finishing the rest in sev-eral huge bites.

"I was hungry," he said, breathing heavily.

"So it would seem." She took an imperceptible step backward.

"Anne, you are, without question, the most intelligent woman your age I have ever met, the best cook, and I have the intuition that you may have been instructed in matters of personal defense."

"What?"

"A man who uses a knife as your father does is apt to demon-strate his abilities to a child. You are the sort of person who would be keen to learn such skills. In short, you have a knife, and you know its proper use."

Anne's shoulders sank. "There is a difference between knowing how to use a knife and sticking its blade into a man's belly."

"Very true." Timon's eyelids were heavy.

"Your lack of sleep," Anne said soothingly, "seems to be catch-ing up with you."

"Indeed." Timon could barely hold his head up.

"I would not be surprised if you fell right to sleep," Anne said softly.

"No," Timon objected weakly. "I must not sleep until—"

He laid his head on the table and began to snore almost at once.

Anne slowly backed out of the room. When she was out in the hallway, she began to run on tiptoe toward the Great Hall. She had seen its lit windows from her room when Timon had disturbed her. She was certain someone must be working there.

She burst from the Deaconage, running faster. The night was black, but Anne raced along the path. She glanced back twice to make certain Timon was not following her.

She reached the doors to the hall and threw them open, panting.

Across the room she could see Roger Andrews, head bowed, pen poised, deep in thought. She hesitated. She could not go to him. He would certainly order her from the building.

A quick look around and she saw Dr. Chaderton sitting in the shadows. Was he asleep?

She edged her way toward him.

"Anne," he whispered. "Be quiet and come here."

She slid along the wooden floor until she stood beside him. He was seated on a bench against a darkened wall.

"I am observing Andrews. I am determined to discover if he is, in fact, the murderer, as our Brother Timon has suggested."

"But that is why I am here," she blurted out. "I have subdued Brother Timon in the kitchen of the Deaconage."

"What?" Chaderton's voice was louder than it should have been.

"He came to my room," she whispered, "acting so strangely, and telling me things that so discomforted me that I did not know what to do."

"So you—what did you do?" Chaderton sat forward, as if he might stand.

"I gave him a dose of sleeping herbs. My father gives me a vial of the concoction whenever he thinks I have been too excited and will not be able to sleep. It works instantly."

"And you gave the medicine to Timon?"

"Ten times the dosage I take."

"Why?"

She thought to herself, because he may well be the murderer.

But she said, "There is something the matter with him. He is driven to distraction. I do not trust him. He told me such things about his life!"

"Perhaps we should go outside," Chaderton said, steadying himself against the bench and making ready to stand.

"Or perhaps you would come with me to the kitchen."

Before any further discussion could ensue, Chaderton's finger touched his lips. He inclined his head in the direction of the cellar steps.

Momentarily baffled, Anne peered into the darkness and was startled to see one of the shadows moving into the hall.

She drew in a breath to speak, but Chaderton pulled her down to the darkness of the bench beside him, out of the ambient light.

Andrews did not appear to have noticed anything unusual.

Chaderton put his lips close to Anne's ear. "Someone has come to meet with Andrews."

"No," Anne whispered, craning her neck to see. "This is just what happened last night when—"

Anne froze. Candlelight caught the sudden image of a knife, a long, thin horror, a meat-slicing device. Gripping that blade was a hooded figure, a monk, a shadow. He inched toward Andrews.

Anne tried to shout a warning, but no sound could be forced from her lungs, a nightmare of silence. She stood but Chaderton grabbed her arm.

The hooded figure leapt over several desks; gravity did not seem to apply to his body. He came crashing down onto Andrews. Andrews shrieked. Both men toppled to the floor out of sight.

A great fit of grunting, strangled cursing, bumping, and scraping ended when a pale white hand flashed into the candlelight and Andrews began to pray. His syllables, loud and ragged, were absent sense, utterly filled with terror.

Anne lurched forward, trying to break free of Chaderton's grip. She could see the hooded arm raised high, the blade catching the candle's flame, then plummet with a sickening thud into the praying man's back.

At last Anne screamed. Chaderton let go of her and called out.

The killer's head shot upward, peering in the direction of the voices. Anne and Chaderton began to shout at the top of their lungs. The killer seemed startled by the intensity of the noise. Through the windows they could see tapers flicker into existence in the windows of other buildings. Other voices, not far off, called out alarms.

The killer froze, staring directly at Anne. She returned his gaze, but her knees began to tremble. A sudden racket of voices arose directly outside the Great Hall, men running, shouting.

The killer seemed to waver, uncertain what to do. Anne felt certain he was on the verge of attacking her, then Chaderton finally managed to stand.

"Stay where you are!" he called commandingly.

The voices outside were nearly at the door.

The killer blew out his breath, turned, and flew back into the shadows toward the cellar door. It slammed closed.

Anne only took an instant to fully realize that the killer was gone before she raced toward Andrews. He lay bleeding on the floor. Behind her she could hear that other men had come in the door.

She only glanced once at the closed cellar door as she came to Andrews, knelt beside him. His eyes were closed; his mouth was open. The wound at his chest continued to spill blood.

Anne gathered him up, determining how best to stop the bleeding. She felt the thick vein at his neck for a pulse. There was none. No breath escaped his lungs. Already his face was paler than it had been. Anne bit her upper lip, determined not to let the events overtake her, but it was clear that her ministrations would be in vain. She looked down at the face and whispered a short prayer for the soul of the man in her arms.

Roger Andrews was dead.

47

*I*t was not yet midnight when Marbury saw his stables by moonlight. Returning from London he had torn open the road before him. With every breath, with every beat of his heart, with every quarter of a mile, his head had filled with evil visions. His torture was born of terror more than of exhaustion. He had done his best to hold it inside as he rode, but at the sight of light blazing from every window of the Great Hall, his last defenses were gone. He allowed himself to give full rein to his fears. Something had happened. No one should be there so late, with all the candles lit.

Marbury barely entered the courtyard before he dismounted from his still-moving horse, shouting for Lankin. Without waiting for a response he raced toward the hall. He scrambled like a madman across the loose stones. He could hear the buzz of voices. Something *had* happened.

Moments later he burst into the hall. The room was lit brighter than day. Marbury had never seen so many candles in the hall. He was greeted by such conflicting sights that his emotions nearly collapsed upon each other.

First he saw Anne and seemed to know her face for the first time. He had seen Raphael's Madonna and Botticelli's Venus, but even they could not remotely capture the miracle, the perfect simplicity, the utter holiness, of his daughter's face.

Anne was all right.

Next, the sight of the rest of the group standing around Roger Andrews's desk confirmed his worst fears. Andrews was the killer.

"Anne!" Marbury called out.

She whirled around. "Father!" she answered, running toward him.

They met and embraced, sharing a look reserved solely for fathers and daughters.

Others turned to see Marbury coming their way.

Then, Marbury saw that Timon stood over the body of Roger Andrews as it lay, quite motionlessly, on the floor. Timon's face was grim.

"What has happened here?" Marbury stammered.

"Roger Andrews has been stabbed three times," Timon said, his voice so clipped that it hurt the very air around him. "The blade was held flat so as to slip in between ribs. The forty-five-degree angle of the wounds was designed to wreck the operation of the heart; to do so very quickly. Blood has flooded from the wounds. This is my fault."

Marbury stared at Timon. Everyone did.

"I," Timon stammered, "I could have prevented this. I should have stood better guard."

"Please, gentlemen," Chaderton announced, "I think that events now make it clear that neither Brother Timon nor Mr. Andrews is the killer. I think it best to leave this place and let Brother Timon do his work."

Anne shot a grateful look in Chaderton's direction. Marbury took note and determined to ask her about it later.

The sleepy men, all in nightclothes, nodded and scratched, agreeing with Chaderton. Even Spaulding was too dispirited or tired for speeches.

Chaderton lingered.

As the rest shuffled toward the door, Anne stood close to her father and said in a low, urgent voice, "There was nothing Brother Timon could have done." Her eyes blazed into her father's. "He was asleep in the kitchen when the murder happened. Dr. Chaderton and I were here in the room and we could not prevent it."

"What?" Marbury drew back.

"I saw lights in the hall," Anne said quickly.

"And I was present, spying on Andrews," Chaderton added with equal speed.

"The killer came from the cellar," Anne interrupted.

"And did not see us."

"He was upon Andrews before we knew what was happening." Anne's voice had gotten higher.

"How could I have been so stupid?" Timon shouted, clasping his forehead in the palm of his hand as if he were attempting to steady his brain. "Why did I not secure the bins down in the cellar—the secret door that leads to the underground passageway? We should have nailed it shut. Damnation!"

"There are a hundred ways into this hall." Anne shook her head. "If the killer wanted to be here for his work and had found his secret door blocked, he could easily have gained access otherwise."

Marbury wondered at his daughter's concern for Timon's guilt. At a loss for words, Marbury stared down at Andrews.

The face was contorted in anger. The eyes were still open. The pale blue doublet was brown-stained. Andrews had a pen clutched in his hand.

"When?" was all that Marbury could muster.

"Scarcely an hour ago," Anne rushed to answer. "I had fixed Brother Timon a bit of supper, and he had succumbed to his exhaustion in our kitchen. That's when I noticed the lights in the hall. I came to see who was here. Chaderton and I saw it all. We called out. The men came running."

"And I *slept* all the while," Timon moaned, self-loathing obvious in every syllable. "Anne had to wake me, to fetch me."

"I—you were asleep while my daughter witnessed *the murder?*" Marbury's exhaustion mixed with a growing anger. "This is exactly what I feared when I left—"

"You have returned from your trip with great haste," Chaderton interrupted Marbury in a low voice. "Did Lancelot Andrews—?"

"We cannot count on Lancelot Andrews for aid in our task," Marbury whispered. "More anon."

Timon stood from Andrews's body and moved to his desk. "What was so important to Roger Andrews," he wondered aloud, clearly irritated, "that he would risk coming here late at night after so many warnings?"

Despite himself, Marbury peered at the desk as Timon held the candle close to several pages. They appeared to be new notes on a mostly blank page. Those notes ended in a long, thick downward scratch of ink, as if the pen had suddenly been torn across the surface of the paper—or the page had begun to bleed.

"'The Devil is permitted to put himself in the likeness of the Saints.'" Timon sighed. "'It is plain in the Scriptures where it is said that Satan can transform himself into an Angel of light.'"

"I know those lines," Marbury said slowly. "They do not come from any book of the Bible. They are words from King James himself, from his book called *Demonology.*"

Timon nodded. "Here is the passage upon which Andrews was working when the killer attacked: 'None can study and put into practice the circles and art of Magic without committing a horrible defection from God.'"

"What can this mean?" Marbury marveled. "Was Andrews attempting to include those lines in some passage of the Bible?"

"And was the killer intent on stealing this page," Timon countered, "or was it mere coincidence that this passage was the last Roger Andrews would ever write? The killer was startled in his business. He had no time for facial disfigurement or to place a note in the victim's mouth. That part, at least, was foiled by your daughter and Chaderton—which is regrettable—"

"There are a thousand reasons to lament Anne's presence at this event," Marbury muttered. "But allow me to say that I am in no condition to explore this matter at the moment. Nor are you, Brother Timon. You have slept—what?—only an hour in nearly two nights. I have had severe shocks to my flesh and mind. I suggest that we take Dr. Andrews downstairs to lie with Mr. Lively and have done with this night."

Before Timon could protest, Anne piped up, "Please. Neither of you will accomplish anything of merit without rest."

Timon sighed, set down his candle, and bent to take hold of Andrews's ankles. "You are correct, of course. My mind is a fog. Let us take this body to the cellar. And let us also secure the secret door down there once and for all."

Marbury nodded. He had other ideas about the tunnel, but held them in abeyance until a more opportune moment.

He helped Timon lift the corpse of Roger Andrews from its place on the floor. Grunting and knocking into desks in the dim light, they made their way to the cellar door.

"Wait," Timon said once the door was open.

He rested Andrews's feet on the top stair and disappeared into the black cave. An instant later, flickering light washed the walls of the stairway, and Timon reappeared.

Without a word he lifted the dead body's feet once more and backed down the stairs. Marbury, holding the body by the arms, lurched after him.

Once in the cellar, they laid the body of Roger Andrews on the floor beneath the table where Lively's corpse rested. Timon then moved to the storage bins that hid the secret door.

"Ah!" His syllable stabbed the air; he pointed to the floor.

"You detect something." Marbury stared at the place where Timon pointed.

"This is fresh." Timon tapped his toe near a pattern in the dust and dirt on the cellar floor. "This is different than before. The killer *did* enter the hall this way. We must find nails and hammers."

Marbury sighed. "In the first place, let us reiterate the need for sleep. In the second, I find your suggestion a bit like closing a stable door after the horse has gone. And finally, if we know the killer's preferred method of entry into this hall, that gives us an advantage we might not want to eliminate by blocking his way, if you understand—"

"What is the matter with me?" Timon's face betrayed genuine confusion. "I am not myself. You are exactly correct in your thinking. We may safely assume that the killer will come through the passage when he tries to kill again. This is an enormous tactical advantage. Why am I—my God. I *do* need sleep."

"As do I," Marbury said gently. "Shall we convene in the morning after sleep knits up our raveled sleeve of care? Over a good hearty breakfast in my kitchen?"

"That—quite suddenly—sounds like heaven. Do you know what a fine cook Anne is?"

"Yes." Marbury turned clumsily to trudge up the stairs.

As Timon moved to follow, he brushed the dead body of Roger Andrews, and the lifeless arm flinched, falling onto Timon's foot. The corpse's hand clutched at his ankle. Marbury saw it.

"There's a sign," Timon mumbled.

"A sign?"

"The dead are summoning me. Perhaps I am soon to join the men I have killed."

48

The next morning came late for Timon, nearly six o'clock. The sun was beginning to rise outside, though his room was still pitch.

He lit the candle next to his bed and was startled to see a bundle wrapped in an ice-white cloth just inside his door. He could detect the aroma of warm bread. His muscles could barely keep pace with his eagerness as he scrambled for the prize.

To his delight, when he had unwrapped the package, he discovered an entire loaf of bread, a corked jug half the size of his head—and something else. Tucked neatly into another cloth wrapping were page after page of ancient Greek—the hidden texts that Anne had kept in her room. At last he would be able to read them!

What would prompt Anne to deliver such a gift eluded Timon, but he sprang back to his bed as delighted as he could ever remember being. He sat upright on his planks, back against the wall, with the bundle in his lap. He uncorked the jug and drank heartily, to his surprise and delight, of good red wine. He tore nearly half the loaf and stuffed it into his mouth.

As he chewed, he turned to the top page in the stack of papers, held them closer to the candle, and read.

There are powers which contend against man, not wishing him to be saved in order that they may feed. These powers do not see those who are clothed in the Perfect Light and consequently are not able to detain them.

Those lines were attributed to the apostle Philip. Timon set the page aside. Unable to content himself with slow and careful study of each page, he longed to take them all in at once, devour them as if they were his loaf of bread. He turned to the final page in the stack and his eyes fell upon the last words there.

He who would know our great Power will become invisible. His soul will be released from punishment.

Timon's fingers began to tremble. He laid aside the bread and set the jug of wine on the floor, holding his breath. He was suddenly seized by a feeling he had not known for thirty years or more. He felt his faith might save his life, and his soul.

He held the bundle of pages tightly, as if he might absorb nourishment simply by touching the letters written there.

Why did my eyes fall upon these particular lines? he asked himself feverishly. And why this moment for me?

Before he knew it, he was on his knees, hands clasped so tightly that they began to ache. How, exactly, to pray? Was there, indeed, a power so perfect that it could make him invisible, that it could release him from punishment? He had once believed so.

Eyes closed, his mind was suddenly assaulted by strange images.

There, beside the candle in his room, stood a boy of seven years, smelling sweet hay as he hitched two horses to a carriage. Beside him stood the man who was waiting for the carriage, a kind man— in many ways the only father Timon had ever known. He smiled and showed the young boy a silver dagger, small, just his size. It was a gift—and it came with instruction.

Suddenly, as Timon knelt praying, another vision attacked. Timon was a young man, perhaps seventeen, crouching low with his back against a wooden post. He was surrounded by half a dozen armed men, and his instructor/father lay dead on the floor beside him. The sight of blood pouring from his beloved teacher so enraged the seventeen-year-old Timon that his own blood became molten iron. Nothing within reach would survive his rage. Walls, posts, arms, eyes, great fat bellies—all tore open, savaged by Timon's impossible blade. When everything around him was dead, Timon collapsed into a heap beside his dead comrade and died himself.

The flood of memories continued. True to his faith, Timon's mind insisted on resurrection. In the memory that followed his collapse, he awoke in a monastery, in a large, clean room filled with books.

Rose light pouring in through the windows like miraculous water. Outside there were grapevines, sheep grazing, a sky wild with high, white clouds in the morning air.

Unannounced, a dark figure entered, carrying a tray, and said, "Do not be afraid. I bound your wounds. We took you in according to your teacher's wishes."

The tray was laden. There was an entire loaf of bread filled with snipped rosemary, also fresh water, soft cheese, barley-scented broth, and grapes dark as midnight.

Timon roused himself from the vision, rubbing his eyes and taking in a deep breath. What could have prompted such a flood of images from his past?

He stood, steadied himself with his hand against the wall, and reached for the rest of the bread before he realized the obvious similarity between the bundle Anne had left him and the tray of food delivered by the young monk so many years before.

God often works in circles, Timon thought to himself as he took a delicate bite of bread. And that work pays no attention to time. An abbey room from so long ago is, indeed, this same room in which I now stand.

He reached for the jug on the floor beside him.

Before he quite realized what he was doing, he had swallowed

49

*M*oments later, clattering into the small kitchen in the Deaconage, Timon was surprised to find Marbury seated at the table there. It was obvious from his expression that something quite serious occupied his mind.

He had changed clothes, dressed in his clerical garb: black robe over black britches, high white collar, skullcap—a stern costume. He sat with his hands folded, an empty plate in front of him, a crumpled white napkin to one side. He was a composition of immaculate decorum.

Timon, on the other hand, was a wreck. His hair was wild, eyes red, robe disheveled. He was clutching loose, random papers to his breast as if they were armor.

"Good!" Marbury said sternly as Timon walked into the room. "I see you have been reading."

"Yes," Timon answered, making his way to the table. "Anne left me these most delightful—"

"Take a seat."

Timon set all the pages down on the table and began to arrange them into a somewhat neater bundle. When he saw the look in Marbury's eyes, he stopped fussing with the pages. "What has happened? You are discomforted."

"I was arrested yesterday by Lancelot Andrews. He thought I was Pietro Delasander. I had to fight my way out. I came home to find another murder has happened while the man who is supposed to prevent them was, as I learn, asleep in this kitchen! Of course I am discomforted!"

"But——," Timon began, staring down at the papers on the table.

"I have not told you the worst of it," Marbury interrupted. "Strange news flies up and down the streets of Cambridge, even this early in the morning."

"People have heard of the murders," Timon guessed, taking a seat.

"No." Marbury's lips thinned and his eyes darted about for a moment. "The reason Roger Andrews was working so feverishly last night when he was murdered is that he, and all the other translators, have been informed that His Holiness Pope Clement VIII has condemned the King James Bible translation as heresy; the devil's work, in fact."

"I—this was to be expected," Timon said slowly. "Surely you knew that the Pope——"

"The rumors have quoted passages from the new translation, from work done here in Cambridge—*word for word*. Whole pages from Harrison, Lively, Chaderton, have been exactly duplicated. Everyone is talking. The remaining translators have turned upon one other—each suspecting the other of betrayal. There is even talk, once again, of demonic intervention. They have decided to halt their work *indefinitely*."

"Oh," Timon whispered.

"That was the reason Chaderton was in the hall last night," Marbury rasped. "He not only suspected Andrews of the murders, but of betraying the work. He suspected that Andrews had revealed our work to Rome. But I believe that you know differently."

Timon's mind raced. He had only given his transcription to the

Pope's men two nights ago. There had not been time to get those pages to Rome, let alone time for a response and a campaign of rumors to begin. This was local work. The Unholy Trio, the men in the back room of the pub, had taken it upon themselves. Perhaps Venitelli had authorized some quick venom that would spread about the streets of Cambridge even as the actual translation was on its way to Clement. It was, he found himself admitting, a clever ploy. It had done its damage. The work on James's new Bible had come to a halt.

Marbury leaned forward with a look of such rage upon his face that Timon knew what he would say next.

"I have surmised that the only way the Pope could know the work of these men in such detail," Marbury began, his words carefully controlled, "is if someone, some Catholic spy, had come into our midst and somehow memorized large portions of the work and later written it all down for the Pope to see. How would a thing such as that be accomplished? I wonder."

Marbury's eyes pierced Timon's brain, and Timon looked away. He tried to recall everything he had said to Anne the night before, what he had given away. She had obviously told her father of his allegiance to Clement.

Timon laid his hands on the pages and tried, for an instant, to reconcile the revelation he had experienced in his room, his waking Eucharist, with his current dilemma.

A year ago, he thought to himself, I would not have hesitated to kill Marbury simply because he knew my true mission here. But today I cannot consider killing him, and I have altered my mission.

Decisions collided, each wrestling the other, until Timon found, once more, that his hands were shaking and his mouth was dry as ancient paper.

Marbury seemed to sense that something had changed in Timon's demeanor. It provoked a choice in Marbury's muscles, if not his mind: a response born of fear.

Marbury stood so suddenly that his chair flew backward and the table lurched forward into Timon's ribs. The blade in Marbury's hand was small, but he held it by the tip, ready to throw it.

Timon took in Marbury's face, the hand that held the blade, the arm that trembled, ready to strike. He could see that Marbury was perfectly prepared. If he threw his knife, it would hit its mark.

Timon sucked in a sudden, loud breath and shot from his chair. As he did, the kitchen table flew upward and into Marbury's arm with such force that it knocked the knife out of Marbury's hand and drove him several steps backward.

Timon leapt over the still-moving table and landed within inches of Marbury. His hand shot into his robe. Marbury flinched backward. Timon grabbed a fistful of Marbury's clerical garb and shuttled Marbury farther backward, all the way to the wall. With deadly certainty his hand snapped out of his robe once more.

Instead of a knife, he held, high above Marbury's head, a strange round instrument, some Inquisition torture device.

Marbury kicked. Timon slammed him into the wall once more and shouted, "This is your answer!" Timon held the odd object directly in front of Marbury's eyes. "This is to blame! This tool and my brain."

Marbury's eyes focused on the instrument Timon held in his hand, a small wooden wheel bearing strange symbols and numbers.

"This is my memory wheel, my own invention. With it, no one on earth has greater powers of memory than I do. It is my *telum secretus*."

"Your secret weapon," Marbury said, swallowing hard, "is your memory?"

"Listen." Timon took a single step backward and released Marbury's garment. "You believed that the trio of men in the public house in Cambridge were Anglicans who found me in order to help you catch a murderer."

Marbury exhaled, struggling to follow Timon's words.

"They are, you must now understand, Catholic agents who hired me to come to Cambridge and memorize as much of the Bible as I could. With the help of this wheel I wrote it down for them so that they could show it to the Pope. I have learned that the murderer we seek is also their agent. I have been instructed to cease my efforts to find or stop him. I am to allow him to finish his work, to kill everyone here. I have even been encouraged to help him. I completed part of this assignment the other night when I delivered to those men, in writing, everything I have memorized thus far. That was the morning I came back to find you and Anne in my room. Clearly the Pope has not yet seen any of the Bible. The Pope's men here in Cambridge have spread these rumors to cause chaos among the translators. And the gambit seems to have been effective."

Timon carefully placed the memory wheel back into its hidden pocket and brushed a thick curl of gray and black hair away from his forehead.

"Why are you telling me this?" Marbury said hesitantly. "Why am I still alive?"

Timon gave Marbury a quick, irritated glance. "I am, it would appear, done with the Catholic Church. I have resigned. I wish to follow the dictates of my own heart."

"And those are?" Marbury steadied himself against the wall, still breathing heavily.

Timon held up three fingers and counted them off as he answered Marbury's question. "Stop the killer; renew the translation; reveal the Truth."

"You are going to catch the murderer."

"I am."

"And you would see to it that King James's Bible is—"

"My best hope," Timon interrupted, his syllables clipped, "is that this Bible will be the first genuine book of its kind in the history of our religion. It will tell the story of our Lord from all points of view. It will give voice to the men *and* women who knew Him. It will emphasize the astonishing message that the true holy work of Christ begins and ends in love. Ours is the only religion on the globe that contains such a wondrous idea. I do not believe that I exaggerate when I say that every soul on earth is at stake."

50

Before either man could comment further, Anne charged into the room. She came to a halt, staring at the overturned table, the scattered papers, and the bare blade beyond. She had wrapped herself in an exquisitely quilted blue robe. It covered her from neck to toe. Her hair was down but tamed by a single clasp at the back of her neck. Her cheeks were flushed and her breathing was labored.

"Your father enjoys challenging me," Timon said. "He drew his knife, that one on the floor there. I toppled the table. But it was in sport. All is well."

He went to the table and took hold of the rough wood, standing it aright.

"You have been fighting with each other?" Anne asked softly, eyes wide.

Before either man could respond, a cry arose outside.

"Deacon Marbury!" a shrill voice demanded. "Hello, the Deaconage! Are you there?"

Timon and Marbury exchanged looks.

"That is why I am here," Anne said quickly, heading for the door of the kitchen. "I heard a strange voice calling. I wonder that you did not. It was coming from the stables, but now it appears to be just outside our door."

Marbury jumped to retrieve his knife.

Timon raced past Anne.

Alarm was in the stranger's voice. He carried vital news—or a deadly threat. Timon produced his blade; Marbury held his aloft and followed after.

Timon burst into the common yard, came face-to-face with the stranger, and said, "Stand where you are," his voice like sand in a mill wheel.

The man halted instantly. He was dressed in ice white and cold blue. His face bore traces of powder, a bit of rouge, and just a touch of purple shading at the eye. His black riding gloves seemed out of place with the rest of his costume.

Marbury exploded through the door the next instant, with Anne close behind.

The man held his arms outstretched so that everyone could see he had only one thing in his hand: a small leather pouch. Tightly tied, it bore the seal of King James.

Marbury and Anne flanked Timon. Only then did Timon glance down at Anne's soft, white hand. It held a thin, round blade, all point and no cutting edge. It was a weapon to dissuade an attacker, not kill him.

The King's man smiled. "Deacon, is this any way to greet the man who saved your life?"

Marbury tilted his head a bit. "Dibly?"

"The King thought it would make matters easier if someone you knew came from Hampton Court. He felt certain you would remember me."

"You know this man?" Timon asked quietly.

"He saved my life," Marbury answered, lowering his knife. "He is the man who gave me the King's antidote when I swallowed poison at Hampton."

"Poison?" Anne lowered her weapon as well.

"This missive contains a matter of the gravest urgency," Dibly insisted, hoisting the leather pouch aloft.

"Of course," Marbury stammered.

Timon alone held his ground—and his knife.

"You must gather all the translators together." It was a command; Dibly's voice and demeanor betrayed his true character, which was built of sterner stuff than his outward appearance would indicate. "What I have to say must be heard by all."

"This is the man who had, on his person, a convenient counter to the King's poison." Timon did not bother to hide his suspicion. He seemed, in fact, to emphasize it.

Dibly turned a withering gaze Timon's way. "This is doubtless the monk, Brother Timon, whom you mentioned to His Majesty. He is, in some small part, a reason for my visit. And may I say it was a difficult journey. You have no idea how exhausting it is to ride a horse from London to Cambridge with only one stop to change mounts. And no one has yet offered me a libation or a crust of bread. What a thankless job it is to serve a king."

Dibly tucked the leather pouch under one arm, removed his black riding gloves, slipped them neatly into his belt, and folded his hands in front of himself, waiting.

"Will you attempt to stick me with that dagger, Brother Timon?" Dibly asked after a heartbeat. "I hope not. I have no antidote for that."

"I have not yet decided what I will do," Timon answered.

"I only ask," Dibly said calmly, "because the news from His Majesty is really most important, and I would prefer not to be distracted by blood on my nice blue doublet."

Timon took note that Dibly did not specify whose blood would cause the stain.

"Might we—we should offer you some meat and drink, then?" Marbury stammered.

"Gather the translators," Dibly insisted, grinding every word to a fine dust, all civility gone from his voice and face.

The demons of curiosity, however, insured that the translators would gather no matter what Marbury or Timon did. First from one door and then another the men appeared, some still dressing.

"We should have realized," Anne whispered, "that if I could hear this man's voice, everyone could."

Running, as best he could, toward the spot where Dibly stood, was Dr. Spaulding, clad in silver. The early-morning sunlight made him almost invisible in its reflection.

"What has happened?" he demanded, out of breath. "Who is this man?"

Dibly reached for the pouch under his arm and held it high without looking back at Spaulding. "This is an urgent instruction from His Majesty for all the translators of his new Bible. If you are not such a man, go back to bed."

Spaulding arrived, slipping in the dewy grass, directly in front of Dibly, who still refused to take his eyes off Timon.

"I am not merely 'such a man,'" Spaulding panted, sneering. "I am in charge here!"

Dibly permitted himself a bubbling bit of laughter. "Hardly."

Spaulding began to sputter his response, but Chaderton, whose sleeping quarters were closer to the Deaconage, had arrived upon the scene. His plain brown robe and sleeping cap were a sober contrast to Spaulding's glinting blaze.

"The royal seal," Chaderton observed to Anne.

"Silence! Everyone!" Dibly bellowed, but his tone and manner were not, even at top volume, entirely impolite. "If you are the King's translators, then let us adjourn to the place where such work is done. I am under instruction to confiscate certain documents, and to insist on a specific course of progress from this day forward. I must have the complete attention of all the Cambridge men working on this translation. Or, I should say, all the men left alive."

Dibly arched a single eyebrow at his last remark. In that instant Marbury concluded that, despite certain impulses to the contrary, he did not really care for Dibly at all.

The other men gathered slowly, variously dressed in blue, purple, gray, and black. They had heard Dibly's declaration and were silent.

A sense of doom seeped into Timon's glorious state of bliss. His ears were assaulted by the sound of hissing as Dibly sighed and flicked a serpent's tongue to slake his lips.

"There has been," Dibly announced softly, "a significant shift in His Majesty's desires. Immediately, certain work will cease. James will manifest his legacy in this manner: the Word of God shall be in perfect concert with the will of the state. And the whims of a king."

"No," Timon protested, before he could think.

Dibly turned to face Timon directly. "Put away your ridiculous knife, Brother Timon. Where is there, anywhere in creation, a weapon that can cut the whims of a king?"

51

*M*oments later the men were seated at their desks in the Great Hall, waiting for the messenger to deliver his news.

Anne had been banished and fumed outside, straining to hear through the door. She clasped her robe tightly about her neck and paced in a pattern so erratic that it frightened the wrens in a nearby hazel tree. They scattered into the air.

Inside the hall, Dibly slowly opened his pouch, a faint smile upon his lips. Spaulding was still sputtering damp protest under his breath. Marbury had chosen to take Lively's desk, and Timon stood beside the seat that Harrison had occupied. He thought it unwise, given recent premonitions, to sit in the dead man's chair.

Dibly had commandeered the station that had belonged to Roger Andrews. He took his time, relishing the discomfort he was causing. Suddenly his right hand shot into his pouch, snatched a page, and held it aloft for all to see. It was affixed with a large wax circle.

"The King's signet seal," Spaulding whispered reverently.

Without further explication, Dibly lowered the page, held it close to his candle, and read.

" 'The translators of Cambridge in the matter of His Majesty's Bible are hereby commanded to hasten with God's speed to complete their work. They are directed to copy, as precisely as their scholarship will allow, the existing Bishops' Bible, altering nothing, adding no new work, deleting none but the most grievous of Catholic errors. This work is to be finished by All Saints' Day.' "

The room exploded.

Anne heard the din from outside, though she could only distinguish unconnected words and phrases: *All Saints' Day, Bishops' Bible, Catholic errors.* She pressed herself against the outer door, listening intently. She debated the merits of crashing into the hall and demanding to know what had happened.

Inside, Dibly raised his hand aloft once more, with a new page waving in the wild air. Flickering candlelight made the paper seem alive.

One by one the men noticed Dibly's tableau, and fell silent.

When tense order had returned, Dibly continued, "*This* paper empowers me to confiscate all of the so-called *secret* texts which His Majesty sent here, and any other documents which I deem aberrant."

"*You* deem?" Richardson demanded.

"I have been told what to look for," Dibly said, lowering his paper authority.

"You are taking all the hidden texts," Timon said simply. "You are retrieving all of the books James sent."

"And any others of a similar nature." Dibly blinked once.

"Pause a moment," Spaulding began, trying to catch up with what was happening.

"Then why did His Majesty send them here at all?" Dillingham interrupted.

"Roger Andrews requested them," Dibly explained. "Our King is currently working on a second volume of his masterwork, *Demonology*. Your Andrews was helping. It is, in fact, the death of

Roger Andrews that prompts my visit—his death and strangely related occurrences."

"Yes," Richardson nodded sagely. "The murders."

"The King is, quite naturally, concerned about the murders," Dibly began hesitantly, "but a more immediate problem has provoked my visit. Only yesterday, the Westminster translators were visited by an infamous assassin, a man named Pietro Delasander. He fought with the guard, made threats upon the person of Dr. Lancelot Andrews, and escaped imprisonment there. Delasander attempted to masquerade as your Deacon Marbury. Dr. Lancelot Andrews informed His Majesty at once. Delasander is almost certainly the man who killed Roger Andrews. And Delasander is a student and known cohort of your strange guest, Brother Timon—who masterminded the murders."

All eyes fell on Timon. Spaulding nodded with great satisfaction. Both Marbury and Chaderton seemed about to speak when Anne, unable to contain herself any longer, burst into the room.

"You must not allow this!" she shouted.

The walls agreed, echoing her ire.

Dibly turned slowly, his grin becoming a disfiguring grimace. "A girl? A girl is raising her voice against the King's command?"

"I see no king in this room." Anne shook her head.

"*I* am the King's voice in this room!" Dibly snarled. "I have come to arrest this Brother Timon."

"I told you all!" Spaulding shouted triumphantly.

"No," Anne said instantly. "I know for a fact that Brother Timon was asleep in our kitchen when Andrews was murdered. And I am a witness to that murder."

"As am I," Chaderton began, "and the killer was certainly *not* Brother Timon."

"Silence!" Dibly demanded.

He whirled suddenly to face Timon, producing a pistol from his leather pouch.

"Powder and ball are in place," he assured Timon. "Flint locked, trigger cocked."

"I do not care for these new weapons." Timon shrugged. "The

ball falls out; the powder fails to ignite. More than half the time, a weapon of that sort does more harm to its owner than it does to the intended victim. But shoot, if you must, or if you can. It does not matter to me. You will not arrest me or take me with you. You may kill me, or you may provoke me to kill you. Those are your only choices this morning."

"Good!" Dibly enthused. "I have always wanted to be able to say that I have killed a man before breakfast. It has such a deliciously brutal tone, and it would surely frighten my rivals."

Dibly took a quick step closer to Timon and aimed the pistol directly at Timon's face.

In the blink of an eye, Richardson swooped up from his chair, tore off his ermine cape, and used it to cover Dibly's head. With the same motion he slapped the pistol from Dibly's hand as if he were disciplining a child who had stolen a sweet. The gun hit the hard floor and the ball rolled out.

Richardson deftly took hold of Dibly's head and shoved it with all his might down onto the top of the nearest desk. A loud thud was followed by Dibly's immediate collapse onto the floor.

"There," Richardson said proudly, smiling at Timon. "I have rendered him unconscious. Tie him up. Splash him with cold water. Get him to tell you who he really is. No one that rude could be an emissary from the King. I told you I would come to your rescue when the time was right, Brother Timon."

"You did indeed, Dr. Richardson," Timon answered, staring down at Dibly. "You are a man of your word. Like the knights of legend."

Richardson glanced at Dibly, brushing his hands together. "What an awful young man."

"Yes," Timon agreed.

"Well." Richardson patted his stomach. "We should have breakfast and sort all this out."

There is England's greatest weapon, Timon thought as he stared at Richardson's face, the ability to forge ahead. Never looking backward, *this* is what I must learn from them.

"Brother Timon and I have already had our breakfast," Marbury said, coming to stand over Dibly. "Perhaps the rest of you would care to go to the dining hall in my Deaconage for such repast and allow us to take care of this unfortunate man."

Marbury's eyes shot briefly to Anne, who nodded once.

"Gentlemen," she began instantly. "Shall we?"

She headed toward the exit from the Great Hall.

"This person, Dibly, may have soiled my cape," Richardson said briskly. "If he has, I do not wish to wear it. Give it away."

"We shall join you in a very few moments," Brother Timon said, kneeling beside Dibly. "Then, as you say, we will sort out all of this business."

"I am hoping for sausages!" Richardson shouted, a wild joy flooding his words. "God's eyes! I *am* famished."

The other men glared at Richardson, unable to keep up with the events as they were happening. Richardson seemed unaware of their confusion and followed Anne toward the door. One by one, not knowing what else to do, the rest filed out. Timon had seen faces like those before. Men too long in combat or hopeless prisoners often exhibited the same demeanor.

When everyone had gone, Timon pulled the ermine cape from Dibly's head. The forehead was caved in and already a deep purple, but there was no blood.

"Is he dead?" Marbury asked, kneeling beside Timon.

Timon felt for a pulse, then licked his forefinger and held it close to Dibly's nose and mouth.

"His heart is still pumping," Timon said softly, "but I can detect little breath. This purple stain on his head means that his brain is bleeding into his skull. He may not survive."

"What to do?" Marbury said calmly. "He saved my life."

"He did that as a ploy, not as an act of kindness. He poisoned you and then gave you the antidote to make you grateful, to assure your allegiance to the King."

"You cannot be certain of that."

"Enough," Timon insisted. "We must concentrate on the moment at hand."

Marbury shook his head. "Concentrate on what?"

"We must have answers from Dibly." Timon slapped Dibly's cheek.

Dibly's eyes flew open, and he exhaled. "Who struck me?"

Timon looked down at him. "Richardson."

"That windbag!" Dibly coughed. "What was his weapon?"

"Harrison's desk," Timon answered. "He pushed you against the corner of a desk."

Dibly smiled. "Good. Let it be said that Harrison struck me. I can stand for the irony of being attacked by a dead man. That is my style."

"Be still," Marbury encouraged, "you have a wound."

"Help me up," Dibly demanded.

Timon held him down instead. "You said that the death of Roger Andrews prompted your visit."

"I did."

"How could you or anyone else in London know of that death even now?" Timon demanded. "It happened mere hours ago."

"That is correct." Marbury let go a pained breath leaning against the nearest desk. "But what if he knew, *before*hand, that Andrews was to be murdered?"

"Exactly," Timon affirmed. "He had such confidence in the killer—"

"—that he considered the murder a fait accompli," Marbury concluded.

Timon looked down at Dibly again. "If you had paused a moment to think, you would surely have realized your temporal error."

"Then . . . is Dibly in league with the killer?" Marbury said, unconsciously moving slightly away from Dibly.

"More to the point," Timon whispered, covering his mouth with his hand, "is King James?"

Dibly suddenly lurched forward, producing a small stick wrapped in cloth with a single briar protruding from it.

Timon pushed himself away in a frenzy. "Poison!" he called.

Marbury jumped as far away as he could, drawing his knife.

Dibly was on his feet, panting, his head beginning to bleed from the wound Richardson had caused.

"Do not allow that fang to touch you," Timon whispered. "It is far worse than any knife."

Dibly squeezed his eyes shut as if he was having trouble focusing. Timon used the moment to grab Harrison's desk by the legs and swing it toward Dibly. He moved it with surprising speed and force, and it crashed into Dibly, knocking him to the floor.

Dibly's hand still held the poisoned briar. He spun the stick; the cloth unwound from around it and flew away. Then he struggled upward.

"He may throw it," Timon warned under his breath.

Marbury retreated farther, but Timon was obviously the object of Dibly's attack. Dibly flung himself with all his might onto Harrison's desk for support. It shoved forward and Dibly was nearly within reach of Timon's face.

Dibly swiped his poisoned claw through the air. In a blur Timon produced two blades, one in each hand, and threw them both.

One buried itself in Dibly's throat, the other in his belly.

Dibly cried out, tried to lunge with his weapon, but it dropped to the floor. He rolled off Harrison's desk and fell in a heap, twitching and cursing.

Timon's boot found Dibly's briar and kicked it away. Dibly's curses became more violent, but the dagger in his neck prohibited clear words. Blood poured from that wound and seeped from the one in his stomach.

"Damn you," Timon whispered, rushing to Dibly's side. "I meant to hit your shoulder."

Marbury was still blinking twenty feet away. "How did you know that the innocent-looking stick was poisoned?"

"It was a favorite weapon of Pietro Delasander's," Timon answered. "His often bore a rose at the end. Its poison is always fatal, greatly painful, and takes hours to kill. It is a devil's tool."

"Is he mortally wounded?" Marbury began.

Timon stooped to Dibly's side. "Are you dying? There is more I need to know from you."

"More?" Dibly managed to gurgle. "No more."

Timon raised his head. "What has prompted King James to

revise his request, to send you here to gather up the manuscripts he first gave to these scholars to aid their work?"

Dibly smiled and shuddered. With one final spasm, he closed his eyes, exhaling his final breath. Timon felt for a pulse, but Dibly lay dead beneath Harrison's desk.

"I say again," Timon sighed, "damn you."

It was almost a funeral prayer

"Another body in this room." Marbury looked about the Great Hall, a great weariness in his eyes. "I cannot bear the number of dead we have accumulated here."

Timon nodded. "Then let us remove this King's henchman from here and bury him beside Pietro Delasander, so that their twin mysteries might keep each other company until the dew of heaven arouses them. This one's part is played."

"He did it well," Marbury said softly, "so well, in fact, that there may be no one alive who knew who he was."

"Assassins and faithful servants are God's best actors," Timon agreed. "Who and what they *truly* are, only heaven knows."

52

*L*ittle more than half an hour later, Timon and Marbury hurried into the dining hall of the Deaconage. The room was well lit by morning sunlight; no candles burned. A third the size of the Great Hall, it could seat twenty at most. The wood-paneled walls looked new, but the rest of the room had seen at least two hundred years. The long table, carelessly set with plates and mugs, was also strewn with crumbs and spotted with ale. Here and there an errant sausage lay scattered from its plate.

Everyone was grumbling. Clearly, the men had been arguing.

"Gentlemen," Marbury announced, "we must act quickly. All of your work is in jeopardy, and a murderer still haunts these grounds."

Chaderton stood. "We have been debating the idea that this person, this alleged emissary from the King, may be an impostor."

"But he is not!" Spaulding snarled. "He had the King's seal. We must obey the royal command. Bring him here. Let him be questioned."

"Alas," Marbury said, handling his words as if they might be glass, "he is dead."

"Oh," Richardson said, wiping his mouth, "I do beg your pardon. I did not mean to kill him."

"Dead, then," Spaulding snapped without the slightest sympathy for the departed. "But the seal on his documents—"

"I should tell you, Deacon Marbury," Richardson plowed ahead, smiling, "that I have revised my suspicions. I no longer believe that you are a murderer. I can see from this man Dibly's visit that chicanery of the most devilish order is afoot. My new theory—"

"I have decided," Spaulding insisted, his thin voice slipping through Richardson's rounder tones, "that we must obey the King's orders! The royal seal is inarguable, and we must return—"

"No!" Timon shouted. "If you obey this so-called royal command, the true words of God's Bible will never see the light of day. The entire history of our religion depends on what you men do now!"

Everyone was surprised to hear such passion.

"You stand on the precipice," Timon continued, struggling for words, "here you are at the beginning of a new universe. You must leap and have faith that God will give you wings. The hour has come to worship the Father in spirit and in truth. God is a spirit, but his atoms are particles of Great Truth, and you must serve that power—not with the leaven of malice and wickedness; but with the unleavened bread of sincerity and truth. Rejoice in the truth, and the secrets of God's heart will be made manifest. You must not handle the Word of God deceitfully, but by manifestation of the truth, commending yourselves to every man's conscience in the sight of God. By the word of truth, by the power of God, by the armor of righteousness."

Silence pervaded the room for too short a moment.

"With this theatrical speech, you *presume*," Spaulding began.

"Brother Timon speaks to us from Corinthians, Dr. Spaulding," Chaderton admonished softly. "He makes no presumption."

"He could be speaking to us from the grave for all I care!"

Spaulding answered. "There have been murders in this place, and I continue to maintain that he is the culprit!"

"There *are* devils here," Timon hissed. "And the murderer in this place does his killing because he cannot abide the truth; because there is no truth in him."

"Why is he going on about the *truth*?" Spaulding demanded of Richardson, who sat on his right.

Richardson responded around a mouthful of breakfast. He alone had continued to dine. "He wants us to ignore the message that the rude envoy delivered. How could he be any clearer?" Richardson reached for another slice of bread. "I believe you are currently working on a particularly relevant passage, Spaulding. 'The words of the Lord are pure words: as silver tried in a furnace of earth, purified seven times.'"

"Heed those words from Psalms, Dr. Spaulding," Anne said, staring the man down. "How can you continue your work if you do not purify everything you do?"

"Mistress, you have no comprehension—," Spaulding began, barely hiding his contempt.

"Please, everyone, we seem to be ignoring the more immediate point." Marbury raised both hands. "Brother Timon and I have, moments ago, devised a plan, one which involves you all. We must move with lightning speed if we are to have any hope. The forces of—many great powers are at work to break the back of our task here in Cambridge. We must not allow that."

"In short," Timon continued, most of his patience gone, "you must translate the Bible to perfection, leaving nothing out, correcting all errors, adding every conceivable true text in order that the Word of God may be restored to all humankind. That is your task now, your only world. My part in this particular scene is to catch a killer. That I shall do. And it will happen, with God's help, to-night."

One by one, Timon read a degree of understanding on every face. Spaulding, to be sure, was clearly reticent. He did, at least, keep still.

Timon looked every scholar in the eye, then continued, "Your task will require all the knowledge you possess. You must also pray for the grace of God's wit. My part will ask nothing more of me than a foolhardy nature and a degree of stubbornness granted to men my age."

"The killer has entered the Great Hall by means of a secret passage," Marbury blurted out.

Timon sighed with a sidelong glance at Marbury. "I will wait close to that entrance—"

Richardson burst out laughing. "A *secret passage*? Honestly? Are we in some sort of devious *play*? Where is this—"

"It is hidden behind the root bins in the cellar of the hall," Timon said simply.

"But, do you mean the underground corridor from the Deaconage to the hall?" Richardson tilted his head.

Timon stared. "You have used that passageway?"

Richardson swallowed a gulp of ale. "We all have."

The others nodded silently.

"But when I attempted to travel it," Timon said slowly, "I was unable to gain exit. There is a stone wall at the end."

"The Deacon didn't show you the latch?" Richardson asked.

"I was not even aware that the tunnel existed," Marbury began.

"The departed Harrison showed me, may he rest in peace," Richardson said.

"He showed us all," Spaulding snapped. "It was common knowledge."

Marbury's eyes shot to Chaderton.

"He did not show it to me," Chaderton said quickly.

Marbury's head sank to his chest. "How is it that I had no knowledge of this?"

"I wonder that myself," Timon said, failing to hide the suspicion in his voice. "How could you have lived for so long in the Deaconage—"

"I have only lived in that building for several months," Marbury said quickly.

"But, you are the deacon—"

"I am deacon of Christ Church," Marbury told Timon, "not these grounds. I was only moved here when His Majesty appointed me to be—what is the word? *Guardian* of the translators? If that is the word, I must face a rather abject failure—"

"You have only lived in your current residence for several months?" Timon shook his head. "How is it that I did not know that?"

"We have both been guilty of distraction."

"Yes."

"But about the tunnel," Anne insisted.

"The killer has used it to escape from me," Timon explained at once. "I need to know about it."

"Of course," Richardson answered immediately. He swallowed his last bite of food, stood, and strode toward the door to the kitchen.

Suddenly Timon remembered the shambles in which he and Marbury had left that room. Loose pages of secret text were scattered everywhere. He hastened after Richardson, preparing to explain. Richardson plunged ahead, through the doorway, and into the kitchen. Timon caught up with him only to find, to his surprise, the kitchen restored to order. A bundle of papers wrapped in a white cloth lay calmly on the kitchen table, no indication whatsoever that they might be the sacred texts.

Anne sailed into the room just behind Timon, offering him the merest smile that explained everything.

Timon nodded his thanks.

Richardson moved to the far wall.

"Observe," Richardson said grandly, loving the role he was playing, "the beauty of this secret. Where do I wish to go? To the root bins in the cellar of the Great Hall. What relief is carved here on this panel in the wall? A bunch of carrots."

He tapped the carrots once, then twisted them clockwise, and the panel of the wall snapped inward, opening a narrow, black hallway.

Timon peered into the darkness to make certain no one was lurking there.

Richardson laughed delightedly. "Fewer than one hundred steps to the hall. Harrison, rest in peace, told me that the Great Hall had once been the chapel for a monastery on these grounds. This Deaconage was the dormitory for the monks. In the worst weather, monks could arrive into their chapel without tracking in mud or snow.

"And from the other side, where you say you encountered a dead end, do you see that raised stone?" Richardson pointed.

Timon peered into the little cave. One stone was raised higher than the others.

"If you feel beneath it," Richardson went on, "there is a latch. Click it once, and you enter this kitchen. It is, indeed, a passageway, but hardly, as you see, a secret."

"Thank you, Dr. Richardson," Marbury said, primarily to prevent Richardson from going on.

"Now, gentlemen," Timon whispered, "please draw near."

The men moved slowly toward Timon. Spaulding took only a few steps.

"As to my part in our immediate scheme," Timon continued softly, "I will set a trap to catch a rat. I will disguise myself tonight as one of you and wait alone in the Great Hall. When the murderer comes, I will subdue and capture him. Now that I know more about this passage, he will not outwit me if he tries to escape this way again."

"I have insisted on being present in the Hall as well," Marbury said quickly. "Anne's recent experience with the killer has convinced me that it is possible to hide quite completely in the shadowy corners of that place."

"Together we will bring the man to justice before the next dawn." Timon's words were bursting with such confidence that several of the men nodded immediately.

"To that end, Dr. Spaulding," Marbury said, a bit of a lilt to his words, "would you select what robe and cloak you deem appropriate for such a masquerade?"

"I?" Spaulding gasped.

"You have informed every man, woman, hound, and worm in the town of Cambridge that you are now in charge of the translation," Dr. Dillingham sighed. "You are, therefore, certain to be the killer's next target."

Spaulding looked around the room as if he had never seen it before, staring into the eyes of the other men, frantically seeking refuge.

"I?" he repeated, like the solitary chirp of a tiny sparrow.

"You wore an unadorned umber coat the other day," Timon suggested, "with a plain skullcap of dark gold, devoid of design or insignia. Do you know the items?"

"I—I do," Spaulding stammered.

"They should do nicely," Timon replied, "if I keep my face away from the candles. And—your desk faces the cellar door, does it not?"

Anne rapped upon the table as if it were a locked door. "Stop! This is your plan? To sit in the darkened hall and wait for a man to come there and kill you? And pray that he does not succeed? The combined brainpower of my tutor and my father has produced this limping plan?"

"If you would lower your voice," Marbury said, hushed, "the killer may not hear you and we can yet have the element of surprise on our side."

"You could have all the elements of nature on your side," Anne stormed, "and this would still be an ill-fated plan! Timon means to make himself a sacrificial lamb. Can you not see that? He blames himself for falling asleep last night. He thinks he could have saved Andrews. This is his penance."

The kitchen was silent for a moment. The men stared at Anne, her face red, her eyes hot. Timon alone was watching the motes of dust as they turned and swirled in sunlight that poured through the single window in the room.

"I have stayed alive for more than fifty years," Timon sighed softly. "In that time, a great many men have tried, in one way or another, to take my life. None have succeeded. There is a divinity that shapes our ends, Anne, rough-hew them how we will. Would you agree? No one can kill me before it is my time. Nothing in the universe has the power to take my life if God does not will it. And, of course, nothing in creation can save me if His plan for me is to die tonight."

53

A few moments later, leaving most of the scholars still arguing in the kitchen, Timon retreated toward his room. He carried the bundle of forbidden writings under his left arm. The desire to read them more carefully was nearly overwhelming. The sound of his boots on the stone floor, the flight of morning light through the high windows in the hallway, even the slow percussion of his breathing, seemed to remove him from the reality of the moment. Though he could not have said why, he felt he might be melting into thin air. Everything was dissolving: the cloud-capped towers of the sky, the solemn temple of his brain, the great globe itself, all an insubstantial pageant, fading.

He opened the door to his room in complete ecstasy.

He was sent plummeting back to the real world by a single piece of paper on his bed. Even from the doorway, he recognized the handwriting. Leaving the door wide-open, he strode to it.

We await the turning of the wheel by the tilling of the wheat, seated, facing east, this afternoon.

A meeting called for the hour of three, when the hands of the clock appeared most like a man seated, facing east. The Unholy Trinity proposed to discuss the progress and timetable of his assignment. But it was too soon for another meeting. The Pope's men had something else in mind.

As he lowered the page, Timon wondered at a certain odd conjunction. The Pope ordered Timon's memory work done by All Saints' Day. King James commanded the Bible to be finished on the same day. What demon had orchestrated that coincidence? What vile contagion moved these events toward the same end? All Saints' Day—was it possible that Pope Clement and King James were in league with one another?

Timon began to pace. If the Pope and the King had combined against him, what chance did he have? Suddenly the plan he and Marbury had concocted seemed, as Anne had intimated, insane. Or desperate. Was he sacrificing himself on purpose?

In his growing panic, Timon was assaulted by a tumbling parade of visions from his past: five dead bodies in Tuscan moonlight; calm Inquisitors with burning clamps; a thousand spiders in a prison cell.

The meaning of these evil portents was clear: he would be dead by morning.

He knew he must calm himself before his meeting with the Pope's men, or he would be dead sooner. He glanced twice at the place under his bed where his box rested, silently beckoning. But instead of taking out his pipe, Timon began to recite aloud from the twenty-second psalm, a personal prayer. "Be not far from me; for trouble is near; there is none to help. I am poured out like water, all my bones are out of joint; my heart is like wax. Deliver my soul from the sword; my darling from the power of the dog."

He stared down at the note in his hand and spoke to it. "You muddle my brain, but not for long. I know what I need. I know where I will find the peace I need to confront your authors."

Without a further thought or word, Timon moved to his desk. He hid the secret papers beneath the loose stone there and moved quickly to his door. He was in the hallway in an instant, headed for the stables.

OUTSIDE, DAY HAD BEGUN—the sun spreading white wings over the bowl of the sky. Timon's boots clapped against the stones in the courtyard as he hurried toward the stable.

The activity he had chosen to clear his mind seemed to him a perfect metaphor. As he walked, he kept an eye out for a dung fork.

Timon arrived at the stables in short order to find them empty of people.

"So much the better," Timon continued aloud, "for mucking out the stalls."

The horses heard him coming and began to stir, thinking they might be in for another breakfast. They sighed, pursing their lips.

The stable had once been painted white, but the wash had long since faded. The building was a comfortable gray. Inside, the seven stalls were solidly built: rough-hewn slats of weathered wood in lines as straight as a plowed furrow. The smell of the morning air mixed happily with the straw and the manure, a clean scent not at all unpleasant, or so it seemed to Timon.

The tool he needed lay nearby, a handle the color of ale and a fork of smooth, tan wood. He took hold of it, staring for a moment, beaming, when a voice from behind assailed the air.

"What do you think you're doing?"

Timon turned to see Lankin, the stable master. He was dressed all in brown, leaning on the entranceway, squinting at Timon. His head was cocked a bit like a hound dog's.

"I heard you talking to yourself."

"Well." Timon hoisted the dung fork. "I thought I might muck out these stables."

"Oh, you did, did you? And what do you suggest I do with the stableboys whose *job* it is to hoist that fork, then?" Lankin asked after a moment.

"Brush a coat, untangle a mane, check a hoof, or any one of the hundred things I know—"

"But what I want to know," Lankin interrupted, "is what the hell you think you're *doing*."

"Mr. Lankin," Timon said, his smile gone. "A monk is used to hard work; a harder life than most men can imagine. I am sickened by the creaking inactivity of the scholars in the buildings beyond this stable. If I do not perform a few hours of honest labor, I may lose what is left of my mind."

Lankin seemed to relax. The grimace he displayed may even have been some sort of smile. "Well, you certainly have said a mouthful there. Them men in that hall, they would never recognize a day's work if it grabbed them by the backside and gave a whistle. What was your name, again?"

Timon hesitated. The smell of the hay, the larks in the high trees, a river's worth of pouring sunlight—all conspired to make him offer what might otherwise have been a foolish confession.

"Giordano is my Christian name."

"And I be Matthew," Lankin said softly, "named after the best apostle." He shoved himself up from his leaning posture and turned away. "I may have to tell them boys to catch us a fish or two since you seem to be taking their measure of work at the moment. I fancy a bit of fish to eat at midday."

He disappeared without another word.

Timon stared after him for a moment, then addressed the instrument of his labor.

"Brother Dung Fork," he said softly, "you and I are both instruments of God, and in this life we have been given similar duties. Allow me to comfort you with a single notion. God will use us whether we want Him to or not. We can perform our task with joy and grace, or we can squall and squabble—but His work will be done." Timon lowered his voice and put his lips close to the handle. "The secret is to surrender to the work and choose joy."

Without another thought in his head for the next several hours, Timon flew through the stables until every stall was scrubbed as clean as a king's kitchen or an apostle's heart.

And when he was finished, he knew what must be done about the Pope's men.

54

Several minutes before three o'clock that afternoon, the market street in Cambridge was spilling noise into the
air: swearing, swaggering, shouldering, shuffling men at work;
women singing. Here and there a cape cast itself open to display the
new clothes beneath, while other cloaks might have concealed a
broken elbow, the ready pistol, or small bits of stolen silver.

But the street in the next block was deadly silent. Timon stood
there, across from the public house where his meeting was to take
place. He sought to be invisible, searching for a way to enter without being seen, some side window or back entrance. An alleyway
was to one side of the house, but he was loath to explore it only to
find a dead end and be trapped there. After a moment a man in a
baker's apron, dusted face to shoe with flour, emerged from the alley carrying an empty tray. He turned down the street toward a
bakery at the far end of the row of buildings.

So there was a service entrance, or perhaps a kitchen door.

Timon looked up and down the street. Satisfied it was empty, he drew his hood over his head, stooped to hide his height, and made for the alley. Once in, he could see, at the very back, a kitchen. He prayed, for some reason, that Jenny would not be there. The alley was wet, a bit chilly, and even quieter than the street. A few steps farther in, Timon could hear the sounds of the kitchen: plates and tankards clattering, grumbling, laughing, sizzling.

He turned his face downward, slumped his shoulders even more, and plunged in through the open door. The smell of smoking meat assaulted his nostrils. Someone by the fire whispered, "Look: another one."

Timon kept walking. As he had hoped, in only a few steps he was in the main room behind the bar. He turned to his right immediately, lifted his eyes only long enough to see the door handle in the dimmer light. He took hold and slipped into the back room through the slightest possible opening.

He stood for a moment with the closed door to his back, listening to the sound of the other three men breathing in the room.

"Ah," a voice whispered, "you arrive precisely."

"If a bit theatrically," another said softly.

"That is you, Brother Timon?" Venitelli asked hesitantly.

Timon drew in a great breath, stood to his full height, and drew back his hood in answer. He clasped his hands before him, though they were hidden in the sleeves of his robe. He stared at his hosts.

The three men sat as before, on the opposite side of a rough table from where Timon stood. The room was slightly more illuminated. Several candles seemed to have been added since the last meeting.

"I must tell you frankly," Timon said, smiling, "I had hoped that there would be much more time between our meetings."

"If you had engaged in *proper* work," Isaiah exploded, "there would be no need for a meeting at all!"

"Why did you allow Marbury to visit Dr. Andrews at Westminster?" Samuel demanded.

Timon's smile never left his lips. "Why did you send Pietro Delasander to kill me?"

The room was plunged into utter silence. All the men had

stopped breathing. Not a single atom moved. Even the candle flames seemed to freeze, fearing what might come next.

"Have I served my purpose already?" Timon continued after a heartbeat or two. "Is that the reason? Cardinal Venitelli's ill-conceived ploy to loose a rumor that the Pope condemned our King James translation—it might have worked. Except that human nature is never quite predictable. We can never be certain whether threats and fears will bend a man's will or strengthen his resolve. It is a tricky business, the molding of a man's soul—and messy."

Venitelli attempted to speak. All three faces at the table had drained of color.

"Delasander misinterpreted his instructions," Samuel began, all hint of authority gone from his voice.

"I deciphered his papers accurately," Timon interrupted. "He was using your code—which, incidentally, I taught him. His orders were quite explicit."

"Is he with you now?" Isaiah barely managed to say.

"No," Timon said immediately. "His body is buried in several inches of dirt in Cambridge. His soul—who can say?"

"Dead?" Isaiah gasped.

"He seemed so when I put him in the ground." Timon's fingers played upon the handle of his knife.

Venitelli, wild panic in his voice, turned to the other two. "I told you!"

Without warning, Isaiah's right arm swung from beneath the table and flung a long, thin dagger with impossible speed. It flew directly toward Timon's heart.

Timon managed to turn slightly to his left and lift his right shoulder enough to prevent the blade from piercing his chest, but it sunk its fang into the flesh of his upper right arm.

Instantly he crouched, yanking the knife from its wound and discarding it. Before any of the other men could move, Timon kicked the table where they sat. It crashed over on top of them.

At one leap Timon landed hard on the underside of the table.

He hit with such force that their chairs splintered and collapsed, and the table came cracking down onto all three men at once.

Venitelli closed his eyes; passed out instantly.

Isaiah gasped for air, struggling beneath Timon's weight, unable to quite reach his other knife. Samuel was unable to move at all. Both of his arms were pinned to his chest by the overturned table. He was directly under Timon.

Timon's arm dripped blood onto the table. He held his own knife in his left hand, sucking in breath through clenched teeth, and put the slicing edge close to Samuel's face.

But he did not move farther. The blade stayed poised over Samuel's throat. Samuel's eyes were mostly white and he seemed to be struggling to speak.

"The difficult thing for a man recently awakened to new faith," Timon calmly explained to Samuel, "is that his old habits are not immediately broken. For the sake of my new self, I do not wish to kill you, but my old self tells me I must. If I fail to do so, you will continue to pursue me. And you will continue to kill other men and women for whom I have some affection. I cannot allow this. Is it right to do a little evil for a greater good? Never. But I believe that this particular moment was ordained by God before the world began. I am already condemned to hell, and so I am the man God has placed here in this room to stop you and your unholy work. I thought you should know this."

Without another word, Timon's blade flashed out and sliced Samuel's throat from ear to ear. The jugular veins on both sides and most of the nerve endings in his neck were severed. Samuel died quickly; without a sound. Timon wiped his knife on Samuel's shoulder and stood.

Isaiah was trying desperately to free himself, kicking, bucking the table; making noises like a wounded horse.

Timon stooped down, tapped Isaiah's head with the tip of his blade. "Look carefully. This is the last thing you will ever see."

Timon held that blade before Isaiah's eyes long enough for Isaiah to fully realize what he was looking at. Then Timon stabbed

Isaiah through the left eye—the point of the knife plunged directly into the brain, and he left it there.

Isaiah thrashed madly, the motion of his head a blur, his tongue out of his mouth but unable to squeeze a word past his lips, even with his dying breath.

Timon turned to the shivering Venitelli and grabbed his hair.

Venitelli's eyes opened halfway.

"Get up and come with me now," Timon said in Italian, "if you want to live out the rest of the afternoon."

Timon backed off the table, dragging Venitelli with him.

Venitelli looked once at his dead compatriots, then kept his eyes lowered, head tucked, waiting for Timon's death blow.

But Timon only pulled his own hood up over his head and said, "You should cover your head too."

Venitelli complied instantly.

Timon took Venitelli by the arm; pulled him over to the exit. He opened the door a crack, surveyed the outer room, judged it safe to pass through, and slid quickly into the public room. He turned left immediately, still pulling Venitelli with him; steered through the kitchen with lightning speed, and out to the alley.

Once there, Timon pulled Venitelli close and whispered into his ear, "When it is my time to die, I will embrace the darkness as I would a bride, full in my arms. But that day is not today. I have more work to do. I do not know how you will receive your own death, but that, also, will not be today. I am sending you back to Pope Clement with a message. The King James Bible will be the first *true* book in the history of our religion. Tell him that sentence exactly. Tell him that nothing will be excluded; nothing will be added. The thoughts and words of our Lord will be plain, in all their confounding splendor, for any human being to read. There is nothing he can do about this because I have read and memorized all the secret, hidden, excluded documents—even Padget's stolen text. Can you remember all of that?"

Venitelli nodded, whispering to himself what Timon had said so that he would not forget.

"Then go now." Timon thrust Venitelli out toward the street with such force that Venitelli tripped and nearly fell.

"You are not going to kill me," Venitelli realized slowly.

"You are not an evil man, Cardinal Venitelli." Timon nodded. "You are not like the inquisitors who tortured me when I was in their jail, the men called Samuel and Isaiah."

"Those men tortured you?"

"You are innocent, and you are stupid. You have been used by other men because of those God-given qualities. Do you think you could communicate one more message to His Holiness?"

Venitelli nodded slowly.

"He may surmise it on his own, but he is by no means the brightest man I know, either, so let me say it plainly." Timon drew in a deep breath. "Tell His Holiness that I am no longer in his employ."

55

That night as the sun was setting, a lone figure walked deliberately toward the Great Hall. He was dressed in an unadorned umber coat and a plain skullcap of dark gold, devoid of design or insignia.

Several stars flickered like candles, and a full white moon began to rise in the eastern sky. Nightingales offered vespers; doves hushed the evening. That particular part of the evening seemed a time for quiet reflection, a lover's whispered call, or the comfort of night's respite.

So when a window on the second floor of the Deaconage scraped open, every fiber of the night turned its attention in that direction.

Anne leaned out of the window and called, "Dr. Spaulding! What are you doing? It was agreed that no one should go into the Great Hall alone. Especially at night!"

The figure paused on the walkway, searched a moment for the source of the racket, and found Anne leaning out of her window.

He made a noise of utter disgust and dismissed the girl with a wave of his hand. Then he continued on his way toward the Great Hall.

"Suit yourself," Anne grumbled, softer. She pulled the window closed.

The lone figure moved deliberately through the common yard, arrived at the door of the hall, and fumbled with his keys. He scratched his skullcap. With a bit of mumbling under his breath, he finally turned the lock and entered. Within seconds a candle was lit. Its flame spilled onto the threshold for a moment before the door slammed shut.

The umber robe moved a bit stubbornly across the floor toward Spaulding's desk.

Once there, the man sat down in the high wooden chair facing the cellar door, placed the candle in its holder, and leaned back to survey his work.

The desktop was immaculate. A single stack of papers lay flat next to a clean white quill in a spotless inkwell. A row of books was lined up side by side at the top of the desk, alphabetically, left to right, according to title.

Order prevailed, but there was no comfort in it. His fingers ached, held at the ready. The back of his neck was an iron rod. The muscles in his face were pinched and tight. He ground his teeth. His ears twitched at every creak of rafter, click of beetle hidden in the shadows; every sigh of wind outside.

He moved the candle closer to the pages that were on the desk and made a great show of beginning to read. He did not realize that his lips were moving.

The first thing he saw was a note that read, *Excluded by KJ*. It was followed by a quote from a secret text, the Gospel of Philip. *The rulers thought that it was by their own power and will, but the Holy Spirit in secret was accomplishing everything through them. Truth, which existed since the beginning, is sown everywhere.*

The absolute perfection of that thought so absorbed his mind that he failed to notice when the cellar door whispered open. He did not immediately see the slouching shadow.

In the darkness outside the candle's influence, a spider of a man crept silently on hands and knees, elbows and feet, drawing ever closer to the lone figure in a round web of light at the desk. A black hood was pulled up over the intruder's head. The space where his face ought to have been was a starless night. Bone white fingers clutched a thin fisher's knife, a long razor of a blade. Dust on the floor lay smeared in the man's wake as he inched ever closer to his prey, utterly without sound. His victim, the man in the light, was absently moving his lips as he read.

He moved around the desk, outside the circle of light, bony fingers and long-nailed toes eking out the distance between him and his prize. Still crouched low to the floor, only several feet away, the murderer drew in a slow, silent breath. He tensed his muscles, ready to spring upward and grab Spaulding from behind.

With no warning, the man at Spaulding's desk stood upright. He kicked his chair backward directly onto his attacker. He spun about with dizzying speed.

"You!" the murderer whispered, clutching his head where the chair had hit him.

Timon threw off Spaulding's skullcap as if to verify the murderer's recognition. He kicked his right foot directly at the murderer's throat.

The murderer barely avoided Timon's blow. He rolled to one side on the floor and flicked his fillet knife. It sliced a deep gash across Timon's boot into the flesh of his ankle. Blood oozed onto the floor.

Timon produced his own knife, backed up, and blew out the candle on Spaulding's desk. The room returned to its natural state, a perpetual, featureless twilight. Timon's years in darkened cells came to his aid. His pupils widened and he could see his attacker thrashing backward, under several desks.

Timon strode two giant steps toward him, ignoring the pain in his right ankle. He flung aside the desks with his left hand, barely grunting as he destroyed the murderer's cover. The hollow wooden desks on the cold stone floor filled the room with deafening explosions.

The murderer responded to the noise by springing upward and producing a thick wooden cudgel. He backed away from Timon, swinging the hard blond wood like a windmill in front of his chest.

Timon hesitated.

The murderer bobbed like a madman, no pattern or method in his movements. Timon stood as still as he could, waiting for the cudgel to swing forward. When it did, he was ready. He needed only a single step to his left to avoid being hit.

Alas, he did not reckon on the murderer's sudden backswing. The thickest part of the wood clapped Timon's knee, and Timon felt the kneecap jar loose. A rake of white-hot fire shot up his leg directly into his brain.

Seeing the damage he had done, the murderer flew forward with the confidence of a man with the upper hand. He thudded against Timon and both men flew backward all the way to Spaulding's desk.

The desk broke apart, sending white pages sailing through the air around the two fallen men.

Timon sucked in a quick breath and stabbed at the man on top of him. The man howled. The blade had slid across his ear, nearly cutting it in half.

Timon kicked his attacker and freed himself enough to roll away. He rose on one elbow in time to see the cudgel flying toward his head. He held up his right forearm and deflected the missile, but a bone in his arm cracked loudly.

Timon rolled once more and sprang to his feet.

The murderer stood too, holding his bleeding ear. Timon could see his face now, just barely. He was a man of thirty years, with rugged features. He wore an unusual briarwood cross around his neck.

Timon took a single step forward, and to his surprise, the murderer jumped away. He landed at a nearby desk that had not been toppled.

It was Harrison's desk, and the man began to bash it with his fists, mumbling a strange incantation.

The murder had clearly lost his mind. Timon moved easily toward him, but before he could lay hold of the man, the desk broke apart and a hidden panel was revealed. Worse: hidden within that panel was a vicious claymore.

The sword's double-edged blade was four feet long; the grip more than a foot. At the far end of the grip lay a wheel pommel, and close to the blade was a guard with a downward slope. The weight of it alone was enough to cleave a man's skull in two.

The murderer held the thing as if it were an extension of his own arm and raised it high above his head.

Timon jumped backward, twisting in the air, and landed with his profile to the killer. He hesitated only a moment before collapsing in a heap on the floor.

From his place on the cold stones, Timon could see the killer lower his claymore. He rested one of its cutting edges on the nearest desk. He glared at Timon, a mass of robe and hands and knees on the floor.

In the next instant a formless demon flew upward at the killer and landed, covering him; smothering him.

Timon had thrown Spaulding's coat.

The claymore thrashed upward once more. The killer's audible breathing seemed to help fling the robe away. He crouched and stared up at Timon.

Timon stood before him a changed man. His hair was in utter disarray about his head, a devil's halo flecked with gray. The whites of his eyes seemed to glow in the darkness. Several blades depended from a belt around his waist. He wore expertly crafted leather breeches and expensive boots. There was blood on his upper right arm in two places, and one of the boots bore a deep gash.

The killer blinked.

Timon's hand flew forward and the killer shrieked with pain. The claymore dropped to the floor as if it suddenly weighed five hundred pounds.

The killer stared at his right shoulder in disbelief. Timon's knife was lodged there, up to the hilt. It was so clean and deep a thrust that not a drop of blood flowed from the wound.

The killer smiled, his eyes rolled back in his head, and he fainted onto the floor.

Timon stepped cautiously toward the body on the floor.

When he was close enough to smell the killer's breath, the claymore somehow managed to appear in the air before Timon, hacking a cut all the way to the bone on Timon's right forearm, just above the place where the cudgel had landed.

The killer was on his feet once more, still smiling. He had pulled the knife from his shoulder, and blood bubbled down his chest. He was holding the claymore in his left hand.

Timon nodded his appreciation of the killer's cleverness and backed away, reaching for another knife.

The killer exploded with incoherent screaming. He surged forward like a mad bull. The claymore was suddenly in both his hands, raised high enough to catch a bit of moonlight.

It was the glint of a death blow.

Timon knew he had no time for finesse. He threw his second knife underhanded and directly at the killer's middle.

The knife found the man's side and blood spurted, but the claymore continued to fall.

Timon crashed backward, trying to turn sideways again, but was blocked by several of the unused desks.

The blade fell toward Timon's face, and he could see it as if in some half-dreamed recollection.

This is how I die, he thought, now I remember.

With the blade only inches from Timon's face, a sudden flash of lightning struck the claymore.

Momentarily blinded, falling backward, Timon heard the killer howl.

Timon grabbed the leg of the nearest desk and pulled himself under it in an effort to protect his head.

From that vantage point he was astonished to see, through gunpowder smoke, Marbury's face.

The killer lay on the floor, his face turned away, groaning.

Standing over Timon, Marbury shook his head. "I thought the

plan was," he said to Timon impatiently, breathing heavily, lowering a musket, "that I would get in place *first*. I would be hidden in the shadows *before* you came in here. I would never have known you had come early at all except that Anne told me she saw you. What were you thinking?"

"I wanted to start early," Timon admitted softly, looking away. "I could not bear the idea that I might fall asleep again."

"No one blames you."

"Is that Lively's musket?" was all Timon could ask.

Marbury smiled. "Yes. A bit of excellent irony, would you agree?"

"After a fashion," Timon said, struggling to sit up. "You shot the killer?"

"No. I shot the claymore. It was about to cleave your head in half. I fired at the blade to knock it sideways. If I had shot the killer, the blade would have continued to fall, and you would be dead."

"I might have dodged the blow."

"Yes." Marbury offered his clearest possible skepticism. "It did seem that you were about to do that."

The killer groaned again and rolled a bit.

Shifting his attention to the killer, Marbury announced loudly, "At last I will see the face of the monster! What manner of demon are you?"

Marbury produced a candle and set the empty musket down. He illuminated the wick of his taper, and a pool of white light spilled onto the killer's face.

Marbury gasped, nearly choking. He took an involuntary step backward.

"What is it?" Timon whispered to Marbury. He peered at the face of the murderer. The man was a complete stranger to him.

Marbury continued to gape, struggling, trying to force his tongue to loosen and his lips to move.

Finally he turned to Timon, eyes wide.

"This is Mr. Harrison!" Marbury gasped in complete disbelief.

56

*H*arrison struggled to sit up. "Deacon Marbury?"

"Mr. Harrison?" Marbury answered, wonder in every syllable.

"Would you be so good," Harrison strained to say, his voice
gravelly, "as to reload that musket and shoot this other man. He is
preventing me from completing God's work."

Timon was surprised by the sound of Harrison's voice. It was
cultured but drenched in a thick Scot's accent, harsh to some ears.
The sound of it was surely an irritant to men such as Lively and
Spaulding. Timon found it full of vigor; more genuine than those
of most of the men he had met in England.

"It—it cannot be you," Marbury stammered.

"And yet," Harrison sniffed, "it is."

"But—I saw your dead body," Marbury rasped. "I helped to
bury you."

"I know." Harrison grinned, obviously delighted with himself despite bleeding from two wounds. "It was rather a good bit of deception on my part, that was."

"How did you . . . ?" Marbury could not find the words to complete his question.

"Damn this pinprick," Harrison said, wincing as he touched his side. He stared down, trying to decide if he should remove Timon's knife. "It hurts, but you missed every single vital organ, *Brother Timon*. Your reputation is vastly overrated."

"I had no intention of killing you," Timon responded, reaching for another of his knives, watching Harrison's hand as it felt around the wound in his side. "Surely you can understand that I wanted to interrogate you."

"You wanted to prevent me from killing you," Harrison corrected.

"That too."

"Which I would have done except for aid from Deacon Marbury," Harrison sighed, taunting Timon. "I have watched you from the shadows. I have learned something of your life. You are alleged to be some sort of great assassin. But you fought me like a little girl."

"An assassin, Mr. Harrison," Timon protested, "kills people. I was trying *not* to kill you. Two separate skills."

"Bollocks," Harrison muttered.

"How did you rise from the grave to commit these murders?" Marbury demanded, eyes still wide. "This is demonic work."

"No!" Harrison twitched. His eyes flashed. "Never say that. *I* devised a perfect plan. Perfect because it was simple. Simplicity is the best rule. Demons had no part of it."

"Your plan does not appear to be *quite* perfect," Timon corrected, "or you would not be lying here, about to bleed to death."

"Chance," Harrison declared. "Hazard. Nothing more."

"Possibly." Timon gave Marbury a casual glance. "Shall we bind this man's wounds and have him arrested, or shall we simply let him die?"

"Your threats mean nothing to me," Harrison said at once.

Mabury, still amazed, could only say, "How?"

Harrison's eyes danced wildly, then he sighed and slumped forward. "In fact, you cannot imagine how I have longed to tell someone what I have done. A man of my intellect must have a certain degree of public acclaim."

"An actor needs an audience," Timon said softly.

"Exactly. I have so much to tell, and no one to hear it."

"Then by all means," Timon said, the gentleness of his voice surprising everyone, "let us have your soliloquy."

Harrison looked between Timon and Marbury several times, obviously trying to decide what to do.

"Please," Marbury said simply.

"Where to begin?" Harrison bit his upper lip for a moment. "Several nights ago, when my mind was made up to take final steps in my holy work, I went to a certain street in Cambridge. I think you know the one. On it there is a public house to which you have both gone."

"How would you know that?" Marbury whispered.

"I was told, it does not matter," Harrison said with a dismissive wave of his hand.

He is the other agent, Timon thought. He is the man of whom the Pope's men spoke.

"What matters," Harrison continued, coughing, "is that I stood there for quite some time in an effort to select the perfect victim."

"Victim?" Marbury's brow furled.

"Hush," Harrison admonished. "I saw him at last, a drunken man who staggered from the very public house I have just mentioned. I followed him to the darker end of the street. The air was quiet and the doorways were empty. I seized him from behind, choked the life out of him, and stuffed him into a potato sack. I then stole a wheelbarrow and hauled him here."

"You murdered a stranger at random?" Marbury gasped.

"Not at random," Harrison answered impatiently. "He had to be of an exact size and shape."

"Yes." Timon leaned against the nearest desk, holding his right forearm. "That victim had to be the same height and weight as Mr. Harrison."

"Exactly." Harrison suddenly took hold of the knife that was in his side and with a wrenching spasm pulled it out.

Timon produced one of his knives and was on the verge of throwing it when Harrison dropped the blade he had just removed. He collapsed back on the floor groaning.

"Plague, that hurts!" he snarled.

"Why did the victim have to be . . . ?" Marbury stopped in midthought. "You brought him back here. You mutilated his face so that no one could recognize it."

"And everyone would think it was me." Harrison nodded, completing Marbury's thought. "I gave him my clothes to wear. I even let him have my briarwood cross. That was a bit of a struggle in the mind. My mother gave me that cross when I was small."

"You seem to be wearing it now," Timon pointed out.

"I dug up my own grave," Harrison responded cheerfully, "and got it back."

"Well," Timon said, his knife still in his fingertips, "it *was* a perfect plan. No one would ever suspect that the first victim was actually the murderer."

"Exactly!" Harrison held his side. "After that, I could kill all the translators here in complete anonymity, one by one. Kill them as slowly or as quickly as I wanted."

How could Harrison possibly be the other agent of the Pope's men? Timon asked himself. How would he know them?

"But now," Timon said softly, "you have been apprehended. You will shortly bleed to death. You are already weakening. You may as well tell us everything before you die."

"Why would Mr. Harrison want to kill the translators," Marbury asked Timon, "except that he is insane? He has lost his senses. Noble minds can be overthrown by excess taxation. Perhaps his work here was too much for his capacity."

"My faculties have never been keener!" Harrison seemed to be insulted by Marbury's contention. "I say I have holy work to do. Despite what Brother Timon says, I may yet have life enough to finish it."

"No." Marbury shivered. "No one but a madman would carve a face as you did. Horrible."

"Delightful," Harrison corrected, "and necessary. As I have said of course, I did it so that no one could recognize the face; everyone would assume that I was the dead man. As importantly: the sight of such a grotesque mutilation would terrify the translators and distract them from their work. And finally, with every slice I uttered a certain curse for King James. Those were also a gift from my mother: curses for his life, his work, his reign, his health, his family."

"But James is your kinsman," Marbury protested. "He is the man who secured your position here with the translators!"

Harrison managed to raise himself up again, red as a sunset in May, and spit on the floor. His face, his voice, his entire demeanor, had shifted. He did, then, appear to be mad, as Marbury had suggested. Clenched fists; halting, gasping breath; a head palsied and shaking, Harrison forced human language from his throat.

"James is Satan," he said at last.

He said it with such rage, such venom, and such utter conviction that both Marbury and Timon were struck dumb.

"Perhaps if I explain it, you will help me," Harrison gasped, exhausted from his bile. "You will aid me in completing my task. You will see the justice of my plan."

Timon saw there was no need for the dagger at his fingertips and relaxed. A kind of pity welled up in his belly.

"I was the child of a large Highland clan when James was King of Scotland. My family lived in a valley called God's Garden, because Eden was all around us. Do you know the words of Jesus: 'The kingdom of God is on this earth, but no one sees it'?"

"From the Gospel of Thomas," Timon reminded Marbury.

"Yes!" Harrison rejoiced. "I hoped you might know the lines."

"Your clan knew James's family," Marbury began.

"No. My clan were all believers of an ancient Way. My mother taught me to know the peace and power of the growing wood. The very earth around us had roots. Within a mile of my home there were a hundred pure water springs, and giant oaks, and scarlet heps.

I knew that Nature laid her fullness before me on each bush and every bough. A hundred times or more I heard my father say, 'Here we do not feel the penalty of Adam. Here we learn everything from the Great Mother. This life finds tongues in trees, books in running brooks, sermons in stones, and good in everything.' "

"But something happened to your family," Timon said softly, "that ruined Eden."

"We human beings are always losing Eden," Harrison sighed with overwhelming sadness. "Over and over again the perfection slips away."

"What happened?" Marbury asked in hushed tones.

"When I was twelve, James began his *research* concerning witches. He knew our clan, and he used our knowledge. That resulted in his book, *Demonology*. When it was done, he proclaimed that our family's ways were a perversion of any true religion. He declared us a witches' coven. Do you know anything of the Berwick trials?"

The Berwick trials. Timon shivered at their mention.

"Fifteen years ago," Marbury said hesitantly, "Scotland—St. Andrew's Church—"

"Seventy people were eventually tried. Most of them were from my clan. The first case convicted my blood relatives of using witchcraft to make a storm to sink a ship."

Marbury gasped. "A ship on which James and Anne of Denmark were traveling. He was bringing his new bride home."

"You have heard the story," Harrison sighed.

Marbury tried to nod. All he could think of was James's rant in the kitchen at Hampton. His mind played over the image of sparks flying from a kitchen log, sent scattering by a poker in the King's hand.

"Confessions were extracted by the most extreme torture. My aunt, Geillis Duncan, was examined by James himself. She was fastened to the wall of her cell by an iron implement that had four sharp prongs. These were forced into the mouth: two prongs pressed against the tongue; the other two against the cheeks. She was kept there without sleep and drawn with a rope around about her head. At last she *confessed* and was strangled, then burned."

"It was said that she had taken a black toad," Marbury said to Timon, nearly in a trance, "and collected from it some sort of venom—collected it in an oyster shell."

"You know the particulars of her case?" Harrison drew himself up a bit more.

Timon stared.

"I was told the story," Marbury said to Timon, "when I was recently at Hampton Court."

Timon nodded slowly.

"It is, in some circles, a well-known tale." Harrison coughed once more. "By and by, James and his henchmen took my parents. He obtained confessions from them by the same methods. It went worse for my mother than it did for my father. It was always harsher for the women. I know this because James tied me to a chair and forced me, by means of the pinching mask, to watch."

"To—to watch as he tortured your parents?" Marbury stammered.

"He said he was teaching me," Harrison answered, his words hollow. " 'This is what comes of witchcraft,' he would tell me over and over again. I shall spare you the details, if you do not mind."

Marbury had the impulse to comfort Harrison somehow. But before he could think what to do, Harrison went on, his voice increasingly lifeless.

"I must tell you that in life my mother had miraculous healing powers. She acted as midwife for nearly everyone in our part of Scotland. The women of Scotland were most destroyed by this madness from James: Agnes Sampson, Barbara Napier, Effie MacCalyan—so many. So many. Can you imagine what happened to our hills when all the women who could birth a baby and stop a death were gone? All ashes. The air above our kirk was gray for a year with the fires that burned them. The smell still clings to the bush and the briar, as if the spirits of all those women held to them as their last hope."

"Harrison," Marbury began softly,

"And then," Harrison raged, gaining hellish strength from great pain, "this monster became King of England!"

"Peace," Marbury entreated.

"James let me go eventually." Harrison's breathing grew more labored and his eyes were vacant. "I changed my name several times. I went to Edinburgh. James began to circulate *Demonology,* hoping to reveal Satan's plan. I began to study the Christian religion, hoping to discover why it would incite a man to murder my parents. I became a great scholar at a young age, and I have spent most of my life attempting to avenge my parents' death."

"You made other attempts before coming to Cambridge?" Timon asked.

"Yes." Harrison nodded as he answered. "There was a certain incident involving Father Henry Garnet."

"The Bye Plot against James!" Marbury swallowed.

"Yes, Deacon," Harrison rattled, his throat thick, "I know you believe that you had a hand in uncovering that plan to kidnap the royal person."

"Believe?" Timon asked at once.

"My compatriots," Harrison said, "are the cleverest of men."

Timon struggled, suddenly desperate to get to his feet. "Compatriots?"

"They are not here in this room, I assure you," Harrison said. "But my cohorts will not cease in their efforts, even if I die."

"Your cohorts?" Marbury whispered.

"Yes. They came to me," Harrison ranted. "They found me at Edinburgh. They told me about this King James Bible. They gave me a perfect means to revenge. They showed me that James's Bible will be a more influential book than *Demonology.* It will, in fact, create generations of Christians like James. It will help to destroy more people like my parents. I cannot allow that."

"These cohorts helped you to obtain a position here at Cambridge in order to murder the translators?" Timon asked, standing at last.

"No. At first I only sought to halt the work by academic means, inserting absurd mistranslations, deliberately using incorrect words and phrases. That is why my three cohorts worked so hard to place me in the position of testing the others in their translation work. But these Cambridge men are all great scholars. Their knowledge surpassed my expectations. It soon became clear to us that the only way to stop their work was to kill them. My cohorts convinced me."

"But, I still do not understand," Marbury said, struggling.

"Christians!" Harrison spat. "This new Bible will create untold ages of believers like James, men who will feel certain of their righteousness. They will murder, torture, destroy in the name of their religion. There will be nothing *good* left on this earth! They must be stopped. They must be *stopped*!"

"But killing these good men is surely not the way," Marbury entreated.

"They convinced me!" Harrison's voice rose, thick and filled with thorns. "My cohorts!"

"Tell us who are these men," Marbury said as calmly as he could manage. "Where are they?"

"They will continue my work!" Harrison too was trying to stand. His face was flushed, and the blood from his arm spattered red rain onto the floor. "They will come for me! You have no idea what loyalty there is amongst the survivors of my clan!"

"God in heaven." Marbury grabbed hold of the nearest desk. "There are others! Men like you have infiltrated the Westminster and Oxford groups."

Timon could see the blood pounding at Marbury's temples.

"*Now* will you understand?" Harrison's voice had suddenly become a whimper. "Now will you come to my aid? My wisdom is right, my sentence is just. Did you not heed the words: 'Wandering through the world as God's hangmen'; 'The enemy of man's salvation uses all the means he can'?"

"God in heaven," Timon whispered, closing his eyes.

"What is it?" Marbury demanded.

"Those are the words found in the mouths of the dead translators," Timon mumbled to himself. "I have only just realized that the notes left were quotations from *Demonology*. I was right to worry about my memory. If I could have recalled sooner—"

"Until this moment," Harrison marveled, "you did not know the origin of my quotes? How is this possible? They were plain as day! I felt certain that you or Marbury would understand. Are you both imbeciles?"

"Those were lines from *Demonology*?" Marbury exploded.

"I thought I was making it *clear*!" Harrison shrieked. "James is responsible for these deaths! James is to blame for the murders! King James is the killer!"

But before Timon or Marbury could reply, the door to the Great Hall burst open, and a shock of white moonlight broke the darkness in half.

57

*M*usket shot!" Spaulding shouted from inside the light. He was utterly out of breath, engulfed in a gray wool coat.

The other translators stumbled in behind him. They all stopped after a few steps inside the doorway. A good thirty feet lay between themselves and the men at the other end of the Great Hall.

Marbury looked down. "This is Mr. Lively's musket. I have used it to aid Brother Timon in capturing the killer. If you would all be so good as to come over here, I think you will find yourselves as amazed as I was."

Spaulding craned his neck. Between the darkness and the desks obstructing his view, he could not see the man on the floor.

Chaderton pushed past Spaulding. "You say you have captured the killer?"

He hurried forward. Quickly, one by one, the others followed, murmuring to one another.

Richardson was the first to arrive in the candle's circle of light.

He peered down at the wounded man beside Harrison's desk. His head twitched in disbelief.

As the others gathered, they gaped in silent wonder.

From the back of the group, a softer voice asked the obvious question.

"Is that Mr. *Harrison*?" Anne stepped forward.

"It is," Harrison answered. "Anne, convince your father to help me. When he tells you my story, you will be on my side. You can imagine what you would do if a king killed your father."

"A king killed . . . ?" Anne's voice trailed off when she looked at her father.

"Mr. Harrison first altered much of the work that the translators have done here," Marbury said slowly, his voice stone-gray, "and then he murdered and mutilated Lively and Andrews—as well as a total stranger from the town."

The silence that followed Marbury's voice had a life of its own. Its tatters fell into the darkest shadows of every corner.

"Why?" Chaderton whispered at last.

" 'By falling from the grace of God, he continues through the world as God's hangman,' " Timon intoned, the fingers of his left hand moving, just barely, " 'and being the enemy of man's salvation, uses all the means he can to entrap them so far in his snares.' "

"These are the words we found in the mouths of the victims," Chaderton said, his voice still hushed.

"They are the words of James himself," Harrison snapped. "But apparently not a single *brilliant* mind in the room could remember them or decipher their meaning. If this is the best England can do—"

"Decipher their meaning for us, then," Spaulding sneered, "*Mr.* Harrison."

"You good men," Harrison spat back. The sound of his voice was sick. "Christians. You call yourselves the followers of the Messiah, but you have no idea what He said. He said that you *cannot* take up a musket and be a Christian. You cannot torture a woman and be a Christian. And you cannot claim strength to rule this world when it was clearly stated that the *meek* were meant to inherit everything. I spit my vilest curse at you men who call your-selves one thing and behave as another."

"I believe that Mr. Harrison means to say that James," Marbury said, his voice faltering, "and any Christian like him, has fallen from God's grace. He is a hangman in this world, and is the enemy of man's salvation."

"And then?" Harrison demanded.

Marbury glanced in Harrison's direction. "There is more?"

"Are you all *idiots*?" Harrison growled. "I left behind a clue *telling* you what I had done; how I would enter this room to kill you. Another quotation from James: 'By what way or passage can these Spirits enter in these houses? If they have assumed a *dead body,* they can easily open any hidden door and enter.' Where did you put the dead bodies? Where is the hidden door? Christ!"

"That was not found in anyone's mouth," Spaulding sneered.

Harrison's wild eyes searched Timon's. "Did no one go through the things in my room after I died? Did no one see *any* of the clues I left? The lines from *Demonology* I laid on my pillow: 'If the dead carcass be handled by the murderer, it will gush out blood, as if the blood were crying to heaven for *revenge.*'"

"I never saw anything from your room," Timon admitted, feel-ing foolish.

"Brother Timon," Harrison moaned, "*you* at least must help me. We must destroy them all. You can see the truth of that."

"He oozes blasphemy and treason!" Spaulding shouted. "He must be arrested at once!"

"Let us arrest him today for the murders to which he has con-fessed," Timon interjected softly, "and worry about the rest to-morrow."

Harrison's elbow faltered, and his thigh slid on the floor. "You will not help me? You will not aid me in finishing my holy work?"

Timon leaned closer to Harrison. "Let us leave it to Samuel and Isaiah."

Harrison's head snapped in Timon's direction. "Do you know them?"

"I know that they are your compatriots," Timon said softly.

"They inspired you to this course of action. They told you of the King's new translation when you were in Edinburgh."

Harrison closed his eyes. His side was drenched in blood. His face was white as milk. "Thank God you know them. Tell them what has happened. They will know what to do."

"I have seen them this day," Timon assured Harrison gently. "They are already doing God's work."

"All of you," Spaulding commanded, "help me lay hold of Mr. Harrison. We must confine him until the proper authorities can be notified!"

Spaulding edged his way toward Harrison's slumped form. Richardson followed, a few steps behind. Chaderton heaved a mournful sigh.

Anne pushed her way past the slow-moving men and flung herself to Harrison's side, her hair in riotous disarray.

"He is bleeding to death," she husked. "His wounds need attention."

"Anne," Harrison rasped. "Help me."

Anne looked around at all the men in the room, her eyes burning. "When the sick and the lame came to Jesus, he did not lay hold of them and contact the proper authorities."

"Take him to my room," Timon told Anne. "Bind his wounds; let him sleep."

"And lock the door afterward," Spaulding insisted. "We shall all go with Miss Marbury to aid her in her ministrations, and to assure her safety."

"Deacon Marbury and I will stay here a moment." Timon's voice was so completely unequivocal that no man dared argue.

As Anne turned to Timon, she noticed that he too was bleeding. "You are also in need of—"

"My wounds are slight. I can bind them myself. I have been doing so for thirty years. Thirty years or more."

The loneliness in Timon's voice caught Anne unaware. She felt a sudden tightening in the corners of her eyes, a quick thickening of her throat. Before she could think what to say in response to her feelings, Spaulding and Richardson were upon Harrison. They tried to get him on his feet without touching him anywhere that blood had stained.

Anne turned sharply and slapped Spaulding's hand away. She took hold of Harrison, heedless of the way his blood soiled her quilted, azure robe.

At that, the others helped her and managed to get Harrison up.

"We will hear more of this, more of what has happened here!" Spaulding ordered Marbury. "And shortly!"

"We shall convene in the dining hall of the Deaconage as soon as you have cared for Harrison's cuts," Marbury agreed wearily.

"And locked him safely in a room," Spaulding assured Harrison, his face only inches away from the wounded man's, "with an armed guard at the door."

Harrison was barely conscious. He searched a moment, found Anne's face, and said again, "Help me."

"That is what I am doing," she assured him softly, clearly not realizing the true nature of his entreaty.

Timon watched the odd assemblage moving haltingly away, across the floor toward the bright doorway. Spaulding was yapping little commands: move this chair, turn that way. Anne continued to whisper soothing things to Harrison, encouraging him to stay awake, to walk forward—a bed and some repose were only a few hundred steps away.

When they were gone, Timon took a chair, sat, and examined his arm.

"Were we really such idiots as Harrison said?" Marbury asked softly. "We did not decode the meaning of his messages; we did not even find half the clues he says he left for us."

"Most of his *clues* were products of a deranged mind. They meant more to him than to anyone else. I, myself, see so many things clearly in my own mind that no other human being alive can fathom, and I am nearly as sane as you are."

"Yes." Marbury stepped close by. "How did you know?"

Timon did not look up. "Know what?"

"How did you know that those men were the ones who convinced Harrison to follow his insane course of action?"

"What men?" Timon asked innocently.

"Samuel and Isaiah—and Daniel," Marbury said unequivocally.

"Oh." Timon nodded. "You heard me say that to Harrison."

"I did."

"It was a guess." Timon's eyes met Marbury's. "But it seemed obvious. Harrison went to the public house where you and I both met with those men when he wanted to find a suitable body to substitute for his own. Why that place? I made the assumption that he had been in that back room with those men."

"Does the Pope know that Harrison is alive—and what he has done?"

"I do not believe that Harrison knew his compatriots were the Pope's men," Timon answered softly. "He was under the impression that they were his friends. They found him a broken man in Scotland. This is their genius, these men: that they know how to use a man's own desperation, how to twist it to their own ends. The men you know as Samuel and Isaiah were expert at that art. They seem to have taken matters into their own hands. It is possible that His Holiness is not entirely aware of the details of *any* of these events."

Marbury smiled at Timon. "You really are quite clever."

"Not clever enough to have remembered that the quotations in the mouths of the murdered men were from *Demonology,*" Timon sighed.

"You do realize what you have done? You have not only caught a killer, you have saved the Bible. You have made it possible to accomplish the impossible. Everything will be corrected. Nothing will be excluded. Ours will be the first true Bible in the history of man."

"There are two other groups of translators," Timon reminded Marbury.

"Yes!" Marbury's enthusiasm was growing. "And we must go to them. Now that we have Harrison's confession, Lancelot Andrews will have to listen to us. So will Dr. Harding at Oxford."

"Have you forgotten that Andrews thinks that you are Pietro Delasander?"

Marbury blew out a breath. "Oh. Well." After another breath he brightened once more. "You could go. You could do what you have done here."

Timon pulled a bit of cloth from his belt and dabbed at the wound in his arm. "I fear I have a bit of a problem."

Marbury peered at the cut. "That cut? It does look bad."

"This cut? No." Timon looked up again. "The problem is that I—this afternoon, in Cambridge, in the public house which we have just mentioned? I am afraid I killed those men, Samuel and Isaiah."

"What?" Marbury's head snapped back.

"In all fairness, they tried to kill me first." Timon raised his sleeve, showing the binding on his upper arm. "This wound came from Isaiah's dagger. He threw it at my heart. I felt justified in killing him with it. Both men sent Pietro Delasander to kill me and would have hounded me until the job was done. They would have stopped at nothing to accomplish their bizarre plans. I find myself in absolute sympathy with Harrison's cause, if not his methods."

Marbury gaped at Timon. A thousand thoughts muddled his mind, none were coherent.

"I let the third one go," Timon continued. "They called him Daniel, but he is Cardinal Venitelli, did you know? A simple servant of the Pope, a man whose duty and honor are pure, however misguided. I sent him with a message to Pope Clement. I told him that I was resigning my commission in the papal armies of the damned."

Marbury managed a smile. "Is that how you put it?"

"Well, not exactly." Timon tied the piece of cloth around the wound in his forearm. The cut from the claymore and the swelling from the cudgel had mixed. "God's blood, this hurts."

"You may not be using that arm for a while." Marbury winced as Timon pulled the cloth tightly around the swelling.

"Yes, well, you see the true problem is that I really *cannot* use this arm at all. I will very shortly be the object of a secret papal injunction." Timon knotted the cloth and pulled his sleeve down over it. "I will be as useless as this arm to the cause you have just mentioned. I must flee England or forfeit my life. Oddly, it is a life which I have come to appreciate only very recently. I must leave tonight, if I can. I will endanger you and Anne if I stay."

"How would your presence endanger us?" Marbury asked slowly.

Timon looked away. "Those men I killed in the public house, they are not the only agents of—there will be others. They would find me. I must lead them away from you."

"Others," Marbury realized softly. "Then it is possible that men like them—and men like you—may visit us again; may endanger Anne."

"And you. And the translators. They would stop at nothing, these men, as we have seen. They were demons, infecting poor Harrison until he was mad, and then using him as their weapon."

"You killed those men," Marbury said, nearly to himself, "and in doing so, you have given up your own life. They will pursue you."

"Yes." Timon drew in a gasping breath and stood, steadying himself on Harrison's desk. Without another word, he headed toward the open door, and the moonlight.

"Wait," Marbury said suddenly. "Wait a moment."

"If I stay, I will be a great hindrance to the work that must be done here."

"Give me time to think."

"Think about what?" Timon said, still striding toward his egress.

"You have saved my life," Marbury said firmly. "I would like to return the favor."

58

*T*wenty minutes later, Marbury pushed open the door to his dining room. As he had expected, Anne and all the translators were arguing around the table. His entrance silenced everyone.

"Harrison is in Brother Timon's room?" he asked of no one in particular.

"Secured to the bed," Spaulding assured him, "with two men guarding the door."

Marbury glanced at Anne, hoping his expression gave nothing away. "Daughter, perhaps you might be kind enough to remove Brother Timon's meager effects from that room—especially from under the bed and the desk."

"Where is Brother Timon?" Spaulding demanded to know.

"Attending to his wounds," Marbury shot back, deliberately exaggerating the irritation in his voice. "Wounds which he received in the process of saving your life."

Spaulding, at a loss for words, looked to Richardson.

"Brother Timon is a true gallant," Richardson announced grandly, "and shall be rewarded."

"His best reward," Marbury said quickly, taking on Richardson's pomp, "would be for you all to resume your work. He fought to save it. Let us complete our portion of the translation as he urged: translating this Bible to perfection, leaving nothing out, correcting all errors, adding every conceivable text in order that the true Word of God may be given to all."

"Let us swear to it!" Richardson roared.

"No!" Spaulding stood, pounding the table. "No, by heaven! We have been given a direct order by our King!"

Spaulding reached inside his gray wool coat and produced the page that Dibly had delivered. He pointed to the royal seal.

"It is genuine," Richardson assured everyone. "I have, of course, seen the King's seal many a time."

Spaulding held the paper before his eyes. "This states, 'The translators of Cambridge in the matter of His Majesty's Bible are hereby commanded to copy, as precisely as their scholarship will allow, the *existing* Bishops' Bible.' " Spaulding looked up. "We are to 'alter nothing, add no new work, delete only the most grievous of Catholic errors.' "

He lowered the paper and cast his eye about the room.

"But, no," Marbury began.

"Do you mean to say, Deacon Marbury," Spaulding said softly after a moment, "that you would subvert the King's wishes?"

"Truly," Chaderton said, his eyes avoiding Marbury's, "if we go against the King's command, there will be talk of treason for us all."

"At the very least," Dillingham sighed, "the King would simply replace us with men who *would* do his will, and the translation would adhere to this command. Any work to the contrary would be, I fear, in vain."

"But the Bishops' Bible," Anne protested hesitantly, "is an instrument of the Crown in the exact way that the Latin Bible is an instrument of the pope."

A long silence coalesced, at last, into assent, an agreement with Anne's assessment.

"We can bring poetry to the text," Chaderton ventured, if a bit sadly. "What has already been done with Psalms and the Song of Solomon—it has a great beauty that was not there before."

"We can correct the most grievous errors in the existing texts," Dillingham sighed. "That must count for something."

"The Word of God is inviolate," Spaulding stewed, his face tightening and his eyes dark. "No matter how it is written on the pages of a book."

"But the murders," Anne protested.

"Those must be kept silent!" Spaulding pounded the table once more. "I have said so from the beginning. We must admit that Edward Lively has died so that all may know why I have taken charge. Let us say that he died of a quinsy, after four days of illness."

"He has left eleven orphans," Chaderton interjected. "Let us, one and all, see to their care. Each of us could contribute—"

"Stop this!" Anne shouted. "You cannot decide in a matter of seconds an issue for which men have died; for which Timon and my father risked their lives. You cannot merely acquiesce to this coward's path without at least—"

"Coward's path?" Spaulding demanded. "What would you have us do? The King has commanded."

"But these beautiful books of Thomas and Philip and Mary," she implored.

"They were expurgated for a reason," Richardson said softly, "by men much closer than we in time and element to the person of our Lord. We would presume too much were we to seek to outguess those immortals."

Anne turned to her father. Her eyes wrote volumes in the air, begged a thousand questions.

Marbury, alas, looked down.

At that, Anne's distress turned to rage. She shoved the chair away from her as she stood and raced for the door.

"Brother Timon must know of your decision at once," she muttered. "He will set a fire under this pile of petrified scholars!"

"Anne," Marbury called, his eyes following her.

The men at the table immediately began to argue once more; the din of their voices rose, sounds of bully challenges that might more readily fill a crowded market street than a hall of learning.

Marbury ran after Anne.

Anne plunged through the wooden doorway and into the black night. Her ire burned her face. Her fists were tightly clenched.

Marbury had to race to catch up.

"Anne," he begged, taking hold of her elbow.

"I will tell Timon this instant."

"No," Marbury corrected, his voice a granite wall. "You will not."

She spun to face him. "Do you think you could prevent me?" Anne's eyes were narrow and her voice was a long needle, a slender thorn.

Marbury drew in a monstrous breath. "He is gone."

Anne was suddenly aware that the night made a net to hold her in place, forcing her to gaze into the infinite sky.

"Gone?" was all she could say.

"I have given him the means to secure passage aboard a ship that leaves London in the morning. He took poor Dibly's signet ring and the King's coach from our stables. I also forced him to take a large sum of money and a letter from me. I wrote it to certain true friends of mine who own a trade ship. In that coach, with that ring and my letter, he will be as safe as the King until he is aboard a ship."

"What trade ship?" Anne stammered. "Surely you do not mean—"

"I will tell you all in the morning, but for now you must collect any documents he might have hidden under the stone at the foot of his desk. He told me to dispose of his box and pipe. He said it was the cause of his falling asleep and allowing a man to die. He is done with it."

"No," Anne sobbed.

"You must believe me when I tell you that all this is done to save his life," Marbury said soothingly. "He is in mortal danger. I will explain the rest tomorrow. Suffice it to say that he is gone. He will not return."

"This trade ship," Anne whispered, "it is bound for—"

"You must never tell a soul where he has gone!" Marbury whispered back. "He would not be safe even there if the truth is known."

"But it is a savage place," she mourned, "filled with wild beasts and murderous half-men. No one should ever go there. God in heaven!"

"It is done, Anne." Marbury suddenly realized that he was speaking to his daughter as if she were seven years old.

"Father," she began.

"Shh." Marbury sighed. He had a sudden longing for that time, which seemed so long passed, when she was a child. His eyes softened and the cold edges left his voice. "He is gone to America. You and I will shortly return to our smaller lives of peace and petty bickering here in Cambridge."

Anne looked toward the stables, her eyes wet. "America. What in God's name can save him now?"

Anne whispered a single prayer onto the wind. She bade that wind to find Brother Timon, wherever he might be, and to fill his senses with the certain knowledge that his student wished him farewell.

59

*J*ust after dawn the next morning, in rose and amber light, London docks were bustling with business. Timon shivered in the salt wind, his back against a post. He had discarded his monk's habit in Cambridge. A thin, white shirt did little to save him from the damp morning air. Years of wearing a black robe had robbed him of his natural, robust nature.

Time will repair that shortcoming, he thought.

The journey to London was a blur. A boy had come to the stables in Cambridge and harnessed the horses, but stable master Lankin had been the driver. Timon was too exhausted to wonder why. He had fallen asleep before the coach had left the courtyard. He had awakened beside the Thames in predawn light. Each baker, bookseller, or beggar there seemed to call to him as if they knew he would never again pass by.

At the end of the journey, on the outskirts of London near the open field of Finsbury, Timon had climbed out of the King's coach.

"Good-bye, Mr. Lankin," Timon had said, giving the man his hand.

"I've been studying how to say this all night," Lankin had answered. "Those men at home in Cambridge? All they know is duty, and fear, and the little tempest that hangs on a disagreement no bigger than a thimble. Worst of all: the good they try to do is nearly always wrecked by the demon of self-preservation."

Timon had done his best to wake up. "What are you saying, Mr. Lankin?"

"I think you understand," he'd said, looking at the horses. "So God keep you. I have to go. Marbury has me on some fool's errand, finding boys in the woods. I'll not see you again."

With that, Lankin had slapped the horses gently, and they'd taken him away.

Timon had then found his way down the Ratcliffe Highway to the north of the Wapping waterfront. Ratcliffe was a filthy street, infested with sotted sailors and wanton women.

The prostitutes were wide-awake, white hands outstretched, inviting. Timon was a rarity to them because he smiled gently and said, "No thank you." One of the women actually sighed as he passed by.

Walking east along Wapping High Street, he had eventually found his way to the Prospect of Whitby. The sign over the door said proudly FOUNDED IN 1520.

Behind its pewter bar stood the wordless, ancient landlord. He clearly thought Timon a smuggler or a thief. There were, after all, several visible daggers at Timon's waist. The old man's eyes were steady; his hand was on a well-used club hidden behind the bar. His apron was nearly as stained as his teeth, and he sucked in a sick breath as Timon approached.

"Francis Marbury sent me," Timon whispered, although he was alone in the bar with the landlord.

The landlord exhaled. He took a second. He cocked his head.

"Deacon Marbury further instructed me to tell you that Bridget Dryden bids you give me the item in question." Timon's eyes remained locked on the landlord's.

Those were the words the landlord needed to hear. He handed over an open passage bill, signed by the proper authorities. The space where the name should have been was blank.

Timon could not help noticing that the landlord's eyes had softened at the mention of Marbury's deceased wife. He wondered what story lay behind that bit of tenderness.

Evoking a ghost to secure an escape, Timon thought to himself, seems a risky portent.

Still, Timon had given the man some money, taken the document, and left the place at once.

After that, Timon wove his way though swaggering crowds, all shuffling, swearing, jostling, jeering. The glut of men and women grew as the light in the east increased: bawds in feathered hats, young men with new beards, spitting. Every voice seemed to raise a noise, building an invisible Tower of Babel all the way to the roof of the dawning sky. Foot by foot, elbow by elbow, he came, at last, to the solitary post against which he leaned his back. He watched as his ship, the *Concord,* was loaded with supplies for the long voyage to America.

Only then did he take time to consider Lankin's odd parting words. "The good they sometimes try to do is nearly always wrecked by the demon of self-preservation."

Would the Cambridge translators ignore fifteen centuries of prevarication in favor of their immediate comfort? Surely not.

Timon was prevented from further introspection. A sailor, barely able to walk, crashed into him. A powdered prostitute was on his arm. Her hand was down the sailor's pants. She smelled sweetly of French honeysuckle.

The sailor growled an incoherent insult in Timon's direction. He shoved the woman away and steered in the general direction of the *Concord*. The woman was the one who had sighed at Timon's passing earlier that same morning. She remembered him and smiled.

"*Concord*'s boarding." Her dainty voice surprised Timon.

He glanced toward the ship. "So it is."

"You going away on her, then?"

"I am."

"Pity," she said softly.

Timon smiled at her once more. "It is a fair morning," he said with a deliberate abundance of manners, "and on another such day I might walk with you along the riverside, if only to see the swans gliding there. But today I am bound away."

He reached in his pocket, produced a silver crown—a gift from Marbury—and held it out to her. "I would, however, like to leave a good impression."

She stared at the coin as if it might bite her. "That's ten weeks' lodging for the likes of me."

"I wish I could give you more." He put the coin into her hand.

"But—," she protested, her fist clutching tightly around the coin.

"All I ask is that you return that sailor's purse to him before he gets aboard our ship," Timon said softly. "I saw you take it from him as he pushed you away just now."

"Oh." She looked down. "You saw that, did you?"

"Yes, but that crown I gave you should more than make up for your loss."

"It does, it does." She looked Timon up and down. "You be a minister of the gospel, then? A priest in some ruffian disguise, is that you?"

"It was," Timon whispered. "Will you give the sailor back his—"

"Johnny!" she sang out.

The sailor stopped in his tracks. He took a moment to find the direction from which the voice had come. He turned, doing his best to focus on the girl.

She held up his purse. "You dropped this in the street, dear."

He patted his pants where his purse ought to have been, eyes popping. He looked around for a moment, then staggered back toward the girl.

"This what you want?" she whispered harshly to Timon.

"I will tell you a secret," Timon said, watching the sailor slowly stumble their way. "A miracle has happened. I have been newly baptized, as surely as if John himself had dropped me in desert waters. Only I have been drowned in *words*. My old self died in black ink. My new self rose up from letters on a page. The oldest words in my religion have brought me to this newest of dawns. I have been changed by the syllables of the saints. Best of all: I remember every single line. I am, you see, the new and living Bible."

The sailor interrupted Timon's soliloquy. Eyes wide, he stood before the girl. "That's my purse?"

"Here you go, sweet," she said a bit impatiently. "You'll need this in America." She sighed and handed him the purse, patting his cheek.

"If ever I return, Nancy," he said fervently, "I swear to make you my bride. You takes good care of me every time I'm in London. I see that now. You could have kept this, but you didn't. That's how good you are. So listen for word of the *Concord* in six months' time. Find me. We shall seal ourselves together. Is that a deal?"

"Done," she said gently, and clearly without the slightest hope that it was true.

The sailor nodded once, tried to kiss Nancy's cheek, missed it, and headed back toward the *Concord*.

She turned then to seek approval from Timon.

But Timon was gone.

She took three quick steps forward, searching the speckled crowd for a thin, white shirt. There were striped sailors, crashing gulls, rioting roisters, a cutthroat with a scar, an apple-squire, and seven doxies, but nowhere among them could she find the one she wanted.

She thought for a moment that she saw his tousled black hair in that throng and called, "Wait!"

But her sailor boy, her Johnny, mistook the word, thought it was for him. He turned back smiling and waving.

"Never fear, Nancy! I'll be back someday!"

She smiled distractedly at him, and when she looked back to see Timon's face, it was gone once more. Into the crowd or onto the ship, she could not tell.

She rushed forward, not really knowing why she so urgently

wanted to see the stranger once more. She searched the faces and the clothes. She stood on the dock for the next hour. She clutched the silver crown in her fist.

Once she fancied she saw him in the street, just out of the corner of her eye. He was not on board the ship at all, but headed back toward London! Alas, when she'd turned that way, no one was there. Surely he had boarded his ship.

The *Concord* weighed anchor and cast off at last. Nancy watched it ease away from the dock, turning seaward. She gazed high at the black-winged gulls circling the middle mast. Her eyes darted everywhere along the ship from bow to rudder, but they did not find the man they sought.

And when the white sails filled with sunlight and the river seemed to swell to help the ship away, she blew a single kiss onto the wind. She bade it find that man, wherever he might be, and fill his senses with the knowledge that a girl named Nancy wished him farewell.

Some Historical Data

The King James Conspiracy is, of course, a work of fiction. There is no evidence whatsoever that Pope Clement VIII employed assassins or anything like them. (The Borgia popes may have employed less than perfect means to accomplish their ends, but theirs is another story.) In this book Clement sends Brother Timon to Cambridge not to kill anyone but to memorize their work. The murders are a result of mad men, some of them associated with the Inquisition. There is ample historical evidence that the Inquisition employed men who were perfectly capable of murder. Additionally, the real Clement was dead by March of 1605, succeeded that year by Pope Leo XI, who died shortly thereafter that same year, and then by Pope Paul V.

James VI lived from 1566 until 1625. He was King of Scotland as James VI until 1603 when he became King of England and Ireland as James I. He succeeded Elizabeth I, the final Tudor monarch of England and Ireland. He died at the age of fifty-eight.

Most of James's dialogue in *The King James Conspiracy* is taken directly from his own writings (paraphrased or quoted relatively accurately). James did, in fact, write *Demonology*; and the portrayal of the North Berwick witch trials of 1590, which included the participation of James, who was (then James VI of Scotland), is well documented in the volume *Newes from Scotland*. A copy of that book exists in the library of John Ferguson (1837–1916), a bibliographer and Regius Professor of Chemistry at Glasgow University. A facsimile of the volume may be seen on the Web site http://special.lib.gla.ac.uk/exhibns/month/aug2000.html.

The Main Characters

1. Brother Timon is the only wholly fictional character in *The King James Conspiracy,* but he is, in part, based on the historical figure Giordano Bruno (1548–1600). Bruno's expertise in the art of memory brought him to the attention of patrons, and he traveled to Rome to demonstrate his abilities to the Pope. He invented a new memory system, based on the work of the medieval scholar Ramon Llull, using circular memory wheels. He was able to memorize thousands of pages of text with perfect accuracy. He lived for a time in England and may have worked for Philip Sidney; was certainly at Oxford University. He was eventually arrested by the Inquisition; for eight years he was kept imprisoned and interrogated periodically. In 1600 he was burned at the stake with his tongue nailed to his jaw, a black bag over his head, and a sack of gunpowder tied around his neck. The specific charges for which he was executed are lost, and his body was so destroyed by the explosion of the gunpowder that it could not be identified with any certainty. The specifics of his memory science are lost to history.

2. Francis Marbury was a deacon at Christ Church, Cambridge. Because he spoke openly about his belief that most of the ministers in the Church of England gained their positions through political means rather than scholarly merit, he was often arrested and spent time in jail. He married Bridget Dryden (an ancestor of John Dryden) and eventually settled into the Church as rector of St. Martin's Vintry, rector of St. Pancras, and finally rector of St. Margaret's.

3. Anne Marbury was born in 1593 and would have actually been fourteen years old at the time of the novel. (While she was considered more or less an adult at that age in her own time, the general thought was that contemporary audiences might not accept her as such.) She was home-schooled and acquired from her father a keen interest in theological studies. She married Will Hutchinson when she was twenty-one and became an avid follower of the sermons of the Puritan minister John Cotton. In 1634, Will and Anne, along with their fifteen children, sailed to America following John Cotton in the hope of religious freedom. As Anne Hutchinson she is often cited as America's first feminist, an early apologist for the rights of women in the colonies.

The Eight Cambridge Translators

1. Edward Lively was a fellow of Trinity College, Cambridge, and King's Professor of Hebrew. As one of the world's great linguists of his day, he was greatly admired by King James and was involved in the Bible's translation from the beginning. Alas, he died in May, 1605, of a quinsy, leaving his children, according to one report, "destitute of necessaries for their maintenance, but only such as God, and good friends, should provide."

2. Dr. Robert Spaulding was Fellow of St. John's College, Cambridge. He succeeded Edward Lively as Regius Professor of Hebrew.

3. Dr. Lawrence Chaderton was born in 1537 into a wealthy Catholic family, and his father sent him to London to be a lawyer, but instead he followed a Protestant religious path. When Chaderton asked his father for economic aid in 1564 for such studies, his father sent him a sack with a groat in it—the smallest possible English currency of the day, and told him to go begging for the rest. Chaderton became master of arts in 1571; and bachelor of divinity in 1584. He was on friendly terms with many of England's rabbis. He died in 1640 at the age of 103, one of the most honored scholars of his day.

4. Dr. John Richardson was born at Linton, in Cambridgeshire. He was first Fellow of Emmanuel College, then Master of Peterhouse. He was fond of the custom of holding public arguments in Latin that displayed his skill, and he likened himself to the ancient knights and Roman gladiators. He died in 1625.

5. Francis Dillingham was a Fellow of Christ's College, Cambridge. He was known as "the great Grecian" after a public debate with William Alabaster conducted in Greek. It was such a famous spectacle at the time that many of the scholars of the age used it as a benchmark from which to date themselves.

6. Dr. Roger Andrews was Master of Jesus College, Cambridge, and became prebendary of Chichester and Southwell, owing to his older brother's influence. He was a famous linguist in his time, but less regarded than his brother Lancelot, who was also the bishop of Winchester and president of the first company of translators.

7. Thomas Harrison was eventually Vice-Master of Trinity College, Cambridge. He was excessively modest though he was, in fact, one of the examiners in the University who tested other professors' knowledge of Greek and Hebrew.

8. Dr. Andrew Bing, not mentioned in *The King James Conspiracy*, was the final member of the Cambridge team, a Fellow of Peterhouse, Cambridge. He was subdean of York in 1606 and was the archdeacon of Norwich by 1618.

Others

1. Lancelot Andrews (1555–1626) was a favorite of Queen Elizabeth. She appointed him dean of Westminster. King James held him in awe, and made him bishop of Chichester in 1605. He topped the King's list of selected translators for the Bible.

2. Pope Clement VIII was elected in 1592, the same year Shakespeare received his first review, Tintoretto painted "The Last Supper," and the plague killed 15,000 in London. During the famous jubilee of 1600, when three million pilgrims visited the holy places, Clement presided at a conference to determine the questions of grace and free will. On February 17 of that same year, he approved the guilty verdict against Giordano Bruno, an advocate of free will, who was then executed. Clement died in 1605 and a Medici was selected Pope Leo XI to take his place.

The Translation

1. From King James's opening address at the Hampton Court Conference in January of 1604, where it was decided that the new King James Bible be created: "I assure you we have not called this assembly for any innovation, for we acknowledge the government ecclesiastical as it now is, to have been approved by manifold blessings from God himself, both for the increase of the Gospel, and with a most happy and glorious peace. Yet because nothing can be so absolutely ordered, but something may be added thereunto, and corruption in any state (as in the body of man) will insensibly grow, either through time or persons, and because we have received many complaints, since our first entrance into this kingdom, of many disorders, and much disobedience to the laws, with a great falling away to popery; our purpose therefore is, like a good physician, to examine and try the complaints, and fully to remove the occasions thereof, if scandalous; cure them, if dangerous; and take knowledge of them, if but frivolous, thereby to cast a sop into Cerberus's mouth that he bark no more."

2. Six groups of translators worked on the King James Bible, two at Westminster, two at Oxford, and two at Cambridge. Each group was assigned a specific section of the Bible to work on, but all the groups shared research at every turn before final decisions were made.

3. From the introduction to the Bible, written by King James: "Translation it is that openeth the window to let in the light, that breaketh the shell, that we may eat the kernel; that putteth aside the curtain, that we may look into the most Holy place; that removeth the cover of the well, that we may come by the water, even as Jacob rolled away the stone from the mouth of the well, by which means the flocks of Laban were watered. Indeed without translation into the vulgar tongue, the unlearned are but children at Jacob's well, without a bucket."

An Abridged History of the English Translation of the Bible

The Christian Bible began mostly in Hebrew and Greek, and thereafter for a thousand years in Latin. The first notable translation into English was produced in the decade of the 1380s by John Wycliffe, made from the Catholic Latin Vulgate.

By 1516, the scholar Erasmus began to correct the corrupt Latin Vulgate and published a revised Greek-Latin Parallel New Testament. Erasmus insisted that the Latin Vulgate had become inaccurate, and that it was important to refer to original languages to create a true English translation.

William Tyndale used the Erasmus text as a source to translate and print the first New Testament in English in 1525. For this work Tyndale was pursued by inquisitors and bounty hunters, but one of his texts found its way to King Henry VIII. Tyndale was eventually captured, tried, strangled, and burned at the stake in 1536. His last words were said to be "Lord, open the King of England's eyes."

That happened, apparently, in 1539, when King Henry VIII funded the printing of an English Bible known as the "Great Bible."

John Calvin published a complete Bible in English in 1560. It became known as the Geneva Bible. It was the first Bible to add numbered verses to the chapters, so that referencing specific passages would be easier. Every chapter was also accompanied by extensive marginal notes and references. This was Shakespeare's Bible, and he quotes it hundreds of times in the plays. It was the Bible most enjoyed by the general population of England.

Queen Elizabeth I tolerated the Geneva Bible, but the marginal notes were a problem. They strongly opposed any institutional church and were critical of rulers in general. She preferred the Bishops' Bible, also in English, a less inflammatory version used by the Anglican clergy.

When Queen Elizabeth I died, Prince James VI of Scotland became King James I of England. The Anglican clergy approached him in 1604 demanding a new translation that might please everyone, priest and parishioner alike. Many proposed a combination of the Geneva and Bishops' Bibles.

From 1605 to 1606 James's scholars engaged in private research. From 1607 to 1609 the work was assembled. By 1611 the first printed copies of the King James Bible were available.

The Name Jesus and the History of Its Translation

Christ's name may have begun as the Hebrew *Yehoshua*, translated into Aramaic as *Yeshua*, then to Greek as *Iesous*, Latin as *Iesus*, and finally English as *Jesus*.

The basic root of the name comes from the Hebrew name Yshua (Joshua), which means *salvation*. There is some argument, however, that a more complete explanation for the name *Jesus* comes partly from the authority of Moses. In Numbers 13:1-16, "the Lord said to Moses, send men to scout the land of Canaan, which I am giving to the Israelites. Send one man from each tribe, all of them princes . . . but Ho-shea, son of Nun, Moses called *Yeho-shua*."

Early Christians cited this ability of Moses to invent names, and invented secret names for the Savior and His twelve disciples (Mark 3:16-19). By the fifth century BCE the name *Yeho-shua* (which means *God Saves*) had been shortened to *Yeshua* (Nehemiah 8:17).

By the first century AD the name *Yeshua* was again shortened, first to *Y'shua*, then to *Y'shu*.

From the Gospel of Philip: "*Jesus* is a hidden name, *Christ* is a revealed name. For this reason *Jesus* is not particular to any language; rather he is always called by the name *Jesus*. While as for *Christ*, in Syriac it is *Messiah*, in Greek it is *Christ*. Certainly all the others have it according to their own language. *The Nazarene* is he who reveals what is hidden."

The early gospels were often written in Greek, and there were two ways of turning a Hebrew name into a Greek name, translation or transliteration. The Greek translations attempted to approximate the sound of the Hebrew name and produced *IhsouV*, roughly pronounced *ee-ay-soos*.

In 382, when Jerome translated the Bible from Greek to the Vulgate or Common Latin Bible, he transliterated the Greek name of the Savior as *Iesus* because of the differences between the Greek and Latin alphabets. (By 1229, the Council of Toulouse made the Latin the official language of the Bible, forbidding translation into any other language.)

Finally in 1066, with the Norman invasion of England, the letter *J*, which had not existed in English before that time, was introduced and began to replace the *I* or *Y* in male names that began with those letters (because, it is suggested, that the J sounded more masculine). *Iames* became *James*. *Iesus* became *Jesus*.

In 1384, however, when John Wycliffe offered the first translation of the New Testament from Latin into English, he maintained the Latin spelling and pronunciation of *Iesus*. Apparently not until William Tyndale's English language translation in 1525 did the name *Jesus* appear in the Bible.

Tyndale had 18,000 copies of his illegal English translation smuggled into England. He was captured in Belgium, tried by the Catholic Church for heresy, and executed in 1536 by strangulation, after which his body was burned at the stake. Eventually King Henry VIII sponsored an English language Bible. This gave James a regal precedent for his translation.

Other Texts

1. From the introduction to *Demonology,* written by King James (exactly as it was written, spelling unaltered): "The fearefull aboundinge at this time in this countrie, of these detestable slaves of the Devill, the Witches or enchanters, hath moved me (beloved reader) to dispatch in post, this following treatise of mine, not in any way (as I protest) to serve for a shew of my learning and ingine, but onely (mooved of conscience) to preasse thereby, so farre as I can, to resolve the doubting harts of many; both that such assaultes of Sathan are most certainly practized, and that the instrumentes thereof, merits most severely to be punished.

2. A book called *Enemies of God: the Witch-Hunt in Scotland* (1981) by Christina Larner is generally considered the standard book on the Scottish witch-hunt. A good discussion of the Berwick trials may be found in *Witchcraft in Early Modern Scotland: James VI's* Demonology *and the North Berwick Witches* (Lawrence Normand and Gareth Roberts (eds.), 2000). I also found it enjoyable (as I always do) to consult Sir James Frazer's *The Golden Bough* (New York: Macmillan, 1922), especially his chapter concerning magic and religion.

    But to hear the details from the horse's mouth, this quote is from "News from Scotland" a historical document reporting the North Berwick witch trials of 1590 in which James was involved. It appears here exactly as it was written, spelling unaltered. "Geillis Duncane took in hand to help all such as were troubled or greeued with any kinde of sicknes or infirmitie: and in short space did perfourme manye matter most miraculous" [*for this activity she was suspected of being a witch,]* "Geillis Duncan was tortured with the pilliwinkes on her fingers and by binding or winching her head with a cord or roape. She did not confess until her tortures declared they had found her 'devil's mark'- it being believed at that time that by due examination of witchcraft and Witches in Scotland, it hath lately beene founde that the diuell doth generally marke them with a privie marke."

3. The gospels of Thomas, Mary, and Philip referred to in *The King James Conspiracy* are quite real. They belong to a body of work often called the Gnostic Gospels. Quotations here come from *The Nag Hammadi Library in English* from Harper & Row in 1977; James Robinson was the general editor.

From *The Gospel of Thomas*:

These are the secret sayings that the living Jesus spoke and Didymos Judas Thomas recorded. 1. And he said, "Whoever discovers the interpretation of these sayings will not taste death." 2. Jesus said, "Those who seek should not stop seeking until they find. When they find, they will be disturbed. When they are disturbed, they will marvel, and will reign over all." 113. His disciples said to him, "When will the kingdom come?" "It will not come by watching for it. It will not be said, 'Look, here!' or 'Look, there!' Rather, the Father's kingdom is spread out upon the earth, and people don't see it."

From *The Gospel of Philip*:

Some said, "Mary conceived by the Holy Spirit." They are in error. They do not know what they are saying. When did a woman ever conceive by a woman? Mary is the virgin whom no power defiled. She is a great anathema to the Hebrews, who are the apostles and the apostolic men. This virgin whom no power defiled [. . .] the powers defile themselves. And the Lord would not have said "My Father who is in Heaven" (Mt 16:17), unless he had had another father, but he would have said simply "My father."

Those who say that the Lord died first and (then) rose up are in error, for he rose up first and (then) died. If one does not first attain the resurrection, he will not die. As God lives, he would [. . .].

No one will hide a large valuable object in something large, but many a time one has tossed countless thousands into a thing worth a penny. Compare the soul. It is a precious thing and it came to be in a contemptible body.

From *The Gospel of Mary*:

[Peter] questioned them about the Savior: "Did he really speak privately with a woman and not openly to us?" The Mary wept and said to Peter, "My brother Peter, what do you think: Do you think that . . . that I am lying about the Savior?" Levi answered and said to Peter, "Peter, you have always been hot-tempered. Now I see you contending against the woman like the adversaries. But if the Savior made her worthy, who are you indeed to reject her. Surely the Savior knows her very well. That is why he loved her more than us."

From *Thunder, Perfect Mind*

I am the first and the last/I am the honored one and the scorned one/I am the whore and the holy one/I am the wife and the virgin/ I am the mother and the daughter.

The Bye Plot

The Bye Plot was a somewhat addled conspiracy by William Watson, a Catholic priest, to kidnap King James and force him to repeal the anti-Catholic laws in England at the time. The plot was uncovered by English Jesuits, especially Father Henry Garnet, who reported it to the Crown. Garnet's motives were not entirely altruistic. The plan was doomed to failure and he feared regal reprisal against all Catholics.

Thomas Dekker

Some of the language describing the London streets is taken from Thomas Dekker's *The Seven Deadly Sins of London*, 1606, "In every street, cars and coaches make such a thundering as if the world ran upon wheels . . ." and *The Dead Term*, 1608, ". . . what casting open of cloaks to publish new clothes. . . ." For Dekker quotes the volume *Shakespeare's England* was used. It was edited by R. E. Pritchard and published by Sutton Publishers LTD Gloucestershire in 2000.

Shakespeare

Though he is never mentioned by name, Shakespeare is quoted by several characters in *The King James Conspiracy*. Included are lines from *Hamlet, Romeo and Juliet, The Winter's Tale, The Tempest,* and *Macbeth.* A great deal of speculation concerns Shakespeare's participation in the poetry (Psalms, Song of Solomon) of the King James Bible. A far-fetched bit of numerology is sometimes cited as evidence. Shakespeare is said to have been born on April 23, 1564, and died on April 23, 1616. The sum of 23 and 23 is 46. The King James Bible was first published in 1611, when Shakespeare was 46. The name *William Shakespeare* can be the anagram: Here was I, like a psalm. And if Psalm 46 in the King James Bible is examined, the 46th word from the beginning is found to be *shake,* and the 46th word from the end is *spear.*

For Shakespeare quotes the *Riverside Shakespeare* was used; published by Houghton Mifflin Company in 1974.

A short bibliography of sources and further reading:

The King James Bible. Plume Books, 1974.

Daemonologie. King James VI of Scotland. Originally printed Edinburgh, 1597. E. P. Dutton & Company, 1966.

The Nag Hammadi Library in English. New York: Harper & Row, 1977. James Robinson, general editor.

Riverside Shakespeare. Boston: Houghton Mifflin Company, 1974.

The quote from Aristophanes' play *The Birds* was recalled from a 1966 production in which I played the part of Tereus, the hoopoe. Alas, there is no memory of which translation was used for that production. The quote has been checked against several current translations of the play and is relatively accurate.

The Nag Hammadi Library in English (Hardcover) by Coptic Gnostic Library Project (Corporate Author), James McConkey Robinson (Editor), Richard Smith (Editor). Boston: Brill Academic Publishers, 4th revised edition, 1997.

The Timetables of History. Bernard Grun. New York: Simon and Schuster, 1991.

Shakespeare's England. Edited by R. E. Pritchard. Gloucestershire: Sutton Publishers Ltd, 2000.

Shakespeare. Anthony Burgess. Chicago: Ivan R. Dee, Inc., 1970.

Giordano Bruno's The Heroic Frenzies. A translation with introduction and notes by Paul Eugene Memmo, Jr. Chapel Hill: The University of North Carolina Press, 1964.

This book came out too late for use in research for *The King James Conspiracy* but is an excellent volume on the life of Giordano Bruno:

Giordano Bruno: Philosopher/Heretic. Ingrid D. Rowland. New York: Farrar, Straus and Giroux, 2008.

Online Sources

The Geneva Bible online at http://www.genevabible.org/Geneva .html

Translators of the King James Bible online at http://www.learn thebible.org/king_james_translators.htm

A timeline of English bible history online at http://www.greatsite .com/timeline-english-bible-history/

Nag Hammadi library online at http://www.gnosis.org/naghamm/ gosthom.html

Life in Elizabethan England online at http://elizabethan.org/ compendium/home.html

Life of King James online at http://www.luminarium.org/sevenlit/ james/jamesbio.htm

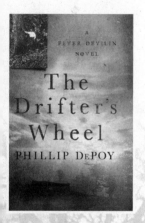
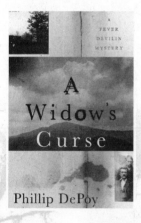
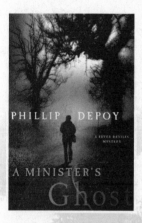
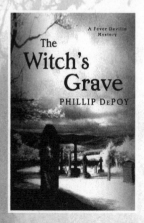